PROLOGUE

SOME CLAIM THERE WAS ONCE MAGIC WITHIN this world, controlled by two factions—those who could see it, the seers, and those who could harness it, the dœwers. But all that magic brought forth was terror, war, and death. So the Great Dœwer sought to bring peace by sacrificing himself to lock the magic away. His power was so vast it not only brought about the end to the age of the dœwers but even shattered the continent into three. However, not even he could end magic completely, and the few surviving seers prophesized that a new age of magic would return and, with it, a new dynasty that would drown the earth in blood.

But others claim this is all just a myth. That there have always been three lands, and they have always known terror, war, and death. They claim that the seers are nothing but cursed beings, like the giants or the dwarfs, prone to hallucinations, and that the Dœwer never existed. That magic is not real.

Who is right is not yet relevant.

This story begins in Ahkebulin, the greatest of the three lands set in the middle of this world. It was once divided by nine warring kingdoms until Aksum Zenzele conquered and unified them all, establishing the Zenzele dynasty. The other eight fallen kingdoms were turned into high noble houses, and for four hundred and fifty-three years, the high nobles swore their fealty . . .

Until a cold summer night, when the Zenzele betrayed one of them.

BHKOSI
IBORI
WAURAIJO

KOSSINAT
TUMELO
KAGISO

JIMULO

NÉRBUA
JANGARI

TIAFRE

AHALON

ZENZELE
ZENZELE

KÉYE
HIWOT

KAZERA

MADADA
LIABREIN
DAKARAI

VOLCANO

AAHAYI

YOENGO
RAAYA

SANNÉ
SKERELE

IDIROJE

SI'ERTAN
DESERT

AODIJO MOUNTAINS

EMYWEI

WINNEBA
NNAMÃNI

No. **1482** of 2,000 copies
of the first edition of

BIRTH

of a

DYNASTY

CHINAZA BADO

Signed by the author

Published by Harper*Voyager*
in association with Goldsboro Books
August 2025

BIRTH
of a
DYNASTY

BIRTH

of a

DYNASTY

CHINAZA BADO

HARPER
Voyager

Harper *Voyager*
An imprint of
HarperCollins*Publishers* Ltd
1 London Bridge Street
London SE1 9GF

www.harpercollins.co.uk

HarperCollins*Publishers*
Macken House,
39/40 Mayor Street Upper,
Dublin 1, D01 C9W8
Ireland

First published by HarperCollins*Publishers* Ltd 2025
1

Designed by Patrick Barry
Map and interior illustrations by Alan Dingman

Chinaza Bado asserts the moral right to
be identified as the author of this work.

A catalogue record for this book is available from the British Library.

ISBN: 978-0-00-869762-4 (HB)
ISBN: 978-0-00-869763-1 (TPB)

This novel is entirely a work of fiction.
The names, characters and incidents portrayed in it are
the work of the author's imagination. Any resemblance to
actual persons, living or dead, events or localities is
entirely coincidental.

Printed and bound in the UK using 100% renewable electricity
by CPI Group (UK) Ltd

MIX
Paper | Supporting
responsible forestry
FSC
www.fsc.org
FSC™ C007454

This book contains FSC™ certified paper and other controlled sources
to ensure responsible forest management.

For more information visit: www.harpercollins.co.uk/green

DEDICATED TO

Those who came before me but did not include me . . .
And those who will come after and will never forget me

AHKEBULIN

BHKOSI
IBORI
WAURAIJO

KOSSINAT
TUMELO

KAGISO

JIMULO

NÉRBUA
JANGARI

TIAFRE

AHALON

KÉYE
HIWOT

ZENZELE
ZENZELE

KAZERA

MADADA
LIABREIN

DAKARAI

AAHAYI

VOLCANO

YŒNGO
RAAYA

AODUO MOUNTAINS

SANNÉ
SKERELE

IDIROJE

SI'ERTAN
DESERT

EMYWEI

WINNEBA
NNAMÃNI

453 AAC

(After Aksum's Conquest)

I

M'KURU

Madada

"WHO ARE YOU?" HIS MOTHER ASKED WITH A wide smile. There was no fear or tears, just joy, something he could not understand, not with the sounds of screams from their maids and servants outside, not with the roars of the soldiers as they struck them down. There was so much blood that it produced a stench in the air that made him sick. How could anyone still keep a smile on their face? And yet, his mother, Lady Mukundi, found a way.

"Who are you?" she asked again, but he could not answer. Instead, he flinched as he heard another shriek for help outside the door.

"I am Neema Mukundi of Madada, the one born in prosperity," his elder sister, who looked like their mother, spoke instead. Everyone said they looked almost identical, with the same round face and birthmark under their right eye. And although their mother was slightly shorter, and her hair held wisps of gray, her skin had not a single wrinkle.

His mother's dark eyes shifted to him, and she squeezed his shoulders once again before repeating her question softly. "Who are *you*?"

"I am M'kuru Mukundi of Madada, the one who climbs over fear and death," he answered softly, his voice barely above a whisper. Despite the meaning of his name, all he felt was fear, and all he sensed was death.

"So, you *can* talk softly." His mother giggled, pinching his ear gently as she always did when he was in trouble or would not listen or when he went around their home yelling. From the day his cries were first heard throughout Madada to this very moment, M'kuru had never once whispered.

"Are you afraid, M'kuru? Is that why your voice has become so? I cannot have that. Tell me again. Who are you? Say it with all the air in your chest."

He stood straighter, held his head high, and spoke louder this time. "I am M'kuru Mukundi of Madada, the one who climbs over fear and death."

"Yes. Exactly." His mother nodded proudly and shook him vigorously. "You are Neema and M'kuru Mukundi, high nobles of Madada, the daughter and son of M'Deba and Esha. You are fierce, steadfast, strong, and born with the wisdom of ages. That is who you are. That is who you will always be. They can never take that from you because it is in your blood!"

She squeezed his shoulders tighter than ever, and M'kuru lifted his much smaller hand to hold on to her wrist, squeezing it in return.

"My lady!"

Four maids rushed in. On their uniform was their family emblem, the Liabrein—the now-forgotten bigger and stronger sister of the lion—with long, curved, saber-shaped canine teeth that protruded from its mouth even when closed. But on their emblem, the Liabrein's mouth was wide open and its head turned upward. So ferocious—and yet it couldn't seem to protect them now. The maids slammed the doors closed behind them as they gripped their blood-covered swords. Lady Mukundi did not answer them, never looking away from her son and daughter, not even as the two maids began to pour oil onto the ground and the walls.

"Break it down!" a voice outside the doors hollered as the other two maids stood before them, lifting their swords.

Only then did Lady Mukundi let go of her son, but M'kuru grabbed her hand again.

"Come with us, Mother."

"A lady stays with her lord to the very end," she said, and drew her hand back. She rushed to the end table, tossed it aside, and lifted the floorboards to show them the way down the stairs. "Go, and do not stop for anyone!" she hollered at them.

Without a second thought, Neema grabbed her brother's hand, took the sword entrusted to her by her father, and ran down the stairs.

"Mother!" M'kuru yelled back as he was dragged into the darkness.

Lady Mukundi's smile as she watched them go never fell or wavered, and the light from her room was the only thing M'kuru could see as it began to go up in flames of red and orange, the heat from the fire so hot he could feel it on his face.

Goodbye was the last thing she mouthed to him before the hidden door shut.

They ran, hand in hand, in the darkness, and soon that darkness felt like hell even though there was no fire in the passage, because the walls themselves warmed, growing hotter and hotter the farther they went.

"We are almost there, Six!" Neema called out to him.

She called him Six for the same reason she called her other brothers One, Three, Four, and Five—to tease them, knowing they hated it, and because as the only daughter of the Mukundi family, their baba would allow her to get away with it.

He didn't complain now, glad she was there with him. So focused were both of them on running, and because it was dark—and everything else that lived in darkness sensed the danger and the heat—she did not notice the snake also trying to make its escape until it was too late, and it bit her.

"Ugh!"

"Neema?" M'kuru called out when she let go of his hand and fell to her knees. "Neema, are you okay?"

She unsheathed the sword, stabbing it into the head of the snake. He was unsure how she could see clearly, even in the dark, but Neema always had the best vision of them all.

"I'm fine. We need to keep going," she lied. She didn't feel fine at all, but nothing could make her feel fine, not in this oven masquerading as a tunnel, so she dragged the sword along the ground with one hand, hoping to scare anything else away, and led her brother with the other.

"Don't worry, M'kuru. We are going to make it out of here. We'll go south to Winneba. You've always wanted to go to Winneba to see the giants, right? Just don't be scared when we meet them. Apparently, they are a very sensitive people, which makes sense, for their hearts are three times as big. The stories of them eating children aren't true. They aren't scary. The giants don't even eat meat. They are vegetarians."

"How do you know?" M'kuru asked. "You've never been to Winneba either."

"I have a friend there. He'll help us," she replied, stopping to take a breath and wipe the sweat from her brow, muttering what her baba taught her, "Run north till you smell the fresh water, then push the lever in the walls."

She could smell the water, so she began to feel against the wall until she hit the lever. It burned, the fire enough to make even this metal hot, but she didn't hesitate, and the ceiling above them cracked open.

"Yes!" she cried, happy at the sight of the moonlight streaming in. Hinging her sword, she reached up and pushed as hard as she could, the earth slipping away. She pulled herself out, then turned back and pulled M'kuru out.

When they both stood on the grass mound of the Bamboo Forest, overlooking their family home in the distance, they just watched as the fire raged through the house, glowing in the night and eating everything it touched. The crackling was so loud and the heat so harsh, even from where they stood on the hilltop it caused the birds to fly away. The smoke was so black it began to blanket the full moon. But to them, the fire was merciful in comparison to the soldiers, who had dragged anyone within their house out, one by one, and set them on their knees before slitting their throats.

"We have to go. We have to go now, Six." Pulling his arm, Neema tried to turn with him and escape into the forest.

"*Zenzele!*"

They both froze when they heard this roar, the hair on their hands rising as their hearts dropped to an even deeper pit in their stomachs.

"Baba . . ." Neema whispered as they both turned back.

They couldn't speak or look away. They just stared at him, their baba, as half his body was engulfed in flames, with arrows in his arms and legs and a deep cut that sliced through his clothes into his chest. The sight of him, still gripping his swords and cutting people down, caused the other soldiers to back up, terrified of him.

"*Zenzele!*" he roared again, with a strength that shook the heavens. Any soldier who dared to step forward was sent straight to hell as his blade cut them down one by one.

"*Zenzele!*"

Even when they managed to stab him, he did not fall. He merely removed their swords from his body and fought on. In his mind, M'kuru could not put that man and the man he'd watched only that morning, who spilled his wine over his hands and handed his mother a flower, together with the man at this moment, who no longer looked to be human.

"Come!" he yelled to the soldiers. When he stepped forward, the soldiers stumbled back in fear . . . all but one.

The man across from him sat on a large black horse, dressed in scaled red armor accented with silver spikes, one on each arm, one on each shoulder, and two upon his helmet. Upon his chest plate was the symbol of a sun with a spear in the center, and in his hands that very same spear with a crescent blade. The soldiers around him were dressed similarly—without silver but with the same red armor to tell everyone they were part of the Red Sun.

M'kuru thought that man in the red and silver armor had to be the Zenzele their baba was calling out to. However, the man moved to the right, showing another man on a horse of white dressed in silver-and-gold armor, and instead of spikes on his shoulders, it was wings.

"You." Lord Mukundi laughed at seeing him. "Tell your father, Prince Effiom—for I swear by my blood that spills upon the earth and the ancestors who watch over us all—your lineage shall weep in agony. You will run to the ends of the earth in fear, and we will find you still. You will cry out for mercy and be given none! The heavens will not forgive, and Madada will not forget! The Mukundi *will* have its vengeance! This is our oath to you!"

Prince Effiom merely waved his gloved hand, and the soldier with the armor of red and silver kicked into his horse, charging forward.

"Let's go, Six." Neema tried to pull her brother away, but he could not and did not want to look away. He watched as their baba's head was cut from his body with a single swing of the man's sword. As Lord Mukundi's body stood for a moment, part of M'kuru still expected him to fight and not surrender, even headless. But there was a limit to even his baba, and M'kuru watched as his baba fell to the ground alongside his brothers.

We shall not forgive.

We shall not forget.

We will have our vengeance.

M'kuru engraved the words in his head.

"*Find the rest!*" Prince Effiom screeched before laughing. "*Kill them all!*"

"We have to go!" Neema said in a harsh whisper, and finally M'kuru turned back and ran with her through the dense forest, the twigs and leaves all breaking under the weight of their feet. His chest burned, his legs grew heavy, and the wind felt like a thousand small needles across his face, but they did not stop. They just kept running as fast as they could . . .

But it wasn't enough.

Soon they could hear the horses behind them. M'kuru looked up to Neema, her curly black hair caught in the wind, whipping around her. When she cried out and stumbled forward, taking him with her, they slipped and rolled down the hill, the bamboo beating against them and the rocks cutting into their skin, tearing at his robes as they fell into a trench by a small stream.

M'kuru peeled himself up from the muddy water, but Neema gripped his arm and pushed him back down. Then he noticed the arrow in her stomach, blood seeping through her dirty white robes.

"Six . . . stay . . . down," she muttered, pushing him up against the dam. She again unsheathed Black Fang, one of the remaining twin swords crafted by their ancestors. The other fang had been lost. The words *Now Our Enemies Rest* were engraved down the black blade, carved like a Liabrein tooth at the tip. She was bleeding too much and, already weak from the snakebite, couldn't fight. M'kuru reached out to take it from her, to protect her, but she drove the sword into the dirt and pushed herself up. "Not yet, Six, but soon. Soon you'll fight, too, but for now you need to hide."

"No—"

"Who are you?" she asked, pulling the sword from the earth and stepping back as the sound of horses reached their ears.

He didn't answer, so with the same smile on her face that their mother had, she answered her own question. "You are M'kuru Mukundi of Madada, the one who climbs over fear and death, a high noble, the last son of M'Deba. You are fierce, you are steadfast, you are strong, and you are born with the wisdom of ages. That is who you are. That is who you will always be. They can never take that from you because it is in your blood. You now must hide and preserve our family, M'kuru, so you can make our enemies weep one day, that has always been your destiny." Tears fell from her eyes, but she still smiled. "Go."

He didn't move.

"Go!"

Picking himself up, he ran through the muddy water but knew

they would be able to track him if he kept running. In the bush, hidden behind the roots of a half-fallen tree, he saw a small burrow of a hole and crawled inside just as the red soldiers broke through. Despite his distance, he could see it all, the six of them surrounding her like a pack of beasts.

"Now, what is a beautiful lady like you doing with such a sharp sword?" The one who asked laughed, and the other five just chuckled.

"I can show you," she answered as she spun like a whirlwind before him, slitting his throat and then jumping back. The air shifted, feeling colder as the others stood in stunned silence before rage filled them, and all five charged her at once. But she did not stop, even as they cut into her, one by one. She reminded M'kuru of their father as she took one of their arms and dropped down, ripping through a soldier's stomach. But when she turned back around, one of them drove a sword through her heart, and M'kuru felt it in his. He felt his throat rumble and placed both hands over his mouth to swallow his screams, his horror, his rage . . . but all of those things broke through the dark of night anyway.

Only, it wasn't from him.

"*Neema!*" a voice echoed through the forest.

M'kuru could see just the hooves of the person's horse above as they came over the fallen tree where he hid. Before the stranger's horse had even touched the ground, he fired not one or two but three arrows simultaneously. Without stopping, the man reached behind him and pulled out three more arrows, firing them all at once at the men around M'kuru's sister, striking them to the ground before rushing to her. M'kuru could tell from his braided hair, which was pulled into a bun and shaved on the sides, and by the seal upon his horse, that he was not from their land. However, he hugged M'kuru's sister and had known her name, lifting her head tenderly now and brushing the stands of her curls from her face.

His voice broke as blood spilled out of her mouth. "Neema . . ."
She let the sword go and reached up, gently touching his face.
"So foolish . . ."

He nodded. "I learned from you."

She laughed and tried to lift her hands as she bit back her bloody
coughs, but they went limp, so instead, she turned her head in
M'kuru's direction. The stranger looked, too, and M'kuru did not
know how, but it felt like . . . like the stranger could see him. But
the man turned away, lifted a rock, and threw it toward his horse,
urging it to go in the opposite direction. The man hugged Neema
to his chest and kissed her forehead then, whispering something in
her ear that M'kuru could not hear but was thankful for because
the look of peace on his sister's face as she closed her eyes meant
more to him now than all the world. The stranger pulled the blade
out of her, then wept and hollered in agony over her body until his
voice broke, and he hung his head.

"Did you kill her, or did you come to save her, Zereen Nnamani?"
a voice called.

It was Prince Effiom, speaking from the mound above, seated on
top of his white horse, ten more men on each side of him.

Before, when he was ordering the death of M'kuru's father, the
prince's face had been obscured. M'kuru could now see it clearly.
It was hard, square, and sunken around his jaw, with a scar on the
side of his neck.

He memorized it with all the hatred he could muster.

"For the sake of your family, your *honor*, think wisely," the prince
was saying to this Zereen. "We have lost one high noble house tonight. Let there not be another."

Gently and with care, Zereen put Neema down on the ground
and rose to his feet, grabbing his sword.

"Zereen Nnamani? There is no Zereen Nnamani, as the Nnamani family will tell you, for he was disowned the moment he foolishly left Winneba, disobeying his father to fight alone against the order of the king," he replied, turning back to face them all.

"All for the sake of one woman?" Prince Effiom questioned, shifting as he leaned farther forward. "Or did you believe the prophecy? 'When Mukundi and Nnamani become one, blood and war shall cover Ahkebulin. Their power will swallow this world, crushing Zenzele under their heel and raising a new dynasty spanning ten thousand years.' Did you truly believe you would become king one day, Zereen?"

"No. I am here for the former." Zereen laughed and shifted his bow to his back as he lifted one of the dead soldiers' swords from the ground, then spun his wrist with both swords in hand. "I'm here just for the sake of one woman, *my* woman. And for that I am foolish— just as you all are for that damned old prophecy. For seventy-seven years, the Zenzele have banned the high noble families from ever marrying one another because you all reek of fear. Yet for all that fear, have you even prepared for a moment such as this? Can you even fight me on your own, *Highness*? Or do you not want to risk it?"

M'kuru was shocked when Effiom laughed then, a sound both full of mirth and coldness. Shaking his head, he said, "All of you and your damn one-on-one challenges. As if I give a damn." The prince nodded to one of the soldiers, and they ran toward Neema, but Zereen easily cut both his arms from his body before twisting both swords into his stomach.

"Fight me on your own, you *coward*!" Zereen hollered back to him. "Stop hiding behind your army! For once, have honor!"

"Honor?" Prince Effiom gripped the reins of his horse. "Where is your honor in disobeying your king? For peace, you should have listened to the law! Her death, all of their deaths, are in the hands of you two selfish idiots. I will have your heads cut and hung on the walls of the capital as a reminder to anyone who thinks they may disobey royal commands." He looked at the other soldiers. *"Bring me her head!"*

When the next soldier moved, Zereen stepped back and cut the arm from *his* body, allowing it to fall right beside Black Fang, still on the ground where his sister had left it next to her.

"Touch her, and you will die," Zereen said, his voice much harsher. "I swear it."

Prince Effiom grabbed a crossbow and shot an arrow into Zereen's arm. "Did you mishear me?" he asked his soldiers. *"Kill him!"*

Every high noble family had their own fighting style, but everyone always said the most graceful and beautiful of all was that of the Nnamani family. M'kuru had never seen a fighting style other than that of the Mukundi, and theirs was always called savage. So as he watched Zereen Nnamani fight, he believed the legends were true. For the Nnamani style was the most elegant and beautiful he'd ever seen. No matter how many soldiers came or how fast they were, Zereen was faster and swifter; he moved like water. He made it look easy, and if any of them had any honor, he would have conquered them all, but that was not the world anymore. In the end, Zereen did not lose by the sword. No, he fell to his knees as arrows rained down on him from every direction, the deadliest of them the second bolt from Prince Effiom's crossbow, striking Zereen through the neck.

M'kuru only wanted to close his eyes when he fell to the ground, but he couldn't look away. He watched Zereen speak, but only gibberish came from him. "Tella . . . ndom . . . Arz.amp.ende . . ."

He had never met the man, but he knew Zereen's was a life worth more than any of those he fought.

I want to wake up. Please, let me wake up, he begged himself.

But the nightmare continued.

"Now that is done, find me the legitimate son of Lord Mukundi!" Prince Effiom hollered at his men. "He is a child, so he couldn't have gone far. Do not rest until you bring him to me—alive or dead, I do not care!"

"Yes, Your Highness."

A large number of the soldiers scattered to find him, even as M'kuru stayed as still as possible. He watched as Prince Effiom finally came off his horse, walked over to Neema and Zereen beside her lying in a pool of blood, and stepped on them both as he reached for Black Fang.

"Your Highness, no!" The man in red-and-silver armor came over—the one who had actually cut down Father—and grabbed the prince's wrist before he could take the sword.

"What?"

"Rumors say that Black Fang, as well as their family seal, is poisoned, and only a person born of their family can wield it," the man said before releasing his hand.

"Is that so?" Prince Effiom tilted his head to the side to stare at it, then grabbed one of the hands of a random soldier, forcing him to grip the sword instead.

"*Ahh!*" the soldier screeched, and wrenched his hand away, gripping it as it burned.

"For once, the rumors are true. How refreshing. Give me her hand . . . just the hand." Prince Effiom smiled and looked back at Neema.

M'kuru watched, numbed to his core, as the man with the red-and-silver armor drove his spear into the earth then pulled out the sword he'd used to kill M'kuru's father and brought the blade down on his sister's hand, cutting it off and using it to grip the sword.

Prince Effiom chuckled as he looked over the sword he held with her bloodied hand in his. "It looks better like this anyway. I'll store it in my chambers. Send the rest back to the capital."

"Yes, Your Highness," the commander replied.

As Prince Effiom got back on his white horse, the quiet rage in M'kuru's heart spoke clearly to the rest of his soul.

I will never forgive.

I will never forget.

I will show them no mercy.

He had not moved from the hole in the ground when the sun finally came up in the morning. His eyes never looked away from the bloody mark on the forest floor, where the soldiers had cut up his sister and Zereen Nnamani, all the while laughing and mocking them for the love they had shared. The soldiers had stuffed them into wooden boxes and carried them away into the night. Now there was nothing left except blood—so much of it that the soil could not hold it, and it pooled to the surface.

He did not eat or drink.

He did not even sleep.

He couldn't feel parts of his body anymore since they had long gone to sleep, but still, he did not move. And so, daylight faded to night, the rain coming along with it, and then it was day again. Still, M'kuru did not move, even though every part of him was wet and cold. All he kept thinking of was his family. Everyone . . . everyone was most likely dead now. Everyone but him. Why him? He wondered. Why was he still alive?

Was it because he was the only legitimate son of Lord Mukundi? No. His baba never treated him differently from his brothers. No one was allowed to be treated differently in their house. Not once had anyone ever said the word "legitimate" to him. He only even realized what it meant after figuring out his mother was his baba's wife and not a concubine. But his mother took care of all his brothers too. So why? Why was he the only one alive now? Why?

M'kuru! He heard his sister's voice yelling at him in his mind. It was only then his eyes regained focus and he looked around still hoping she was still there somehow. She wasn't, and he couldn't look for ghosts; he needed to leave.

But to where?

Should I go to Winneba? Zereen is dead, and he said he'd been disowned. Does his father support the king? Even if he doesn't, will he put the rest of his family at risk for me? What if they send me to the king? His mind just kept reeling and thinking, trying to find a way to save himself. Where could he go? Where could he hide? He knew he couldn't stay in that hole for much longer, but he also had no plan. Clearly Neema had meant for them to meet with Zereen, and that meeting had ended bloody.

So that left . . . what?

Where is the best place to hide? M'kuru asked himself, not so much an actual question but a rhetorical one, a puzzle like his tutors used to put before him. Then, slowly, he realized where he needed to go:

Under the feet of the person searching.

I need to go to the capital.

To Ahalon.

It was madness, but it was *something*. A direction. Except now that he knew where he wished to go, he tried to move, but it still took his body a second to remember how. His bones ached, and he was weak—both in body and spirit—but finally he crawled out from the fallen tree. His legs wobbled when he tried to stand, though, and he nearly collapsed. He caught himself, planting his feet firmly in the stream. He wanted to gather himself, but then he heard something that caused panic to spread through him.

Hooves.

He tried to crawl back into the hole, but his legs would not budge. When the dark brown horse finally reached him, M'kuru turned back in horror, only to see the horse had no rider. That horror turned to recognition—M'kuru knew that horse. He had just seen it. The saddle on it, with the symbol of the Golden-Crowned Crane, belonged to Zereen. *Had* belonged to Zereen, he thought bitterly. The horse ignored him and walked over to where its master had fallen and started to smell the ground before kneeling down, like it was waiting.

It couldn't know Zereen was never coming back.

Slowly, M'kuru stumbled over to it, resting his body on it when he reached its side.

"Your master is gone. I'm sorry," he whispered, and with fading strength, M'kuru grabbed the reins and threw himself onto the back of the horse. But it didn't move. "Please . . . go."

It would not budge. Closing his eyes, M'kuru remembered the sound Zereen had made with his lips, and he made the same sound. It was only then that the horse rose. It got up off the ground but didn't begin to run. Again, M'kuru thought back and did it again, gently kicking into the horse's side. It took off faster than he expected, forcing M'kuru to hold on as tightly as possible. All too soon, the green of the trees began to blur together as his body finally demanded the sleep that was withheld from it.

It was only then that M'kuru closed his eyes.

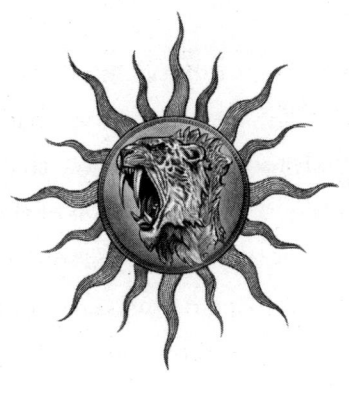

2

M'KURU

Madada

FOOD.

Not just food.

Meat.

It was that smell that woke him up. His vision was blurred, and he felt heavy. And for a brief moment, he didn't understand why. For a brief moment, he wondered where everyone was, his mother, his baba, his brothers, Neema . . . then that moment ended, and he knew exactly where. His vision cleared, and the sound of the horse as it chewed on the grass under him was almost as loud as the birds in the trees above.

They are dead.

My family is dead.

He remembered.

He saw it over and over again in his mind, and pain returned tenfold. *Why am I the only one left? Why did I have to be the only one left?* He didn't know the answers to those questions, but he knew he had to live, if only to avenge his family, to keep them from suffering in the afterlife, but how? It took at least thirty days to ride to Ahalon by horse, and depending on where he was now, he'd have to keep himself hidden in the forest the whole time.

"Ugh . . ." he groaned when his stomach grumbled.

The horse bucked, forcing M'kuru to slide off his saddle. He was so weak that he just lay there, looking up at the blue sky in the space between the trees.

"Luckily, the forest is your food," M'kuru muttered to the horse. M'kuru was so hungry and tired, he was ready to fall over, and then he smelled it again—meat.

Hope got him up off the ground. He tried pulling on the horse, but it didn't budge. He even made the same sound again, but the horse still wouldn't move.

"Fine, stay here," he muttered to it. Holding on to the trees as he stumbled through the forest, he licked his lips and swallowed his saliva to ease the ache in his throat as he followed his nose.

"No . . . stop! Please! Stop!" a woman cried out, her voice carrying through the trees as he reached the source of the smell.

It was a small camp by the stream, and there was a woman on the rocks, with one man holding her down as another one ripped off her clothes. The men weren't dressed in armor, their clothes old and tattered. Their hair was wild and unkempt, filled with dirt. When the men removed their clothes, they tossed their daggers to the side, unknowingly closer to M'kuru.

He almost didn't notice, so entranced was he by the smell, which he saw came from spitted rabbits roasting over the fire.

"*No!*" the woman screamed, managing to fight one of them off of her only to be beat by another man.

M'kuru had heard so much screaming, he felt numb to it. Yet it shook him from the shame of thinking of food over this woman's plight. Not that anyone would have known—the men were so focused on being beasts that they did not notice him. But *he* knew. And the way they laughed and took pleasure in hurting the woman made him think of Neema. He remembered how weak and useless he was to her and how he couldn't fight then—everyone else fought for him, and that was how he had lived.

Now that he was alone, he had to fight for himself, he had to be able to protect someone. Just like . . . just like his mother and sister protected him.

Reaching over and grabbing the silver spiraled hilt of his dagger so tightly his knuckles dug into his skin, he slowly crouched down, breathing through his nose, and stepped closer to them. His heart beat faster and faster, like drums, until he was right behind one of them. Without a second thought, he drew his blade and stabbed the first man in the ear with all the force he could muster. When he pulled it out, the man's blood was warm as it hit M'kuru's face. He'd never felt blood on him before . . . it startled him.

"*Ahh!*" the man screamed, and reached up to his ear.

"You filthy rat—" The other man lunged at him but M'kuru stabbed him in his neck, right under his hairy chin, and when M'kuru pulled the knife out, blood poured down his hands. Both men rolled off the woman, trying to stop the bleeding, and then the first man tried to run away from M'kuru.

If he gets away he'll do this to someone else. He could tell someone he saw me, M'kuru thought, and with that thought he chased after him.

"Ughhh. . . ." The man coughed when M'kuru attacked him, knocking them both to the rocks.

Taking the dagger, M'kuru stabbed into the man's chest not once, not twice, but four times before he got up and saw the second man trying to crawl away.

"Please . . ." The man gurgled, blood already filling his airpipe. So even though the man was as good as dead, M'kuru stalked toward him.

"My father once said that killing a man is not easy. I think he lied, for it's very easy," M'kuru said coldly. His blood-covered hands became even bloodier as he stabbed the man in the neck once more, dragging the blade through. It was only when the man fell at his feet that M'kuru turned around and headed straight for the campfire, grabbed the stick with the rabbit on it, and bit into it. It burned, but he kept eating as fast as he could while the woman behind him could only weep.

"I wish I could cry, but I can't yet," he told her, then found the woman's water and drank from the leather pouch, water spilling down his face.

He ate and drank and ate even more, hoping he wouldn't be hungry for a while, not once looking away from the trees nor letting go of the dagger in his hand. He even listened to the woman behind him carefully, so when she finally stopped crying and he heard the rocks shift, he quickly got up, holding the dagger with one hand and the rabbit with the other. Her brown face and neck were swollen and covered in bruises as she hugged herself. Her hair was cut short, and she was shaking but still reached out for him. Her dark eyes were wild and crazed.

"Khalil," she called as she reached out for him. When she stepped forward again, M'kuru stepped back and took another bite of the rabbit but kept the knife out in front of him too. "It's okay. You're okay. Your mama is okay. You saved me."

My mama? My mama is dead . . .

"Khalil, it's okay. We can go home now. Take my hand, and come. It's not safe here, so we need to go." She beat her chest with one hand and reached for him with the other. "Khalil, please don't leave me again."

A voice called out from the trees before he could tell her he wasn't who she thought he was.

"Femi? Femi?"

Hearing the deep voice calling out, M'kuru grabbed the pouch of water and another rabbit before taking off without another word, running straight toward the trees with the dagger clutched in his hand.

"No, Khalil! *Khalil!*" the woman screamed behind him as he ran right into something—no, *someone*—and fell to the grass.

"Who are you?" a man with gray-black hair asked him, his eyes pure white and half-shut.

"Ugh." M'kuru groaned, looking down at the cut on his hand where the dagger had sliced him when he fell.

He tried to get up, but all of a sudden, a pair of thin, fragile arms wrapped around him.

"Khalil!" the woman sobbed, holding M'kuru. "Why do you keep trying to leave me?"

"Get off me!" M'kuru yelled, trying to peel her hands from him, but she would not let loose. "I said get off."

"Khalil, stop it. We are going home!" she screamed at him, trying to pull him with her. "No more running—"

"I am not him. Let go!"

She froze, and he was able to break loose and crawl away from her. When he turned back, he saw the old man holding a needle right in her neck.

"Ay . . . Khalil . . ." she tried to say before she closed her eyes.

The old man's gaze then shifted to M'kuru, and before M'kuru could move or say another word, he felt the pinch at the side of his neck. M'kuru reached up to pull out the needle that was so thin it looked like silver hair.

"What . . . what did . . . you do?" M'kuru whispered, his eyes heavy. "Stay . . . back."

The man didn't answer, and everything began to melt away. M'kuru's eyes were too heavy to stay open any longer, but still he tried to fight it, to get back up.

"I . . . can't . . . die . . . now." Everything faded to darkness, and in that darkness, he heard the voices of his family.

Who are you?

You now must hide and preserve our family.

The heavens will not forgive, and Madada will not forget! The Mukundi will have its vengeance!

Who are you?

Not yet, Six . . . but soon you fight . . . now you need to hide.

Fierce, steadfast, strong, and born with the wisdom of ages.

Zenzele!

Who are you?

Go!

It was as if he were falling through a dark void of his most recent nightmares. There was darkness all around, but he saw his mother's face at the end of the tunnel. He wanted to move toward her but was frozen in place.

The tunnel started to close, and he screamed, but no sound came out.

He heard only the sound of her voice.

Goodbye.

———

WHEN HIS EYES SNAPPED OPEN, he first saw ginger and herbs—rows and rows of ginger and herbs hanging from the thatched roof above him. He couldn't help but stare at them momentarily before sitting up. And when he did, he noticed his hand was wrapped up, his clothes were changed, and the dark-colored garments he now wore itched a lot.

"Stop that," the old man said, smacking M'kuru's hand and forcing him to stop scratching. The man then lifted a clay bowl to M'kuru's mouth to drink. "Drink . . . the rest."

M'kuru didn't even get a chance to stop scratching before the man forced it into his mouth. It was cold, bitter, and slid down his throat slowly, making him cough as it hit his dry throat. It tasted like grass, old grapes, and dirt mixed together in water.

"Who . . . are you?" he managed to ask, trying to clean his tongue. "And where am I?"

"Kazera."

Kazera? The village among the hills? It was one of the most important farming villages just north of his family's private lands, beyond the Bamboo Forest and only a day and a half away. He sat up and watched as the man moved over to the other corner of the house, picked one of the herbs above him, then stuffed it into his own mouth before sitting down. His gray-black hair was cut short but his similarly colored beard was long, his half-closed eyes were directly on him. The man picked up a fan and waved the incense over the screaming woman from the stream, now curled asleep beside him with a cloth over her face.

Again M'kuru asked, "Who are—"

"How old are you?" the man asked.

"What?"

"How old are you, child?"

"Ten," M'kuru answered slowly.

"From now on, you are nine."

"What?"

"Khalil." He sighed, still fanning the incense. "I am already blind, so you cannot be deaf, or else people will think we are a comedy."

"I am not deaf. I just don't understand what you are saying. Why do you people keep calling me Khalil?"

The man yawned as he lifted a knife. "Because that is your name."

"No, it is not."

"Then what is your name?"

M'kuru opened his mouth to answer but realized he couldn't. He didn't know who these crazy people were or what they wanted. All he knew was that Prince Effiom and all the kingdom would be looking for him, so he couldn't expose himself.

"Exactly," the man said, nodding. "So, until you can answer that question, you are Khalil, a nine-year-old boy, and I expect you to do all your chores and help your mother as she recovers—oh, and help me with my patients, of course." He said it as if it were the most logical thing in the world. "Now, fetch me my palm wine."

The man pointed to the red-colored jar sitting closest to him.

"Are you both insane?"

"Tsk." The man hissed at him and reached into his clothes, re-moving one of those needles again. He held it up almost casually, but the threat was as clear as day.

M'kuru got up quickly, crossed the room, and picked up the man's wine, then set it right in front of the old man's legs.

He grinned like a madman and uncorked the wine, inhaling the strong scent for as long and hard as he could before exhaling happily.

"There is nothing sweeter in this world," the man said, hold-ing his hand out.

"What?"

"Is that the only thing you know how to say?"

"That isn't the only thing I've said," M'kuru muttered, scratching himself again, but the old man smacked his hand away from his neck.

"I told you to stop that—" the man started to say, but he stopped and turned his head to the side. Frowning, he recorked the wine and set it back on the ground.

"What?" M'kuru didn't mean to say that again, but he didn't get an answer.

The old man rose from the ground, his bones cracking as he did.

"Stay here," the old man said to him, and walked out before M'kuru could have a chance to ask another question.

M'kuru set the wine back in the corner then looked down at the lady with the brown cloth over her face. Closer now, he could see some type of green mud on her arms and even her foot. She breathed in slowly, and on the side of her face, the only part he could see of her skin, tears fell from her closed eyes onto her ears. M'kuru froze and immediately glanced over his shoulder as he heard someone coming. He felt sick, and his heart began beating faster.

It wasn't long before he heard a man's voice yell out, "You!"

"How can I help you, soldiers?" he heard the old man's voice reply. "Do you need medicine—"

"Have you seen a lost boy around here?"

"I am blind, so I cannot see any boy at all."

"Do not joke with us, old man. We are looking for a lost boy. Have you heard anything, since you cannot see?"

M'kuru rose and moved closer to the door to hear more clearly and glanced around for a place he could hide.

There was none.

"A lost boy? No, I have not. Who is lost?" the old man replied.

"That is none of your concern. Is this your home?"

"Yes. My daughter and grandson, but they are very ill——"

"Call them out!"

"They require rest."

M'kuru heard the sound of swords being pulled from scabbards.

"I will not ask you again, old man!"

"Khalil," the old man called.

M'kuru didn't answer. He didn't know what to do, but he felt like the old man was trying to help him. Why, he wasn't sure, and he had very few options.

"It's all right, Khalil. Come out now."

Swallowing the lump in his throat, M'kuru turned and stepped out, covering his eyes because the sunlight was so bright. Eventually his eyes adjusted and he saw three soldiers in their red armor, the emblem on the center a spear within the sun, making it clear exactly who they were and who they were after.

"Is your mother still asleep?" the old man asked him.

M'kuru glanced up at him and then back at the men, who all now seemed to step back from him. Reaching up, he scratched his neck again as he answered, "Yes."

"Do one of you want to check inside for yourselves?" the old man asked them, stepping to the side for them to enter, but they all covered their mouths and stepped back even farther. The one in the center kicked the man to his left, nodding for him to check before backing away. The old man grabbed M'kuru by the collar and pulled him close as the soldier poked his head inside.

"What is wrong with the boy?" the man on the horse asked.

What is wrong with what boy? M'kuru wondered. *Me?*

"We aren't sure, but I am determined to find a cure for him." The old man nodded happily and added, "Do not fear, for it is not contagious."

What's not contagious? M'kuru asked himself.

"There is no one else in there but the mother." The soldier rushed back out.

Nodding, the man in the center turned to leave. "If you hear of any strange boys in the woods, you are to report him to the local guard."

"I will." The old man nodded.

They all left through the gates, and M'kuru watched them go before turning to face the old man. "Cure me? What are you talking about?"

The old man just pointed to some buckets over to the side.

"The sheep need water, and I need wine," was his only reply, and he went back into his home. When M'kuru tried to follow, the man just pointed again. "Chores, remember?"

Frowning, M'kuru headed to the buckets, only to see his reflection in the water . . .

No, this can't be me, he thought, because . . . it was a monster looking back at him. As he backed away, he fell down. He reached up to touch his face, his brown skin covered in red hives and peeling.

"What did you do to me?!" M'kuru yelled at the man.

"Shh!" the old man snapped. "Do you want to bring them back?" He added under his breath as he entered the house, "It will clear up in a few days."

"Why are you doing this?" M'kuru asked him.

"Doing what?" The old man sat back down in the corner.

"Letting me stay here." *Helping me?* M'kuru wanted to ask, but held back. He didn't want the old man to think he needed help.

"I'm blind," the old man said as if that were an answer to M'kuru's question, and he pointed to the jar.

If he is blind, how did he know I put the jar there?

Picking up the jar, M'kuru set it back in front of the man.

"Your mother is sick. I'm not letting you stay here. I'm making you *work* here. You are a servant."

"A servant?"

He took a long drink of the wine then wiped the corner of his mouth. "Yes, a servant. You don't expect an old man and sick woman to be taking care of you, do you? What are you, nobility?"

Yes. "No," M'kuru lied.

"Then go tend to the house. Don't forget to milk the sheep afterward."

Milk sheep?

"Careful. Moujo bites."

He couldn't be serious. And yet, in looking at the old man's face, it was clear he was.

"I'm not going to milk your sheep. I'm heading to Ahalon—"

"How?"

"What do you mean how? With my . . ." M'kuru paused, thinking back over the farm. He'd seen everything but a horse. "What did you do with my horse?"

"You didn't have a horse."

"A large brown horse, with a saddle emblem of a crane—"

"How could you afford a horse with a saddle? You are the son of a poor, sick woman, and a blind man's grandson."

Exhaling angrily, M'kuru tried to stay calm. "I borrowed—"

"You *stole* a horse?" There was a mocking lilt to the man's astonishment. "You know the punishment for theft is a hand. You may lose both your arms if not your life for a horse, of all things." The old man shook his head. "Can't have that. Who will milk Moujo?"

"Who's been milking Moujo all this time?"

"You, Khalil."

M'kuru just opened his mouth, but no words came out.

"Are you going to do your chores or just stand there?"

Inhaling again, M'kuru tried once again: "I cannot help you, old man, because I am needed in Ahalon. I appreciate your help, but I bid you goodbye."

"Did you hear the high-noble family Mukundi were slaughtered in their homes by the king's army?" the old man asked him, and M'kuru froze in front of the door. "That's why those soldiers were here. They said the army slaughtered everyone, even their horses, and their home was set ablaze. Nothing and no one survived except for the lord's youngest son. That's who all the soldiers are looking for."

Slowly, M'kuru turned to look at the old man.

"If *you* were that boy, Khalil, where would you go?" the old man asked. "I think you might be tempted to go to Winneba. After all, it's said that the boy was able to escape due to Zereen Nnamani. His family emblem is the crane, isn't it? It would be on such things as their saddles."

"Who are you?" M'kuru whispered.

The old man just snickered and poured himself a glass of wine. "Who am I? Can't an old grandfather talk about the stuffy nobles with his grandson? They are the best form of entertainment."

M'kuru made a fist. "The massacre of a whole family in the middle of the night, while they were to head to sleep, is entertainment?"

"For some people, yes." The old man drank, and M'kuru clenched his jaw. "Though I am sure many people are weeping in Madada now. The Mukundi family was held in the highest respects in these lands, and many still call them the true kings. To kill them all in such a manner will never be forgotten. I hope this lost son does not act recklessly and endanger himself and that he swallows his rage, his anger, and pain. I hope he holds it down and allows it to fuel him forward and not burn him up. He should hold on to all of it, trap it inside of himself until one day when he is big enough and strong enough to open his mouth and swallow the sun, fulfilling a prophecy set in motion long ago."

There was silence in the air.

M'kuru remembered his sister's words to him: *Not yet, Six . . . but soon you will fight . . . now you need to hide.*

He couldn't just hide in a hole in the ground somewhere in the forest. And there were only so many places out there he could hide from the Red Sun Army and still survive. But here, he could be right under their noses . . .

It still felt too far from the king, he thought. How would he get his revenge while on a farm?

How can I get revenge if I'm dead?

"Is such a thing possible? To swallow the sun?"

"What has been done once can always be done again. . . ." The old man hiccupped. "He who swallows the sun brings forth darkness, and in darkness comes a new light."

M'kuru frowned. "What are you talking about? And how is any of what you're saying possible while on a farm?"

The old man laughed. "What kind of question is that?"

What kind of conversation is this? M'kuru thought, but tried to refocus the man. "So, if that lost son found himself here, what should he do?"

"He definitely shouldn't go to Ahalon. A boy with no connections but who can read, ride a horse, speak with manners, and have smooth, unworked hands could not possibly be a servant or slave. Such a child would stand out no matter what he did or said. And to be an orphan in this world is a horrible thing, especially under the Zenzele hierarchy. One needs connections, a background, and a story of who they are and where they came from—such as a farm, one where many people will remember him.

"So you should go do your chores now, *Khalil.*"

M'kuru wasn't sure what to say, but the old man made sense and had already helped him. Why? He didn't know. All he knew was that no matter how long it took, he would kill every last person in the Zenzele family when he got the chance. He swore it on the souls of all his family, all those who died, and yes, even their horse.

And if I cannot, let me be cursed and ripped to shreds, he thought.

"What are you waiting for?" the old man asked.

"Nothing . . ." M'kuru paused before adding, "Grandfather."

I am M'kuru Mukundi of Madada, but I cannot be M'kuru Mukundi, he thought.

So until I can once more, I will be this Khalil.

3

KHALIL

Madada

BY THE DAY'S END, PLACES ACHED THAT HE didn't realize it was possible to ache in. Everything hurt, even his eyes. He never realized taking care of animals would be so hard. But he finished the chores. He didn't just have to take care of the sheep but also fifteen chickens, four goats—one brown and the rest white and black—all trapped behind a wooden fence in the corner near the house in the open, rolling valley in the center of the woods.

And that didn't even account for taking care of his "mother" and "grandfather."

When Khalil went back inside to lie down, the old man said to him as he sat in his corner, grinding something over a gray stone, "You are very slow."

Frowning, Khalil lifted his arms to show the old man the dirt and bite mark his stupid brown sheep gave him, but realized he couldn't see it anyway.

"Your sheep bit me," Khalil muttered instead, returning to the straw mat to lie down.

"I told you she would. Moujo bites people she doesn't like."

"Well, I don't like her either," Khalil answered, annoyed—the nerve of that weird sheep. It was the smallest of all the ones on the farm, but it was the only one with a white belly and brown coloring for its head and legs and it had one broken horn. "What happened to her other horn?"

"The more important question is, what did you bring back for supper?"

"For supper?" Khalil repeated, looking back at him, confused. "You want me to get supper too?"

The old man poured a few drops of wine on the rock and rubbed the purple-brown paste with his fingers, then nodded. "I'm hungry."

Khalil stared at him, too tired and not sure what to say.

So the old man kept talking, "You're not well enough to go hunting. I was waiting for you to finish, but you took so long. So just this once, you can kill one of the chickens to eat. Don't forget to build a fire."

"You want me to kill a chicken?" Khalil asked in disbelief. He had just fed all the animals. Then he'd milked the sheep, cleaned their little sheep house, and put them back in it. Now the old man wanted him to kill a chicken. He had never worked so much in all his life.

"You killed two men, didn't you?" said the old man, and Khalil was surprised by the reminder, because he had forgotten. *Had that only been a day ago?*

"The woman inside . . . is she okay?" he finally thought to ask.

"You mean your mother?"

Khalil felt like frowning at that but he had already decided to live like this for now. "Yes, is she all right?"

"As much as she can be. Now, go before it becomes too dark for you to see."

Khalil said nothing and turned around, stepping outside and looking at all the chickens still walking around. He wasn't sure what to do, so he just tried to grab one, but it darted right out of his grasp, and because it started running and flapping its wings, the rest of them all started to run and flap *their* wings.

"Get back here," he muttered, and ran after them, chasing them up and down and all over the place. Khalil jumped to catch one, only to land on his stomach in the dirt.

"Have you never caught a chicken before?" asked the old man, standing outside with his rock in his hand.

"Does it look like I have?"

"No. It looks like my grandson is lying in the dirt instead of getting my dinner ready."

Khalil grumbled at that, pushing off the ground as the old man set the rock down. "I *am* going to catch one," Khalil said.

"Hopefully before I die of hunger."

Khalil ignored him and looked over to the chickens, and this time, he walked up slower before bending and reaching out to snatch it, but once again, it ran. Breathing through his nose, he picked up a stone to throw at one of the hens as hard as he could but then he heard the old man speak from behind him.

"Determination is to be commended, but in your case, you only look more foolish for it."

When Khalil turned to face him, a chicken was at the old man's feet, eating whatever the old man had ground up and put on the rock. The old man knelt in front of it and snapped its neck before

Khalil could blink, and then without a word, he sat down in front of the door and started to pull the feathers off it. Khalil sat down in front of him and watched.

"Sometimes, you do not have to chase things but simply wait for them to come to you."

"Why didn't you tell me sooner?" Khalil muttered, annoyed.

"You didn't ask." The old man snickered, throwing a fistful of feathers onto the ground. It was the first time Khalil noticed how wrinkled and scarred the old man's hands were.

"Will you answer my questions if I ask?"

"Yes." The old man nodded.

This was his chance to figure out more about him, and he wouldn't let it go. "Who is Khalil?"

"You're asking me who you are?" the old man replied.

Khalil frowned.

Fine, I'll do it his way.

"Yes. Who am I?"

The old man nodded and turned the chicken upside down before pulling a knife from his sleeve. "You are Khalil Rausi."

Khalil froze, hearing that surname. His hands balled into fists as he remembered the man in red-and-silver armor. "My family name is Rausi?"

"Yes."

Khalil clenched his teeth, shaking his head as the old man began to cut around the back of the chicken. "Rausi is the family name of the head adviser and Great General of the Red Sun Army."

"He is. The Rausi family goes back almost as far as the high noble families. Their ancestors swore a blood oath of loyalty to the Zenzele dynasty."

Khalil did his best to swallow his rage. "If that is true, and I am a Rausi too, why am I here and not in Ahalon or any other Zenzele land—"

"All of Ahkebulin is Zenzele lands," the old man interrupted him to say, turning the chicken once more before continuing. "This land belongs to the king, and the king is Essien Zenzele. He could come here and remove us from this farm if he wanted."

The old man held the chicken's neck and pulled the skin tightly before slitting the bird from the backbone to the top of the neck.

"The king wouldn't," Khalil said, pulling his feet back so as not to get any of the chicken on them. "The king would give the command, but the Rausi family would be the one to come with their army to kill everyone . . . just like they did with the . . ."

"The family of Mukundi," the old man finished for Khalil, separating a small white line in the chicken's neck and pulling it completely away. "Some say that although the Rausi family are just nobles, they are even more powerful than the high nobles. For that reason, they command the army of the Red Sun. Their blood oath of loyalty is without question or compromise. Some have even killed their own children on command, as the oath cannot be broken."

"To impersonate them or a high noble is a death offense," Khalil whispered, remembering when his baba had even taken him to see a man being punished for that crime . . . they pulled him apart with four horses.

"You know a lot about nobles, it seems," the old man said, and cut the neck off the chicken's backbone.

Khalil didn't reply.

"But then again, you are the illegitimate son of one, so I'm sure your mother told you all about it," the old man said when Khalil did not reply.

"The illegitimate son . . . of a Rausi," Khalil repeated slowly and then looked around at the place they lived in.

"Not just any Rausi, the head general and lord of the Rausi family." The old man sighed deeply. "I do not know which is crueler, fate or people."

"People," Khalil answered. "Because people make and spread fate."

"I see you do not believe in prophecies." The old man smiled even as he reached inside the chicken to scrape the intestines loose from the top and sides.

Watching him do this for some reason made Khalil think of his sister, Neema, and how they had cut her to pieces before him. It made his stomach turn and he was no longer pleased with the thought of eating the chicken.

"I believe the seers are crazy people, and everyone should stop listening to their hallucinations. It only causes pain and trouble," Khalil muttered, clenching his fist.

"You believe their power to be nothing more than hallucinations?" The old man chuckled.

"Yes. My ba— I mean, I heard once that seers claim they can only see bits and pieces of things to cover up for all the times they are wrong."

"That may be true. Some seers see mere flashes of things, but some see—"

"We are better off not listening than figuring out who might be right. Their words are dangerous and cause innocent people to die." Khalil repeated what his father had taught him and what he now held to be the truth after what he had overheard.

The old man nodded. "And if you were to know a fire was to come and kill many innocents, would you keep it to yourself?"

Khalil did not answer, just gawked at the dead chicken.

"If the Mukundi family had a seer, maybe they could have been warned."

Khalil snapped, yelling as he rose, "Innocent people should not need warnings! The Mukundi family was innocent!"

The old man paused and glanced up at the boy, not seeing him but feeling his pain. "Aren't rabbits innocent?"

"What?"

"Was this chicken not innocent?" the old man asked before lifting his hand.

"Those are just animals—"

"If a rabbit or chicken learned to speak as we speak and told us about themselves, would you think twice about eating them?" Khalil stood stunned, silent, his eyes wide as he looked at the chicken. The old man continued: "What if the leaves, grass, and grain learned to speak too? Would the rabbit or a chicken stop eating them?"

"I . . . No?" Khalil finally replied.

The old man nodded. "Why?"

"Because they have to eat," Khalil whispered.

"Exactly. Khalil, this world does not care if you are innocent, just, or kind. It cares if you survive. The wolf will eat the rabbit, and the rabbit will eat the grass and the leaves, just like you will eat this chicken. Why? Because you have to eat. You have to live. It is all unfair, and the innocent can only adapt and try to find a measure to survive. For some, the seers are that measure, a gift from the gods, the only hope humans have to fight back injustice. They are one of the few remnants of magic left in this world."

"You believe in magic too?" Khalil frowned now, very worried he was betting his life away on a crazy man.

"Have you not heard the tales of the dœwers?"

"What? You mean the fables lowborns tell their children about the world?"

"Fables, you say?"

"Yes. Lowborns cannot understand the great writings and so made up stories to entertain one another." Lowborns could not read or write, and his father had said too much knowledge hurt their minds. So they preferred outlandish stories of magic to truth. "There is no such thing as dœwers."

He chuckled. "Maybe not today; but they can exist tomorrow."

"No, they cannot, old man. I do not know why you wish to confuse me with such things. But you will not convince me to believe what is not true. Like I said, there is no such thing as dœwers, and seers are——"

"Having hallucinations that are sometimes right?" the old man asked, and shook his head. "Whichever you believe, if your mind is closed to all the tools given to you in a fight, you are also to blame for your loss."

"What does that mean?"

"The world is greater than even the greatest of writings. Maybe that is why the lowborn live and the highborn vanish."

Khalil hung his head, then slowly sank to the ground, rubbing his chest. "Why are you telling me this? All I . . . I just want . . ."

"I know what you want, because everyone wants it." Khalil glanced up at the old man as he continued speaking. "The power to protect what we love."

At that, Khalil smiled, but it was a bitter smile. "No, I want the power to avenge those I've lost, nothing else."

"Bitterness should not come from children." The old man snickered to himself. "What job will be left for those who are old?"

"Gutting chickens?"

The old man's eyebrow went up as he stuck the chicken and knife out for Khalil to take. "Cut the feet off. We'll save them for later."

Khalil at first did not want to cut the chicken to pieces, but then remembered what the old man had said. He had to eat, so he had to cut it. He took the chicken and bloody knife, holding it the way the old man did, and started to hack away at it. "Why is a Rausi—I mean, why am I here?"

"You are here because I now think *both* fate and people are cruel." The old man laughed, rising to his feet. "A woman fell in love with a great general, rising from a simple maid to his most favorite concubine. And for that, she found herself and her child poisoned, so sick they were sent away by that general's wife back to her hometown, her father's home, until they are cured of their sickness, of course."

Khalil moved to cut the other leg off and stood up as well. "So, when I am cured . . ."

"Yes, you cannot stay here. After all, you are a Rausi, and illegitimate or not, your duty is in Ahalon, defending the king and this great dynasty."

Looking from the chicken to the old man, Khalil asked, "How long until you cure me?"

"I do not know. There seems to be something wrong with your mind, and you do not remember me or your mother. So, until you are fully Khalil Rausi, you will remain here. But never forget that one day Lord Rausi will want his son home," the old man replied, and walked past Khalil toward the large wells of water.

Khalil lifted the bloody chicken to his face and stared at it, then looked back at the old man.

He had one more question.

Is he a seer?

"Are you just going to hold it all night or are you going to wash it so we can eat?" the old man snapped.

Khalil frowned but stepped forward when he heard a footstep beside him.

"Khalil?"

The woman from the river stood at the door, her round face no longer as red but still bruised, her short hair matted, and her brown skin seeming to have a pale gray tone to it that he hadn't noticed before. She seemed small, even to him—a child. Her eyes were hollow . . . like she wasn't awake or was looking right through him.

Khalil quickly lifted the chicken for her to see. "We are about to cook—"

"Khalil!" She threw herself onto him and hugged him tightly, falling to her knees. He held the chicken and the knife away from her body, not sure what to do. "Mom will be good. I'll be better. I promise. Don't go again, okay? Don't go, please. I need you. I can't go back without you."

Khalil looked to the old man, but the look he got in return was inscrutable.

So all he could do was nod as the woman cried on him.

4

PRINCE EFFIOM

Madada

WHEN THEY ENTERED HIS TENT, THE SOLDIERS fell to their knees before his table as he finished his painting. Beside him sat a woman with skin so dark it could not be called brown but black like the night sky. Upon her head was a braided wig, the tips locked with gold and the top a ring of puka shells.

She sat mixing ink over a plate.

"You did not find the boy?" Prince Effiom asked them, not bothering to look up from the image he was creating, a masterpiece he planned to hang up.

"Your Highness, Commander Rausi sent out search parties, but the sun is about to set—"

"Leave me," Prince Effiom interrupted the soldier, and only when the soldier backed out of the tent, the folds of the entrance closed once more, did the prince speak again.

"This is not what you foretold, seer."

"In this world, there are two streams, what is and what could be, and the ability to draw from one to another can only be done with the help of a seer, from a single ripple comes a new course—"

The stirring plate fell from her hands when he reached over and grabbed her small throat and squeezed, jerking her forward.

"Spare me your tales, seer! I do not care how it is done! I only seek to know the outcome of these events!" The prince hissed slowly into her face. "If you cannot see that far, Sauda, it is because you are not as powerful a seer as you presented yourself to be. Words cannot cover your failure. And if you fail, I have no use for you. I do not keep things I do not have a use for."

She struggled as he squeezed tighter. "I—"

"Be of use!" He threw her body onto the ground, allowing her to gather her breath. "Speak!"

"Since the great prophecy, your grandfather and now your father have tried to find a way to rid the world of the Mukundi and Nnamani families, tried and failed . . . until now. I helped you with that." She coughed, holding her throat. "It was because of my vision that you, Prince Effiom, have done what kings of the past could not! I *am* of use!"

"But if one of them lives, the deed is incomplete!" he yelled. "As long as he is alive, there is still a risk, and if there is still a risk of that stupid prophecy, my brother will use that to undermine my achievements here. So you will need to do better."

Sauda held her neck, rubbing it before sitting back up. Inhaling through her nose, she closed her eyes as if she were sleeping while sitting. However, Prince Effiom knew she was merely beginning to truly open her eyes.

He stood over her, watching as she trembled at the vision, but the longer she took, the more impatient he became. "Well? They say fear or pain helps you see. Would more of each help?"

When she opened her eyes again, she sat up straighter. "No—I have seen. And you are right. The prophecy can still come to pass. So when you return to the capital, you will not call this an achievement."

Prince Effiom's teeth and hands clenched. "I will not go back without utter triumph. Look for the boy! Can you not see where he is now or where he will go?"

"The son of Mukundi is lost from my sight or is being protected by something. You may search, but you will not find him—"

"Who!" Prince Effiom slapped his hand across her face with such force she was thrown back on the ground.

"I do not know," she muttered, wiping blood from her nose. "I've never experienced this before."

"Sauda," Prince Effiom said, frighteningly gentle. "If you do not start telling me what I want to hear, I will become angry."

"My prince, a seer can only tell you what we see, not what you want."

"And that is why my grandfather cut off the heads of your kind. Should I continue the legacy again with you?"

She bowed deeply. "My life is at your mercy, my prince. If you wish for my head I shall give it to you. But know all is not lost. Something can be done."

"What?"

Prince Effiom watched as Sauda pushed herself up from the ground and shifted to his table, where she lifted a brush and fresh scroll before writing. "The prophecy says when the Mukundi and Nnamani became one, yes? But the only daughter of Lord Mukundi was killed with her love, so the only other pair that can exist in this generation lies with the last son of Lord Mukundi and the only daughter of Nnamani."

He lifted the scroll, reading the name she had written. "Zikora Nnamani."

"She is eight years old now. Lord Nnamani has no living siblings, so she is the only daughter of the Nnamani family. Lady Nnamani is not able to bear any more children. Whoever is protecting the last son of the Mukundi family does so in vain if that girl is in your grasp."

Slowly Prince Effiom nodded as he understood how to have his victory, a small smile spreading over his lips. "Zereen Nnamani, disowned or not, betrayed us, so the Nnamani family should pay the consequences for that." He glanced over the scroll, then back at her.

"And just like that, you have become useful again, Sauda."

"You must act quickly before the crown prince does," she whispered. "Also, the Nnamani family—"

"Guards!" he hollered, cutting her off as he looked to the front of his tent. Two soldiers entered.

"Yes, Your Highness," they said together, their heads bowed.

"Tell Commander Rausi to call off the search. We are returning to the capital tomorrow morning," he ordered.

"Yes, Your Highness," they repeated, bowing once more before leaving.

Prince Effiom looked back to the seer. "I don't need you to know that the Nnamani family will denounce their son and declare loyalty to the king. With Zereen's public declaration that he disobeyed his father, they cannot meet the same fate as the Mukundi family. Not yet, at least, or the other high nobles may unite against us out of fear. I will take the girl diplomatically."

"Carefully, Your Highness," she said in return. "Just as you did with the family of Mukundi, you must make the king feel as though it is *his* plan—"

"I know how to work my father," he snapped at her. "It is my brother who is my major concern. Did you see how he will react to this?"

The seer nodded. "The crown prince will . . . seek to take me."

He turned to her, his head tilted and eyebrow raised. "Take you? The crown prince is to cause a rift with his brother over a servant, a former slave? Does he know you are a seer?"

"He suspects so but has no proof. As you rise, Your Highness, so do I. But I will never forget whom I serve." She shifted back and knelt before him, bowing her head to the floor. "You saved me. You believed my words and my power. I swear I shall never betray you. Our fates are connected. Just as I saw that day, and even still now, you will become crown prince and then king of Ahkebulin."

"Exactly what I want to hear. Therefore, I am also wary of you, Sauda, as you always know what to say. So, I shall remind you that should you betray me, no force on this earth shall be great enough to save you from my wrath," he stated coldly.

If she could have sunk lower into the floor, she would have.

"Your Highness, it is the curse of a seer never to see their fates. I neither know what is or what could be with me. But I would rather take my own life than betray you."

"Good." He looked over once more, then returned to his seat. "Now, how will the crown prince seek to tempt you?"

She nodded her head on the ground. "The crown prince shall threaten you upon your return to the palace. He will accuse me of being a seer, poisoning your thoughts, and suggest I be in his custody to judge my true nature. It is because you are there that my fate was in this. If not—"

"Enough. Rise." Prince Effiom sighed with boredom, looking at his ruined painting and then crumpling it into a ball and throwing it aside. "Should my father even hear the word 'seer' he will condemn you, which is surely what the crown prince desires."

Since the beginning of their known history, seers had always been hunted down and treated either as monsters or the mentally depraved. Mothers were celebrated for drowning their own children should they claim any visions. That had always been the way till the Great Seer saved his grandfather when he was young from a foreign ambush and warned of the Wytjreia's coming invasion. His grandfather was pleased, so he proclaimed that any man who harmed a seer would be put to death. However, the Great Seer's protection was short-lived once he foretold the prophecy. In both anger and fear, his grandfather had the Great Seer, his family, and every other seer within Ahalon beheaded, and their heads displayed on spikes on top of the palace gates.

Throughout his grandfather's entire reign, he feared a single man's words enough to ban marriage between high nobles. His grandfather lived in fear of something that would never come to pass in his lifetime. It had yet to come to pass under Effiom's father's reign either. Nevertheless, throughout the land, people to this very day held the Great Seer's word as absolute, and it drove Effiom's father to near madness whenever the people were displeased and whispered, "Do not forget the Great Seer's prophecy. The end shall come for the Zenzele."

His father, Essien, was still wary of the seers. The king had ended their compulsory death sentences, because he believed killing them only made men seek them out more. Instead, the king wished to have all the world believe them to be nothing but madmen. Something Prince Effiom would hinder if it were known he kept a seer so close to him. However, it made no sense to Effiom why he should lose such an asset over old words.

"Your Highness," Sauda whispered, gaining his attention. She nodded over her shoulder at the walls of his tent, where he saw the slightest shadow of a person beside it. *A spy,* she mouthed.

His eyes narrowed, and his fist clenched before he reached for his sword.

The seer shook her head and touched his wrist to stop him, then spoke again seductively. "My prince, please allow me to stay with you tonight. I cannot bear to be without you."

Prince Effiom released his sword, adjusting to sit up higher, cupping her cheek and kissing her. They shared a long kiss before he flipped her onto the ground. They continued on as such until the seer whispered into his ear. "He is gone."

"Who put spies around me?" he questioned angrily, pushing her off him and sitting back up.

"Who else but the king?"

"He is testing my patience." And truthfully, Prince Effiom had half a mind to kill his father and his brothers and be done with these games.

"Remain strong, nevertheless, Your Highness. Your dreams can only be realized by remaining steadfast," the seer replied, and closed her eyes once more. "The king must be the one to make you crown prince. If not, the current crown prince will have the support of the court and your other brothers, thus sending the kingdom into war—one you will lose. The king's reign is quickly coming to an end. During that time, you must gain his favor and that of the other officials, then slowly bring the crown prince down to his own ruin. Once it is done, no one will stand in your way to the throne."

"Quickly is not quick enough. My father took the throne when he was nineteen," Effiom whispered in annoyance.

"The king had the support of the elders and no siblings to get in his way," she reminded him.

"Because he killed them! Have you never wondered why there are so many females in the Zenzele family, why I have so many aunts and great-aunts, yet no uncles?" the prince muttered but nodded. "Because they killed one another. My father got rid of them all yet preached to his sons to revere one another. Hypocrite."

"Your Highness . . ."

"Enough. You need not explain again." He waved her off. "I shall have patience—one step at a time. You will keep a lookout for that boy, just in case. If someone is hiding him, you must get better at uncovering him. I will not have the people whispering behind my back when I rule."

"Yes, Your Highness."

"Leave me," he said to her, and she rose, bowing to him before taking her leave.

When Sauda left, Effiom set a fresh piece of paper out in front of him, smoothed out the sheet, then lifted his brush and wrote the words he had dreamed of hearing since childhood.

Effiom Zenzele, the protector and the wrath, the lord of all lords, the lion that turned into the sun in the sky, the King of Ahkebulin.

When he was done, he turned to the beautiful box on the table and lifted the lid. He then removed the hand contained within, which sat on a bed of white cloth wrapped in preserving oils, and lifted the Liabrein seal of the now-fallen Mukundi family. His hand shaking, Prince Effiom dipped the seal into the ink before stamping the corner of his dreams.

One down. Seven more to go, he thought, but as he moved to put the seal on the page, his finger touched the corner of it, and it burned him.

"Ah!" He clenched his jaw and threw the seal and hand back into their box. He rested his left finger, scorched and bright red, on the table as he stared down at the paper. "Damn the entire family. I hope you all are burning as well."

"Your Highness . . ."

Had anyone else called and interrupted this moment, he would have had them caned one hundred times, but he knew that voice.

"Enter," he said as Khalaf Rausi, commander of one thousand men and future general of the Red Sun Army, entered.

His brown face was devoid of all emotion, which made it seem even more fierce. The scar on the side of his neck, one of many he'd acquired in his short twenty-one years, looked painful to anyone else, but for the Rausi, battle scars were a thing of pride. His hair was cut low, as all men in their army, for their helmets. Every part of him was built for war.

"Your Highness," Khalaf said again, and bowed before approaching Prince Effiom's desk, holding a small jar. "Lady Sauda said you would need this for your hand . . . and now I see why." Khalaf looked over the paper before him.

Prince Effiom merely snickered. "You disapprove, Khalaf?"

Khalaf did not answer him, merely reached for the sheet, but Prince Effiom used his good hand and stopped him.

"Leave it," Prince Effiom ordered.

"I cannot. My job is to protect Your Highness, even if it is against yourself sometimes. You know that for something like this even to exist is treason," Khalaf muttered harshly.

Only then did the prince release him, allowing Khalaf to immediately take the paper to a candle, where he watched the fire burn it.

"You are so dramatic, Khalaf. It's merely a dream unless you report it to your father," Prince Effiom stated as he dipped his finger in the cream.

"Which I shall," Khalaf answered.

"Disloyal," Prince Effiom replied.

"The fact that you know I will tell him and still let me enter means you know my father will not tell the king. Therefore, you have nothing to worry about," Khalaf stated coldly.

Prince Effiom smirked. "You are starting to sound like a seer."

Khalaf's displeasure was obvious. "It does not take a seer to know the obvious."

"What is obvious?"

"You will not hurt the king," Khalaf replied. "You need the king to make that paper a reality, so when I tell my father, he will conclude the same thing and keep it to himself. We exist to protect the king and this dynasty. The power struggle between you two princes is not our concern."

"Do you resent having this blood oath?" No matter how often the prince asked, the answer never seemed to satisfy him.

"No, for it is our nature. Just as birds fly, water flows, and the sun rises and falls, the Rausi are loyal to the Zenzele," Khalaf said before moving to leave.

And this was why it never satisfied him. Their reasons for loyalty were too earnest.

"Khalaf," Prince Effiom called before the soldier could leave the tent. "When I am king, your family will finally have the status it deserves, that of high noble."

Khalaf bowed his head. "Your dreams honor us, Your Highness . . ."

"But?"

Khalaf stood straighter. "To be a high noble is to be like a king. Such an honor cannot be given to my family, for it would interfere with our duty."

"Is that all?"

"Your Highness wishes for me to offend him with the truth?" Khalaf replied emotionlessly.

"The truth does not offend me."

Khalaf nodded to himself and simply answered, "High nobles cannot be made, Your Highness, and you know this. Either they do or do not exist, but no other family can rise to that status."

"Would your father say the same?"

Khalaf did not answer, and Prince Effiom smiled.

"Does your silence imply you don't know or that you know he would not say the same?"

"As I am here and represent my family, I say no such honor is needed," Khalaf stated.

"I shall tell you a secret, Khalaf. Step closer." Prince Effiom leaned in, and when Khalaf leaned in also but didn't step closer, he held up his burnt finger to show him. "Even if I have to sacrifice all my fingers, I swear the other houses will be no more."

For the first time, Prince Effiom saw the slightest crack in the stone-faced Khalaf as he tried to understand.

Khalaf's eyes searched the prince's before he spoke once more. "Your Highness seeks not just to end the Mukundi, but *all* of them?"

Prince Effiom nodded. "They have existed for four hundred and fifty-three years too long as it is, Khalaf. They should have been destroyed outright, as they make Ahkebulin weak. They all still see themselves as separate kingdoms even after the conquest. Even more so now. The continent is so vast, and our true strength as a dynasty does not affect them, as warring cras did. Now, after watching two generations of kings fearful over that prophecy's threat, they have too much pride. Before Zereen Nnamani died, he said the Zenzele reeked of fear. That is the legacy that my grandfather and father have created. If the king is weak, the kingdom is weak. If the kingdom is weak, why would a high noble bow? Right now, they think we are a dynasty by *their* allowance. But soon, there will only be one great house. You can tell your father that if you wish."

"I will not," Khalaf replied, and he stood straight up. "For now, it is only the ramblings of a prince."

"One day, it will be the command of the king. So keep that blade of yours sharp. It has only just begun," Prince Effiom replied as he sat back. "You may go."

"Yes, Your Highness. I've put out orders that we will leave at first light to return to the capital."

"Excellent."

Khalaf then bowed his head before taking his leave, and the prince looked back to the seal tilted in the box.

Prophecy or not, there could be only one Ahkebulin and one family to rule it.

His.

5

ZIKORA

Winneba

"PULL BACK . . . TAKE A DEEP BREATH . . . NOW."

The moment her dabir—teacher—said go, Zikora released the arrows from her bow, only to have the first one strike right outside the red dot in the center, while the second fell to the ground beside her feet.

"Well done, young mistress—"

"I missed. Twice." Zikora frowned as she picked up the arrow that had fallen. "That's not well done."

"Young mistress." Her dabir sighed. "You are only eight, and hit near the center with a double arrow—"

"When Zereen was eight, he could shoot a double arrow and hit dead center with each!" Zikora exclaimed, then pouted, looking up at her dabir.

"Of all the brothers you have, young mistress, why must you compare yourself to Zereen?" he asked her.

"Because he's the best." She grinned. "And I want to beat him."

She knew if she could exceed Zereen, she'd be one of the best archers in Winneba, and then she could convince her mother to let her officially train with the Seh Llinga Amazons.

"You will—"

Her dabir's words were short, interrupted by the two arrows that flew right past them both, the first arrow hitting the center and the second striking just below. Zikora spun around, her smile turning into a full grin as she saw her second-favorite brother.

"Why don't you work on beating me first, Zikora?" he called out to her.

"Because if I beat Zereen, I beat you anyway, Zeihra." She stuck her tongue out at him. However, she then noticed the engraved, handcrafted wooden bow, the ends plated in gold and marked with the crowned crane. "That's Zereen's bow. He's going to be upset you took it!"

"Dabir Ayubu, it is not fair if you go easy on my sister just because she is a girl," Zeihra said to the teacher to distract her, and it worked.

"*Go easy?*" Zikora gaped in horror and looked at her instructor. "Dabir Ayubu, is that what you're doing? Because that *isn't* fair! Baba said I can learn."

Dabir Ayubu looked between the two youngest Nnamani children and shook his head. "Yes, but young mistress, your mother said only to teach you the basics. And you've long since gone beyond the basics." He turned to look at Zeihra. "And young master, she may be your sister, but she is still a noble lady and must focus on her other lessons."

"Other lessons?" Zikora asked, confused.

"Yes, young mistress, you have weaving, sewing, cooking, and making—"

"Weaving? Sewing and cooking?" Zikora frowned, shaking her head. "Dabir Ayubu, they're not lessons—they're torture. Why do

I have to learn them? I'm not going to need such 'skills' when I'm one of the Seh Llinga."

"She'd be better with a bow than a needle, that's for sure," her brother said. "The last time she tried to learn to sew, she and Nanny Urenna started to cry!" He laughed.

Zikora kicked his leg.

"Both of you?" Dabir Ayubu gasped at her.

Zikora nodded and lifted her fingers for him to see all of them were still wrapped. "Nanny Urenna started to cry because she got frustrated, and I cried because I kept hurting my hands on the weaver. I started bleeding."

"Really? Or did you hurt your hand on purpose to get out of weaving?" Dabir Ayubu asked, crossing his arms as he questioned her.

"What? I would never! That would be a *bad* thing to do!" Zikora replied dramatically, and when his eyes only narrowed, she elbowed her brother to help. However, her brother didn't say anything. She looked at him, but he was only staring at the bow in his hand, completely lost in his thoughts. "Zeihra, are you all right?"

He looked between her and Dabir Ayubu, then forced himself to smile before loudly saying, "Dabir Ayubu, have mercy. Think of her poor fingers! It is also much safer for her to learn to fight than to unleash her on our food! We'd all end up sick!"

"Hey!" Zikora stomped her foot. "I won't be that bad!"

"So, you *are* just faking it then," Dabir Ayubu said.

Zikora froze, and Zeihra shook his head at her. Zikora, trying to think, slowly offered her dabir a smile, and her voice got higher as she said sweetly, "Dabir Ayubu."

"Yes, young mistress?" Dabir Ayubu tried not to laugh at her.

"I promise, if you teach me like you taught Zereen, I'll tell you what I heard Nanny Urenna say about you—"

"Zikora!" Zeihra yelled, because everyone knew Dabir Ayubu was in love with Nanny Urenna.

"What? Don't you want to know, Dabir Ayubu? It was really nice—"

Zeihra placed his hand over her mouth and just smiled at Dabir Ayubu, who was now coughing, trying to hide his embarrassment at being unable to correct her. "Dabir Ayubu, why don't you come back for lessons tomorrow."

"Good idea." He nodded to them both before quickly looking to run away.

"Ah! Zikora!" Zeihra pulled his hand off her mouth when she bit him. "This is why people say you are like a wild cat!"

Zikora brushed her hair from her face. "I thought that was because my eyes are big, and I like to climb on things."

"That too," he muttered.

"Zeihra!" She pouted before laughing. She pushed him and tried to make a run for it, only to notice he wasn't following her. "Zeihra, what's wrong with you today?" she asked when she saw he wasn't looking at her. Instead, his attention was taken at the sight of his "older" twin brother, Zesiro, on the top level of their home. Zesiro and Zeihra looked the same, with round and smooth faces and dark-brown skin, were the same height, and they even sounded identical to almost everyone but Zikora. The only difference was in their clothes and that Zeihra wore all of his braided hair up and not in a ponytail like his brother.

"Zesiro, come down and play with us!" Zikora called up to him, waving and smiling.

But Zesiro said nothing, just turned and walked away on the upper platform of their home.

"Did everyone eat something bad?" Zikora grumbled, and then

looked back at her other brother. "Why are you all acting weird today?"

"There is an important council meeting—I have to go." Zeihra swallowed hard before turning to his sister and giving her his brother's bow. "Hold on to this for me?"

"A meeting?" Zikora took the bow for him. "Can I come—"

"No!" he yelled, and it was the first time he'd ever sounded so serious, which made Zikora jump. Putting his hand on her head, Zeihra said, much quieter, "Just stay here and practice. Zereen said you could use his bow before he left. I forgot to tell you. I'll come back once the meeting is done, okay? Just stay here."

Zikora nodded and watched Zeihra whisper something to her maid before he left and went into the house. Zikora glanced down at the bow in her hand. Their great-grandmother had given the bow to Zereen. It was his favorite, and he had named it "the weeping crane" because of how it sounded when he released an arrow from it. He loved it so much that he rarely fired it. So Zikora knew Zeihra was lying, for their brother wouldn't let her use it—he wouldn't let anyone *touch* it. But even though she knew it was a lie, she was still tempted to keep it. She ran her hand over the engraving of their ancestors on the side before she lifted it, put the arrows in place, looked at the center of the target, then pulled back and let the arrows fly. She heard the sound of a cry in her ears and grinned as she looked at the bow.

She wanted to keep it.

But knew she couldn't.

"Where are you going, young mistress?" the maid asked, blocking her way as she tried to go inside.

Zikora stared at her, confused. Maids did not ask where she went; they just followed. However, she replied, "I'm going to return Zereen's bow to his room."

"Why don't you practice with it more, young mistress?" The maid smiled and now stood directly in front of her.

Zikora stared at her maid. She had a weird feeling but didn't know what it was. Her brothers had been acting strange, and now this. "I'm done practicing today."

Zikora tried to step around the maid, but the woman blocked her again. "But I barely got to see you and would like to watch. I hear you are very good—"

"Are you trying to keep from going inside?" Zikora frowned, and when the maid's eyes widened, Zikora knew she was right. "Why?"

"Of course I'm not. I—"

"That's a lie. If you don't tell me, I'll run," Zikora said. She tucked the bow under her arm, picked up her dress, then stepped back, ready to bolt forward.

"Okay. Okay," the maid replied, leaning in closer. "I was ordered to keep you here for now. Until the meeting is over."

Zikora dropped her dress and adjusted her stance. "Why?"

"I do not know. Really. So please, stay here for me so I am not punished," the maid asked gently.

Zikora nodded. "Okay. I'll practice more."

Walking back to the practice mark, Zikora took out another arrow, pulled back, and let it fly, then watched as it hit just off-center again. Feeling the maid's eyes on her, she grabbed another and let it go, allowing it to hit even farther right then the last one.

The third time, she pulled back harder and firmer than she was supposed to and didn't release correctly, letting the string cut her hand.

"Ah!"

"Young mistress!" The maid rushed to her as Zikora dropped the bow and held her hand as it bled.

"Hold on, young mistress," the maid almost cried, putting a handkerchief to her wound. "I'll get the doctor. Wait here, okay?"

"Okay." Zikora nodded. She held her hand and waited until the maid was out of sight before putting the bow on her arm and rushing into the house. She ran down the opposite side toward her room. She put the bow beside the window as quietly as she could before pushing the window open and crawling out. She grabbed hold of the tiles, ignoring the cut in her hand, and pulled herself up as she had done dozens of times. Her mother had removed the hooks she'd used to climb before, but now she was good enough without them. Carefully, she made her way onto the roof. The roof of the palace of Winneba was an intricate series of diagonal beams and spirals, mostly designed to guide all the water from the heavy rains each year down either to barrels or back to the earth. There were only two types of weather in Winneba, humid and very sunny or cold, heavy rain.

Zikora did not know there could be anything else.

She carefully began her walk to the other side of the estate. She ducked low so none of the servants could see her. When she reached her destination, she crawled along on her stomach until she reached the top and carefully peeked over the edge into the courtyard to where the meeting was being held.

Like so much in her young life, it just wasn't fair that she was the only one who couldn't go. She wanted to know what was going on too! Moreover, the maid had lied to her. She knew what was happening but didn't want to tell. In fact, the more Zikora thought about it, the more everyone seemed to be acting weird today. She was a child, but she was not stupid. Something had happened, and she wanted to know what. It had to be something big, because when she looked over the edge, she saw that Master Uzolin was there, and he never came to any of her baba's council meetings even though her baba had made a special entrance and seat for him to sit in on the council. No, the giant stayed high up in the mountains, past the place of the mist, in Aoduo, with the other giants, and just sent a messenger eagle for meetings. He only came down two times a year, for the New Year and the Nnamani Lantern Festival.

To see him here now was startling.

Not as startling the first time she saw him and his wife, though—Zikora had never been so amazed to see people so large. It was like staring at a man with three more men on his shoulders! What made it even more amazing was that Master Uzolin told her he was one of the shorter giants! Her mouth had fallen open, making her mother mad at her, but it was marvelous, and she begged to see the rest of the giants. She even sent notes to the mountains hoping she could invite them down. None ever came, but she tried every week.

Master Uzolin never told her to stop asking, though, even after she secretly told him what she was doing. And now here he was.

And it wasn't just him. All the masters from the other families her mother always told her to behave like a young mistress in front of were here. They sat in the council square, which had risen up and over the bed of water, whispering to one another. Every one of them had the same hard look on their face, even Zeihra, who sat with Zesiro. Sitting in the first seat, ahead of them both, was Zakee, the second oldest, and he sat with his eyes closed.

Was he meditating here too? Zikora thought. Zakee meditated a lot. And she noticed that the maids didn't speak to him as they set his drink beside him. Zesiro nodded to his maid but didn't speak—he normally said thank you at least. Zeihra shook his head when the maids came to give him his, flipping his cup upside down and looking away . . . right at Zikora. Because of course he'd see her, and of course he knew she'd find a way to come. Smiling at him, Zikora put her finger to her mouth to tell him to keep quiet.

He instead turned his head and whispered something to the maid, whose eyes almost came out of her head when she turned to see Zikora. The maid rose and stepped behind Zeihra back into the house, sliding the door behind him closed.

What is wrong with him? Zikora frowned, hurt by her brother's small betrayal. Still, it would be some time before anyone could actually get her down from the roof. And Baba was already starting.

"I thank you all for coming," her baba said. His long braided hair was held back with a single wooden hairpin through it, and he stepped out into the square, walking to his mat in the center of the platform.

Everyone was silent.

"Young mistress." Zikora heard the maid whisper from below, but she ignored her. "Young mistress, please come down. That is dangerous."

Zikora waved her bloody hand for the maid to go away.

"The stories which have most likely reached you all by now are true. I sent one of my men down to Ahalon, and he sent a report in turn," her baba said, looking at everyone. "A little over three months ago, I told my son, Zereen Nnamani, if he left to aid the Mukundi family, he would never be welcome in Winneba, nor would I ever look upon his face again."

Baba? Zikora frowned, not understanding. *What does that mean? Zereen left? Wasn't he just gone for training?*

"Young mistress, please, we will be punished—"

Leaning in more, Zikora watched as her baba put his arms behind him and held his head high. "Zereen Nnamani left anyway, and he is now dead. As well as the Mukundi family, by order of the king. All of their heads were hung outside the walls of Ahalon. Neither the Nnamani family nor Winneba have been given any punishment for Zereen's actions, but that very well may come. I, Zikobi Nnamani, Lord of Winneba, head of the Nnamani family, seek your forgiveness for raising such an unfilial and traitorous son. Never shall I speak his name again."

When he got down on his knees and hung his head, and when Zakee, Zesiro, and Zeihra all hung their heads with him, Zikora cried out, "*No!*"

She didn't mean to, but it came out all the same.

"Young mistress!" the maid screamed up at Zikora.

All of the council turned their heads upward to look at Zikora, and she looked back at them, shaking her head and repeating the words even as her baba glared at her.

"No!" she declared again, since she was already caught. "Baba, what are you doing? How can you say that about Zereen? Zereen loves everyone the most. Why are you saying this, Baba?"

"*Get her down!*" her baba snapped at one of the guards, and two of them had already climbed onto the roof to try to get her, but she got up and started to run.

"Zikora, get down. It's dangerous!" she heard Zeihra yell.

"*No!*" she screamed at him, her eyes burning with tears and rage. "He's not dead, and he's family! Why are we sitting here? We need to go help him! He's in trouble, right? We won't abandon him. We need to—"

Her foot slipped, and she slid down the dark-blue tiles of their house.

"Zikora!"

"Young mistress!"

Before she fell off, she was able to grab the edge of the roof, gripping on as tightly as she could though she winced as pain shot up her still-untreated hand. Nevertheless, she kicked her feet back and forth, trying to pull herself back up, but before she could, one of the guards grabbed her tightly and he jumped down, holding her.

"Are you all right, young mistress—"

"No. You knew!" Zikora yelled, pushing the guard away and wiping her face. "All of you knew! And no one told me! You all said it was nothing! You all said nothing was wrong—"

Slap.

The side of her face burned, and when she looked, her mother stood there, dressed in a beautiful woven skirt and top. Upon her head was her favorite beaded crown, and she was covered in jewelry. Her clothing was bright and colorful, as if she were celebrating something, but that did not make sense to Zikora.

"Mama—"

Slap.

Her mother smacked the other side of Zikora's face, and tears fell from Zikora's eyes as she looked back at her. When her mother raised her hand to hit Zikora yet again, all the maids and the guards fell to their knees.

"Forgive her, my lady," they said.

Slap.

Her mother hit her so hard that Zikora fell to the ground.

"Forgive her, my lady!" they yelled, louder.

"How often must I remind you to behave, Zikora?"

Rubbing her face and biting her lip, Zikora tried to speak through her tears, "Zereen—"

"Does not exist," her mother replied in a harsh voice. "I have only four children, and if you ever disgrace your father, your brothers, or yourself in this manner ever again, I shall have only three."

"Mama—"

"Do you all hear me? There is no Zereen Nnamani, and never shall that name be spoken again. And you will not cry here." Her mother looked at everyone else before turning from Zikora, lifting the robes to enter the house again. "Lock her in her room without food or water, and she will not be released until the morning."

When her mother walked away, Zikora lay there and rubbed her cheeks, her eyes burning, but none of that was even a rock among mountains to the pain in her chest.

"Will you throw me away too?!" Zikora yelled angrily at her mother. "If you could just throw us away, why have us at all? Why are you a mama at all?"

"*Take her away!*" her mother screamed at the top of her lungs.

The guards picked Zikora up and dusted her off, then led her from the council square, kicking and screaming.

6

LADY NNAMANI

Winneba

WILL YOU THROW ME AWAY TOO?

The words gutted Lady Nnamani so deeply that she held her chest. She lifted her head and stared at the ceiling to keep the tears from falling.

That girl.

Never mind bow or sword, her words always cut the sharpest. Nothing Lady Nnamani did seemed to tame her daughter's mouth. Other daughters from less prestigious families were sweet and soft-spoken, and they listened to and respected their mothers. On the other hand, Zikora had been disobeying her ever since she learned to walk and talk on her own. What was worse was that Zikora was blinded to the effects of her words in turn. Lady Nnamani knew her daughter could never see beyond her feelings. She also knew that might have been everyone else's fault for making her that way—including her own.

As the only daughter, Zikora was all but a princess here.

Everyone, from the maids to the commoners and her brothers and father, treated her as if she were sent from the heavens. Everyone loved to see her do things she should not do, like hunt, climb up trees, run on the rooftops, and question everything and say whatever was on her mind, regardless of what anyone might think. The innocence of her emotions and the simplicity with which she could tell what was wrong and right when no one else could made Zikora the treasure of Winneba.

People seemed to forget that treasures were often burdens too.

That sentiment became more obvious when Lady Nnamani stepped into the square, sitting to the right and behind her husband, watching the looks on everyone's faces: the anger, the pain, and frustration, but also the understanding that they clearly felt the way Zikora felt.

They all wanted to yell *No* and do something for Zereen.

But her husband, her family, had no other choice. Lord and Lady Nnamani needed to rip their son, their firstborn and most-beloved scion, from their hearts, and for the sake of Winneba and their other children they had to do it for all the world to see.

Closing her eyes, Lady Nnamani hung her head and fell to her knees, stretching out her hands before her. She said the words for them and all the world to hear: "Forgive me for giving birth to such a son."

In her mind, however, she wept and said, *Forgive me, Zereen, for betraying you.*

But she could not show her pain. She could not mourn him the way she knew Zikora would, but till the day she died, her heart would scream out in agony for the son she lost.

"It has been weeks, and there has been no word from the king," Master Uzolin said, causing Lord and Lady Nnamani to look up. Lord Nnamani rose to his feet while Lady Nnamani sat upon her knees, listening though all she wished to do was return to her chambers and close her eyes.

"No," Lord Nnamani said to them. "But after . . . he left . . . I wrote to the king and assured him of our continued loyalty to the Zenzele dynasty."

"But will that be enough?" Master Jahi, Lady Nnamani's baba, spoke next. He was short with an even shorter temper and was the oldest man there, his white beard stopping at the center of his chest.

"What do you mean, Master Jahi?" Lord Nnamani looked at him, calling him master instead of Baba insaa out of respect for the council.

Master Jahi leaned closer. "I mean, we do not even know what crime the Mukundi family committed that led to their executions, for an explanation was not given."

"The king needs no explanation, Master Jahi," responded the snake-faced man, Master Oglik of the southern bother cities bestowed to him by the king and not by the Nnamani family.

Suddenly, the other masters all began to speak over one another.

"The Mukundi family has ruled and protected Madada for thousands of years! They were high nobles. Surely, even a king can see why this would be questioned—"

"Questioning is not our place. We follow our king."

"There is order, and there is law. The king rules all but is bound by a blood oath to adhere to civility and respect the high nobles—"

"The king deemed the Mukundi family traitors, so we must—"

"Are we all truly going to pretend as if we do not know the cause?" Master Dayo yelled out, his loud and deep voice rising over all the rest, causing everyone else's voice to fall silent. Master Dayo lifted his cup with his left hand because he no longer had a right arm. "Lord Nnamani, is it true that Zereen loved and sought to marry the daughter of Lord Mukundi? Was that why he went to Madada?" he asked before drinking his tea.

All of them looked at Master Dayo, their faces a mixture of pain, anger, and disappointment, and Lord Nnamani nodded only once.

"He did."

"Then we all know the reason, and we are all avoiding this truth," Master Dayo repeated. "The family was executed to prevent the prophecy!"

Some of them groaned in annoyance, while others began to whisper among themselves. Only three nodded in agreement.

"*If*," Master Oglik called out, "the king cared for such a thing, then why punish the Mukundi family only and not the family of Nnamani? The traitor Zereen Nnamani broke the king's law and sought to marry her!"

Lady Nnamani forced herself to remain emotionless at his words, not blinking or giving him the satisfaction of seeing her pain.

Lady Nnamani's father, however, could not conceal his rage. "Who in Ahkebulin does not know that Winneba has the second-strongest army in the most unconquerable land, with the giants and the mountain of Aoduo in the west and the Si'ertan Desert in the east? Yes, the southern lands had swamps, but we all know that Madada and the Mukundi family were also our barriers. It is rumored that the king plans to get rid of his current queen and marry the daughter of the Jangari family, making Nérbua an ally. He has already had the crown prince marry the daughter of Hiwot of Kéye, another ally. Now he has rid himself of the Mukundi family, ending conversations about that prophecy, we are their next target. They *will* make some excuse to come for us next."

Lady Nnamani agreed, though she did not show it. He was right.

If the Nnamani family fell, who else had the power to question or fight back? All the other high nobles would live in fear of the king and not just tolerate him as they did.

"Did you summon us here, Lord Nnamani, to prepare for rebellion, treason, and war?" Master Oglik asked, his eyes never looking away from Lady Nnamani's baba. "Because that is what it sounds like—"

"The Zenzele dynasty swore always to keep peace with the high nobles so long as there is loyalty," Master Uzolin interrupted, and due to his size, his voice echoed like thunder when he spoke in anger. "Zereen was young; to execute him for something that may not have even occurred should he have gained more wisdom is not peace, Master Oglik."

Lady Nnamani bit her tongue in anger to keep from screaming when Master Oglik replied, "Even Lord and Lady Nnamani held him as a traitor, and as such, the king's choice was sound. Is that not right, Lord Nnamani?"

Lord Nnamani was reduced to silence, and Lady Nnamani wished he would hold it but knew he could not. Eventually he nodded once and spoke, "I have said it once already, and I shall say it again. The Nnamani family is loyal to the Zenzele dynasty. Our king is good and fair—I know this. So I do not fear for this family nor Winneba."

Lies, Lady Nnamani immediately thought. She knew everything he just said was a lie and could tell from the way he stretched out his fingers, which he now held behind his back. She also knew many of them also realized he was lying, but what could anyone do? Declare war? Rebel? That would not bring back their son and would cause only more death.

"I am sure the king will explain more at the next meeting of the high nobles in a year's time. Until then, one of Lord Mukundi's sons managed to escape—the youngest, M'kuru Mukundi," Lord Nnamani said to them. "Should any of you know or hear anything about him or where he may have gone, speak now."

Silence.

"I shall take you all at your silence then," Lord Nnamani spoke again. He glanced over his shoulder to Lady Nnamani, and understanding his look, she rose from the ground and took the bell from the floor beside her.

"You all must be weary from your journey. The maids will show you to your rooms," Lady Nnamani said softly, then rang the bell. Behind them, all of the doors slid open.

The council turned and entered the main house one by one, and only then did Lord Nnamani turn back to his wife. He did not say a word as he walked, he did not even meet her eyes, but she knew exactly where he wanted to go.

"Zikora is in her room and is to receive no visitors or dinner," Lady Nnamani said, and he stopped. She glanced at her sons and repeated, "*No one* is to go to her."

"But her hand looked injured—" one of the boys began to say, but she cut him off quickly.

"I said no one."

They all pretended to find something interesting in the sky to avoid her hawklike stare. She stepped up beside her husband, and it was only then that his gaze met hers. His big eyes were tired, heavy, burdened, and filled with pain, so she knew he wanted to see his favorite child.

Lord and Lady Nnamani had been married so long that no words needed to be said anymore. Lord Nnamani just nodded and sighed and was again about to leave when a maid rushed toward them.

"Forgive me," she said, falling to her knees. "I checked on the young mistress because she cut her hand, but she is no longer in her room!"

Lady Nnamani exhaled and clenched her hand. She heard a small snicker from one of her sons behind her.

"We'll find her, Mother!" Zeihra tried not to laugh as he took off, dragging Zesiro with him.

Lord Nnamani glanced at his wife, fighting the small smile threatening to appear on his lips.

This is not funny! she thought. "She acts this way because of all of *you*," Lady Nnamani whispered, and turned to look down at the maid. "If she is not found, you will pay the price."

That stubborn girl! Lady Nnamani shouted in her mind as she stomped off, realizing that she should have anticipated Zikora would act this way.

She was *her* daughter, after all.

7

ZIKORA

Winneba

"DID YOU NOT ALMOST FALL OFF THE ROOF earlier?"

Zikora looked down to see Master Uzolin looking up at her, the top of his head level with the branch where she sat.

"Master Uzolin, how did you know where to find me?"

He lifted the big scroll. "I didn't come to find you. I came to paint."

"You like to paint?" Zikora questioned.

He pointed to the valley that was deep green from all the trees as far as her eyes could see, and as it did every day, the mist hovered around the green-covered mountains in the distance. On the sides of the hills, seven waterfalls fed into the snake-shaped river below, leading from Winneba to Aoduo. The sun, like always, beat down heavily upon everything. The mountains looked so close, but Zikora knew they were far away because it took Master Uzolin seven days to come to their home, and he had giant steps.

"With a view like this, how can anyone not paint, young mistress?"

She thought about it. "They could be bad painters."

He laughed, and it made the birds fly out of the tree. The grin on her face only got wider as she watched the birds come out of the side, and then she remembered her brother Zereen. He'd loved this place too. He was the one who showed her this spot and taught her how to climb this tree, and her eyes started to burn with tears.

"Young mistress?"

"Is Zereen really dead?" Zikora whispered, hugging the bow she had taken with her when she ran away.

"Do you think your father would lie?"

She shook her head. "But still, he could have heard wrong, right?"

"I'm sorry for your pain, young mistress."

She nodded and rubbed her eyes as she tried to stop crying, but her tears still came. "Master Uzolin, how do you become a giant?"

"Why?"

Again, she glanced down and spoke, "Because no one messes with the giants."

"You'd be surprised. But alas, you cannot be made into one. You are born a giant, young mistress, just as you are born a high noble. No matter what, your blood will always define you," he said. "But I'm sure you would have made a fearsome giant."

Zikora's gaze focused on the valley and she watched the birds take to the sky, how free they were.

"If my brother is ever born again, I want him to be a giant," Zikora told Master Uzolin, then sniffled and held her hands to her face.

"Did you come here to cry, young mistress?"

"Yes. My mom said I could not cry for Zereen at home, but I can cry here, right?" she asked him hopefully.

He reached up and put a handkerchief half the size of a table-cloth on the branch. "Yes. You lost your bother. You should cry."

Zikora's lip quivered, and she bit her lip. "The king—"

"I am a giant, and you are the young mistress of giants. No one will, as you said, mess with you as long as I am here."

"Thank you, Master Uzolin . . . ugh . . ." The tears started to fall, and she grabbed his handkerchief, held it to her face and cried into it.

"My brother . . . was . . . not a traitor . . ." she said. And she would not forgive anyone who called him one.

Master Uzolin didn't speak and just let her cry into his handker-chief. Her tiny cry carried through the leaves, over the hills, and into the valley until she finally stopped to breathe.

Master Uzolin stretched a hand out for Zikora. She looked at him, and he spoke gently, "Your brothers have come to get you."

Zikora looked down and around her tree. "Where?"

It didn't take much longer before she heard them.

"Zikora?"

"Zikora!"

Zeihra and Zesiro called from below as they came running out of the trees toward her, but they slid to a stop when they saw Master Uzolin standing beside the tree. No matter how often Zeihra saw him, he couldn't help but stare, wide-eyed, which made Zesiro elbow him in the side.

"Master Uzolin, I hope she did not bother you." Zesiro stepped forward and nodded to the giant.

"I was here first and did not bother anyone!" Zikora yelled at her brother.

"Zikora, don't be rude!" Zesiro yelled back at her.

Master Uzolin smiled and shook his head. "She is right, young master Zesiro, for she was here first and did not bother a soul."

"See. Told you," Zikora said to him, carefully climbing onto Master Uzolin's hand so he could bring her down to the forest floor beside her brother. Master Uzolin knelt before them both as Zikora held up his handkerchief as much as she could because it was large.

"I promise to return it, Master Uzolin. Thank you! Oh . . ." Remembering why Master Uzolin was there, she quickly asked, "Can I see your painting when you are finished?"

Master Uzolin laughed. "It's not very good, young mistress."

"I'll see and tell you." Zikora grinned up at him, wondering how quickly she could go from pure pain and tears to joy and grins.

"Zikora." Zesiro elbowed her on her left and whispered, "You're supposed to say it will be good no matter what."

"But what if he's right and it's not good?" Zikora asked Zesiro, causing both her brothers to sigh.

Zeihra shook his head and put his elbow on her head. "Don't you know by now that she is like this, Zesiro? She always does and says the things everybody knows not to say."

"Get off." Zikora tried to pull her brother's arm off her head.

"I think she does it on purpose," Zesiro muttered, frowning at her as he put his elbow on top of Zeihra's, still on top of her head.

"*Hey!*" Zikora yelled at them. "Master Uzolin, they are bullying me!"

Zeihra turned to Master Uzolin and smiled. "Us, her brothers, who love her so much, bullies? Never, Master Uzolin. After all, we came out here just to bring her back home so our mother does not send an army out here. Right, Zesiro?"

"Right." Zesiro nodded, and they both pushed down on her head.

Zikora swung the bow to the side, hitting first Zeihra in the stomach and then Zesiro.

"Ugh!" they both groaned, stumbling away from her.

"Bye, Master Uzolin! Paint well," Zikora said to him, bowing her head quickly before taking off running.

"Zikora!" her brothers yelled at her.

She made it deep into the rainforest, running farther and farther, but just as she was about to jump over one of the fallen logs, she saw a shadow. Zesiro flipped right in front of her path, spinning around and pointing his dagger at her. Instead of slowing, Zikora captured his arm in the bow and turned it and herself underneath him, then took out her hairpin to point it at his cheek.

"Good. Good. You both can defend," Zeihra called out breathlessly as he put his hands on his knees. "But can we stop running?"

"Zeihra!" Zesiro broke away from his sister and ran over to his twin as he leaned against the tree. "Are you all right?"

Zeihra smiled and waved him off. "Me? I'm all right. Give me a second, and I'll be right behind you guys."

Zikora frowned, stepping up beside her brother.

Zesiro turned to her angrily. "Why is it so hard for you to be considerate of others? You know his heart—"

"Don't yell at her," Zeihra snapped at him, clenching his fist when Zikora hung her head. "You ran, too, Zesiro."

"I'm sorry." Zesiro sighed and took a seat beside him. "We'll sit here and wait a bit, Zikora."

"Sorry, Zeihra," she whispered, and sat with her brothers beside the tree. "Am I really odd?"

"Yes," both her brothers said. She looked at them wide-eyed, and Zeihra started to laugh.

"See why it's better not to always say what is on your mind?" Zesiro told her.

Zikora frowned, looking away into the forest. "Well, I think you both are odd too."

"Zeihra is definitely odd. I'm the most normal of all of us," Zesiro muttered, picking up a stick and digging into the ground. Both his siblings laughed aloud at him. He looked between them both. "What? Do you not agree?"

Zikora and Zeihra shook their heads.

"Zikora, you spend your days hiding from Mother and your nanny, fighting and joining our training lessons! You are also the worst liar ever. You don't even lie. You just twist sentences! You don't act graceful at all. You're lucky you are pretty, or you'd never get married," Zesiro said.

"I don't plan on getting married. I am joining the Seh Llinga!" she shot back at him.

"When will you get it that it is impossible for you, Zikora," he replied.

"Why?" She huffed angrily. "It's not fair! Every other girl can begin training and go—"

"Because you are not every girl, Zikora. You are a Nnamani," Zesiro replied.

"Mama is a Nnamani, and she is a Seh Llinga!" Zikora said.

"She wasn't a Nnamani when she joined," Zesiro tried to explain to her. "How long are you going to keep being this stupid!"

"Hey!" Zikora moved to smack him.

"That was mean, Zesiro," Zeihra snapped at him, blocking his sister. "Apologize."

"No. When will someone tell her the truth?" Zesiro replied and then looked back at Zikora. "No matter how good of an archer you become, even if you learn the spear or the sword or become the best warrior in Winneba, you can never be part of the Seh Llinga. And you know why?"

"Zesiro, stop. She'll understand later——"

"Why?" Zikora asked quietly, looking at her brother. "Why can I never be part of the Seh Llinga?"

"Because all the Seh Llinga are the concubines of the Lord of Winneba," he said.

"No . . ." Zikora wasn't exactly sure what concubines were, but she knew other people had them, like her grandfather, and they were like wives. "You're wrong. Baba only has Mama. And the Seh Llinga are female warriors. I've seen them."

"He's not wrong, Zikora," Zeihra said gently. "The Seh Llinga was created back when Winneba was a kingdom. To ensure the king was never without protection, all his wives had to be warriors, so even at night, someone would be there. When we became high noble houses, they began to protect and serve the Lord of Winneba. Some things have changed over the years. But the Lord of Winneba still chose his legitimate wife from them, and the rest are still considered his concubines. So, it is impossible for you. Right now, you are the daughter of the Lord of Winneba. In the future, you will be the sister of the Lord of Winneba. You can never be a concubine, so you can never be Seh Llinga."

The twins both stared at her because they knew that since the very moment she saw the Seh Llinga, she'd wanted to join them. She wanted her hair braided with gold, since the Seh Llinga were the only women permitted to wear their hair as such. Due to the humidity, most other women wore their hair in knots or cut it short. It was Zikora's dream, and she had been too young for them to explain it before, so they'd simply let her dream and practice . . . until now.

"I know this is——"

"Stupid!" Her whole face bunched up as if she had bitten into a lemon. "Can we just stop doing that then?"

They stared at her like she was crazy.

"You want Father to get rid of hundreds—no, thousands of years of tradition so that you can become a female warrior?" Zeihra asked her.

Zikora nodded like that was the most rational thing in the world. "Yes."

They laughed at her.

"I don't even know why we bother!" Zesiro shook his head and lay back down.

"Laugh all you want. I'm going to talk to Baba!"

"You really believe you can just go up to him and ask?" Zesiro questioned. "You may be the favorite, but you are not *that* special."

"Yes. I will tell Baba to change the rules for the Seh Llinga. I want to be a warrior."

"What if your future husband doesn't want you to be one?"

"I won't marry him."

Zesiro shook his head. "We should be more worried about who will want to marry you. You run wild all the time. Look at your hand! You don't even take care of yourself."

Zikora looked down at the dirty, unraveling bandage she'd quickly put over her hand before leaving the house.

"The maids always say it doesn't matter how I look or if I am graceful or not because someone will marry me anyway because I am a Nnamani."

Zeihra and Zikora glanced at each other and then Zeihra spoke up. "Did they say this to you, or did you overhear them?"

"I overheard them," Zikora admitted.

"Zikora"—Zesiro shook his head—"they were making fun of you."

"They were?" Zikora asked, tilting her head to the side to think about it and making both of her brothers sigh.

"Add 'slow' to her list," Zeihra muttered to his brother.

"Hey!" Zikora glared and pointed him. "What about him? He's odd too."

Zesiro nodded. "Yes, he is. He's a child born with an old man's heart. He tells the worst jokes that no one laughs at except himself, and his feet always smell funny."

Zikora smiled, nodding to herself.

"What?" Zeihra crossed his arms, looking down. "They do not."

"They do," Zikora and Zesiro said, causing Zeihra to frown and pull his feet back.

"Why is his list shorter than mine? I'm odder then Zeihra!" Zikora said angrily.

Zeihra crossed his arms. "Are you trying to say I am the weirdest?"

"Zakee is the weirdest," Zesiro replied, writing his brother's name in the dirt ahead of Zikora's name. "It goes Zakee, Zikora, and then Zeihra, and finally . . ."

He stopped talking.

"Zereen?" Zikora spoke what both of her brothers didn't want to say. She looked down at their names in the dirt. "Zereen wasn't odd at all! He was the best!"

Both of her brothers glanced at her.

Zeihra swallowed and nodded. "Zereen was the best swordsman, the best at archery, hunting, fighting, he memorized all the great books, and he could even sew and cook. He was too good at everything to be normal."

Zesiro took the stick and wrote Zereen's name in front of Zakee's. "I was wrong. Zereen was the oddest. He was good at everything. He had everything and gave it up just for some girl, and it got him killed."

Silence came upon them all again, and Zikora put the bow in the center of the three of them.

"Why did no one tell me?" she asked.

"Because Zereen is your favorite brother, and everyone knew you would do exactly what you did today," Zesiro snapped at her.

"I didn't do anything—"

"Yes, you did!" Zesiro went on. "We are all sad, yet you thought you were the only one with grief. But we can't be sad because if we are, the king will think we were trying to betray him too! Then we could all die. Is that what you want, Zikora—"

"Stop yelling at her!" Zeihra threw some dirt at him.

Zesiro got up, dusted his face, and started to walk away, grumbling, "I'm going back. You guys can stay here."

Zikora hung her head. "I don't want anyone to die."

"Don't mind him, Zikora," Zeihra whispered, then lifted his head to yell toward his brother: "We all know he's not really leaving!"

Zikora nodded. "Zesiro really loved Zereen. He was always copying everything he did."

"That is why Zereen played tricks on him." Zeihra started to laugh. "Do you remember last winter when Zereen said he goes swimming in the river right before it rains with all his clothes on because it made his bones stronger?"

Zikora started giggling and nodded. "Zesiro jumped in and started to scream at how cold it was."

"He came out shaking so badly, his teeth were making noise, and he had to change behind one of the bushes." Zeihra broke out into a fit of laughter.

"I can hear you!" Zesiro yelled from behind one of the trees. "I hated his tricks. He only did them on me."

"Because you were the only person who fell for it over and over again. Even Zikora figured out when he was just joking," Zeihra replied, shaking his head, and his laughter slowly stopped.

"We shouldn't be talking about him," Zesiro replied, but still didn't show himself. "Mother said not to."

"She said not to at the house," Zikora whispered.

"Then we will talk about him out here. Any objections, Zesiro?" Zeihra called out, adding, "Come back already. You look silly hiding behind that tree."

"I'm really leaving you both," Zesiro lied, and Zeihra just looked at his sister and shook his head, making her smile . . . or at least tried to.

"So, it's settled then. The order is Zereen, Zakee, Zikora, me, and then *normal* Zesiro hiding behind that tree because that's what *normal* people do," Zeihra teased and laughed.

"Did Zereen love that girl more than us?" Zikora asked randomly, picking up a stick too. "That's why he left us—for her."

Zeihra's smile faded as her words sank in. "Zikora, read the environment. I'm trying to make everyone laugh, and you are dragging us down."

"Sorry—"

"He must have." Zesiro returned to them and picked up the bow she had put down. "He knew he was going to die. That's why he left this here, in Winneba, so that it could stay with family. It belongs to Zakee now. He's the oldest."

Zikora frowned and held on to the center of the bow. "Zakee doesn't like bows or swords. He says they are all violent. I should have it."

"If we aren't going in order"—Zeihra gripped the other end—"I think it should be mine. After all, I am the best archer of us three."

He tugged at it, but both his siblings held on. "Zesiro, you like swords better anyway!" Zeihra added.

"The iron dwarfs handcrafted this bow, and the bow string is made from golden silk, the hair of Ludo sheep, and musk ox twisted together. It's a treasure—"

Zikora and Zeihra shared a glance before asking, "Really?"

"If Zakee does not want it, then it goes to me because I'm the next oldest," Zesiro said, tugging on the other end of the bow.

"Only by a few minutes, and you were so big you squeezed your poor little brother, which is why I have a bad heart. You should feel bad and want to give it to me—"

"You little—"

"Baba says brothers should never fight," Zikora reminded them both, causing their heads to turn to her. "And if he found out you were fighting over Zereen's bow, he would take it away. So, I think I should have it—"

"No," they both said to her.

"Okay, I'll tell Baba and ask for it, and then I won't share it with you both anymore," she told them, and they eyed her. Zikora smiled, leaning in. "We can share it, but I get to keep it . . . Baba will not take it from me."

Her brothers looked at each other again.

"She's right. I took this out of Zereen's room because Father was having all of his things locked away," Zeihra whispered. "He won't take it from her."

"She gets away with everything," Zesiro muttered back.

Zikora leaned in. "So, do I win?"

Sighing, both brothers let it go, and she fell back with the bow in her hand as Zesiro got up. "Only if Zakee doesn't want it. He's the oldest now, and he might want it."

Zikora grinned and got up, hugging the bow. "He won't. He wants to travel all across the world."

"He can't," Zesiro said as they all began to walk back. "He's going to be the next Lord of Winneba."

Zikora frowned at that. She didn't talk much to Zakee because he was always so quiet and meditating, but she knew he really did want to travel the whole world and planned to. He must have been even more sad now.

"Let's make a promise," Zeihra said when they saw their massive home sitting on the open hill in front of Emywei, the capital city of Winneba. Her baba noted that in other lands, high nobles built their palaces in the center. But the house of Nnamani was part of the walls, as they were protectors meant to stand between it and any that came toward their people. The walls stretched across the plane, shaped like a maze around the city. They were so massive in both height and length that Zikora had never actually walked it entirely and stayed only in the family quarters or those of the guard.

"Let's promise never to put anyone else above family again?" Zeihra said, looking at them. "We can't ever do what Zereen did. We can't lose one another, promise?"

"Promise." Zikora locked her pinky with him then looked to Zesiro, who looked away but gave his pinky too.

"Promise," he muttered.

"Aww, he's shy." Zeihra poked his brother's face.

"Stop that!" Zesiro made them laugh, but then he pointed to the small green-tailed hawk as it dove toward the family quarters. "All the masters are at the house already, so who is sending a hawk?"

"It is not coming from inside Winneba." Zeihra's face darkened as he looked at his brother.

Zikora looked between them, but they weren't looking at her, so she asked, "Is this bad?"

They did not reply.

8

LORD NNAMANI

Winneba

HE COULD FEEL HIS WIFE'S EYES UPON HIM, HER silent panic and fear, but he had nothing to say to her. Instead, he lifted the message he had gotten from the hawk and held it up to the flame in his chambers. He allowed the fire to burn through the paper slowly before he dropped what remained of it on the tray on his table. Turning back around, he saw her as she sat silently, her beautiful brown eyes watching the message momentarily until she lifted her gaze and focused on him.

He wished to say so much but knew this was not the time to tell her. He knew her far too well. So instead, he said nothing and walked toward the doors.

"At least tell me how long we have until whatever is coming is at our gates?" came her voice softly from behind him.

He thought about it. He wanted to tell her, he truly did, but her emotions were already fragile as it was.

"We will speak on it later," he replied softly.

"You do not give my father enough standing," she whispered. "He only wishes to protect all of us, including you. He is not just your father-in-law but your mentor. He isn't after more power."

Lord Nnamani frowned. "Everyone is after more power."

"Even you, Zikobi?" she asked.

"In this world, there are two types of people separated by a thin line—those who want power for the sake of power and those who wish for power to protect what they love," he replied, then opened the door and stepped outside. "You know I am the latter."

He was Lord of Winneba. He held riches and had armies that were second to none, other than the king. Lord Nnamani had never sought more power than what he had been born into because he had all that was enough to protect himself and those he loved—until now. Now everything felt like it was slipping through his fingers, making him wish to hold on tighter and longer to his loved ones.

Can I only do this much? Do I have no other options? he momentarily thought as he stepped into the family courtyard. Closing his eyes, he felt the gentle breeze brushing past his face. In his mind, he saw his son and wondered about the pain Zereen must have felt and the anger he carried in his heart . . . an anger Zikobi now carried with him.

"Baba?"

When he opened his eyes, his daughter was staring at him from the middle of all the flowers, her knees covered in dirt, her hair filled with leaves and tossed every which way, and she dared to stand before him as if this were perfectly acceptable. Hearing the sounds of footsteps, he glanced into the corner and saw his sons, the twins, hiding behind the beam, trying to pretend they were not there.

"I was wrong," Zikora told him, and hung her head.

"About what?" her mother asked as she stepped out of their quarters and stood beside him, her face hard. "Is it the foolish way you acted this morning? The foolish way you ran away, or the foolish way you now stand before us? Look at yourself, Zikora. Is this any way for a young mistress of this family to look?"

"I do not know," Zikora muttered, "because I'm the only young mistress of the family."

Zeihra snickered from his hiding spot while Lady Nnamani tried to control her annoyance. "You—"

"Guards!" Lord Nnamani called out. Immediately, three guards appeared from the corners of the courtyard, swords in hand and bows on their backs. "Arrest the young mistress and have her thrown into the southern prison."

Lady Nnamani's gaze whipped from their daughter to Lord Nnamani. "Zikobi!"

"Father!" Both of their sons jumped out of their hiding spot, staring at their father with the same confused and horrified panic as their mother.

None of the guards moved, so he opened his mouth and asked, "Did you not hear me? I said arrest her."

"*Stop!*" Lady Nnamani yelled, then turned and stepped in front of her daughter, putting herself between daughter and husband. "Zikobi? What are you doing?"

He looked into his wife's eyes and asked, "Is this any way the *lady* of this family should act? Zikora not only disrespected my word in front of all the council, but she disobeyed you and ran away. Are there no consequences for her? If you cannot control your daughter, I shall teach her what happens to those disobeying my word. She will learn to act as a young mistress should."

Lady Nnamani's brows knitted together, and she turned back

to look at her daughter before stepping aside. The guards stepped forward, but now the twins ran into the courtyard and knelt before their father, bowing their heads to him.

"She was wrong. We will make sure it will not happen again!" they both said.

They all wished to disobey but knew better—all except Zikora. She was still a child and was confused, but she was not afraid. She approached one of the guards and lifted her hands to him. He was a fearsome warrior, twice her size, who had killed many. He would have killed many more, but staring down at Lord Nnamani's daughter, the warrior froze.

So Zikora leaned in and whispered, "We have to go, or Baba will get mad."

The man nodded slowly, then took the rope and wrapped it gently around her small child's hands.

"You two remove yourself from my face before I have you beaten a hundred times," Lord Nnamani said to his sons, and they rose from the ground, looking at their little sister as the guard with the rope slack and a slow pace began to lead her away.

"Hurry up and take her," he called to the guards. "She is to get no food or water, and anyone who tries to help will die," Lord Nnamani snapped before turning and entering the home again.

Again, he wondered if he had no other options. But he wasn't sure he did—not if he were to protect his people and his family . . .

Especially his daughter.

9

ZIKORA

Winneba

THE FIRST THING ZIKORA NOTICED WHEN SHE
was brought down into the dungeons was the smell. It was so harsh,
strong, and foul that she took a step back into the legs of the prison
guard.

"Young mistress," the guard said, and patted her on the back of
her shoulder.

Swallowing hard, she slowly stepped forward. She couldn't help
but stare at the men in their cells, dressed in dirty clothes and their
hair a mess, some covered in blood and each chained at their feet.

"This one," the guard said, opening the only empty cell. It had
one table, and straw covering the floor. When she walked in, another guard came over with chains.

"What are you doing?" A guard with a deep scar across his hand
grabbed the first guard's arm.

"Lord Nnamani said to . . ." The first guard's voice drifted off
after one look at the other guard's face.

"Young mistress, I am Hanif Akintola. Don't be afraid," he said, removing the ropes from her hands.

"I'm not afraid," she said, rubbing her wrist. "It smells bad, but I'm okay now."

The guard stared at her, not sure if he believed her. But he didn't say anything more when she moved to sit behind the table, looking into the cells of all the other prisoners as they lay on the ground, groaning aloud. When the guards stepped out, one of the prisoners reached forward.

"Food," the prisoner demanded, straining to grab one of the guards, the skin of his hands so dry and cracked and breaking against the chains around his wrist. The guards just ignored him.

"Young mistress," Hanif called to gain her attention, and knelt outside the bars of her cell. "If you are scared or need help, just blow on this." He held out a wooden whistle marked with a white owl. She took it from his hand and held it carefully.

"Lord Nnamani said to leave her," another guard said.

But Hanif stared him down, and the other man just walked out of the dungeon.

"Thank you," Zikora replied as she looked it over.

"Go," Hanif said to the rest of the guards, and they all walked down the dark hallway and back up the stairs, closing a hatch behind them. The candle lights were dim, and the sound of groans came from every direction.

"If Lord Nnamani does not even spare his only beloved daughter, what hope is there for the rest of us?" said the man in the cell across from her, the same one who had demanded food. His hair was gray and black but matted in different sections. Which was strange to Zikora because all prisoners she had ever seen always had their heads shaved.

"Who are you?"

Not looking at her, the man said, "No one."

"But you can't be no one if you are speaking."

"Little one." The man looked over to her, and it was then that Zikora winced at the healed burn all over his face that had melted his brown skin, his eyes wide and wild, his lips cracked and bleeding also, yet still, he spoke, "Being someone has nothing to do with speaking and everything to do with the condition of your soul."

"What does that mean?"

"Good question." He coughed. "You will figure out the answer one day . . . or not."

Zikora shifted a little closer to him. "Are you a bad person? Is that why you are here?"

"Are *you* a bad person? Is that why *you* are here?" he asked in return.

She frowned and pouted. "I made my baba angry."

"What a coincidence. So did I."

"My baba or your baba?"

The man snickered, for not only was she not afraid, even in this place, but she was also a bit sharp. "Both."

"Then you are a bad person," Zikora stated firmly. "What did you do?"

"How are you sure I am bad?"

"Baba is good."

The man stared at her for a long time, and not once did Zikora dare to break that gaze. "Your baba is a coward, Zikora."

Her jaw set, she stood up and moved to the edge of her cell. "Take it back."

"Or what?" He grinned as he stood and moved to the edge of his cell as well, and in so doing, he showed his full height, which was even taller than her father. "Shall you break out of your cell and into mine?"

"Take. It. Back," she demanded.

"No," he said in return. "Never. Your baba is not even brave enough to kill me. Instead, he leaves me in limbo to compensate for his guilt."

Zikora didn't understand what he meant, but neither did she back away. Instead, it was in her nature to lean in. "My baba doesn't hurt people without reason, and he is not a coward."

Again, the man laughed madly and leaned on the bars. "Your baba was born a coward, raised a coward, and will die a coward."

"He is not! Everyone says my baba is a good man, the best in all of Winneba!"

"A good man?"

"Yes."

"Really? Then let me ask you"—the man leaned closer, looking at her—"what kind of good man disavows his kin, then throws his daughter in the dungeons for speaking out against him? Doesn't he know how dangerous it is for you to be here with us insane and *bad* people? He doesn't care about his family—"

"Not true!" Zikora yelled back at him. "You don't even know him!"

"Oh, but I do!" the man stated, gripping the bars tighter and pressing his face into the gaps. "Little one, I know Zikobi better than anyone. You want to know who I am? Ask him. I want to see your face when you find out what type of man your *baba* truly is."

"I will!" she snapped. Then she moved to the center of her cell, tucked her knees to her chest, and held on tight to the whistle in her hand.

I am not afraid. Baba is coming, she declared in her mind.

She was sure of it. Even as the prison became nearly pitch-black when the candles began to go out and her stomach began to grumble, she sat and waited . . . and waited, never once losing faith.

Hours had passed, and just as she was about to nod off to sleep, she heard his voice.

"Have you learned your lesson?"

"Baba!" She smiled as she got up and rushed to the bars. "I am hungry!"

"Have you learned your lesson?" he asked her.

She nodded and tried to be serious. "Yes, sorry, Baba."

"Here," her father said, giving her a golden cup, his face still cold. "Drink."

"Thank you," she replied without hesitation, and drank all the sweet-smelling liquid as if it were juice. But it was not, and she did not seem to notice until she tried to hand back the cup. It slipped from her hands and she couldn't feel them anymore.

"Baba?" she cried out as she fell to her knees and then onto her side. Her eyes were wide as she stared up at her father.

"Poor little one," the man opposite her cell said, sitting upright, breathing in the scent as well. "See why we don't trust people so easily. Baba or not."

Zikora struggled to speak, but she could only watch as her father stared back at her, frowning.

"Baba . . . ?" Zikora reached out to him again, as she was sure it was him. However, before she could ask what was happening, her eyes closed, but still she heard him speak.

"Shh, you will be fine. I promise it will be over soon."

"Who needs your useless promises? They've never been able to save anyone, little brother," the prisoner said.

Little brother? She didn't understand. All she knew was that she was scared for the first time.

Baba!

10

Lord Nnamani

Winneba

"YOUR DAUGHTER IS PROUD BUT WEAK. AND IF your children are weak, it is because you made them so," his brother whispered, sitting back down in his cell as Zikobi laid his daughter on the ground in her cell and brushed her small braids from her face. "Isn't that what Father always said, *little brother?*"

Turning to face him, Lord Nnamani nodded. "You are right. He did say that. But do you still think what you did came from strength, Zeikel?"

"Lord Nnamani, they came for your son, they cut him to pieces, hung his head from the walls of Ahalon, and you *bowed* before them. You are not worthy to ask me what strength is!" Zeikel snapped.

"I am not you," Lord Nnamani calmly replied, looking at his daughter. "I am not willing to sacrifice hundreds of thousands of men, making them also suffer the loss of their children—"

"Then you are still a fool. Like Father. Who is going to protect

the people of Winneba when our family is gone? Or are you waiting for the day that cursed army of theirs massacres your wife and
children? Until you are like me?"

"It was an accident——"

"Poison is never fed to anyone by accident!" Zeikel said with a
hiss. "Nor was the fire used to cover it up."

"You had no proof, and the man you captured . . ."

"Was silenced by our father, who wanted to avoid a war with
the king. And here you are doing the same thing," Zeikel sneered.
"Making the same mistakes as him."

"I understand——"

"You lost one! I lost *everything*! You do not understand yet, but I
have a feeling you soon will."

Lord Nnamani swallowed and breathed through his nose. "I
think you're the one who doesn't understand. Back then, you nearly
started a rebellion."

"Oh no, little brother, I *did* start one." Zeikel held on to the bars,
squeezing them as tightly as he could. "You can't see it, but I'm
sure you can feel it as I feel it. Our people have pride too. How long
do you think they will stay quiet as they murder us? You thought
hiding me away here, hiding or killing anyone who dared to stand
and fight, would stop their anger? Impossible. Now that Zereen is
gone, you and I know there is no avoiding what is to come. The king
will send his army one day, and you will see that we should have
rebelled long ago."

"You're right," Lord Nnamani said, inhaling deeply before facing
his brother one more time. "About all of it, you were right. The king
will not stop until every threat to his rule is gone. But you are a fool
if you think you are still strong enough to lead an army to fight back
now. You are old and broken, brother, and so am I."

"If only you had an elder son with the fire——"

"How dare you?"

"I dare now, just as I dared then. Just as I would dare again! Give me a sword, and you will know I have not aged a day."

Lord Nnamani snickered and shook his head. "A dead man does not need a sword."

"I am not dead yet."

"Zeikel Nnamani died from his wounds twenty-five years ago," Lord Nnamani reminded him. "All those who sought to join his rebellion were put to death also. There is no undoing what has been done."

Zeikel smashed his fist against the cell. "Weak! You and Father both! You could not even manage to kill me. Instead, you keep me here locked up like a dog."

"Better a dog in here than a wolf out there."

Zeikel exhaled through his nose and gritted his teeth. "How is it that we manage to have the same fight every time you come here?"

"When it comes to stubbornness, who in Ahkebulin has more than the Nnamani?" Lord Nnamani replied with a tired smile on his face.

"Those damn iron dwarfs," Zeikel said, leaning on the bars. "Have you at least brought me wine? And I mean good wine. That last bottle you sent was an insult."

Lord Nnamani snickered and handed over the small jar he had been hiding.

Zeikel glanced down at it and then at his brother. "This is also an insult."

"You do not have to take it—"

Zeikel snatched it from his brother. "I have very little pride left, so I shall take this anyway."

"Of course you will."

"Well, are you going to tell me why you are here or not?" Zeikel asked, then took a drink from the jar. He passed it back when he tasted the sweetness of it. "There is so little of it that I'm more annoyed you gave it to me in the first place. What is the point of wine if I cannot indulge in it?"

"I need you sober."

"I'm dead, remember?" Zeikel snorted and waved his hand around the cells. "What need do I have of sobriety? What are you expecting me to do? Surely you did not come for advice."

"My daughter is here," Lord Nnamani replied, though it did not answer his brother's question.

"And you put her here. Why?"

Lord Nnamani stood a bit straighter. "Because they are coming for her. The king is going to ask that my daughter live in Ahalon at the palace."

"And how do you know that? You've enlisted a seer?"

"If I could, I would, but can find none. No, I was sent word by an ally in Ahalon."

Zeikel shook his head. "So the king had your son killed, and now he's taking your daughter hostage? But still you will not rebel."

"I never said that."

Zeikel paused, then slowly took a seat on his straw bed. He tilted his head to the side and looked at the rage in his brother's eyes. "You never said that? You have been saying that for almost three decades now."

"I am not saying that right now, am I? I only said you are old, and I do not wish to carelessly waste men in war," Lord Nnamani said. "Do you really think you are what you once were? What any of us once were? The years have made us all soft."

"Ah . . . this generation has known more peace than any of us," Zeikel replied, thinking it through quickly. "So, if we are soft, so must be the cities and villages in Winneba. How long has it been since the walls have been fortified and prepared for war? Could they even last a week in a siege?" he mused.

"Now you understand me," Lord Nnamani replied.

"You *are* rebelling," Zeikel said, a grin slowly spreading across his face. "But you need time, so bow now, strike later? You, the great and honorable Lord of Winneba? I do not believe it. Who knew all it would take was one dead—"

"Do not invoke my son's memory again."

"Why? Does the guilt rip you up inside? Does it poison your soul? Does it leave you hollow to know he wanders unavenged?" Zeikel asked. "Know that there is no peace, no end . . . just dull agony from now on for you."

"You delight in this, don't you?"

"Zereen was my nephew. Whether I met him or not, he was kin, and he was slaughtered, so no, I do not delight in the death of my own," Zeikel replied, balling one hand into a fist as he glanced up at his brother. "But I will not pretend as if I did not warn all of you. The council, Father, and all of the masters—with the exception of Master Jahi—disagreed with me. Now look at us."

"When it comes to war, my father-in-law would agree to it under any circumstance and now has the support of most of those on the council." Lord Nnamani frowned but stood upright, never wavering.

"His connection to our families is strong. Of course they will listen to him."

"Even over me?"

Zeikel did not answer, instead asking, "You have always fought for peace, not war. Now you come to me suddenly with a change of heart? Why?" Zeikel looked his brother over carefully, still not believing.

Lord Nnamani nodded, his face hard and his hand gripping his wrist behind his back. "They took my son. I bowed down and disowned him. Now they are coming for Zikora. Why? Because they failed to murder all of the Mukundi, and they fear if that boy comes to us, we will unite against them, fulfilling that ridiculous prophecy. I will be disobeying a royal decree if I say they cannot have her, which will be treason, and war will break out. We will lose. If I say yes, my daughter may never return home, and there will still be war. We may win, but she is in their hands, and I may never see her again. There is no avoiding this, so if this is the course we must walk, then I must be the one to decide on how to go forth."

Zeikel clapped his hands, his chains jingling. "How brave you are, little brother. And yet you will not release me, as all the world believes me dead, and changing that would cause chaos here. So I must ask again: why go through so much to speak with me? You're free to come down to this prison whenever you please, since you are the lord here. Why lock up your beloved daughter? There is something else. What is it?"

Lord Nnamani looked at Zeikel, then stepped back and called with a stern voice, "Bring it!"

His most-trusted guard, Hanif, came forward holding a large golden urn engraved with broken wings on a tray. Right behind him was a small beyond-aged woman with a hunched back and face so wrinkled and worn that her eyes seemed to protrude. She was dressed in all white and blue, and she held a tray upon which lay a gold dagger, a bowl of oil, feathers of the crowned crane, and a familiar round red-and-violet-colored fruit.

"So, you have, in fact, come for my help," Zeikel said as he took this in.

Lord Nnamani opened his daughter's cell and lifted her into his arms, then walked over to his brother's cell.

"She is headstrong, proud, honest, and good. She is strong but will need to be stronger. I fear . . ."

"Their palace will eat her alive." Zeikel nodded as Lord Nnamani brought the girl to him. "Between their power struggles, the lies, those who just want to harm us or cause war, and the faults they will pin on her, she might not make it a year there."

"Exactly."

"You cannot save her, so you seek to sacrifice—"

"I am not *sacrificing* my daughter," Lord Nnamani snapped as his brother reached the cell bars.

"But you are. The moment you threw an innocent girl in here, you knew that," Zeikel muttered, leaning against the bars. "The difference between us is that I am always quick to anger, to fight, whereas you and Father tread carefully as if this is a match of wit and not a blood sport."

"The truth is that it is both—a match of wit and a blood sport— which is why we both have taken losses," Lord Nnamani replied.

"I'm afraid your losses have only just begun. Just as mine have finally come to an end," Zeikel replied.

Lord Nnamani laid his daughter at Zeikel's feet.

"The Rite of Blessing can never be taken lightly." Zeikel frowned, looking over to the small girl as she slept quietly, then at the old woman, who was already preparing. "I am surprised you approved of this, Elder. Especially in a cell, of all places. Is it not supposed to be done in the tower of kings?"

"It matters not where the rite is passed," she whispered as she opened the urn to turn the ash with the end of the feather. "So long as it passes."

"There is no precedent for passing the rite onto a girl. She could die," Zeikel said, looking at his brother. "Are you prepared for that?"

"She will not. Unlike me, she is strong," Lord Nnamani said ruefully. "Give her the blessing. As you know, my own was a farce, which was why I never held the ritual for Zereen."

"Yes, you had nothing to give. And Zereen would not have been able to fake it like you," Zeikel replied coldly.

"They are all too honest." Lord Nnamani often took pride in his children's honesty, proof that he'd raised worthy and honorable children. But now it looked like foolishness, and all the good and honor he'd tried to hold on to had weakened him.

"If you had killed me then, as Father demanded," Zeikel said, "you would have been Father's heir and able to pass the blessing down to your son. Now, because of your softness, this girl has to carry the burden of men."

"Maybe it's fated, and if it is so, she will be our glory," Lord Nnamani replied, remembering the day she was born, one month too early and in the midst of a storm that nearly flooded several villages and cities. He remembered waiting in the western wing as the thundering sky drowned out his wife's screams, the rain beating down so heavily it sounded like drops of stone and not water. But most of all, he remembered the young boy who stood in the storm before the gates of his home. The guards had told the boy to leave over and over again, but he remained silently watching. He could see the child from the window, and just as his daughter was born, the boy got on his knees and prostrated himself three times.

There were only two reasons to perform this obeisance—a ceremonial greeting to one's parents or a proper greeting to the king and queen.

Lord Nnamani had looked away from the window for only a moment when the maids came to tell him of Zikora's birth, and when he looked back, the boy was gone.

Over the years, he'd searched but could never find him.

Lord Nnamani feared he may have met the fate all seers faced—death.

Zeikel stepped forward and looked into his brother's eyes. "Swear to me, Zikobi, that when this rebellion—this war—begins, you will not waver. You will rid yourself of any weakness. You will not stop till they pay for what they have done to us. Swear to me, little brother."

"I swear upon all that I love and my dead son's restless soul that we will have vengeance and then peace," Lord Nnamani said.

"Peace . . . does it exist?" Zeikel asked as the elder presented the oil to him. Dipping his right fingers into it, he coated them, then placed them on Zikora's small forehead and drew the crown of the crane. He then drew its wings on her cheeks.

Stepping back, the elder placed the black fruit in her mouth and lifted the golden dagger. Zeikel offered the same oiled hand to the elder, who sliced into his palm until blood pooled. Walking around Zikora's body, he allowed his blood to fall. When the circle was completed, he spoke: "With my blood and the blessings of our ancestors, I, Zeikel Nnamani, true Lord and *King* of Winneba, declare you, Zikora, daughter of Zikobi, my heir. All I have I leave to you, and all I know I leave to you."

Then the elder nodded to Hanif, who proceeded to pour the ashes of Zeikel and Lord Nnamani's father on top of the small girl.

"May your ascent be to the sky; may your death be fertile to the ground, and in your rebirth, you are so crowned," both brothers whispered as her whole body was engulfed by a mound of ash.

"Now we must wait," the elder told them.

"Thank you," Lord Nnamani muttered to his brother, looking into Zeikel's eyes as he took Hanif's sword and drove it deep into Zeikel's gut.

"Finally." Zeikel grinned, not bothering to look at his wound but staring directly at Lord Nnamani. "What do you think Father will say to me when I arrive? 'Welcome, my foolish and stubborn son'?"

"I hope he says he is sorry . . . as I am," Lord Nnamani replied, pulling the blade from him.

"Ahh . . . Father never apologizes," Zeikel reminded him as he fell forward. Zeikel's eyes glazed over, and it was as if Lord Nnamani were staring through his brother instead of at him.

"Then I apologize for him and me both. We were weak," Lord Nnamani muttered.

"I see them." Zeikel's grin widened. "My wife . . . my sons . . . I see them."

"Good . . . tell them we have not forgotten them."

Then Lord Nnamani bit down on his lip, trying to hold back his agony and hold his brother as they slowly slid together to the ground.

"Tellandom Arzampende. Little brother," Zeikel murmured.

"Rest well big brother," Lord Nnamani said, knowing Zeikel could no longer hear him. They stayed like that for only a moment before Lord Nnamani gently rested his brother's body on the ground. Rising to his feet, he inhaled deeply and stepped back.

"Take him and do what needs to be done," Lord Nnamani ordered.

Hanif stepped forward. "What of his ashes, my lord?"

"He is to go where he deserves to be . . . in the tower of kings," Lord Nnamani replied.

"Yes, sir," Hanif said, lifting the body onto his shoulders.

Lord Nnamani had a mind to tell him to cover Zeikel's body at least but then remembered that although through his own eyes, Zeikel was his brother—a noble lord, the true lord—to anyone else who might see him now, he would look like nothing more than a prisoner. No one would even spare him a glance.

As he often did, Lord Nnamani wondered if he deserved to be lord.

"The fact that it saddens and disturbs you is proof enough that you deserve to be our lord," the elder said from beside him as if she could read his mind.

When Lord Nnamani turned to her, she was sitting before the ash dome covering his daughter. Slowly, he sat down as well.

"If it disturbs me, and I do it anyway, am I still any better than anyone else?" he asked.

"Yes. But only barely," she replied honestly.

"If Winneba knew of what I had done, they would . . ." He did not know, or maybe he did but feared to say it.

"They would look to her as she is now: the true ruler here," the elder said, watchful. "Should she arise from the journey of kings, that is. We have never done such a rite as this in my hundred years."

Which was his fault, Lord Nnamani knew. Because he had let Zeikel live. The rite was to be done when the heir reached maturity, for the journey of kings was a severe test to see if one were worthy of the blessing and worthy of leading Winneba. It was said to be too much for a child, but Lord Nnamani truly believed Zikora was not just any child.

He *had* to believe it, for it was the only thing that helped him manage his guilt.

"She will arise, for the heavens have a greater destiny for her," he muttered.

"I will pray that it is so," said the elder.

So will I.

II

LADY NNAMANI

Winneba

THEY SAT IN LADY NNAMANI'S CHAMBERS around her morning table, where three small cups of bitter wine were laid out. Master Jahi was the first to pick up his cup, followed by Lady Nnamani and, finally, Zakee.

"You are now the heir of Winneba, Zakee," Master Jahi said, lifting his cup to him. "If you ever need anything, you know you can come to me?"

"Thank you, Nna Baba," Zakee said softly, bowing his head.

Lady Nnamani noticed the look her baba gave him, a look she often got as a young child, so she gave her father a stern look in return, warning him not to go any further than that. He merely drank then, and the rest of them did as well.

"Your dabir tells me you were meditating on the river stones all night?" Lady Nnamani asked, and Zakee simply nodded.

"Last night, I saw there was a waning moon to the right of double stars. It was beautiful." Zakee smiled and took another sip.

"Does that mean anything?" Master Jahi frowned as he watched Zakee.

"Nna Baba, it means everything. The stars are how the gods speak to us—the waning moon means letting go and surrendering, and the double stars mean the approaching vision, the coming destiny of heaven," Zakee replied, looking out the window at the clear blue sky. "I think there is order in all of this, even if we do not understand it all yet. And that gives me peace."

"Peace?" Master Jahi gripped his cup tightly.

"Father—"

"Your brother was murdered. Where is the order and peace in that?" Master Jahi snapped at Zakee before Lady Nnamani could get another word in.

Zakee blinked a few times then bowed his head. "Forgive me, Nna Baba. I only meant that we should look to the future—"

"Zakee," Lady Nnamani interrupted him quickly, placing a hand on his. "Why don't you go check on your brothers. I haven't seen them all morning."

He glanced at her, and she offered him a small smile, nodding for him to go.

"Yes, Mother." Zakee bowed to them both before getting up and leaving the room. When the doors closed, Master Jahi sighed deeply, shaking his head.

"That boy will not be able to lead us," he muttered, taking another sip of wine.

"As you said, Baba, he is still a boy," Lady Nnamani replied, pouring more wine into his cup.

"At fifteen, I had already gone to war. Zereen was his age two years ago, and he spent his nights training and studying from the masters, not looking up to the sky, waiting for the gods," he scoffed. "How they could be so different is a wonder to the world."

"Because one was born and raised to be king, and the other never thought such a burden would fall to him."

"Which is why Zereen's death is all the more—"

"I will forgive you, Father, for saying that child's name again, but remember—it is now forbidden. Speaking it is against Lord Nnamani's orders." Lady Nnamani spoke gently, lifting her own cup to her lips.

"I will not speak his name, but I will say that child was the best of the best of them, and many are disappointed to see his life cut short so soon—"

"*Baba*," Lady Nnamani begged, doing her best to remain calm. "Please—your words add to the pain you know I cannot express."

"Forgive me." He nodded and placed his hand on his chest. "I understand and am hurt too. I just lack your dignity in this situation. I always knew you were born to be a great lady. You walked and spoke with elegance from the age of three."

"I was not three." She smirked and looked down into her cup. "I had to be at least four."

He chuckled at that and nodded. "Fine, four—it feels like ages ago."

"I am not that old, Baba," she reminded him, then thought about it. "Though I swear my daughter is trying to make me so. I do not know how to handle her. You saw what she did yesterday at the council meeting."

"She spoke the truth."

"Since when is truth a matter of politics?" She shook her head. "But that is not the point, and I'm surprised to hear you spout such apologies for her, too, Baba." Lady Nnamani sighed and put her cup down. "She should not have even been there at all, let alone on the rooftops and yelling like she is insane."

"True. Was her nanny not with her?"

Lady Nnamani shook her head. "Zikora managed to trick her by cutting her hand while practicing her archery. She knew they would leave her to get a doctor and took that chance to attend the council meeting."

"Clever girl." Master Jahi chuckled. "I didn't know you were still permitting her to practice archery."

"Her father was . . . along with swords, hunting, fishing, and climbing—anything that girl can think of to prepare herself to become one of the Seh Llinga." Lady Nnamani shook her head. "When you forced me to train, I hated it all, the fighting, the practicing . . ."

"And yet you did it anyway, as the Seh Llinga was the only way you could become the great lady you always dreamed of being." Her father smiled. "The irony of your daughter, born a great lady and wanting to become the warrior you never sought to be."

"Irony aside, it is a waste of her energy because it can never be. I am trying to get her to focus on the only path open to her. I've gotten her strict nannies, but she hides from them, tricks them, or worse, complains to her father, and they are removed. I have gotten her kinder nannies, and she somehow manages to get them to take orders from her instead. I do not know what to do with her."

"She's still young and is playful. Your older sister was like that once, but as soon as she married, she could have outmatched you in grace. Give Zikora time and strict punishment, and she'll straighten herself out," Master Jahi replied, placing his cup down.

"Yes, but whatever punishment I come up with now is going to be useless compared to Zikobi throwing her into the southern prison," Lady Nnamani told him as she finished her drink.

Master Jahi's eyes narrowed, and he immediately looked at her. "Zikobi put her in the southern prison yesterday?"

"Yes, and she is still not out," she replied angrily, placing her cup down with some force. "I did not think it warranted punishment that severe, but then again, yesterday was important, so he must want to show everyone how serious he is. But even still, it has been hours, and he has not returned either."

"He went with her?"

"I have no idea where he's gone."

Master Jahi chewed on that for a moment. "He said *southern* prison?" her father asked.

Noticing the look on his face, she nodded but asked, "Yes, the southern one—why? Isn't it just the prison for the insane ones? The other prisoners are in the northern section—"

"Has anyone been down there to check on her?"

"Father, what is it?" Lady Nnamani leaned in. "Why do you look so concerned?"

"Nothing." Her father shook his head. "It was just the thought of her being in there. You are right. That is very severe."

Lady Nnamani knew her father well enough to know he was lying, but she heard hurried footsteps outside her door and her name being called before she could press the matter further.

"Your ladyship!"

"Enter."

The doors slid open, and for the second time in two days, Nanny Urenna rushed in, then fell to her knees in front of her.

"What is it?" Lady Nnamani rose to her feet.

"The guards have spotted a messenger's envoy . . . they have the sun emblems . . . they are from the king."

Lady Nnamani inhaled through her nose, then looked at her father, who poured himself another cup of wine.

"And so it begins," he muttered, then tossed the drink down his throat.

"Where is his lordship?" Lady Nnamani asked her.

"I have not seen him today, my lady."

Lady Nnamani drew her eyebrows together. Ever since Lord Nnamani had gotten that letter yesterday and sent their daughter to prison, he'd disappeared. He refused to tell her what was to come, and now it had come, and she was without him to face it.

"Have someone find him. *Now!*" Lady Nnamani hollered, her hands shaking. Nanny Urenna fled.

"Remain calm. Better a messenger than an army," her father reminded her as he rose from his chair.

"He knew something was coming, Baba, but he didn't share it with me," she whispered, hanging her head. "I do not know where his mind is anymore."

It was true she had always wanted to be a great lady, which was why she and so many others joined the Seh Llinga. She knew it was rare for a lord or even former kings to favor all the Seh Llinga. Normally, there was always a wife and maybe one or two others. The rest truly were warriors, and upon the lord's and king's death, were free to live their lives or marry. When Zikobi had chosen her, it felt like a dream, and when he sought no one else but her, she thought she was divinely blessed. He shared everything with her. Every dream and thought—or at least, she'd always believed so. But lately she was starting to see there were things he'd hidden from her. She just didn't know what.

"You and Zikora are a lot more similar than you think," her father said with a snicker, drawing her attention back to him. "You both are very good at sulking."

She smiled. "Forgive me."

"No need, daughter." He bowed to her and stretched out his arm for her to go forward. "But remember, you are the Lady of Winneba."

She felt quite silly that after all these years, she still needed to be talked up by her father. But it had helped and, composed, she moved to the door.

Stepping out into the hallway, she saw all the servants on her wing of the house had paused and waited for her, lining the halls, their faces stern and backs straight.

Lady Nnamani said not a word to them as she walked forward with her head held high. The farther she walked, the more of them she saw, all of them bowing to her as she passed. It was so silent that she wondered if they dared to breathe. She did not rush the five minutes it took to walk from her room to the front of their estate. When she arrived, she saw all three of her sons standing, waiting. Zikobi and Zikora were the only two people not there.

Stepping beside the twins, who always had information on their sister, she asked, "Where are your father and sister?"

"She's still in prison," Zesiro whispered, never looking away from the gate.

"I saw Father go last night before bed. I thought he had taken her out, but I think he's still there," Zeihra added.

"At the prison?"

"Yes."

What in heaven's name are you doing, Zikobi? Lady Nnamani called out in her mind, but her face remained solemn as the gates opened and a large carriage, drawn by four horses, entered before them. It was not a royal carriage, she knew for sure, but it was far too grand for any simple messenger. Especially with the ten guards, armed to the teeth, who surrounded it.

When the doors opened, however, it was indeed a simple messenger, judging from the state of his clothes. He was a short man with a thick beard and bald head who nearly slipped coming out of the carriage, which made Zeihra snicker.

"Silence," Lady Nnamani hissed at him.

They all waited for the messenger to adjust himself before marching over to her. Looking down at him, Lady Nnamani said, "Welcome to Winne—"

"Yes, yes, thank you, my lady. Where is your lord?" he asked, glancing around her.

"He is otherwise indisposed, as we did not hear a word of your arrival until just moments—" She was caught off guard by the man's series of coughs and the phlegm in his throat that he spat out on the ground—the ground of her noble house—as if it were a barn. He snapped his hand, forcing some other poor aide who'd arrived with him to hand him a handkerchief.

"How much longer must I wait for him? As you can see, the air here does not agree with me at all." He blew his nose into the same handkerchief before throwing it back to his aide and giving a deep sigh. He was sweating so much his head shone. "Well?"

She had never once been tempted to use all the knowledge she had gained on how to kill a man, not till that very moment.

"Do they speak another language up here?" the short man asked, looking to his aide. "I—by the heavens!"

The man stumbled back as he saw Master Uzolin's giant form arrive at the gates, the mere sight of him making the horses shriek almost as loud as the men upon them. Each of them, the messenger, his aide, the soldiers, and even the carriage driver, stared dumbstruck.

"As I was saying," Lady Nnamani spoke once more, getting the short man's attention, though he did glance back over his shoulder at Master Uzolin. "I welcome you to Winneba. I am Lady Nnamani."

"Yes, thank you for your welcome," the man spoke more mannerly. "I am Szatu Osavadah, the royal messenger of her most gracious and humble majesty, Queen Nasera."

"And for what reason does Her Majesty send you to us?" Lady Nnamani asked him gently, even offering him a smile.

The short man looked up at her and, realizing she was the only one to speak with, said, "The queen thinks of your daughter, the young Lady Zikora, and has asked that she come to the capital to spend time with her and other young ladies of the palace."

The smile dropped from Lady Nnamani's face. Almost instantly, it felt like the earth beneath her feet was spinning. She did not know what she had expected, but this was not it; this was not it at all. She could not breathe, but the short man kept speaking.

"I congratulate you, madam, for raising such a fine young lady to achieve such an invitation. It is a great honor for her and your family, an honor many can only dream of—life within the royal palace. Queen Nasera even sent this carriage, as well as guards to ensure the young lady's comfort and safety during her trip to the capital. Of course, you may add whatever more you see fit. It is at least a seven-week journey, and I am sure she will need a maid or two, as well as other . . . things, I assume. How long will this take you to sort out? We hope to return on the road in a matter of days—"

"Never!" Lady Nnamani nearly spat down at the wretched man, gasping for air to calm her anger. It was only then that Szatu noticed the looks of every last person around Lady Nnamani, the fury in their expressions, how all her sons' hands had balled into fists, how the house guard gripped their swords, and the glare of hate in the eyes of everyone who looked at him.

He stood straighter before her. "Lady Nnamani, I hope you understand that even the *king* has approved this. It is not an invitation to be declined."

"Then it is an order?" Zesiro spoke up, his hand trembling. "The queen is ordering our sister to come to Ahalon to stay with her."

Szatu smiled at the boy, who was already taller than him at thirteen. "Who in this world does not wish to meet their queen? It should not be seen as an order but a chance of a lifetime."

Lady Nnamani swallowed the rage in her throat. "Tell her *most gracious and humble* majesty that we——"

"Are honored by this invitation."

Lady Nnamani turned and looked at her husband as he finally arrived, in the same clothes he had worn yesterday, his face unsurprised. Immediately, she remembered the letter. She remembered how harsh he was with Zikora and slowly realized why he did not tell her. Staring at him, she shook her head gently, begging, her eyes already beginning to burn from holding back tears.

Don't! Please, don't!

"Zikora is still very young and is in need of the best education," Lord Nnamani stated as he came forward to stand beside her, and still she stared at him. When he did not look at her, she grabbed his sleeve. "Who better than the queen herself? That said, it shall take us a few days. Zikora has caught a slight fever and is unfit to travel. When she is, we shall see to everything else. Until then, you all may rest from your journey. Prepare their rooms!" Lord Nnamani ordered, and Lady Nnamani used this command to let go of him and turn back to their home.

To flee from this ambush she had been caught in.

Dazed, everything around her was a blur as she walked, but she fought to keep her head high. The farther she walked, however, the more her legs trembled. It felt like ages had passed before she finally made it to the door of her room, and she collapsed onto her knees once inside, covering her mouth with her hand and sobbing. She screamed into her palm as tears slipped down her face.

She did not know how long she stayed there, but she did not rise until she heard the door open. Only one person could be coming to her at this point.

When she turned and saw him, she felt nothing but rage.

"I—" he began.

Marching up to her husband, she slapped him across the face, and he stood and accepted it. She pushed him, and he accepted it. When she struck him again, he still accepted it.

"You *knew*!" She tried to scream, but her words turned to sobs. "And you immediately accepted giving her up. You coward—"

"There is nothing to be done—"

"I am tired of hearing that!" Lady Nnamani cried aloud. "They killed my son, and you said, 'There is nothing to be done, Eziama.' They beheaded him and hung him from a wall to be mocked before the whole world, and you said, 'There is nothing to be done, Eziama.' You told me to dress up in all the best finery, just to bow my head and abandon him because you said, 'There is nothing to be done, Eziama.' Now they have come for my daughter, and you say it to me again. *Again*, Zikobi!"

"They will not kill her—"

"You do not know that!" Lady Nnamani screamed as she pushed him once again. "All the rumors that float around about those people! We do not even know how long the queen, who is summoning her, will be queen if your sources are true—we all know that's not a position one sits in for long in Ahalon! Let's not pretend this isn't the work of the king and his greedy court. And that's who you send Zikora to? Do you know when they will let her come back? *If* they will let her come back? Even if they don't kill her today or tomorrow, do you truly believe any will care for her there?" She shook her head, venom and tears warring against each other, threatening to come out. "They treat girls as mere toys in their land. How many have died in that palace already? They will abuse and destroy her!"

"They wouldn't—"

He tried to speak, but she was not to be silenced. "If not physically, then mentally, and if not mentally, then spiritually. They will take everything good in her and *break* it. No! I would rather we all meet the same fate as the Mukundi than just hand her over. If you don't fight, I will!"

"I *am* fighting!" Lord Nnamani hollered back to her, and his vehemence was enough to give her pause to at least let him finish. "Not just for Zikora, but all of us!"

"I do not believe you any longer," Lady Nnamani snapped, stepping away from him. "They are *not* taking her. I am not letting you give her away. Do they think ten soldiers are enough to keep a mother from protecting her daughter? From me, they will learn what it means to face a Seh Llinga."

"Eziama, she must go," Zikobi repeated softly, trying to hold her, but once more, she pushed him away, showing *him* the strength of Winneba's Amazons. Catching himself against a table—the only thing that kept him from falling—he said, "It's the only way we can buy more time."

She froze at the way he had said "time" now—it was different. "Time for what?"

He stood there like he was made of stone.

"Time for what, Zikobi?" she asked once more. When he did not answer, she knew in her heart what it meant. "You are . . ."

"We need more time," he muttered more to himself. "So she must go."

"Time, sure. But your daughter isn't time. She isn't a distraction or a diversion. She's a child," she whispered back, shaking her head.

"She's more than a child. She's *our* child. The daughter of the House of Winneba. If we do not let her go, her time will come to an end here anyway, as they will declare war first and march on us before the end of summer. Winneba will be a battlefield, and her childhood will be steeped in the blood of it, the same with Zakee, Zesiro, and Zeihra. They are all too young. We need *time*. They may be hard on her, but she is strong." He looked his wife in the eyes.

"And nothing is harder than war."

Lady Nnamani understood . . . but she could not do it. She had heard too many stories of the horrors that young girls and women had been subjected to in the capital. She always pitied them. Now she was expected to send her own child? She could not sacrifice her daughter for *anything*. She placed her hands over her face, wanting to scream once again.

"I swear to you, we will not abandon her, and one day, she will return home alive. But for now, we must bear it," Lord Nnamani replied, hanging his head.

Her head jerked up at that. *Bear it?* How could he stand there before her and say such words? How could she bear losing another child? Who could simply bear that? "I need to see her. Where is she? Have you returned her to her room? You said something of a fever? Was that a lie?"

"Yes," he admitted. That was all she needed to hear before attempting to walk past him. "She does not have a fever, but she is not in her room."

"What? Where is she?"

"You cannot go to her."

"I *will* see her."

"You—"

"Zikobi, why can't I go to her?"

"Do not ask me more—"

"I will ask you one more time! Where is my daughter?"

When he tried to walk away from her, Lady Nnamani jumped

into his path. Once more, he tried, and she stepped in his way again. He inhaled through his nose.

"Eziama—"

"You are sacrificing her, and now you will not let me see her?" she demanded.

"Prepare her things, Eziama. Hanif's daughter, Tuliza, is around her age, so she will accompany her to Ahalon as her handmaid. Now, let me pass—I will not discuss this any further!" Lord Nnamani snapped, walking past her and out of the room, the door slamming behind him as he went.

Lady Nnamani stood for a second longer, shocked and unbelieving . . . then fell to her knees and wept. She wept until she had no more tears. Then she stood up and went to her mirror, where she cleaned her face and took a breath.

"One day, we will make them pay for this."

12

LORD NNAMANI

Winneba

LORD NNAMANI SAT AT THE HEAD TABLE OF THE dining hall, eating to avoid engaging, as he knew they all wished he would speak. Despite the music and even with the sun shining down, everything felt dim and burdened with sorrow.

"Good morning, Your Lordship, Your Ladyship," said the queen's messenger, Szatu, as he entered the hall, bowing, turning the somber morning sour. He was dressed in the embossed robes of Ahalon, which explained why he was sweating, but to balance that, he had his aide behind him fanning the air.

"You are welcome. Please sit," Lord Nnamani said, but in his heart, much like his wife did, he felt utter disdain for the short, bald man and the queen he served. He glanced at his wife as if in commiseration, but she was eating and refused to make eye contact.

"Your Lordship," Szatu called once more, not going to his seat. "Unfortunately, the food here does not agree with me."

"Does anything?" Zesiro muttered under his breath, causing his brother and the servants behind him to snicker. Szatu had been here for three days now and spent more than half the time complaining about how nothing in Winneba *agreed with him*—whether it was his rooms, the air, the clothes, or the food.

"Her ladyship figured as much and sent for another cook to create your meal special. They are also from Ahalon, so please enjoy," Lord Nnamani said, causing his wife to look at him, for she had not done that. He was sure she would sooner feed the man dirt.

"Someone else from the capital is *here*?" Szatu's eyebrow rose as he went to his seat. "I suppose I could try."

Lord Nnamani nodded to the servant at the door, who returned to fetch the royal messenger his food.

"I thank you for your efforts, Your Ladyship," Szatu said to Lady Nnamani.

Lady Nnamani just stared at the man, her eyes devoid of emotion, which Lord Nnamani knew was much more dangerous than anger.

"Is your daughter still unwell?" Szatu sked. "It has been days, and I have not seen her even at meals."

"Yes. She is still ill," Lord Nnamani replied, and ate quietly.

"If that is the case, maybe it would be best to have her come to the capital as she is, for we have the greatest doctors—"

"My daughter will go when we determine she is fit!" Lady Nnamani snapped, causing Lord Nnamani to look at her sternly. They glared at each other until she finally inhaled. She swallowed before speaking more calmly: "As you said, it is a long road to get to Ahalon's great doctors—eight weeks or more, is it not? What shall you do if she is not strong enough for the trip?"

Szatu's meal arrived, saving him from answering her. He examined the tray as though it were art. He fanned the smell of the soup under his nose and nodded to himself, then lifted his spoon to taste it with the tip of his tongue, making Zesiro and Zeihra roll their eyes.

"It is decent!" Szatu announced with approval before taking a proper spoonful.

"Must you pamper them as well? A whole new cook?" Lady Nnamani muttered to Lord Nnamani from behind her cup.

"It is the same cook," Lord Nnamani whispered back, causing her to glance at him. "I simply directed her to create something strange."

The corners of her lips turned up as she chuckled, which was the first time he'd seen her amused in days.

"Father," Zesiro spoke up, drawing his attention. "I would like to visit Zikora."

"Later—"

"When later?" Zesiro snapped, speaking louder and interrupting him. The tone of his voice caused everyone to stop and look at him.

"As your mother said, when we determine so." Lord Nnamani's voice was stern as he sat up straighter. "Now, sit and finish your food."

Zesiro did not sit, though. Nose flaring, he glared at his father. "I am finished, Father. May I—"

"You may not. Now, *sit*," Lord Nnamani commanded, watching Zeihra grab his brother's arm to yank him down, but Zesiro still would not sit down.

"I will not!"

"Zesiro!" Lady Nnamani sat up straighter, eyes wide. "To whom do you think you are speaking? Apologize now, and sit down as your father ordered you to, or—"

"Mother, if I am to be punished, throw me into the southern

prison," Zesiro demanded, head raised, clearly stating the intent behind his disobedience.

His sister.

Lord Nnamani expected this sort of behavior from Zeihra, but Zesiro?

"If he goes, I go too," Zeihra said, rising as well.

Both their eyes were on Lord Nnamani, daring him.

"You—"

"The southern prison smells bad!"

At this, Lord Nnamani's heart nearly stopped. He would have thought it was his imagination had it not been for everyone else's reaction to the sight of his daughter as she skipped into the room wearing her second-favorite dress and hair scarf, Hanif and her nanny following behind her.

"Zikora!" Lady Nnamani rose from her seat and moved to their daughter. She hugged her tightly before releasing her and cupping her little face to check her all over. "Zikora, are you all right?"

"Yes, Mama." Zikora grinned. "I am late, but can I still eat?"

Lady Nnamani chuckled and nodded. "Of course, you can have anything you like!"

"Zikora!" Zesiro and Zeihra called as they rushed to her and hugged her too.

"You are squishing me!" she yelled at them.

Lord Nnamani glanced over to Hanif, who was now coming around the side to speak to him. He sat up straighter when Hanif stepped beside him and whispered into his ear.

"She arose only a few moments ago. She appears to be the same and does not seem to remember anything. After we cleaned her off, I sent her to the nanny, saying the young miss ran away, but I caught her, and Zikora didn't deny the story."

Lord Nnamani nodded, watching as his family gathered around his daughter.

"What happened to you?" Zesiro asked.

"Are you sure you are okay?" Zeihra asked at the same time.

Lord Nnamani and his wife watched Zikora carefully, as she was very bad at lying—so bad that she almost always told the truth anyway.

"I'm fine now. Just hungry!" Zikora said, and ran to her seat, where Zakee, who had sat silent this whole time, was already giving her his own plate. "Thank you!"

"What do you wish to do with the elder?" Hanif asked Lord Nnamani quietly.

"She will not say anything, so leave her," Lord Nnamani replied, at which Hanif nodded and stepped back. Lord Nnamani glanced at his daughter, who looked to be herself and was talking quickly, even as she ate and made fun of her brothers.

His wife sat beside Zikora, patting her head gently and possibly still checking to see if anything had changed or was wrong with her.

"I am quite pleased to see you are well, Lady Zikora." Szatu had also moved from his seat, and his voice reminded Lord Nnamani of his presence, destroying the air of joy that had begun to rise.

All of his sons stood around Zikora, and his wife hugged her.

"Who are you?" Zikora asked him.

"I am Szatu Osavadah. The queen has invited you to the capital, and I shall be the one to take you now that you are much better," he said with a smile.

"Mr. Osavadah, she is only just recovered," Lady Nnamani said. "We will discuss this later—"

"Can we go once the rains have stopped?" Zikora asked as she took a bite of her bread, causing her whole family to look at her.

"It's not raining, Lady Zikora," Szatu said.

Zikora swallowed before answering, "When the air is like this, it usually means a big rainstorm is coming. The roads will be very bad."

"Zikora." Lord Nnamani watched as his wife turned Zikora to look in her face as she said, "Do you understand what he means? Do you know how far Ahalon is from here?"

"It's about two months away on a good road." Zikora nodded and reached out with her hand to dip her bread in the jelly though her mother still held her face.

"Zikora, you might be there for a long while," Zeihra said gently to her. "You would be going without us."

"Okay," Zikora said, and took another large bite, then mumbled with her mouth full, "Is there fish?"

"Marvelous . . ." Szatu nodded to himself. "Though the queen might want us to teach her table manners on the way."

Lady Nnamani glanced at Lord Nnamani, her eyes wide and confused. Their daughter would never just agree to be taken away. She loved being in Winneba; it was her world. Moreover, this sense of geography was new—Zikora had never even bothered learning about the other lands because she only cared about trying to be part of the Seh Llinga.

"Bring her favorite fish," Lord Nnamani ordered the maid. "And Hanif, take Zesiro and Zeihra. They are to kneel in the courtyard for the rest of the day with no food or water."

"Baba!" they both called out to him.

"And if they are still standing, maybe . . . just maybe, they will get their wish and go to the southern prison," Lord Nnamani said with a huff.

They stared at him with their mouths agape.

"You have the worst timing, Zikora," Zesiro grumbled when Hanif arrived at his side to take them.

"What did I do?" Zikora asked, jelly around her mouth.

"Nothing." Zeihra exhaled heavily and glared at his brother. "I told you to wait at least another day."

"How was I to know?" Zesiro shot back as they were being led from the hall. However, they stopped when they heard the thunder.

"See, the rain is coming." Zikora hummed, and her big eyes lit up as her fish was brought to her.

Lord Nnamani grinned as he watched his daughter, the feeling both pure and bittersweet. Her presence alone had made everything brighter. And when she looked up at him and smiled, he smiled in return, desperately wishing the coming rain to fall forever if that meant she could stay with them, knowing that the sunshine would bring the darkest of days.

13

ZIKORA

Winneba

ZIKORA SAT WATCHING THE RAIN FROM HER window. It was dark out, but she wasn't tired, even though she'd spent time playing around her brothers. Not with them, since they were still kneeling. After it was clear they wouldn't break their punishment to play with her, she'd walked with her mama instead of attending classes. The day seemed to go so fast to her, and she wanted to do many more things.

"What are you looking at?"

Zikora turned to see her father coming behind her. "Baba!"

"Zikora!" Lord Nnamani exclaimed as he sat down beside her. "Are you all right?"

"Everyone keeps asking me that today." Zikora made a face.

"Would you rather them not care? It's polite to ask," Lord Nnamani said, poking her forehead.

"Over and over? It's annoying. Mama says, 'Are you all right?' I

say, 'Yes.' Then Zesiro says, 'Don't get sick again.' And I say, 'Okay.'
Then Zeihra says, 'Are you okay?' And I say, 'Yes.' Then Zakee says
something odd about the stars, but I think it also means 'Are you
okay?'" She sighed dramatically and put her face in her hands, and
her father laughed.

"Fine, I will tell everyone not to ask," he replied. "But then you
shall complain no one is paying attention to you." Zikora made another face, which made him poke her forehead again. "You should
enjoy everyone worrying, for soon you will be . . ."

He stopped, and Zikora watched as his face fell. So she reached
up and poked his forehead.

"It's okay, Baba," Zikora said to him gently. "Don't be sad."

"Do you know what is making me sad?"

She nodded and said softly, "I have to go to Ahalon."

"Does that make you sad?" he asked. "Everyone is asking if you
are all right because you didn't get sad. You didn't cry."

"Hey, I don't cry a lot!" She huffed and spun around to face her
father. "I don't want to go to Ahalon, Baba, but I must."

"Do you know why you have to?"

"I don't know. It hurts when I try to think, but I know I must
go." She rubbed her head, feeling it ache for a moment. "If I stay,
something bad will come here."

"Something bad?"

"Yes, to Winneba. But if I go, it feels like it will be better," Zikora
stated, and when her father just stared at her, she looked him over.
"What, Baba?"

"Was it the same feeling that told you it would rain?"

She nodded.

"Zikora," her father spoke seriously, petting her head, "when
you go to Ahalon, you must listen to this feeling, all right? Even if

someone tells you you're mistaken or tries to convince you otherwise. Always listen to your feelings. They will guide you the right way."

"Yes, Baba," she answered.

"And you must send as many letters as you can to us. Tell us everything that happens to you, okay?"

"Because you will miss me?" Zikora grinned, thrusting her face toward him.

He nodded and gripped her cheek hard.

"Ahh! Baba!"

"Yes, exactly that!" Her father smiled and pulled harder, then let go.

Zikora rubbed her cheek, then grabbed his cheek, pulling as hard as she could. "I will miss you too!"

When Lord Nnamani reached over and tickled her, Zikora squealed and tried to escape, but her father only picked her up and held her.

In between her laughs and her father spinning her around, Zikora had another feeling. She didn't like this one, because it told her this would be the last time her baba could carry her.

So she held him longer, spoke to him more, and asked for several stories before finally falling asleep.

IT RAINED FOR FIVE DAYS, which meant they had to wait an extra two days for the roads to dry, which Zikora noticed was much to Szatu's disappointment and everyone else's glee, and the last week had been her best. She no longer had to go to her lessons, her mama did not lecture her, she was free to eat whatever she liked, and everyone kept giving her gifts to take with her. But her feeling was right, for her baba did not pick her up again after that night. In fact, she had seen him the least due to all his meetings—something about the king's new demands for tributes. However, she knew he came to sit by her bed every night, as she heard his voice even in her dreams.

The sun shone brightly on the eighth day, and the queen's messenger's carriage stood before the gate, waiting for its guards, her nanny, another carriage for her things, plus ten more soldiers from Winneba that her father had chosen to accompany her.

"Young mistress." Hanif stepped before her with a girl her size, with light-brown eyes and skin, short-cut curly hair, and ears pierced two times, beside him. "This is my daughter, Tuliza. She is just a year older than you and will be your handmaid now."

Zikora looked at Tuliza, who bowed her head once then set her gaze on the ground, her jaw tight.

Before Zikora could speak to her, Hanif asked, "Do you still have that whistle I gave you?"

Zikora nodded. "Yes. Sorry, I forgot to return it—"

"No, keep it. It's yours now." Hanif smiled, bowing as her baba came.

"Thank you, Hanif," Lord Nnamani said, and they nodded and walked to the carriage to wait. "Are you ready?"

"Where is Mama?" Zikora asked, looking behind her.

"She is—"

"Here," her mama said as she came forward. Lady Nnamani's eyes were red, but she smiled. Surrounding her mother were Zikora's brothers, but they hung their heads too. "Come on."

Zikora held her parents' hands as she walked toward the carriage, where Nanny Urenna held open the door for her.

"Zikora," her mother called, then bent down to her, her eyes watering, but once more, Lady Nnamani smiled. She took off her beaded gold bracelet with a small brown feather at the side. She placed it on Zikora's arm. "This is my favorite bracelet. I am letting you borrow it, but you must return it to me when we see each other again, okay?"

"Yes, Mama. Thank you!" Zikora grinned, holding her wrist.

"We left you things too," Zeihra muttered.

"Things you have to give back!" Zesiro added.

"I will!"

It felt like the thousandth time she'd hugged her brothers.

"We will all be waiting for you," Zakee whispered to her before letting go.

There was no more time and nothing left to be said, so Zikora entered the carriage first before her nanny and Tuliza.

"What are we?" her father asked her.

"Unbent and outstretched above all, we fly," she replied to him.

"On your journey, Zikora, check the trees," her father said as the door closed. "Some other people wanted to say goodbye to you too."

"Who?"

"Just check." Her father smiled and leaned in, kissing her forehead. "Be safe, little one."

His voice cracked for a moment before he stepped back, and then the last person, Szatu, came waddling up into the carriage.

"Fear not, my lord, for she will be in the best care!" Szatu called out happily. Sticking his hands out the window, he waved. "Go on!"

But the carriage did not move until Lord Nnamani nodded for the gates to be opened. Zikora stuck her head out and waved to her family, even as they got farther away.

"Oh, thank the heavens." Szatu exhaled and leaned against the cushioned seat. "I thought we would never leave."

No one spoke to him, although that didn't seem to bother the man. Zikora wasn't interested in him, though, and instead kept her eyes trained on the trees as her father had told her. She wasn't sure what she was supposed to be seeing until she saw a pair of eyes, then another, and then several more before she heard a loud chanting that caused the whole carriage to stop.

"What is going on?" Szatu hollered.

The voices only grew louder as dozens of women came from the trees, with feathers, threads, and gold in their long-braided hair, more gold around their necks, and their shoulders bearing striped paint while behind their backs were several more feathers that looked like short wings. Each carried a spear as they stomped into the earth with their feet. All the while, they called out.

"Guards!" Szatu hollered when he saw the women's spears pointed at them. The royal guards encircled the carriage, about to pull their own swords, when Tuliza called out before Zikora could, already at the window to see.

"It is the Seh Llinga!" Tuliza grinned from ear to ear. "They are performing a war dance!"

"Who are they at war with?" Szatu complained.

"No one," Tuliza mocked him. "It is also done as a goodbye."

Zikora watched, grinning along with Tuliza as the women gathered around them. They said words Zikora had never heard but understood anyway, so she bowed her head to them.

"Not fair," Tuliza whispered as they disappeared into the trees.

"What is not fair?" Zikora asked, glancing at her.

"I should be there—"

"Tuliza," Nanny Urenna snapped at her, making her cross her arms and look away.

But Zikora pressed. "There? You mean with the Seh Llinga?"

Tuliza did not answer.

"Leave her be, young mistress," Nanny Urenna said, adjusting her skirt.

Zikora was not good at leaving things be, however. "Your ears, they are pierced two times on each side. You get the third one when you are accepted as a Seh Llinga mentee, right? Then you can get your hair braided."

"I was almost there!" Tuliza snapped at her, glaring. "I've been training all this time. I was sure I would be picked for the next line, but now I must go to stupid Ahalon with you."

"Stupid?" Szatu exclaimed.

"Watch your tone!" Nanny Urenna pointed a warning finger at Tuliza. "You are talking to your mistress. Be respectful."

"What are you going to do? Send me back?" Tuliza mocked her. "Please do."

"I will!" Zikora replied, causing the other girl to look at her strangely.

"What?"

"If we are still in Ahalon when we are older, I will send you back by yourself," Zikora repeated, glancing out the window and resting her head on the frame. "As long as you can still fight, you can take the test and be chosen. No rule says you must be trained in Winneba—just born in Winneba. There was once a warrior trained in Kossinat for almost twenty years before returning and joining."

"How do you know that? No one knows what the rules are to be chosen," Tuliza asked, causing Zikora to pause.

"If no one knows, how do you know you were almost picked?" Zikora teased her. "You do not know. You just think so."

"I am strong."

"Strength is not the only thing they look for," Zikora replied in a singsong voice.

"How do you know that?"

Zikora shrugged, and Tuliza glared at her, so Zikora smiled back.

"It should be said that the queen does not like chatterers," Szatu said, reminding them he was still there. "Instead of worrying about how to join a bunch of wild women in the forest, you both—especially you, Lady Zikora—should be preparing to become *proper* young ladies. The capital is very different. Women are seen but never heard. And if they are heard, they speak very, *very* softly."

Zikora tilted her head to the side, not understanding. "Why? Is there something wrong with their voices?"

"No. That is simply how they talk."

"But I do not talk like that."

"I noticed," Szatu said. "However, that will need to change. In fact, everything you have learned so far is wrong and will need to change. But do not worry. With the proper masters, even the roughest stone can be polished smooth."

Zikora's face bunched up. "Is that what happened to your head?"

Her nanny and Tuliza bit back a snicker as Szatu glared at her, annoyed. Quickly, Zikora looked away. She could not see her home anymore.

She wondered about everyone there already.

She had been holding it together without realizing it, but the truth was, she was a little scared. And sad.

Nothing would be the same again. And she wouldn't be home again for a long time.

She could feel it.

456 AAC

(After Aksum's Conquest)

14

KHALIL

Madada

"YOU ARE TWO KOBERS SHORT . . . *AGAIN*, SIR," Khalil grumbled to the large man before him. He might have had muscles that were nearly as big as Khalil's head, but still the boy outstretched his palm, waiting for the rest of the copper coins.

"Be grateful you even get that," the man said, slamming the wooden door in Khalil's face.

Balling his hand into a fist, Khalil gripped the coin and knocked on the door with all his might, so hard that the whole frame shook.

"*What?!*" the man hollered as he snatched the door back open.

"You are two kobers short! *Sir! Again!*" Khalil yelled at the top of his lungs, causing everyone within hearing distance to pause and watch.

The man grabbed Khalil's shirt, yanking him forward and nearly off his feet. "Are you deaf? I said to be grateful."

"Are *you* deaf? I said you're short, which means you owe more.

Besides, why should I be grateful? I am not the one sick and in need of my grandfather's medicine." Khalil sneered even as the man's grip tightened. "Four kobers is your total . . . *please!*"

They stared each other down, man to boy, and the boy held the unflinching and cold gaze of the man.

"Just pay the boy, Ollaze. Everyone knows Khalil is more stubborn than the king's damn tribute collectors," a neighbor hollered over.

"Maybe it's because no one teaches this little bastard a lesson," Ollaze snapped, and yanked Khalil closer this time. Khalil was used to this with Ollaze, and though Khalil was growing taller, Ollaze was still big and strong enough to pull him off his feet.

"If you don't pay, how can I afford any lessons?" Khalil shot back, making those now watching hope for a real show. *This is what you get for being such a kober-pincher,* he thought.

Ollaze drew back his fist, ready to beat Khalil's face, when a small, thin, fragile woman appeared at the door.

"Here are your kobers, Khalil," the woman said, then began coughing.

"Ina!" Ollaze roughly threw Khalil to the ground and grabbed the woman. "What are you doing out of bed?"

She coughed once more, then smiled and stretched her skeletal hand out to Khalil. "We apologize . . . for missing so . . . many payments. Thank your grandfather for me. I noticed he gave me extra this time around. And tell your mother I said hello."

Ina managed to get this sentence out without coughing but immediately began to again, which caused her to drop the coins on the ground in front of her.

"Ina, sweetheart, go rest, please," Ollaze said, guiding her back into the house. Before following her inside, he glanced down at

Khalil, who had bent down to pick the coins up. "You have no shame. Let me not see you here again, Khalil!"

Khalil ignored the man as he bit into the copper coins, something he'd learned to do after being cheated nearly five times.

"See you next week, *sir*," Khalil said, then turned to walk away.

"This is why bastard children burn in the afterlife!" yelled Ollaze.

"See you there then!"

It wasn't Khalil who said this but Ashon, a boy whose skin was white, his hair golden, and his eyes blue like the sky, making him stand out everywhere he went.

"What was that, you mongrel?" hollered Ollaze, marching out of his home and making Ashon stumble back quickly, trying to use Khalil's body as a shield, but Khalil kept walking, unbothered.

"Nothing, sir! Have a good day!" Ashon half laughed before running to catch up to Khalil, who was counting the coins from all his deliveries.

"How much did we make today?" Ashon asked him. "Is it enough for some chicken?"

"*We* did not make anything, and no, it is not," Khalil said as he put the coins back into his pouch.

"Khalil, what are we going to do for food then?"

Khalil ignored Ashon in the same way he'd been doing since he met him a month after his arrival in the village. His "grandfather" had just then started to make him do medicine deliveries. Khalil believed it was his grandfather's way of making sure people began to believe he was who he said he was. The last stop on his first day of deliveries was to an older couple who lived in a rundown hovel at the far end of the village. That was where he first met Ashon, who was hiding behind his grandmother's skirts, though neither of the grandparents looked like Ashon.

Upon seeing the boy, Khalil remembered a map of the three lands he'd seen with his elder brothers once long ago. They had told him that across the Great Thundering Sea was Wytjreia, a land covered in ice whose people's skin was pure white and hair gold in color. His brothers told him they were cruel and savage people who feasted on the bones of man and beast alike. In his books of the wars, they were all drawn more like crazed animals than people.

So, when he saw Ashon, he thought to find out more. However, upon learning that Ashon was born in Ahkebulin and had never so much as set foot out of the village or beyond the hills for that matter and was pretty much exactly like him in every way except his skin, eyes, hair, and utter cowardice, Khalil lost all interest. Nevertheless, ever since then, Ashon had followed him around *every day*.

"What if we do not get a full chicken? What's the price for, like, a thigh?" Ashon asked him desperately.

Khalil sighed. Whether Khalil spoke or not did not really matter to Ashon. So Khalil did his best not to listen.

"We should hurry, not that there will be much in the market. Did you hear about old man Yuma?" Ashon asked, looking at him. "The king's tribute collectors took his last goat yesterday! He tried begging and asking for more time but got hit upside the head with a rock and started to shake! They say white stuff even came out of his mouth."

Khalil did know, as he had been forced to run across the village with medicine. Thanks to his grandfather, Khalil had ripped the strap of his shoe again but managed to make it in time to save old man Yuma just as the soldiers were leaving.

"Everyone's complaining and angry about it." Ashon sighed, lifting his arms to his side. "My grandparents gave everything we owned today, which wasn't much, for this year's collection. It's just the hovel now. I'm going to have to find new work without the farm. What did they take from you this time?"

"The chickens," Khalil grumbled.

"The chickens? *All* of the chickens?"

"It was either that or Moujo, and my grandfather refused to give her up."

"He gave up the chickens to save the sheep? *One* sheep?" Ashon gasped and looked at Khalil as if he were insane. "The chickens lay eggs and give you more chickens or food."

Khalil had said the same thing to his grandfather, but the old man refused to listen. Much had changed since the slaughter of the Mukundi family. The king had passed a new decree for tribute, calling for half of all the livestock, poultry, and grain to be sent to Ahalon every year, which meant there was less and less available for the villagers. It was starting to affect everyone directly, and every other day, there were thefts, fights on the roads, or deaths from hunger.

"What will he do next year to save that sheep?" Ashon asked Khalil. "I doubt he will sell enough medicine to pay the tribute instead—how much does it cost to pay again?"

"One gold aksum," Khalil replied as Ashon kicked a rock on the path, laughing.

"I've never seen an aksum in my life," Ashon shot back. "How much is that again?"

"One golden aksum is sixty silver suns or one hundred and twenty half-suns, which is two hundred and sixty-four copper nyah, that equals one thousand, one hundred and sixty-four copper nuliks, and that comes to five thousand, one hundred and twelve half-copper kobers," Khalil repeated with ease, slightly annoyed, as he had tried to teach Ashon over and over again.

"Five thousand, one hundred and twelve half-copper kobers." Ashon shook his head in disgust. "They might as well just tell us they never expect us to pay with coin. Everyone says they are forcing us to give up half of everything until we have nothing left so that we are in debt and become slaves."

You would think Ashon spoke to many people, but he didn't. He did his best to stay away from them so as not to get hurt. And yet, somehow, he always seemed to know what the village was thinking or talking about.

"Slavery is forbidden in Madada," Khalil reminded him.

"Yeah, only because the Mukundi family stopped it from coming here. Now with them all dead, they took slaves in Xauri, and that's only a day's walk north of here." Ashon sighed heavily, and Khalil did his best not to react though his fingers felt tense. "I heard some people have been attacking the soldiers too. People are saying—"

"Stop listening to people—"

"If it isn't the bastard and the mongrel of Kazera!" called out a group of boys as they rushed onto the street, circling them. Immediately, Ashon stepped behind Khalil, who glanced around at the six of them.

"We do not want any trouble, Chuks!" Ashon yelled from behind Khalil.

Chuks, who was fifteen and the oldest, tallest, and pretended to be the smartest, was the leader of the group of orphaned boys in the village.

"Shut up, mongrel!" Chuks sneered back at Ashon. "It's now twenty kobers to go this way."

"Twenty! You raised the price!" Ashon gasped, sticking his head out, which got him a glare, and he bent back down.

Chuks held his hand out to Khalil. "Pay up."

"I'll use another road then," Khalil replied, and turned, but when he did, the other boys ran in front of him.

"You know it doesn't work like that. You are here now, so you have to pay."

"It is against the law to demand tribute on top of the king's tribute," Khalil stated, looking back at him.

"You say that all the time. Who are you going to tell? The king?" Chuks asked, making the rest of them laugh. "Hand it over. I know you went to deliver medicine today."

"And if I don't?" Khalil stated.

"Then you're going to need medicine!" Chuks replied, pounding his fist into his palm, and the boys around him started to do the same. "Last chance, so hand it over. I'll count to three. One . . . two . . ."

Khalil punched Chuks right in the nose before he said three, which then caused all the other boys to jump on him. Over the last three years, Khalil had gotten stronger thanks to his daily chores, running the farm on his own, and secretly training at night with a tree branch he made into a sword. He did it so he would never forget his family's fighting style. The only problem was that he could never use it in public, and the battles he fought weren't with a sword or a branch but with his fists. And while he had gotten much better with those, Chuks still beat him almost every time.

"I tried to be nice!" Chuks hollered from above him, shocking him. "Hand it over!"

"Get off him!" Ashon hollered, and tried to throw his body into the older boy but was grabbed by the rest and pinned to the dirt. One by one, they began to stomp on him.

Khalil yanked the coin pouch at his waist and held it up.

Chuks grinned and snatched it from him. "I thought so."

"How much does he have today?" one of the other boys said, rushing over as Chuks poured the contents of the pouch into his hands, but with the coins came powdered dust.

"Why is this dust mixed with it?" Chuks snapped.

"It's not dust," Khalil said, rising to his feet. He dusted off his hands and cleaned the blood off his nose. "It's poison. Now that you've touched it, you won't make it through the night."

All the boys froze, staring at him, and those who hadn't touched the dust stepped away quickly.

"You're lying!" Chuks yelled.

"Let's wait until tonight, then," Khalil replied, picking Ashon up from the ground.

"My hand is turning red!" the boy screamed, dropping the coin he had. One by one, they all checked their hands, panicking.

"Khalil!" Chuks yelled.

"There is a cure," Khalil replied to them, reaching back into the medicine bag behind him. "But it will cost you."

"How about I promise not to pound your faces into the ground," Chuks said.

"I would like that, as well as ten kobers on top of the twelve you stole from me," Khalil declared.

"You—"

"Or you could die, and then I never have to worry about it again," Khalil stated.

"Murder is against the law!" said one of the boys, coughing.

"Who are you going to tell? The king?" Ashon mocked them with his arms crossed over his chest, no longer standing behind Khalil.

Khalil fought the urge to roll his eyes at Ashon's temporary bravery.

"Well?" Khalil asked them, lifting the bottle of medicine for them to see. "Take it or leave it."

Chuks and the rest of them dumped out their pockets, only managing to scrounge up eight kobers among them all.

"That's not ten," Khalil stated.

"That's all we got," Chuks snapped.

"Guess you are dying then," Ashon said, and their eyes widened in fear.

Khalil threw the bottle to the side. "Take one each, and from now on, leave us alone. Find some other people to mess with."

"We'll get you back for this, Khalil," Chuks grumped as he stuffed a seed into his mouth.

"I have more of—"

"Let's go!" Chuks called out to the other boys before picking up the bottle and running away.

When they were gone, Khalil picked up his coins from the powder. However, Ashon rushed and grabbed him first. "What about the poison?"

"What poison?" Khalil asked, blowing the coin clean. "Just grinded osrenyebore."

"Os . . . osren—what?"

"It's a flower," Khalil stated, putting the last coin in his pouch. "It can sometimes make your hands itch, but it's harmless."

"If you were just going to trick them, why did we have to fight!" Ashon huffed.

"We?" Khalil asked, looking at him. "I fought. You got beat up."

"And we could have avoided all of that if you just gave it to them—"

"Chuks is stupid, but not that stupid. If I didn't fight him, he'd know something was wrong and would check inside first instead of just dumping it out on his hand," Khalil replied and checked the coins. "We have enough now for food."

Ashon's eyes lit up, and he nearly jumped. "Finally, chicken!"

"I only have eight kobers, so soup," Khalil said as he started to walk farther into the heart of the village.

"I thought we had twenty now."

"The rest belongs to my grandfather," Khalil said as he walked.

"Right." Ashon sighed heavily. "What if—"

"No."

"You don't even know what I was going to say!"

But Khalil did. Because Ashon always suggested the same thing: claim they got robbed. The only thing was, his grandfather would know and even if he didn't it was dishonorable to steal . . . especially from someone who helped you.

"No."

"Fine."

They were just about to reach the only food stalls for those in the village who couldn't afford the tavern or the alehouse when Khalil saw from the corner of his eye, for the briefest of seconds, a symbol he had thought stomped out by the Zenzele.

The Liabrein.

It had to be. There was no other family emblem in Ahkebulin that held any saber-tooth creature but the Liabrein . . . and that was his family's.

"What are you looking at?" Ashon asked, stopping beside him to look in the alley beside the inn.

"Go on ahead of me and get your soup. I'll be back," Khalil said, giving him some kobers before taking off and running down the alley. However, when he turned the corner, Khalil saw nothing but drying sheets on the lines. He stepped around them, trying to see where to go, but it was a dead square.

Did I imagine it? he thought to himself, frowning. Khalil was about to walk back to the alley when he paused and glanced at the water well for no special reason other than the fact that the rope to lift the bucket was badly frayed and tied wrong. He knew a lot about fetching water from his work on the farm, and the last thing you wanted was for your bucket to go plummeting down the well and having to fish it out without falling in.

Walking over to it, he checked around again, then lifted the bucket to the top. He wasn't sure his hunch was right, but his heart started racing when he looked down the well and saw spiral stairs descending instead of water.

His family was dead. He knew that, but he couldn't help but hope. Khalil quickly stepped down and closed the lid above him. It wasn't pitch-black. There was a glow of light, and the farther down he went, the larger the space was. At the bottom was a corridor, and he quietly crept into it, hearing voices as he went. He paused and glanced around the corner only when the light was so bright he could see his hands again. And what else he saw he knew couldn't be real. It was a massive stockpile of swords, shields, bows, and spears, but that wasn't the strangest thing to him. It was the fact that all the weapons had his family seal on them.

"How many did they take?"

Khalil leaned in at the sound of a man's voice. The man had his family's seal on his shoulder. He saw four men all together, but none of them he recognized, around a large table, with what looked to be a map in the center.

"We counted forty imprisoned from Xauri, another twenty in Tasam, and eighty-seven in Laru!" replied another man whose face was the smoothest and the youngest-looking even though his hair was pure white. He was pointing up and down the map of what Khalil realized was Madada.

"It is no longer a rumor or speculation, Hamisi. The Zenzele are doing exactly what they wanted to do since the beginning. If we do not stop them now, it may be too late," said another man with long twisted hair, dressed in dirty brown clothes and wearing a belt that held twin silver swords at his waist.

"Mbwa is right, Hamisi. Once a man is broken and enslaved, it takes too long to repair him. The people of Madada want to fight. I see it on the streets every day. Kazera has the best natural defense. Outsiders cannot easily make it up those hills. The people are strong, but the loss of M'Deba and the Mukundi has paralyzed everyone. Seeing the boy will give them hope and strength to fight now."

The boy? Khalil wondered. *Do they mean me?*

"The problem is he is still a boy." Hamisi, apparently their leader, with a clawlike scar across his face, sighed and crossed his arms over his chest.

"He is the last Mukundi. Boy or not, his life alone will inspire everyone to join us. He can unite Madada." The fourth man with four tribal marks around his mouth and on his hands spoke.

"It's too early! We put too much at risk," Hamisi snapped.

"It's almost too late!" the man with the gray hair hollered back. "He is the last Mukundi, and whether it is today or ten years from now, this will always be a risk. How do you not understand, Hamisi? You cannot keep him hidden from us or the world forever! Even I am starting to doubt the boy lives at all—"

"As sure as I stand before you, the boy lives!" Hamisi replied.

That hope in Khalil, the joy in him, made him lift his foot to walk forward when, all of a sudden, he felt a blade at his neck.

"Anyone ever warn you about the dangers of eavesdropping, boy?" whispered the man with the shaved head, his sliver blade pressing deeper, pinching Khalil's skin.

Before Khalil could reply, he felt a sharp blow to the side of his head, and everything turned dark.

15

KHALIL

Madada

"WHAT ARE WE GOING TO DO WITH THEM?"

"How in all hells did they even get down here?"

"No matter how they managed it, we cannot risk keeping them alive."

"We should at least find out if they are working for anyone or said anything?"

"They look nearly the same age as the young one you want to lead us."

"That is not the same, and you know it!"

All the arguing woke Khalil up, his vision blurred, and his head ached. It took him a moment to realize his hands and legs were bound . . . and that a body was beside him. He didn't need to see clearly to know it was Ashon. His blurred white skin was still white, and only one person in the village had that.

"Mbwa, do we know anything about them? And how is a Wytjrein in this village?"

"The white one is the grandson of Kendi and Sabra of the family Kanumba. From the talk in the village, his mother left and returned heavily pregnant one year later, claiming she'd married a man with the family name of Wakhunzi and then gave birth to the child before passing. Back then, Lord Mukundi apparently ordered that no harm was to come to the child or his family. And the child was to live with his grandfather until his father's village was found."

Khalil had not known his father knew of Ashon or ever ordered such a thing. But it did explain why the villagers never killed him, no matter how afraid or worried they were about him.

"The other boy is a bastard, though no one knows who his father is. His mother is a madwoman and drunkard. They both live with her father, the old medicine man," the voice continued.

"Doesn't seem like much of a high threat," another man said.

"No, the threat is what they will say going forward." All of a sudden, Khalil felt himself being yanked from the ground. "You are awake, aren't you, boy? Still eavesdropping? Should I cut off your ears before you understand the danger?"

Khalil opened his eyes to see the one good eye of a very muscular man staring at him, so Khalil glared back, not saying a word.

"What is up with that stare of yours?" The man nearly snarled as he shook Khalil by his shirt.

Khalil didn't answer.

"Put him down, Eko." The order came from the man who stood at the head of the table, Hamisi. The muscular man dropped Khalil, allowing him to fall back on the ground as the man with the claw-like scar across his face stepped forward and lifted one of the swords from the arsenal.

"Do you know what this emblem is?" the man asked Khalil, tapping the Liabrein at the center of the sword.

"Hamisi, the kid got lucky—"

"To defeat the Zenzele, no one else can afford luck but *us*, Oringo!" Hamisi said angrily as he threw the sword onto the table. "It does not matter how many weapons we gather, how many hideouts we have, or how many people support our cause, because the Zenzele have thousands more to spare. Do you not understand? Do you not see? Even the slightest crack on our path could destroy us—could destroy everything we have spent years working for."

The silence among the men only grew heavier as they hung their heads. Khalil opened his mouth to speak, but a trembling voice beside him beat him to it.

"If . . . if you need luck . . ." Every pair of eyes turned to Ashon, who Khalil hadn't realized had woken up. Ashon swallowed under the intensity of everyone's gaze.

"What?" Hamisi snapped at him.

Khalil tried to shove Ashon with his foot to tell him to be quiet, but Ashon continued. "Um, ugh, if you . . . you . . . need luck, Khalil's got a lot of it."

Now Khalil looked at him as if he had grown seven heads.

"How does the bastard have luck?" Eko asked.

"I don't," Khalil answered quickly, then whipped a look back to Ashon, mouthing for him to shut up.

"Well?" the man pressed.

Nervous, Ashon's mouth opened, and words just fell out quickly. "I mean, that's what my grandma tells me. He and his mom were sick, he couldn't even walk, and he was covered in bandages when he first came to the village. Everyone said he was going to die. But he didn't. One summer, a disease killed all the animals, but all the ones Khalil cared for lived. He was kicked in the head by sheep, and it was said he'd be messed up in the brain, but he's the smartest in town. He can do math, read and write, and knows much about medicines. He can fight, and he's good at tricking people, too, like Chuks and all his—"

The men laughed.

And Khalil hung his head, not sure what else to do or say. *That* was supposed to be his luck? He didn't die, and he got kicked in the head by his own sheep and didn't lose his mind.

"We should keep him around, then. With that type of luck, who knows what he could save us from?"

"Yes, if we ever have a run-in with a herd of wild farm animals, he would be our savior!"

Khalil sighed heavily and glared at Ashon.

"Eko, untie them," Hamisi said, his voice dull as he walked back to the head of the table to where their map was.

"Just like that?" asked Eko, whose nose was broken and still bleeding from the headbutt. "It could be dangerous—"

"If everything is undone because of two little kids, then we never had a chance from the beginning," Hamisi replied, and glanced between both Khalil and Ashon. "If either of you want to keep living, go home and forget everything you've heard and seen. Do you understand me, boys?"

"Yes!" Ashon said quickly.

Khalil rubbed his wrist and rose when the ropes were cut off him.

"Are you deaf, bastard? I asked if you understood—"

"How do we help?" Khalil asked him seriously.

"Help?" Hamisi repeated.

"This is a rebellion," Khalil stated.

"Khalil!" Ashon grabbed him to make him shut up. The thing about cowards is they always knew when they were in over their heads. But Khalil was not a coward.

A part of him didn't want to say anything, but a greater part felt better among these men with his family's crest. Whether he knew them or not didn't change what they were doing. They wanted what he wanted, and that was to destroy the Zenzele.

"You—"

"The Zenzele destroy everything!" Khalil snapped, angry. "They should pay. They have to pay. I'm going to—"

"You are going to do nothing. As you have and are nothing," Hamisi said in reply.

"Then give me something—"

"That is the problem. Children need. Men give. This moment is for men, not children."

"I—"

"Get them out of my sight," Hamisi ordered.

"I got them." Mbwa, the man with long, twisted hair, said as he grabbed both the boys by the back of their necks.

Khalil tried to speak again, but when he did, Mbwa pinched down hard and pulled them away.

"Do not push your luck," Mbwa muttered as he led them toward a corridor. It was not the same way they came, via the water well. "Even I'm shocked Hamisi didn't kill you both. I doubt it would be hard. He could make it look like you came across some bandits on the road or a wild animal."

"You are not going to scare me," Khalil grumbled as they walked through the dark, the light behind them fading.

"That's good for you, but what of me?" Ashon muttered beside him, and Mbwa chuckled.

"What is the matter with you? Didn't I tell you not to follow me?" Khalil said to Ashon, though he could barely see him through the dark.

But he didn't care about the boy's answer. Because as they

walked, it reminded him of the night he escaped his home with his sister. There were a lot of underground passageways in Madada, but they were very hard to navigate for almost anyone who wasn't part of his family, as some of them were designed to lead to dead ends or traps. Khalil had never learned all of them. He didn't even think it was possible to learn where each one was throughout their land, so he found it odd that these men he'd known nothing of had the skill to navigate them, especially in the dark.

"Who are you people?" Khalil asked him.

"Just a moment ago, you were asking to join us, and only now you think to ask?" the man replied.

"I didn't need to know who you are to know who you are fighting against."

"Ahh, so you believe the enemy of your enemy is your friend?"

"Am I wrong?"

"Not at all," Mbwa replied, letting go of their necks and brushing past them. Khalil wasn't sure what he was doing or where he was going until he heard a soft knock. There was a second before a dim light peeked in above them.

"Up you go," Mbwa said as he rapped on the wooden step at the base of the hole with his knuckles. The first one up like a bat to freedom was Ashon.

In the light, Khalil could see that Mbwa was dressed in dirty and ripped brown clothes—much more so than the others—and with the long, fang-shaped twin swords on his waist, he watched him carefully.

"How can you trust we won't say anything?" Khalil asked him.

Mbwa grinned. "I'll be watching you both now. Do not worry. Now, up you go."

Khalil frowned as he went up the ladder. Ashon reached down

to help him, but Khalil ignored him, climbing out of the hole and onto the patchy grass field by himself. When he turned back to look at Mbwa, he was gone, and just as Khalil was about to stick his head down the hole to check where he had gone, a rumble slithered over the ground.

"Khalil!" Ashon pulled him back quickly. The hole they'd just escaped from filled with muddy water.

"What in the——" Khalil sat on the grass, dumbfounded. *Did they flood the passageway? How?*

"Oh God, that was close!" Ashon exhaled, lying back on the grass. "I thought we were going to die. Khalil, what were you——"

Khalil didn't spare Ashon a second glance or even another word. Instead, he took off running. They had come up right outside the village, and he could see the candlelight coming on for everyone in their homes. It was dark, and he was supposed to have been home a while ago, but Khalil was sure his grandfather already knew what was happening. There was no way he wouldn't know about this.

Running as fast as his legs could carry him, Khalil nearly knocked over the drunkards who'd been turned out onto the street for the night. Still, he kept running with all his might, not stopping until he burst through the wooden gates of his home. He dashed into the medicine room, where his grandfather was always crushing herbs.

The moment Khalil saw his grandfather, all he could think to ask was, "*Why?*"

His grandfather only paused to add the bright-yellow petals of calendula flowers under his stone before resuming his work. "You missed supper, so water and bread are all that's left for you."

Khalil tried to speak again but was out of breath. He marched over to his grandfather when he finally felt he wouldn't keel over.

"Every time there are rumors . . . every time we get word that people are fighting back, you tell me it's nothing. You tell me not to pay attention to gossip. You tell me to keep my head down and focus on the farm!"

"Hand me the foxglove—"

"No!" Khalil yelled down at him. "I am done taking care of the sheep and picking flowers and . . . They have weapons, not pickaxes or farm tools but swords and armor. They have—"

His grandfather rolled the stone over his flowers slowly. "Was the Mukundi family lacking in any of these things? Were they lacking swords and armor?"

"No, but they were caught off guard. The Zenzele knew they couldn't win in a fair fight. Madada's strong. Once there is a war, they will fight—"

"And they will lose." His grandfather's voice was barely above a whisper as he lifted his head in Khalil's direction. Khalil stared blankly. But the man spoke on. "If war breaks out now, they will lose not only their lives, Khalil. They will lose everything."

"You do not know that for sure!" Khalil said.

"Are you willing to risk everything when you do not know for sure either? You are willing to trust your life, your future, on men you have only just met?" his grandfather continued, dropping his head and focusing on his stone once more. "When the time comes Khalil, it will be you who decides."

"What does that mean? I am deciding now, aren't I?" Khalil asked him, but his grandfather didn't answer. "I hate when you do that."

"I know that too." But this time, there was a touch of sadness to his grandfather's tone.

Khalil left him and stepped out into the yard again. He glanced at the moon. He did not believe the whole world could be predestined. There had to be a way for them to win. He did not want to wait until he was older to get Madada back. He wanted . . . he wanted justice, and he wanted it now.

He needed to learn more about those men and what they knew about the "last son" they were talking about.

"I don't care what you say . . . I'm going to do something now," he muttered.

"Khalil!" His mother stumbled out of her small room holding a jar, her long hair scattered, tossed around and covering her face, her dress nearly falling off her shoulders. She lifted the jar for him to see. "I'm out of wine. Bring me more."

He thought she'd had enough already but didn't care to deal with her when she was sober, as she either cried or screamed.

"Coming," he said dully.

"That's my boy."

He glanced at her as she stumbled back inside. Inside, where the lies were thick and he was tucked away from what he really wanted: truth and revenge.

More, though, he just wanted this nightmare of a life to end.

16

KHALIL

Madada

THE NEXT DAY, KHALIL SKETCHED ALL HE COULD remember, which wasn't a lot, but enough. He knew their names, and knew what they looked like. On the day after that, he tried to search for more clues and even went back to the well, but he found the rope had been changed and the well was now just a normal well again, filled with water.

He had so many questions, so much hope, and so much consternation.

He tried to calm himself but couldn't when he thought of the weapons.

Someone would have had to have made those, and they would need coin—gold coin—to forge weapons like that. No normal citizen could spend that much without getting the attention of a Zenzele officer. So that had to mean someone was helping those men. *Maybe the other high nobles?* Khalil wondered. Perhaps the Nnamani, who might be secretly trying to get vengeance for their son? Or maybe there was an even bigger plan in the works, which was why it was taking so long to start this rebellion.

Khalil's mind was spinning with so many possibilities that he could barely pay attention to his chores.

"Ouch!" Khalil yanked his hand away from Moujo's mouth, which was filled with the hay meant for her pen. "If you bite the hand that feeds you, you don't get food, Moujo!"

Moujo kicked the milk bucket with her foot.

"What's that supposed to mean?" Khalil moved to lift the bucket. "If I don't let you bite me, you won't give me milk?"

Moujo stared as she ate, her mouth gnawing away at the hay lazily. But when Khalil stepped forward to milk her, she skirted off to the other side.

"I am not doing this today," Khalil grumbled.

At that, the sheep took off running. Khalil groaned and tossed the bucket to the side. "Now that the chickens are gone, you think you are special. Fine! I'm not chasing you! Sick of chasing you! I'm sick and tired of cleaning your pen, and truthfully, I would love to make you into a nice, hot sheep stew!"

Moujo bleated from across the small farm, running to hide under the deck of the house. Rolling his eyes, Khalil moved to the fence, where his journal and a piece of bread awaited him. He'd just wanted a little milk to drink with it for his lunch, but no, his grandfather just had to have the most temperamental sheep in the world.

There was a time in his life that he was slowly starting to forget was real, where all he had to do was wake up, and there would be any sort of milk, juice, or food he wanted waiting for him. It had only been three years, yet it felt like a lifetime ago; he'd gotten used to wearing clothes that didn't fit and itched and eating stale bread or not eating at all. He didn't remember what it was like to be full or not to ache or to bathe daily. People used to help him wash his hair! It used to be very soft and even had a nice curl. Now it was dry and flaky. The roughness of his hands and the aches in his body all felt so familiar to him that they did not bother him anymore. There were no more discussions with the elders, his brothers, or his baba about the world, though, and that still bothered him, but not as much as it used to. No, now he had conversations with a sheep about how she felt because it was more important that she was in a good mood than him so he could have milk to drink.

He was more concerned about milk than pretty much anything else.

This wasn't his real life, and yet this was his life.

And he hated it.

"I need to find them," Khalil muttered, looking at the sketch in his journal.

"And who might *them* be?"

Khalil spun around so quickly that he nearly hurt his neck. Standing beside the sheep house, outside the gate to their property, was Mbwa, dressed in his tattered brown clothing, dirt on his face, a large round straw hat upon his head, and a piece of hay in his mouth.

"You—"

"Shh," Mbwa cut in, snatching Khalil's journal from his hands.

"That's mine!" Khalil called out, jumping to his feet.

The man's weapons were no longer on his waist, but a dagger was pointed right at Khalil's eye as Mbwa flipped through Khalil's journal with his thumb. "I told you I'd be watching, and I grew curious about what you were sketching so fervently. Good thing I took the risk and came to check."

Before Khalil could reply, the dagger was gone as the man tore pages out of Khalil's journal.

"Hey!" Khalil tried to reach for it again, only to have the dagger at his neck.

"Your conversations with the sheep had me worried about your sanity, but I didn't think you were stupid, Khalil of Kazera." Mbwa gazed down at him. "Are you planning on reporting something?"

"No!" Khalil replied quickly, moving forward despite the blade. "I want to help. I've been to—"

"You think putting our faces on paper helps us?" Mbwa snapped. "The village is still crawling with guards for the tribute collectors."

It was only then that Khalil realized what he meant. "Do they know of you all? No one ever looks at my journal, and I keep it hidden. I use it mostly to remember the herbs and flowers my grandfather tells me to go look for."

"Does my face look like herbs and flowers to you?" Mbwa asked as he tossed the journal back to Khalil. He continued to rip up the papers he'd torn from the journal.

With all the dirt on it, yes, Khalil thought, but said instead, "It won't happen again. I have been searching for you all."

"I noticed." Mbwa frowned. "Also, not a smart move on your part. In fact, I wonder why I believed you were smart at all."

Khalil ignored that, inhaling through his nose as he glared at the man. "I can help."

"There are those eyes of yours. Tell me, what did the Zenzele do to make you hate them so much?" Mbwa asked as he gnawed on the hay in his mouth, reminding Khalil of Moujo. But before Khalil could answer, he heard the door to his home open.

"You have to go!" Khalil whispered to Mbwa, then rushed to the front of the house.

"Khalil," called his grandfather as he stepped out of their home, his hands behind his back and looking in a completely different direction. "Where are you? Who are you speaking to?"

Khalil had a feeling his grandfather knew already but lied anyway. "Who else would I be talking to but your stupid sheep?"

His grandfather was silent, and from the corner of his eye, Khalil saw Mbwa's straw hat as he walked in the direction of the village. However, before he could get far, a familiar blur of white came running frantically toward the gate.

"*They are back!*" Ashon yelled as his body collided with the gate.

"Get off our gate before you break it *again*," Khalil called out to Ashon. "And who is back?"

"Never mind the gate, Khalil, the tribute collectors are back!" Ashon exclaimed as he gripped his knees to catch his breath.

"What?" Khalil asked. "Why? Aren't they finished with the collection? They should be leaving now."

Ashon shook his head, sucked in air, and stood upright. "Apparently, the whole village is short on the tribute this year or something, so people are saying they are coming to collect more."

"If they take more, we won't have anything left now or for the dry season, and if we don't make it through the scorch, we won't be here for next year's collection. That doesn't make sense," Khalil replied. "You must have heard wrong."

"They are meeting and calling all the heads of the families into the village now!" Ashon hollered, stretching out his hand. "My grandfather is already going."

Khalil whipped around to his own grandfather, only now noticing that he wasn't barefoot as usual but wearing his worn-out leather sandals, his walking stick leaning on the frame of the house.

He already knew.

"Grandfather, I will go by myself," Khalil said quickly.

"You are not the head of the house. You are a child," his grandfather said as he grabbed his cane and stepped out.

"You are an old, blind elder, so you do not need to leave. I can find out whatever it is myself," Khalil said as he quickly went to his grandfather and took his elbow.

His grandfather huffed, smacking Khalil's hand away with his cane. "If you are going to help, grab my bag!" It was then that Moujo came out from under the house. "No, no, Moujo, you can't help me either."

"Are you sure? She's a very fat sheep," Khalil said as he grabbed the bag. He saw Ashon pet her head. "With bad judgment."

"And you wonder why she keeps biting you." Ashon laughed.

Khalil ignored them as he followed after his grandfather. When Ashon caught up to Khalil, he couldn't help but ask, "What is your family going to do? If worse comes to worst, we can still give them Moujo."

"I don't know," Ashon whispered back. "That's why I came here."

Khalil understood. Everyone respected Khalil's grandfather because he'd helped almost everyone in the village at one time or another with some ailment or illness. He wasn't the village chief, but he was considered an elder, and even a guard would respect that. So, if he begged on their family's behalf, it would mean something. At least, that is what Khalil assumed Ashon must have thought. However, Khalil didn't trust any army or guard loyal to the Zenzele to even offer a person air, let alone a reprieve.

And when they arrived at the village square and saw nearly all the villagers there, silently waiting, Khalil knew no one else trusted them either.

"I'm going to my grandfather," Ashon whispered before weaving through the crowds, careful not to push or touch anyone.

"How bad is this going to be?" Khalil asked his grandfather quietly.

"Do I look like a seer to you?" the old man replied, and Khalil looked up at him, annoyed, as he hated when his grandfather pretended not to know anything. Over the years, Khalil was certain his grandfather *did* have the power to see into the future. However, Khalil didn't know exactly how far or if there was really any way to change it.

Still, it was always riddles and obfuscation, and he was tired of it.

"Okay then, as an elder, are you sure we don't need Moujo?" Khalil asked when he saw some people had a few valuables in their hands, such as shoes or jugs of milk. Some had even cut their wives' hair to give.

"Why don't you ask your friend with the straw hat, since you are more eager to listen to him than me," his grandfather replied, and Khalil's jaw set. He knew it! The old man was only pretending not to know who he'd been talking to.

"I don't know what you are talking about," Khalil lied.

"Well, you are about to learn," his grandfather whispered back as a man dressed in a fine blue kaftan, a white kufi hat, and matching shoes was led to the center of the square by soldiers in light-brown armor. "Watch. See for yourself how the strands of fate connect us . . . how the unbridled greed and selfishness of men cause a chain of events that ruin the lives of so many."

Khalil didn't understand, but that wasn't new. So he remained silent and watched as a man with long, curly hair stood on the raised platform, adjusting his blue sleeves and looking at them all as if they were rats.

"Greetings, people of Kazera. I am Okereke Djimon, chief tribute collector of central Madada." The man said his name with an air of importance that did not fit someone who had to say his own name.

The people were quiet, still waiting. The man seemed startled by the eerie silence and adjusted his sleeves once more before speaking. "Unfortunately, this year's tribute was . . . pitiful, to say the least, and unconscionable to present to the king, to tell the utter truth. And frankly, I do not understand why, when Kazera is considered to be one of the more flourishing villages in the area."

It was then that the chief of the village, a tall man, no more than forty years old, stepped forward to face the man. "Collector Djimon, fever struck the villagers and animals, and we are only just now getting back on our feet. We do not have much to give. However, to make the difference—"

"Chieftain, only one tribute can make up the difference for this year's utter failures," the collector interrupted, his voice rising as he glanced around the crowd. Everyone had heard the rumors and knew what the king really wanted. Almost as one, they all tensed. Never had Khalil seen old men ball their hands into fists so tightly.

"And what is that?" the chieftain asked, breathing through his nose.

Collector Djimon smiled. "Fear not, good people, as Kazera is important to the king. Which is why I wish to ask a special tribute from here: a representative of Kazera to present to the king."

There was muttering from the crowd, but when the chieftain raised his hand, they were silent again. "Only *one* representative? That is enough to make up the tribute?"

"Yes, and I already have the one in mind. I've been told you harbor a Wytjrein?" Collector Djimon replied.

Khalil's eyes immediately widened, and he looked over to where Ashon was and saw his eyes had widened too, and Ashon was looking directly back at him. What was worse, however, was the fact that all the people of the village made way so that the collector could see Ashon too.

"Ah, there he is!" Collector Djimon replied. "Step forward, boy."

Ashon's eyes shifted to his grandfather, whose grip on his shoulder seemed tight from where Khalil stood.

"Is he deaf?" Collector Djimon asked as he waved to Ashon.

"Ashon, come," the chieftain ordered, and when Ashon tried to move, his grandfather held on to him, pulling Ashon closer.

"Collector Djimon," Ashon's grandfather called out. "He is not Wytjrein. He was born here in Kazera. I was there on the day of his birth. As were you, chieftain."

The chieftain nodded. "He speaks the truth—"

"I do not care!" Collector Djimon snapped. "His skin is white, he is rare, rare is expensive, and expensive is what uplifts your tribute, making it worth presenting to the king. Now, bring the boy forward."

"Collector, my wife and I are old, and we have no other living descendants—"

"Take another, *younger* wife then. You are not that old," Collector Djimon replied. He then snapped his fingers, and the guards moved to get the boy.

"I'll go!" Ashon replied, breaking free of his grandfather's grip and dashing to the center before the guards reached them. "Sorry, sir, for not coming fast enough."

"Ah, you can speak." Collector Djimon nodded. "How old are you?"

"Eleven, sir."

"Still young enough to—"

"When does he come back?" Khalil wanted to find who spoke but found that it was himself, and now everyone's eyes were on him as he spoke again. "Can he come back? This is his home."

"He is a tribute to the king," Collector Djimon stated as Ashon was walked to a horse. "He doesn't come back. And you all should hope he doesn't, since that would mean your tribute was rejected.

In fact, you all should be grateful he alone has won you all more time for next year!"

"A person is not a tribute!" Khalil called out again, wanting to grab a stone and throw it at the man's flat, ugly face. "You can't just take him away forever! That is slavery!"

"Who are you to tell me what I can or cannot do?" Collector Djimon snapped, and the guards beside him stepped forward.

Khalil sought to speak up again but was grabbed by the man beside him.

"Shut up, boy," another man grumbled.

"Elder, tell him to be quiet before he gets the rest of us sent off as well. Who gives a damn about the mongrel? Better him than us," said yet another man, sneering at Khalil and his grandfather.

But his grandfather said nothing. Khalil looked at him, expecting him to do something, anything, but his grandfather was just silent. How was this supposed to teach him anything? Didn't he care? Khalil tried to think of what to do, what to say, how to stop this, when he heard a voice no stronger than his own call out.

"And how will we be able to make up for him next year?"

Collector Djimon turned his head toward the new voice, a clear grimace now on his face. Khalil could not see through all the people, but it took only a second to see another boy step forward. Khalil thought he knew everyone by now, especially someone his age and dressed up in finery, but Khalil didn't recognize him.

"What is with the young boys of this village? They speak back to their betters any way they wish? Have you all been too sick to teach them manners?" Collector Djimon demanded angrily.

"Forgive me for being rude, sir, but you still did not answer me!" the boy yelled as he stepped forward even more. "What happens next year? When Kazera's tribute isn't enough, and we have no more white-skinned people to make up the difference?"

"Let's hope you work harder this year so that is not the case—"

"But it will be!" the boy proclaimed, and then looked to the crowd, who were stunned and confused as to who this child was. "Don't you see what is happening? This is how it starts. You have all accepted giving a *person* as a tribute! There is nothing else you could ever farm or make that will be worth more! Today, they have asked for one boy . . . one *rare* boy. Then next year, they will say, 'Give us twenty regular boys, since you do not have a rare one.' And then next, it will be fifty, then one hundred, and then Kazera will have no boys, so they will take the girls, the women, and the old— anyone. Then there will be no more Kazera and no more villagers, just slaves. This is how our freedom ends!"

The dots were lined up right before their eyes, and once more, all the villagers tensed up, and a man from the crowd yelled, "Slavery is forbidden in Madada!"

"We cannot give you the boy!" another called out.

"A person is not a tribute!"

"It is forbidden!"

"We will not allow it!"

"Chieftain!" Collector Djimon hollered as the guard unsheathed their swords. "Do you speak here, or does this child? I wish to know whom to report this *insolence* and *insult* to!"

"Then let it be clear what my name is for you, sir!" the boy hollered at the very top of his lungs. It was then Khalil saw Hamisi as he stepped up behind the boy, men behind him carrying all sorts of weapons. Eyes wide, Khalil looked to his grandfather, whose eyes were closed and his head down, just as the other boy proclaimed, "I am M'kuru Mukundi of Madada, son of M'Deba!"

17

KHALIL

Madada

IT WAS DAYTIME, BUT THE SOUNDS OF SCREAMS, the smell of blood, the clashing of swords, and the sight of fire re-minded him of that night—the last night when *he* was M'kuru Mukundi.

But now someone else was M'kuru. It had happened so quickly, yet it felt as though everything was moving in slow motion. The moment that boy claimed to be him, to be M'kuru, the soldiers rushed to attack this strange child, and the people of Kazera all rushed to defend. It didn't even matter or occur to them where the swords, bows, and shields came from. They just picked them up—old men, young men, and even a few of the women who were there. Everyone had something in hand, and those who didn't had the pent-up anger of a people who'd had their necks stepped on for too long.

They fought.

Because there weren't enough soldiers to defend against the whole village, it was a slaughter.

"You are rebelling!" Collector Djimon screamed when there were about five soldiers left trying to protect him. "This is a rebellion! I am an officer of the king! You think he will let you live if you harm me? He will burn this whole village down! Forget slavery, for you fools will be dead—"

"Better dead than slaves!" the impostor M'kuru yelled, which made the villagers scream the same as they encroached upon the collector, who shuffled back as his eyes shifted from side to side, his nose flaring as he tried to breathe.

"And better you than us!" screamed a woman.

"Stop! Think about what you all are doing! Don't let this boy lead you to make a—"

"*Kill them!*" the crowd hollered.

"*Please!*" Collector Djimon cried out as they clobbered his soldiers to death, one by one, their blood painting the soil red.

Khalil looked to his grandfather once more, but he was no longer there. Khalil spun around to find where he had gone but couldn't find him as the crowd charged forward.

"M'kuru!"

Khalil paused and turned back as if he were the one called, but it wasn't him they were looking to. It was the impostor. The collector was on his knees in the blood, his fine blue clothes soaking it in until it looked purple. Hamisi stood behind him, holding a sword out to the impostor. And for some reason, the boy froze, which caused Hamisi's face to harden, reminding Khalil of the look his former teachers used to give him when he didn't do what they asked. But whatever disappointment Hamisi harbored disappeared just as quickly with his shout.

"My lord!" Hamisi's voice boomed over the crowd. "I will not allow your sword to be wasted on such fools! Allow me to rid this world of all the king's dogs!"

"*No!*" the collector screamed once more, but Hamisi swung the sword down at the man's neck when the impostor nodded. The blood splattered up over Hamisi, coating his hands and chest.

"Now your enemies rest, my lord!" Hamisi proclaimed, and the crowd roared again.

Khalil looked around at the townspeople. He was very good at remembering faces, yet he didn't recognize any of them. He'd never seen them like this. Some of the men were kicking and spitting on the dead guards, while others were already trying to strip the bodies of their clothes.

"And just like that, a rebellion begins," said Mbwa, standing beside him. Khalil wasn't sure how he got there, but when he looked at the man, Mbwa was smiling and shaking his head, his arms crossed. "Why are you looking at me like that, boy? Isn't this what you wanted? A war."

This *was* what he wanted, yet something didn't feel right to him. Khalil didn't understand why it felt so wrong, though. He didn't care about the damn collector and was glad no one, not even Ashon, was taken away.

This is right, isn't it?

Khalil wondered.

"Ah, here comes the big speech," Mbwa said, drawing Khalil's attention to the center of the square, where everyone slowly seemed to calm as they saw the impostor stand on the same platform the collector once did, with Hamisi now beside him.

"Three years ago, the king's people, the king's murderers, killed my family. From that day until this, I have watched as, over and over again, they destroyed the lives and families of Madada—as they pressed our faces into the ground and stripped us of our food, our land, and our freedom. My father taught me that Madada does not bow its head by choice and never by force! That we are the bravest and the strongest of the nine lands. So even though I am still just a boy, I will fight. Even if it is just me, I will fight! But I hope you will fight alongside me!"

There was silence for a moment, and then, one by one, like a disease that spread through the air, the crowd responded.

"I will fight with you, my lord!"

"I am with you, my lord!"

"For Madada, my lord!"

The more they said it, the sicker Khalil became.

"Khalil!"

For the first time since this whole mess began, Khalil saw Ashon, who ran up with a grin so wide a bird could fit in his mouth and lay a nest.

"Khalil, did you see?! Of course you saw, but see! Look! It's really a Mukundi!"

What did he know about the Mukundi? Why were they all so ready to fight for his family? When the king's men slaughtered his family, no one said anything. They made jokes and whispered among themselves. They all just moved on with their lives, yet now, behind an impostor, they were all ready to fight? Was it now because their lives were at risk that his family suddenly mattered again?

"He saved my life," Ashon replied, looking back at the impostor. "I really didn't know what to do . . . but he saved my life!" he repeated. Ashon stepped forward and threw his fist into the air, yelling, "I will fight with you, my lord!"

Khalil, however, stayed silent.

While everyone cheered as they dragged the now-naked collector and their guards away, and as word spread of this fake M'kuru and people came running to see him and swearing their loyalty into the evening, Khalil stayed silent. He just followed behind Ashon and tried to find out where everyone was going. Mbwa had left Khalil's side the moment Ashon came, so they were on their own, and because they were not as big as the other men, they couldn't get closer to the impostor.

"Khalil, keep up!" Ashon snapped at him, trying to yank Khalil forward with him into the meeting hall. Ashon being ahead of him was a first.

"My lord," a voice said.

Khalil knew the voice, but the tone threw him off. So he squeezed through to the front of the meeting hall to make sure it really was him—the kober-pincher Ollaze, and he was on his knees. "My grandfather fought with yours in the last battle of Abeera. No matter what happens, I will fight with you as well."

For some reason, seeing the big, mean, and scruffy-haired Ollaze on his knees, bowing to a boy around Khalil's own age with such respect and deference made Khalil chuckle. And when he thought about the fact that Ollaze was bowing to a fake, it made Khalil outright laugh.

"What are you doing?!" Ashon whispered, and shoved into him.

"What is so funny, bastard?" Ollaze called out to Khalil, and upon hearing himself being called a bastard, Khalil laughed even more.

It was just funny.

He was the real M'kuru. He wasn't a bastard. He wasn't a farm boy or a medicine-runner. He was really who these people were looking to fight with, and they were bowing to some boy.

"I asked what is so funny?" Ollaze growled, now in front of him, and grabbed Khalil by his collar. "It's about time you learn some respect, boy!"

"Sure," Khalil replied, serious now as he gripped Ollaze's wrist.

"I will give my respect to the person who earns it. Some stranger, whom none of us have ever seen or heard of before, *claiming* he is M'kuru Mukundi, deserves it? Have any of you thought that maybe he could be lying?"

"Why would anyone lie about being a Mukundi—"

"Maybe to get a big oaf like yourself to bow down to him?" Khalil rejoindered just as Ollaze lifted his fist to him.

"Release him!" Hamisi said with his hand upon Ollaze's shoulder. And Ollaze huffed and threw Khalil back as he let go of him. "I can vouch for our lord."

"And who are you?" the chieftain spoke up as he entered the meeting hall with three other men behind him. "Other than one of the men who has pushed us into a rebellion against the king?"

"My name is Hamisi Udaku, son of Hodari, the former western general of the Mukundi Army."

Instantly, Khalil remembered Master Hodari. He came to their home once a year with the other generals and noblemen for his father's council meetings. He could see the similarity now when he looked up at Hamisi's face and didn't focus so much on the scar.

"My father was with the Mukundi that night and was killed along with them," Hamisi replied as he reached into his shirt and pulled out a saber-tooth-shaped medallion. Khalil recognized that too. His father gave it only to the masters who served under him. "As most of you know, the Zenzele raided all of the generals and commanders of the Mukundi Army, and those who did not swear loyalty to the king and denounce the Mukundi—as well as give up their weapons—were put to the sword."

"And they all denounced the Mukundi and did not put up any other fight," the chieftain replied.

Khalil hadn't forgotten or forgiven that either.

"Because the greater fight was protecting the last son," Hamisi stated, glancing around the room. "Everyone knows that the Mukundi had secret passageways built. That is how he escaped, and that is how we found him. We've been protecting him ever since, and we would have kept doing so if not for the fact that the Zenzele have no conscience, and their greed knows no bounds, seeking to turn us all into their slaves. We cannot allow them—"

"No one has been able to stop them!" the chieftain hollered, causing the air to stiffen. "You think we do not hear the rumors? You think we do not know what the Zenzele have done? But as the son of a general, what army do you see here? Because all I see are farmers, miners, regular men—and boys—not warriors! It is the same from village to village. The Red Suns alone could take this village within a day."

"But it will take several weeks for the Zenzele to realize what has happened here," Hamisi replied calmly. "By that time, more will come to join our cause, just as you all did upon hearing our lord was here. What will you have everyone do, chieftain? You were already willing to let one of your boys go. Do you want to know what happened to the boys they took in Tasam or the eighty-seven they took from Laru? Do you wish to see your people dragged away with chains around their necks and feet like cows?"

The chieftain's hands clenched into fists, but he turned and looked to the impostor, who had not yet spoken but instead stood just watching. When the impostor was far away and speaking, Khalil thought he'd sounded older or bigger for some reason. But now that Khalil was closer to him, the impostor looked like a kid—a scared kid.

"Everyone out!" the chieftain hollered to the crowd, but no one moved, so he yelled once more. "As your chieftain, I command you to leave for the night. Return to your homes! The young lord and the son of Hodari have much to discuss before the morning. Do not try to leave the village, for guards will be on patrol. We are to speak about none of this!"

All the older men nodded as they began to leave, and slowly, the younger men followed.

"Thank you for speaking up for me," he heard Ashon whisper before bowing his head to the impostor. The impostor smiled, but it was short-lived, for when he saw Khalil staring at him so intensely, the boy froze. So Ashon elbowed Khalil, but Khalil simply turned and walked out of the meeting hall with everyone else.

For the first time, Ashon didn't follow immediately, and Khalil just shook his head. There was no true loyalty to anyone. Wherever the winds were going was where people went. They did not say anything when his family was slaughtered. They didn't do anything. But now, when they worried over their own families, they all thought it was best to rebel. And he was confused, because he wanted to rebel. He wanted to defeat the Zenzele, but . . .

"Khalil!"

Khalil heard Ashon yell but kept walking as though he did not hear him. However, because Ashon seemed to be under the same spell as everyone else and was acting unlike himself, Ashon ran right into Khalil's back, causing him to fall to the ground.

"What in all the hell is wrong with you?" Khalil yelled, glancing back up at Ashon, who grinned and stretched out his hand.

"Sorry, I thought you would dodge."

"Does it look like I have eyes in the back of my head?" Khalil snapped, ignoring Ashon's hand and getting up off the ground himself.

"You always heard me coming before," Ashon replied.

Rolling his eyes, Khalil started to walk away, and Ashon was right behind him again. "Thanks for trying to help me too."

"Are you sure you don't want to bow your head one more time to that impo— to M'kuru?" Khalil grumbled.

"You can't call him by his name, Khalil!" Ashon exclaimed.

"And why not? Isn't that what names are for?"

"He's a high noble! The last Mukundi!"

By my ass, he is, Khalil thought.

"And I think you might have offended him. My grandmother told me if you were ever blessed enough to meet a high noble, even if they are the same age as you, you must stop and bow and call them my lord, or you will be cursed if you don't."

Then you are most definitely damned a thousand times over already, Khalil replied in his mind. *Actually, that might explain why you almost ended up a slave today.*

"I can't believe he's actually still alive. Lord Mukundi—"

"He still could be a fake," Khalil muttered, walking faster.

"Why are you so annoyed by him?" Ashon asked as he caught up. "Isn't this good? Think what could happen if we become friends with him. We could become his generals! Live in a big, fancy home with servants and fine clothes, and you wouldn't have to milk Moujo!"

"I'd rather marry Moujo than be that boy's general. Did you see him? After causing a whole rebellion, he didn't say another word and just looked so . . . small. Yet everyone is bowing to him."

"I never thought I'd see it." Ashon then started to laugh, which made Khalil turn back.

"What?"

"You are jealous!"

Khalil's eyebrow rose. "What?"

"You are jealous of Lord Mukundi. You wish it was you, don't you? You tried to get everyone to stop the collector, but they ignored you and listened to some outsider before you. So you are mad."

Khalil paused. Was that what was wrong with him? It couldn't be.

"It is nice to see you jealous for once. It's only ever me," Ashon said.

"What?" That was the third time Khalil said it, but Ashon just shrugged, backing away.

"I should go home. My grandparents must be worried again! See you tomorrow!" Ashon said, and ran off before Khalil could actually form a reply.

The rest of the way home, Khalil wondered if Ashon was right. That he was jealous, and that was why he was upset. He wanted to stop the collector, but didn't have the power to do it. Then came this impostor, using Khalil's name, and all the villagers respected the impostor, coming to him and treating him like . . . like a Mukundi. It was annoying, but even if it wasn't true, that didn't mean this was the wrong thing. No . . . This felt wrong because it was a lie, not because he was jealous. An impostor could not restore his family's honor. He did not suffer for all these years hiding for his bloodline to be claimed by a stranger. But perhaps if he worked and helped the impostor, became a general, and used him as a shield, he could one day reveal himself? Would anyone believe him?

"So, you are back?"

He was already at the gate of his house, and his "mother" was lying outside with several jars of wine. "Where is the old man?" she asked.

"He's not back yet?" Khalil asked, rushing inside to search.

"You lost him." She giggled, then snorted. "Serves the liar right! I hope he trips over a nest of snakes!"

"I'm going to go look for him!" Khalil said, already turning back to leave.

"You look for things that are lost, and I am not lost. Just wished to speak to some old friends of mine once more," his grandfather said as he came up the path to the gate.

Khalil quickly went to help when, all of a sudden, he heard a crash.

The jar of wine went right past his head and hit the gate.

"*Liar!*" his mother screamed.

"Do not break the jars, Femi," his grandfather said as he entered the yard.

Khalil quickly went to pick up the broken shards before one of the animals could cut their feet . . . again. Then he remembered there were no more animals besides Moujo.

"Damn the jars, damn the farm, damn you, and damn me!" she replied as she lifted the other jar, but that one was still full, so she drank instead. She drank first and then spoke: "You said that this hell would come to an end soon . . . that it would be over soon!"

"It shall be. But no matter how far you run, this will always be your home, Femi," his grandfather replied as he petted Moujo.

"This is not home. This is a prison, and you know it. You—"

"Enough, Femi," his grandfather said softly. "Enough."

She scoffed and lifted herself off the ground. "You told me all I had to do was keep my son alive. There he is. Alive. I did it. Why am I still suffering here?"

"Don't worry, Femi. You'll soon be leaving this hell for another one," his grandfather replied as he walked into his room. Khalil had no idea what they were talking about, but that was normal. Everything about this night was frustratingly normal.

"Khalil, come," his grandfather said.

Khalil, listening to his grandfather, took off his shoes before entering. His feet were dusty, cracking, and hurt, but when he saw his grandfather's feet, which were far beyond repair at this point, Khalil didn't feel like he had any room to complain.

"Did you see it?"

"What?" That was now the fourth time he had said that, and it made him annoyed with himself. "I mean, see what?"

"The unbridled greed and selfishness of men," his grandfather replied as he took a jar from his basket that held dried herbs, jars of paste, and heaps of ginger. He sat in front of his straw bed. Khalil could hear the man's bones crack and pop on his way down.

"Do you mean how the villagers were ready to let the collector take Ashon to save themselves?" Khalil asked as he sat down as well.

"No, the first person's greed was the tax collector himself."

"What do you mean?"

"The tributes this year were just barely enough. But the tax collector wished to take some of the goods for himself, so he told the village it was not enough. He planned to use Ashon to replace what he planned to steal."

"And that caused his death. So, all because of one man's stupid greed, the whole village is in a mess."

"He's not the only one who is greedy and selfish."

"Who else?"

"Many others. But also you."

"Me?"

"Yes."

"How?"

"Because you wanted to expose that M'kuru. It didn't matter if he was doing what you wished to do, that he was saving your friend.

At that moment, when you looked at me, you knew it and were angry," his grandfather replied.

Khalil frowned, then muttered, "It's a crime to pretend to be a noble, especially a high noble."

"So you've told me once before," his grandfather said, uncorking the jar. "But is that justice more important than the justice you really seek?"

Khalil was seething at the accusation. "If you let a lie live long enough it becomes the truth."

"A lie will always be a lie. Even if no one else remembers, the heavens will."

At that Khalil scoffed. "The heavens . . . let me guess: you are going to ramble on about something I don't understand, and I'm just supposed to have faith. No. Things should be done right—"

"You let your greed for glory and your desires trump everything else."

"It should not be called greed if it is owed," Khalil muttered, and hung his head.

"And good men should not have to die because of the whims of bad men. But that is the nature of the world. Have you forgotten all I have taught you?"

Khalil clenched his fists for a long time, and he felt like screaming, but instead he let out a deep breath and relaxed his hands.

"So, what would you do, Grandfather?"

"I would focus on who I am and never forget my own purpose. No matter who anyone else is, you are you."

The corner of his lip turned up as he glanced back at the old man. "And who am I, again?"

"I recall having this conversation once already with you."

Just once he wanted to catch the old man; have his grandfather call him by his real name.

"You are a strange old man, Grandfather."

"Many in the village think you are strange as well," he replied, handing Khalil a drink for the very first time.

"Why would they think I am strange?"

He didn't answer, just held out the wine. "Drink."

Khalil sniffed it, and his face bunched up in disgust. "Can I not?"

"No. You must. Only a sip is fine."

He didn't want to, but he quickly brought the jar to his mouth and threw his head back. The moment the liquid touched his tongue, Khalil gave a jerk, turned his head, and began to cough.

"What in all the hells is that?" Khalil asked.

"Wine."

Khalil's eyes widened, and he looked at the jar again. *Is this what Femi drinks? How is she still alive?* he wondered.

"The more you drink bitter wine, the less bitter it becomes, and it can even start to taste like water," his grandfather said, and he took the jar back.

"That is *not* water." Khalil tried to get the taste out of his mouth.

"Because you have not drunk it enough."

"I don't want to drink."

"That may work with wine but not with life," his grandfather replied, taking an easy gulp from the jar. "In life, sometimes we must do the bitter thing. And you must do it over and over and over again."

"Why?"

"To survive . . . to prevent a worse thing from happening. It will never be easy for you, Khalil, because you will always be stuck choosing between two evils."

Khalil sighed. "I really hate when you speak like this. I don't understand what you mean exactly."

"Then I will tell you in a way children can understand things . . . in a story."

"I do not want another story. All you ever do is tell me stories. Talk to me like an adult," Khalil said.

"Adults can drink bitter wine." His grandfather chuckled, so Khalil reached for the jar, but his grandfather stopped him. "Either way, let me tell you this story. This will be the last story you and I shall share."

"Why?" Khalil glanced him over. "Is something going to happen?"

His grandfather ignored the question and began, "Long ago, there was a boy just a few years older than you. His elder sister was a beauty with a voice that made even the birds stop in amazement. Their family was not very wealthy, so she often went to sing for noble families. One day, she caught the eye of a young nobleman, and he wanted her for himself. She refused over and over again. Soon, she never returned to that noble's home when he called. This enraged the young noble, so one day, when she was returning home from another day's work, he dragged her into the forest, beat her, and took her by force, then left her for dead. The girl's father was enraged and went to the high noble and begged for justice. The high noble was also furious but did not want to anger the young nobleman's father, as he needed his help, so he punished the young noble only slightly, demanding the girl's family be paid retribution as she did not wish to marry the young noble."

Khalil was completely confused, but he didn't say anything.

"The young noble didn't like that he was punished even slightly. And when he heard that she and her family were leaving their village to start over with the money they had gotten, the young noble had bandits attack them once they were many days away from their village. The young boy ran, seeking help. It just so happened that a general was hunting with his sons nearby, but the bandits had already killed the boy's parents and sister by the time the general reached them. The general put the bandits all to death right there before the boy's eyes. With the parents now dead, the general took the boy into his army, and he grew to be a very skillful warrior. As the years went by, everyone had forgotten about that poor, simple family—everyone but that boy, who was now a man. And he could not rest until he got vengeance on behalf of his sister and parents. The general allowed the young man to search for the young nobleman to kill, so long as he sent information back to his general whenever he could. Then one day, the young man found him."

"And he killed him? The end?" Khalil asked, his hand clenched in anger as he remembered his own sister.

His grandfather shook his head. "No, he became his friend, and they worked together on a new mission."

"You don't become friends with the people that kill your family." Khalil shook his head. "This story isn't right."

"So what do you think he's doing?"

"Pretending to be his friend?"

"Why would he do that instead of just killing him while he could?"

Khalil shrugged. "Something must be stopping him from doing so? Or maybe he has new orders, right?"

"You are smart," his grandfather replied, and moved to lie down on the straw mat.

"So . . . am I right? What happened next?" Khalil questioned

"The story is not finished yet."

"Then why did you start to tell it?!"

His grandfather just closed his eyes to sleep.

"I swear you never make any sense, old man!"

18

KHALIL

Madada

THE SOUND OF HAMMERING WOKE HIM THE
next morning. Normally, it was the chickens, but since they were
gone, Khalil wondered what his grandfather was doing so early
as he rolled onto his side and put his hands over his ears. But the
sound only felt as if it were growing louder. Grumbling, he sat up,
rubbing his face.

"Can I not sleep in for once?" he sighed.

"No one woke you."

Khalil jumped at the sound of his grandfather's voice. He wanted
to groan again when he remembered who he would be delivering to
once he rubbed his eyes and saw the old man packing herbs.

"More deliveries? I thought I did them all for the week?" Khalil
asked.

"Is that good morning?"

"Good morning," Khalil replied, then sat up, looking for the
source of the sound. "What is that noise?"

His grandfather didn't answer, and Khalil didn't want to ask again, so he put on his worn-down sandals before stepping out. However, the world he stepped out into was vastly different from the one he'd gone to sleep in. Their farm was quiet and far from the main center of the village. No one really came this way unless they sought medicine from his grandfather or wished to leave the village. Rarely did that ever happen, and when it did, it was normally only one or two people. And yet, outside their farm now were at least ten men, and they were not leaving. Instead, they stood there hammering and tying together wooden spikes at the edge of his grandfather's land.

"Have you rested enough, bastard?" Khalil turned and saw the giant figure of Ollaze, along with two more men beside him.

"It is hard to with this noise," Khalil replied as he stepped closer to his gate. "What is going on?"

Ollaze reached down and grabbed him by his shirt. "Are you slow in the head, boy? Did you forget we are at war?"

Khalil frowned, not understanding, until he recalled the day before and the impostor.

"I suggest you put the boy down," said none other than Mbwa, dressed in the same dirty clothes, the twin swords at his waist.

Still not releasing Khalil, Ollaze glanced up and down at the grimy-looking man before him. "We were ordered by the chieftain to seize this land."

"What?" Khalil snapped angrily. "You cannot take our land!"

Both Ollaze and Mbwa ignored him.

"What I believe your chieftain said was to speak to the elder here about using his land and home for the time being, as it is an easy entry point into the village that quickly needs to be fortified," Mbwa replied.

"That is what we are doing," Ollaze snapped.

"No, it seems as though you are bullying a child."

"I am not a child," Khalil grumbled, finally able to break free of Ollaze's grasp.

"Whatever! We don't have time for this," Ollaze said as he pushed himself inside the gate along with the two other men. "We must speak with the old man. Where is he, bastard?"

Khalil just pointed to the room, and they walked in with their shoes still on like they owned the place. They were dressed no better than him and his family, yet they acted as if they were head army officials already. At the sound of snickering, he turned to see Mbwa shaking his head.

"It's amusing how a man's back strengthens the moment he's given a purpose."

"What?"

Mbwa glanced down at him. "Where is your mother? Tell her to pack all that she can carry. Hamisi has ordered all those unable to fight to be moved to the center of the village."

Maybe it was due to how early it was and how fast everything seemed to be changing, but Khalil felt lost.

"Who is this Hamisi? And what right does he have to order me?" his mother asked as she stumbled out of her room. As always, the sight of her would have been embarrassing to Khalil if she really were his mother. She was nothing like his true mother—poised, strong, and always dignified.

"Your chieftain has given him such right—"

"The chieftain?" She laughed. "He has a habit of making the very worst choices. Do you—"

"Enough, Femi," his grandfather said as he stepped back into the open. "Pack your things. You wished to leave, remember?"

She stared at him for a long time, frowning. "This is not what I meant, and you know it!"

"Khalil, help her, and gather your things as well." His grandfather's voice was stern as he stood there, staring at all of them with his sightless eyes. Khalil was a bit dazed by the sound of his grandfather's voice. "Now, Khalil."

Nodding, Khalil went to his mother first, taking her wrist and pulling her into her room, where the ground was littered with empty wine jars. Grabbing the longest piece of cloth that he could find among her things, he spread it out to wrap the rest of her belongings.

"The world truly is run by fools," she scoffed as she looked among the jars for any that still had anything to drink inside. "They've started a war on a whim, and now they rush to build defenses? Idiots."

She laughed as she found a jar not yet emptied.

"Would you rather they bow their heads?" Khalil asked, annoyed, dumping her clothes into the large cloth on the floor and searching her room for anything else worth taking with him. He rarely came in here, and she rarely came out. He wasn't surprised to find only more jars.

"I could not care less what they do with their heads. And apparently, neither do they," she replied as she drank. "Soon enough, many of them will hang outside the walls of Ahalon. No, their heads are not even worth that much to the Zenzele. They rule the world for a reason, and a bunch of farmers—"

Khalil kicked one of the jars angrily, shattering it, and turned to her, his teeth and hands clenched. But he swallowed his rage along with the words he truly wished to speak. "Is there anything else you need, *Mother*?"

Instead of answering, her eyes widened and she rushed toward him. He didn't understand why until he looked where she was reaching: toward the broken jar. There he saw a dagger among the pieces, and not just any dagger. It was encased in silver, and on the hilt at the center there was a white diamond with thin, flat spikes around it, making it sort of look like an eye. He could not make out more of the symbol as she snatched the dagger and held it tightly to her chest.

"Have you gathered everything—"

It was the voice of Ollaze.

"*Go away!*" she screamed at the door.

"Femi, we do not have time for your drunken games—"

"We will be out in a moment!" Khalil called, then looked at his mother, who gripped the dagger tightly, her eyes wide. "Mother?"

She flinched, then looked at him and rushed to the center of the room, where he'd packed the rest of her things. She quickly wrapped the dagger in the cloth and tied it all together.

"Let's go."

Khalil reached to grab everything, but she held on to it. "I have it, Mother."

"No. Go pack the food we will need," she ordered.

He was curious. He was sure that dagger looked far too expensive for her to have simply bought it on her own. Where did she get it? Why did she get it? And why was she now hiding it?

When he glanced back up at her, she was once again muttering to herself.

He had no idea what made her like this sometimes but did his best not to push her, or she would truly begin to lose her mind.

She stepped away, waiting by the door, and he moved to go pack his own things, but his grandfather stood there with another packed bag.

"I have everything you need. You both get on," his grandfather said, holding the bag out to him.

"Both? Aren't you coming?" Khalil asked him.

"This is my home, so I am staying. Besides, who will milk Moujo?" his grandfather replied, petting Moujo's head.

"What? Then I am staying—"

"Khalil. You say you are not a child, then do not act like one."

Something didn't feel right to Khalil. Truly, the whole morning had not felt right. He felt as if he were being moved by something out of his control.

"Grandfather—"

"Remember the story I told you last night?" he said. Frowning, Khalil nodded, not sure how that mattered now. "Good. Go on."

Khalil didn't say anything and took the bag.

"I'll lead them and any others on the way," Mbwa said as Khalil and his mother walked out the gate. Then to Ollaze, he noted, "Those barricades must be up before I return."

Khalil glanced back at his grandfather one more time, but the old man wasn't facing him. Instead, he was feeding Moujo from his medicine pouch. Yes, something was certainly not right. His grandfather was acting odder than normal. Something was going to happen. But what?

He glanced around the farm once more, hoping to see what else he could be missing, but nothing brought anything to mind.

"Come on, kid—let's go." Mbwa nudged him forward. "We will see if we can find your white friend."

"You have to tell me the rest of the story later, Grandfather!" Khalil called out to the old man as he began to walk.

The old man shook his head as he petted Moujo. "You'll be the one to tell me."

How can that be? Khalil wondered. He wasn't sure, but he was glad that at least it meant he'd still see his grandfather again. That was good enough.

"You still need bedtime stories, bastard?" Ollaze chuckled. "And here I thought I heard you say you were not a child."

Khalil glared, muttering a curse under his breath. Mbwa laughed a little too jollily as they walked.

"What? Why are you laughing?" Khalil asked him. "What is happening right now?"

"You ask far too many questions. Aren't you afraid? The other children, even some of the adults, all seemed to be in shock. Though after the bloodshed yesterday I am not too surprised."

Khalil ignored this and continued pushing for answers. "Why are you going with us and not staying with them? They aren't very bright. They might need your help."

"I am to take you to Hamisi before returning," Mbwa said, then started whistling to himself.

"Hamisi? What for?"

Mbwa didn't reply, and as he walked, Khalil noticed Mbwa's twin blades again. But this time, his attention was caught by the hilt of one of them. At the tip he saw a white diamond in the center of flat spikes, which were pointed in different directions. Khalil stared at it, then glanced over to his mother, who walked silently, dazed and gripping her bag for dear life. It was very similar but not the same. Which made Khalil want to believe he was wrong.

Maybe he was mistaken. He hadn't seen many swords or daggers, so maybe this was a common design. He wanted to ask Mbwa, but after how his mother had reacted, he could not bring himself to do it. Instead he walked silently until they reached the center of the village, noting how the men of the village now patrolled with weapons, spears, bows, and anything they could get their hands on. The village center was filled with even more people than the day before.

"Khalil!"

He turned toward the voice and saw Ashon pushing through the crowd to get to him, a large grin on his face. "Do you see this? It's crazy. Oh, everyone is preparing—Ugh, sorry, I did not see you. Good morning, ma'am."

The boy waited for a response from Khalil's mother, but she ignored him and warily looked all around her.

"What is going on? Where do we go?" Khalil asked.

"There are some people up front that tell you—"

However, before Ashon could say another word, Mbwa came over to them. "You two, follow me."

"My mother—" Khalil started, but some woman was already speaking to Femi.

"She'll be with the other women. Now, come," Mbwa said, already walking up ahead.

"Mother, I will be back," Khalil called to her, but she ignored him also.

"Where is he leading us?" Ashon asked as they fought through the crowd of people coming toward the center.

Khalil didn't reply, as he was trying to keep up. They went through alleyway after alleyway, farther and farther away from the crowd, until they reached a similar well to the one he'd gone down just a few days ago. This one, however, was guarded by men now wearing the Mukundi crest on their red-and-gold armor. It felt completely different from the villagers and their weapons.

"Whoa," Ashon said, gaping at them all.

They didn't stop at the well, either, however. So Khalil made sure to focus on the path in front of him, which led them into a house, in an area of Kazera he wasn't familiar with. It was simple enough, yet seeing his family crest on a flag hanging over the building was strange and brought back a feeling in Khalil that he'd nearly forgotten: hope.

"In you go," Mbwa said to him as the guards stepped aside.

Ashon hid behind Khalil as they entered. It turned out the building wasn't a house, but a pub. Except all the chairs were gone, and maps seemed to cover every table instead of jugs of wine. But the largest map was the one on the ground, and only one man stood tall beside it, arms crossed behind his back.

When the door shut behind them, Ashon jumped and nearly knocked Khalil over. Khalil glared at him.

"Sorry," Ashon whispered.

"Khalil of Kazera. Ashon Wakhunzi," Hamisi said, raising his face to show them the claw-like scar across it. "Do you know why I sent for you two?"

"No," Khalil replied. "Why?"

"I have an important job for you both," Hamisi said, and crossed to the farthest corner of the room. He pushed the wall, and to their surprise, it opened. "Follow."

"Is this a good idea?" Ashon whispered to Khalil.

No. Yes. How should I know?

Because Khalil wasn't sure. However, he followed Hamisi anyway. And the first thing he noticed when he entered were stairs. And as they went down into the darkness, it smelled just like the well.

Hamisi did not speak, so it was only by his footsteps that Khalil could follow. He had no idea how far down they had gone, and he tried to bury the memories that were rising.

Maybe it was his family's crest . . . seeing it on the men, on the flags, it made him remember the words of his father, his baba: *The heavens will not forgive, and Madada will not forget! The Mukundi will have its vengeance!*

Madada hadn't forgotten their family. Even if it was an impostor. That was a good thing.

When Hamisi pushed open another hidden door, allowing the sunlight inside, Khalil did not flinch from the brightness as Ashon did. Instead, Khalil stepped inside and tensely looked around but saw nothing but a small camp. In the center, a boy his age was being fed a bowl of soup and bread by a woman no older than Femi, and four warriors stood around them.

"My lord!" Ashon exclaimed happily, then bowed his head almost to the ground. When Khalil did not do the same, Ashon smacked his shoulder. All the other adults seemed to be looking at him as well.

"Have you not been taught manners, boy?" Hamisi asked Khalil as he stepped up beside him. "You stand before M'kuru Mukundi of Madada, son of M'Deba. Show your respect."

Khalil looked back at this M'kuru, a boy about the same build and height as him, with dark-brown eyes and low-cut hair. Nothing about this M'kuru stood out. Then again, nothing about Khalil stood out either. If Khalil told everyone the truth and told them who he really was, who would believe him? What good would it do? His grandfather had told him, *Focus on who you are and never forget your own purpose.*

It didn't matter what he did, didn't matter what other people said, even what he said. No one could ever make him forget he was the real M'kuru Mukundi of Madada.

So he bowed his head, but only slightly, and said, "My lord."

"What's going on, Hamisi?" said the woman beside the impostor. She stepped forward with her hands on the impostor's shoulder. "Why did you bring them here? It's not safe—"

"Nowhere is safe, Chima." Hamisi walked toward the center of the tent, motioning for Khalil and Ashon to follow suit. "Aren't you the one that said he needed friends? Well, here they are. My lord, this is Khalil of Kazera and Ashon Wakhunzi."

Before the impostor could step forward, Chima grabbed him and pulled him back, shaking her head. "The bastard is one thing. But the Wytjrein draws too much attention—"

"The boy needs friends with drive and intelligence," Hamisi replied as he poured another portion of soup into a bowl. "You saw them yesterday. This village was ready to give a child to save themselves. Men twice their age, cowering in fear, giving no thought to the future. Weak and spineless. The Wytjrein was ready to sacrifice himself for them. The bastard spoke up, was willing to go against them to save him. What better qualities for friendship than that?"

"Even still—"

"Has anyone bothered to ask us if we wanted to be his friend?" Khalil replied, already seated in front of the pot of food, taking the bread that rested on the log by the fire. Ashon's eyes widened at him, but Khalil simply took a bite. "Or are you going to keep talking as though we aren't here and can't hear you?"

The woman scoffed. "You are a very disrespectful child. Has no one taught you—"

"Will you be my friend?" asked the impostor, now away from his keeper's side and standing in front of Khalil, a smile on his face.

"Of course, my lord!" Ashon grinned wide.

"No," Khalil replied, looking around him and Hamisi. "I do not want friends. I want to fight. Why do you want friends? How would that be helpful to you?"

"Don't take it personally. He doesn't say he's my friend either," Ashon whispered to the impostor.

"Really? But you seem close," the impostor replied.

Ashon nodded, resting his hands behind his head. "Yeah, he's a little grumpy, but if you just stick around him, you get used to it."

The village was preparing for war, and those two were chatting like girls—no, worse than that. The girls in Kazera were probably doing something useful to help, making food or something. Meanwhile, they were all cowering here.

"What have you seen?" Hamisi asked, recalling the question he had put to Khalil the first time they had met, but handed Khalil a bowl of soup and took a seat beside him.

"What?"

"Something must have killed the child in you. Otherwise, you'd be standing with them," Hamisi said, and they both watched Ashon and the impostor laughing, chatting unendingly. "So, what was it?"

Khalil glanced at him. "I have seen the village is preparing for war. Can you really just be sitting here?"

"That's not it," Hamisi said, shaking his head. "But it's of no matter at the moment. What does matter is *here*. Here is very important," he continued. "I have been planning this moment for years. It may feel as though your world has shifted overnight, but for me, it has been many nights. Too many. So trust that there is nothing I've overlooked. You said you wished to help—well, this is how. You are to protect our young lord should anything go wrong."

"You're asking *us* to protect him? Isn't that what you have these guards for?" Khalil indicated the men around their camp.

"They are our first line of defense. Should anything happen, they are to buy you time to help him escape. I'll explain more later. But know that this isn't a game. This is the most important task of your life."

It wasn't.

Not by a long shot.

But right now, it was all he could do.

So he nodded, ate his soup, and wondered if they expected him to give his life to save this lying little boy.

If so, they would be greatly disappointed.

19
KHALIL

Madada

KHALIL STOOD IN THE MIDDLE OF THE VILLAGE square, amazed beyond words.

It had been only two days, yet Kazera looked nothing like it once had. It had changed from a quiet, rather poor, boring village to a bustling one. The drunks who had sat around the inn all day gambling with chicken bones were now lookouts perched on the rooftops. The ladies who used to blow kisses with their skirts hiked up in the alleyway were now collecting hay and bringing it to the sewing house for some reason. And old men, like Ashon's grandfather, were polishing the weapons on the other side of the square.

All the while the younger men who were able to fight, like Ollaze, were being trained by Eko, Oringo, and a few more of Hamisi's warriors who had arrived. The boys, like Chuks and his gang, were bringing up more and more weapons from the tunnels under the supervision of Mbwa. The women who frequently worked in the sewing and cleaning houses, like Ina, Ollaze's wife, were now creating quilted woolen coats to wear underneath armor. The young women and girls who weren't sewing or cleaning were cooking. Everyone was working together . . . *desperately.*

Everyone but Khalil.

He had never seen the village like this before, and it had certainly never felt like this. It made his body shake with a sense of pride and excitement. It felt like they could really do it. It felt like finally, *finally,* Madada would have its vengeance. He wanted to believe it, to get to work just like the rest of them. Yet there was this dread inside of him, and he knew who was responsible for it: his grandfather.

Khalil hadn't been able to see him since he'd left the farm, and for some reason, his grandfather didn't have to stay in the village center with everyone else.

"Khalil?"

He turned to see Ashon beside him, his blond hair combed, his white face washed clean, and his clothing looking neat as well. The clothes weren't new, but they had been patched up, and he wore them with so much confidence, which was strange to Khalil.

"What happened to you?" Khalil asked, looking him up and down and frowning.

"What?" Ashon said, looking over himself as well. "Is something wrong? My grandmother spent so much time helping me get ready this morning. I even took a bath."

"I can tell," Khalil said, though he wasn't sure when. "What did you tell your grandmother? We aren't supposed to be this obvious."

Their duty to be "friends" with the impostor was a secret, and here Ashon looked like he was about to dine with the king's cup-bearer.

"I know. I'm not stupid. I told her Hamisi has a special job for me."

"And she didn't ask what that was?"

"No. She just told me to do my best. Did your mom ask you?" Ashon tilted his head and then looked around the courtyard when he didn't see Khalil's mother with the other women preparing to split their work for the day. Ashon's grandmother was there, and she smiled and waved from the door of the sewing houses. "Where is your mom anyway?"

"Sleeping." Like she always was at this time of day. But he was grateful because he was allowed to go check on her when no other woman was in the room. And because she was such a heavy sleeper, he went through her things, searching for that dagger. It was far too expensive for her to have gotten it in Kazera. So where . . . ?

"Sleeping? But doesn't she—"

"Let's go," Khalil interrupted, already turning to walk. Just then he heard a familiar cry and was knocked to his ass right in the middle of the square. Beside him, biting at his arm, was none other than . . .

"Moujo?"

"Damned stubborn sheep!" A fat, reddish-brown-haired woman came rushing over and grabbed Moujo and lifted her onto her shoulders.

"That's our sheep," Khalil said as he got back on his feet, staring at Moujo's head, her single horn gone and a dried bloody stub in its place.

"Do not worry, Khalil. I promised I'd have her back in one piece," the lady huffed as she held the sheep with all her might. "We are rounding up all the sheep and goats we can get to shear them. We need the wool."

"You didn't do anything else to her?" Khalil asked rather pointedly.

"Anything else?" the lady asked. "Like what? Oh, the horn? She was like that already."

"Okay," was all he said in reply. Because she had no reason to lie, and he was too confused about why his grandfather would ever dehorn his most-beloved sheep.

"This one, though, ugh!" She gritted her teeth as Moujo jostled and fussed in her arms, trying to break free. "This one is a bit stubborn. Any idea how to calm her down? She's making the others restless."

"She likes me," Ashon said, trying to help by reaching for Moujo, only for her to bite at his hair. "Ah!"

Khalil chuckled. Finally, everyone else saw what he did: that damned sheep was a menace.

"A little help here?" Ashon said, trying to reclaim his hair.

"Are you two just messing around?" It was the familiar and unwelcome voice of Chuks, from only ten paces behind them. Chuks stood beside a pile of swords and was covered in sweat from head to toe. "Come over here and help!"

"We are busy!" Ashon yelled back, finally able to free his hair and letting out a sigh of relief.

"I'll be busy rearranging your faces if you—"

"They have other jobs," Mbwa's voice was clear as he stepped up beside Chuks. Once more he had a hat on his head and was chewing on a piece of straw. "You two hurry up and go ahead—"

"No!" the woman yelled as Moujo finally broke away and made a mad dash straight toward Chuks and Mbwa. Khalil rolled his eyes, really not wanting to spend his morning chasing Moujo again, but she had been his responsibility for three years, and he was sure he'd be the only one to corral her. He expected to have to start running but, instead, found the sheep joyfully playing around Mbwa.

He walked over as the large man calmly waved the piece of straw from his mouth and then offered his hat to the sheep, taking a knee in front of her.

"Now, what's the matter with you, girl?" Mbwa asked, petting her head softly. "Do you not want a haircut?"

"She's just dramatic and spoiled," Khalil said as he reached to take her rope. However, as he leaned in, Moujo kicked her legs furiously. Khalil was used to it, but with Mbwa being so close, she ended up kicking his waist, knocking one of his double swords onto the ground.

"Shh . . . relax," Mbwa cooed to the animal.

Khalil's gaze was now on the sword at Mbwa's feet. Now that he was so close to it, he was finally able to see it clearly. As he thought, every detail of the hilt was exactly the same as his mother's dagger, except the direction of the spikes.

Nearly mesmerized, Khalil reached to pick it up when, all of a sudden, another hand beat him to it. When he looked up, Mbwa was grimly staring at him.

"Sorry about that. I got her now," the woman said, holding Moujo. "Thanks for calming her, sir."

As she spoke, Khalil was frozen in place. It was as if his mind had simply broken down, and all he could do was stare at Mbwa. Maybe he wanted it to break down. Because when it worked, his mind told him the only way a sword could have the same exact hilt is if they were made in the same exact place. But his mother had only lived in two places: Kazera and . . . the capital.

"Ay, bastard, are you just going to stand there staring?" Chuks snapped at him, drawing his attention from the sword. "We got work to do. Or are we going to spend all morning on your stupid sheep?"

"As I said, Hamisi has another job for them," Mbwa said, and

Khalil met his eyes. The smile on Mbwa's face was cheery once more, which was as bewildering as anything else that had happened in the last few minutes. "You two hurry on."

"Yes, sir," Ashon said as he tried to fix his hair. "Bye, Moujo."

Khalil walked forward, trying to stay calm. Trying to think reasonably about the sword and the dagger. Could it just be a co-incidence? It wasn't so odd to see similar markings on weapons. Many people lived in the capital. Many fine blacksmiths must have a trademark on their work. But that was usually because the style was ordinary. Cheap and easy to make repeatedly for customers. The detail of that eye, the rays around it, that was far too expensive to just be made en masse. Then again, Khalil hadn't exactly been inspecting the hilts of many weapons. All he knew was from what he'd learned from his real family and what he'd seen done by the ironsmith in their small property.

Khalil didn't know everything and had barely seen anything of the world other than violence, death, lies, and poverty. So maybe he was overthinking things. He desperately wanted to believe he was overthinking things. However, the last few years with his grandfa-ther taught him that wasn't the case. In fact, his grandfather had told him repeatedly that coincidences were merely fate in disguise and that the simplest answer was usually the correct one.

So when he asked himself why his mother and Mbwa would have a weapon with similar emblems, the simple answer was they came from the same place. But what place? The same blacksmith? Or was it from a house? Every prestigious family had an emblem. Khalil knew all of the ones for the high nobles. The Liabrein for his family. The Golden-Crowned Crane for the Nnamani of Winneba. The Three-Headed Monkey for the Ibori of Bhkosi. The Broken Scorpion for the Skerele of Sanné. The Black Fire Lilies for the

Tumelo of Kossinat. The Gpzebui Mask for the Raaya of Yoengo. The One-Eyed Elephant for the Jangari of Nérbua. The Headless Eagle for the Hiwot of Kéye. And the Red Sun for the Zenzele.

He could still see a picture of all of those sigils within the old *Book of Kings* on his father's desk. Khalil wasn't sure if it was funny or sad how some things faded from his mind, like what some of his brothers' faces looked like, while other things, such as drawings within books, he remembered clearly. Nevertheless, he did. However, his education hadn't gone further than the high nobles. He didn't know all of the lower nobles in each land, but they all had to have their own crest and sigils also.

"Khalil. Khalil? Khalil!"

After he blinked a few times, his vision focused on the white face staring directly back at him in confusion. "What?"

"We're here."

"Here?" Khalil repeated, looking around to see they were a few short paces away from the impostor's camp. Two guards stood at the entrance to the tent, and two others sat under the trees, holding their swords as they slept.

When had they gone through the tunnel? He had been so lost in thought that he didn't even realize how far they had walked. But Khalil was even more shocked that Ashon had been quiet the whole way.

Ashon leaned in and whispered, "You need to get it together. We are about to see him."

Khalil frowned. The world really had been flipped on its head if Ashon was the one lecturing him.

"I'm glad you two remembered your way." The woman they'd met the other day appeared at the front of the tent, and right beside her was the impostor, dressed in a brown coat with a Liabrein crest on his chest.

Ashon immediately bowed his head low as he spoke, "Yes, ma'am, thank you."

Like the other day, Khalil didn't bow, just stared at them, and when Ashon noticed, he tugged on Khalil's sleeve—hard. Khalil bit the inside of his cheek and just gave a short nod.

"Have you guys eaten?" the impostor asked with a smile on his face. "Chima made fresh fish soup!"

"Uh . . ." Ashon didn't know what to say, as they had only been given a small corner of bread and watered-down milk in the morning, so they were still hungry. But Khalil knew that he was worried about eating the impostor's food. Khalil didn't share that worry in the slightest.

"We are hungry," Khalil replied as he walked up to the tent. When he entered, the smell of the soup hit his nose, and he found himself by the pot. The woman came over and Khalil noticed she was dressed in a long skirt that had watery mud on the hem. She glanced up at him, a smile on her face.

"Everyone is always a tough guy until they are hungry," she replied, lifting a bowl for him to take, along with a wooden spoon.

Khalil took the bowl from her, then sat on the ground and began to eat.

"What he means is thank you!" Ashon kicked Khalil's foot as he moved in for a bowl too. Khalil shot him a glare, and Ashon made a face back. Khalil wasn't sure what was giving Ashon all this confidence, but he was sure he wasn't a fan of it.

"Thank you, and sorry, he normally has better manners," Ashon said to the woman as he sat down beside Khalil with his soup.

"Are you my mother?" Khalil grumbled to him, taking another bite. However, upon doing so, he paused, remembering his last breakfast with his real family in the dining hall, his baba and mama at the center high table, and he by his mother's side. His brothers teased him for being a baby, for still clinging to his mother. But Mama had whispered that they were just jealous, that even though they were his brothers, they were the sons of concubines and could never sit at the center high table.

Take pride in these moments, Libini. He hadn't heard her voice in so long, at least not like that, and he'd forgotten she called him Libini—the Liabrein's cub.

"Do you not like it?" the impostor asked Khalil.

Khalil stared at him, unable to speak.

"If he doesn't like it, I'll take it back!" Chima snapped, reaching for the bowl, but Khalil hugged the soup to himself and turned away from her.

"I like it," Khalil said quickly.

That made them all laugh.

"Then eat it as if you like it!" Chima ordered him sternly.

"Yes, ma'am!" Ashon replied, stuffing a large spoonful into his mouth. Her brown eyes narrowed on Khalil, and he quickly took another bite, pushing down the thoughts of his family.

"Isn't her food good?" the impostor asked, sitting across from them. "Chima's family were cooks for my family for hundreds of years."

"Really?" Ashon asked, and Khalil looked again at the woman with the short, braided hair, tending to the rest of the indigents in baskets before her.

Were they really? Or was the impostor lying?

"Why do you sound shocked?" she asked as she pulled apart bay leaves. "Have you never had fish soup so good in your lives before? It's my family's secret recipe."

So many people had worked in their house that Khalil couldn't remember them even when he was living there, but he did know one thing. "Didn't the Zenzele kill everyone in the house of Mukundi that night? How did you escape?"

She froze right there before them.

"Khalil . . ." Ashon warned as he shoved him.

"She . . . escaped with me!" the impostor said quickly.

"No, I didn't." She frowned, hanging her head, and put the leaves down. "I ran off that night. I was tired. It wasn't my job to do most of the cooking, but I had to go every day to collect fresh ingredients either from the market or straight from the river. My mama was very picky about what she served on our lord's table. Everything had to be checked and double-checked. Handpicked. And she always sent me, even though they had so many other people that could go. She said it's what made us such great cooks. We could pick out the best ingredients to store and prepare. I'd spent all day getting the best fresh fish from the river. Fish I didn't even get to eat."

"You didn't get to eat it?" Ashon asked as he took another bite. "Why?"

"You can't eat the same food as a high noble." Chima laughed and shook her head. "My mother worked and worked, even into the night, just to prepare the next meal. All the while, she forced me to be by her side. I was tired. I didn't want to help her debone and season the fish that night before bed. So, I snuck off. I was going to have just that one night to myself. I went into town, watched a play, bought candy apples, and lay in the field looking up at the stars, never realizing—all the while . . ."

"They were being attacked," Khalil whispered as he, too, took another bite. "Your mom . . . she died."

The impostor was lying. But he believed Chima. Simply by the taste of the food he knew, she had to be telling the truth.

"She was *murdered*," Chima corrected angrily, gritting her teeth. "Everyone remembers what happened to the Mukundi, but no one remembers all those who served there."

Khalil gripped the spoon tightly out of shame, because she was right. He never once thought of those people.

"I do," the impostor said, drawing Khalil's attention. "Your mother's name was Camara Yacouba. I remember her and her food."

Chima bit her lip and nodded, then bowed her head to him. "Thank . . . thank you, my lord."

Khalil saw the joy on her face and how tenderly she stirred the soup as the conversation went by. And again, stared at the impostor . . . how did he know the name of their cook? As he listened to them all speak, he could not help but feel like *he* was the impostor. He'd never bothered to learn any of the servants' names.

He rarely even saw them.

Was that not shameful?

All the pride he had in being M'kuru, and he couldn't even remember the names of the people who took care of him.

I promise I'll avenge them too.

20

KHALIL

Madada

THE SUN WAS SETTING BY THE TIME THEY RE-
turned to the center of the village. They hadn't done much other
than sit around and talk. Well, Ashon and the impostor spoke while
Khalil listened, shocked by how much the impostor knew about
Khalil's family and life. He couldn't help but wonder if it was maybe
Hamisi's doing. And as he thought about the scar-faced man, Khalil
realized he had been completely out of sight today, him and the
chieftain. Khalil hated being young. It meant no one told them
anything but where to go, to sit down, and shut up.

"I can't believe it." Ashon sighed, happy, as they walked. "We are
really friends with a high noble."

"We aren't friends," Khalil muttered.

"Not your choice to make. He already said we were friends!"
Ashon stuck out his tongue at him.

"You are getting more annoying."

"No, you are. What is wrong with you? You've been acting . . . weird all day."

"I am fine. It is you who is acting like a—"

"Who do you think you are?!" an angry voice cried out.

They both stopped as they heard the scream, but they didn't have to wonder where it came from as they saw what looked to be a fight brewing outside of where all the women were staying.

"Who died and made you a queen? We all have to work here!" a woman hollered as she pulled the other woman's hair. The women around them tried to separate them—at least, some of them did. Others seemed more intent on seeing how this played out.

"Get off me, you stupid bitch!"

Khalil hung his head, as he recognized that voice at least, and he wished to turn back around the louder she screamed. "If you all want to waste your useless lives collecting sheep hairs, be my guest! But I refuse to be part of your pitiful delusions!"

"Isn't that your mother?" Ashon asked him.

Khalil watched as all the women turned against her and took a deep breath. He couldn't act like he didn't care. He was her son. So he ran into the circle pushing with all his might and yelled at the top of his lungs, "Let go of her! *Let go!*"

He could feel the women beating on his back, blow after blow coming like rocks as he pushed to get to Femi.

"Enough!"

The bellowing roar came from behind them. It was the chieftain. It took a moment before Khalil could finally see his mother through the bodies. She was on her knees, covering her face with her arms, her clothes tattered and torn.

"Mother!" Khalil rushed to her side and tried to help her back to her feet.

"Chieftain, we have been working all day, and all she does is lie there and drink!" the first woman Femi had been fighting with screamed. "Insulting us, no less!" Khalil ignored her, pulling straw from whatever they beat Femi with from her hair.

"Femi, is that true? You aren't working?"

Only then did Khalil see the chieftain and Hamisi standing side by side, the crowd of women parting for them. Khalil tried to get his mother up, but she would not budge. She stayed on her knees and looked up at the chieftain, her eyes filled with rage, not tears.

"No, I am not. Are you going to kill me?" she sneered.

"Mother," Khalil muttered, trying to get her to stop talking. Where had she gotten any wine to drink?

"She has no respect for anyone, not even her chieftain!" another woman said. "She's better off—"

"Silence!" the chieftain roared, and once more, everyone was quiet. More reserved, he said, "Femi, out of respect for your father, I will ignore your actions today. But tomorrow, you work."

"And if I don't?"

"You will be shackled to the stocks in the middle of the square like an animal," he declared angrily.

"Fine with me!"

"Mother!" Khalil tried to move her again.

"And your son will be there right beside you. Is that what you want for him? How much more humiliation will you place on your boy? Or do you really not care about anyone but yourself?" the chieftain asked.

It was then she clenched her jaw and slowly picked herself up. She ripped at her clothes and just glared at the chieftain. "You want me to sew and cook, fine. You want me to collect hairs, fine. You want me to lift a donkey onto my shoulders, fine. But tell me, chieftain, or better yet, you"—she turned to look at Hamisi, who regarded her with disgust—"tell us, since you started this, will it make any difference? Is my help the key to your victory? Everything you have these poor idiots doing . . . will it really make any difference?"

Hamisi stepped forward. "We wouldn't be asking you to work if it didn't."

"Liars," she scoffed. And she turned, limping as she went back to the house.

"I do not want to see such foolishness again!" the chieftain declared to the rest of the women. "Khalil, go tend to your mother's wounds. Your grandfather sent down medicines for you both earlier."

"My grandfather?" It was then Khalil remembered he still hadn't seen him. "Where is he?"

"The old man refuses to leave his farm. He said to make sure to use it." Ollaze tossed him a basket, as it seemed more people had gathered around.

Khalil caught it and stepped forward, hoping to get the men to talk to him, but they were already walking away. Khalil wanted to go after them, demand some answers, to know what they were planning and what was happening, but why would they listen to him? Who was he to question or even talk to the chieftain, let alone Hamisi? He could see it in the way everyone just sneered or scoffed at him. He was a bastard. He was the son of the drunk crazy woman. Khalil should have been used to it. Truthfully, they'd always treated him like this, but it had never bothered him because he knew who he really was.

Yet at this moment, it did.

Biting the inside of his cheek, he turned and walked inside. The furniture had been cleared from the house, and all that remained were the women's beds all rolled up, lining the sides. Well, with the exception of his mother's. She sat on her unrolled bed in the very corner of the room, an oil lamp to the side of it. She leaned against the wall, her clothes tattered, her eyes closed, holding the cloth from the bundle of things he'd packed the day they left the farm to her chest as if she feared it would be stolen from her.

And then Khalil remembered the dagger—the eye.

Khalil had never really had many conversations with his mother before. She had been very ill when he first met her, and then after she got better, she was nearly always drunk and ordering him to get her more drinks. But she had to have known something. She didn't have anything worth protecting but that dagger.

Slowly, Khalil came over and sat before her. When he opened the basket, he heard her snicker bitterly but didn't say anything.

"What is funny?" Khalil asked, picking up the first jar.

"Nothing is," his mother grumbled, so he stirred the wound paste and spread it onto some small pre-cut bandages. "That old man . . . he could have at least given me wine."

Khalil looked in the basket. Everything in it was for treating cuts and bruises, with the exception of a small brown glass vial that he'd never seen before.

"Grandfather guessed you'd get in trouble," Khalil said, ignoring the vial and moving to roll up her sleeve—the one not holding the wrapped dagger.

"You still think all he does is guess?" She let out a short laugh, then grimaced as Khalil placed the bandage on her.

"What else could it be?" he asked, pretending not to understand what she meant.

She stared at him for a long time before placing her hand on top of his forehead, her whole expression softening. This happened sometimes. One moment, she'd be angry and ready to fight. The next, she'd be so gentle—like a mother.

"Look what they've done to us," she mumbled, her eyes filling with tears. "What they've reduced us to. Don't be sad, okay? They'll regret it. One day, they will regret it. We just have to wait until he comes back for us."

"Who . . . who will come back for us?" Khalil whispered, leaning in closer. "Father? My father?"

"It's not time yet." She clenched the dagger and looked away, her eyes expressionless even as tears came. "When it's time, he'll come back . . . I have this, and we can use this to get back."

Khalil stared at the cloth, his heart pounding in his chest, making it harder and harder for him to breathe.

"Mother . . ." The words felt like poison on his lips, but he kept going, reaching for the cloth. "Mother . . . what is this?"

"I can't tell. No one can see." She shook her head and tried to hide it behind her back.

Khalil grabbed her wrist. "Mother, it's me. Your son. You can tell me."

Once again, she stared at him, or through him. "Do you know who you are?"

"Yes." *M'kuru Mukundi of Madada, son of M'Deba*, he said in his mind, but with his lips, he whispered so low he barely spoke the words, "Rausi. Khalil Rausi."

At that, his mother smiled wide from ear to ear, quickly shoving the covered dagger into his hand and nodding vigorously.

"That's right." She held on tighter, then opened it for him to see. He watched as she pushed the spikes until all the points made a circle around the eye. "The sun sees all."

The fish soup came back up his throat. Because it all made sense now. The symbol, it wasn't just an eye.

It was an eye within the sun.

The Rausi were devoted, blood-bound to the Zenzele. So, all of their family emblems and war flags were drawn within the sun, as they claimed to serve nothing other than the house of the sun. He remembered a lesson he'd had once, long ago, about the Great General, how in battle, when he was near, he was the sword within the sun, and when he was far, he was the eye that kept watch.

The eye that was on her dagger . . . and Mbwa's sword.

"Khalil, you can go now!" A woman's voice came from behind him, making him start. "She can't be hurt that badly. Head back over with the other boys. We need sleep."

"Okay," he said, quickly shoving the dagger into the medicine basket. His mother tried to reach for it, but he shook his head, whispering to her, "I'll keep it safe."

Rising to his feet, Khalil turned to the woman at the door. "You all aren't going to attack her again, right?"

The woman scoffed. "Get out before you need medicine too."

Normally he'd reply how he'd heard that one before. But he was silent. Khalil gripped the basket for dear life. His mind spun as he tried to think. He quietly walked, and all the while, those words repeated in his mind: *The sun sees all.*

"Khalil! Over here!" He glanced up and saw Ashon standing next to none other than Chuks and the rest of his followers.

Khalil didn't want to go over to them. He wanted to take the basket and run. To hide the dagger and pretend he'd never seen it.

"Are you coming over or not?" Chuks hollered.

Khalil walked over and stood before them all, forcing himself to act as he normally would. "What's going on? Another tax?"

"No. Chuks's sister made us this!" Ashon said, lifting a cup to him. "It's tamarind juice!"

Khalil didn't have time for this. "Next time. I need to see my grandfather."

"Hey! I'm trying to be nice here!" Chuks stepped in his way. "Don't know why. We were stuck doing all the heavy lifting while you guys were—where again?"

"We were working too!" Ashon snapped back, and took a drink.

"Really, with what?"

"Can't tell you!" Ashon stuck out his tongue, forgetting who he was dealing with. Chuks immediately grabbed him by his collar.

"Do we need to get the chieftain out again?" They all turned to see Mbwa there, as if from the shadows, gnawing on his straw.

"No!" all the boys said quickly, with the exception of Khalil, who just stared up at the man.

"Good. Wait, what is this?" Mbwa came over and picked up the jar of juice and sniffed it.

"Tamarind juice!" Ashon said.

"My older sister made it," Chuks added quickly.

"Hmm." Mbwa lifted it to his mouth, drank, and nodded. "Not bad. Now you need to head to sleep. It's almost curfew."

"I need to go to my grandfather," Khalil said.

Mbwa's eyebrow rose. "Why?"

"Most likely for a bedtime story!" Chuks laughed and looked over at him. "Ollaze said your grandfather still tells you them."

"So?" Ashon challenged. "What's wrong with stories?"

"Nothing if you are a baby!"

Mbwa chuckled. "I see you are all close."

"We are not," Chuks and Ashon declared at the same time, which only made Mbwa chuckle harder, but his eye drifted back to Khalil.

"You and that stare, boy. You look as though you are ready to kill, or have you already?" Mbwa asked him.

"Who, Khalil?" Ashon laughed. "He's all glare."

"I have," Khalil declared, glaring up at him.

"What?" Ashon gaped at Khalil.

"He's lying." Chuks huffed, crossing his arms. "Don't go pretending to be all tough—"

"A few years ago, some men attacked my mother by the river. I took their dagger and killed them." Khalil didn't know why he was confessing this. But for some reason, he wanted to show he wasn't scared. He wanted Mbwa to know he could kill too. But instead of the reaction he expected, Mbwa bent down and placed his hand on his shoulder.

"You did the right thing," Mbwa said to Khalil, his face stern. "Men have to protect their family. If only I had your courage when I was your age."

"My age?" Khalil asked. "Were you a coward at my age?"

"Khalil!" Chuks and Ashon gasped at the same time.

Mbwa nodded, standing up straight and holding both swords at his waist. "Yes, and a coward with a sword is useless. But a boy with courage and no sword is also useless. Now, all of you go to bed. Tomorrow will be a busy day."

"Yes, sir—"

"Mbwa!" called Oringo, the man with short gray hair and beard, as he walked over to them. "Hamisi is calling for you."

"Again?" Mbwa sighed, and Oringo simply shrugged, laughing at the man as he turned to go.

But Khalil didn't want him to go. He still had questions he didn't know how to ask, but knew he couldn't ask them if Mbwa went away.

"You all go! Now!" Oringo ordered.

Once more, Khalil's head hurt. He looked down at the basket. He really needed to speak with his grandfather, but there was no way he could go now, not without drawing attention to himself, and the last thing he needed was more eyes on him.

The eye in the basket was causing him enough trouble as it was.

21

COMMANDER
RAUSI

Madada

"WE HAVE BEEN HERE BEFORE, HAVEN'T WE, Khalaf?" Prince Effiom asked as he sat upon his horse, the quiet, unexpecting village beneath him. As far as he knew, neither of them had ever been to Kazera, but that was not what Prince Effiom meant.

"Yes. The night is familiar," Khalaf replied, looking at the full moon. It had been the same way three years ago when they had brought down the house of Mukundi.

"Three years, and I am exactly where it started because of a little boy." Prince Effiom scoffed with little to no humor as he glared down at the world below him. "Is that not pitiful, Seer?"

The prince spoke to a woman dressed in deep purple, strings of puka shells in her long hair, standing to his left. Even in the dark, they could see her eyes searching over the village desperately. The longer she stared, the less human she looked. It was no wonder the rest of the army avoided her, though they did so believing she was the prince's most precious concubine and feared doing or saying anything to get themselves killed.

Only Prince Effiom knew the truth about her . . . what she truly was.

"The boy is here," she whispered into the darkness.

"Do you think I would have wasted my time and army coming this far if I did not know that?!" the prince snapped at her, shaking his head. "A single spy has done me more good than you of late. Khalaf!"

"Your Highness?" Khalaf bowed his head.

"Let's not have everything be the same. This time, we attack in the morning. Send word to your spy."

"It can be done, sir, but do you not wish to continue waiting?" Khalaf asked. "From what I have been told, other nobles, maybe even high nobles, will be sending soldiers. This Hamisi has already sent out a call to armies on behalf of the boy. If we hold, we could crush all your enemies here once and for all."

"We could. But then again, I do not feel like waiting another month or more in this horrid, forsaken forest to see who may or may not be stupid enough to start a war for a boy. We've already been following your spy throughout Madada for weeks, waiting for his signal," Prince Effiom replied. He pulled on his horse's reins, turning to face his general. "I'm done doing that. By the time those fools even think of joining their cause, Kazera will no longer exist, and neither will that child. Their little rebellion isn't worth my time. I want the last son and to close this chapter once and for all. I will not go back to the capital a fool again."

"Yes, Your Highness," Khalaf replied, backing up as the prince moved off with his horse and without his "concubine" who had a horse of her own. Khalaf waited until they had all but disappeared into the forest before letting out his breath and glancing to his right. "I am sure you heard him."

"Clearly, Commander," the man replied as he came from the shadows of the trees and knelt beside Khalaf's horse. "Though it is such a waste."

"On your feet," Khalaf ordered, and looked into the man's eyes as he stood. The man shifted the twin blades at his side to his back and adjusted the straw hat on his head. "Has anyone answered Hamisi's letters?"

"It's only been three days since the incident at the collections, so I doubt—"

"My father may give you leeway to do and act as you think best, Mbwa," Khalaf injected coldly. "But I am not my father. You do not withhold information from me. Two old noble houses of Madada have already pledged support. Why didn't you tell me?"

Mbwa hung his head. "Forgive me. I did not know that."

"*Why* did you not know? You've been at this Hamisi's side for two years. He still does not trust you?"

"If he did, it wouldn't have taken me so long to verify his claims or know the location of the boy. Hamisi keeps secrets from everyone. He doesn't tell us who he's been in contact with, how many former Mukundi army still remain, and if there are more weapons caches. I know for sure he has at least a hundred soldiers within the tunnels and around the village now. That is double from the day before. And from his confidence level, I'm sure more will come, because he has no plans to really rely on the villagers to rise up. He moved them all into the village center as bait. They don't know it, but they are really there as a barrier for the tunnels."

Khalaf mused on this. "So if we attacked the center now, before they are ready, he is still hoping by the time we get through the bodies, they can make their escape if need be."

"Exactly."

"How well do you know these tunnels?"

"I only know half of them well enough to lead you through. Many of them have entrances throughout the forest, but I still haven't uncovered all of them yet."

"What of the one that leads to the boy?"

"I'm not certain yet. Hamisi's only taught the route to two boys. If worse comes to worst, though, we'll take the boys and they will lead us."

"That is not a very solid plan," Khalaf snapped, thinking it all through again. He had no doubt the Red Sun Army would win swiftly and easily, but that meant they would not be able to crush the Mukundi loyalists for good once again. Those men knew the tunnels. So, he couldn't send his own men down there, for they'd be lost or slaughtered.

Once again, he wished he had more time. When his father had gotten the information from Mbwa a year ago about some former noble's son seeking to start a rebellion, claiming to know the whereabouts of the last Mukundi son, his father passed it on to him. Khalaf was not sure if it was because his father had no interest in stalking a child through the forest or if he wished to see how well his son could prove himself, but here he was now, with nothing but loose information and a shaky plan.

The boy was important, but he was still a boy. Prince Effiom was rash, but he wasn't stupid. So, let the prince deal with the little high noble. He would fight the men of the army.

"The soil of Madada will swell with blood again," Khalaf whispered as he stared down at the village. All those people would be brought to their death simply because of him. "You will bring the boy to Prince Effiom tomorrow—*alive*. My men and I will smoke out the tunnels. If they know how to get in, they will know how to get out. My men and I will be waiting for them in the forest."

"When it begins—"

"It has already begun. Do not fail me, or I'll cut you apart with those swords of yours myself."

22

KHALIL

Madada

KHALIL COULDN'T SLEEP.

He had waited for all the other boys and men to start snoring before quickly reaching inside the medicine basket for the dagger. However, the moment he did, he yanked his hand back as what felt like liquid fire spread across his palm. As he bit his lips closed to keep from screaming, he stared down at his hand to make sure it really hadn't been burned off. But it looked completely fine and the same as always. So he sat up more and looked into the basket to find what had burned him as the pain was now fading.

The only thing not in place, outside of the dagger, was the small brown vial. It had broken, and whatever had been inside must have spilled out onto his hands. To make sure that was what burned him, he used his other hand to touch one of the wet, broken shards, and it burned once more.

What in all hells has that old man given us? Khalil grimaced, holding his hand again. Now he was even more determined to see his grandfather and get answers. Grabbing the dagger, he tucked it under his shirt at his waist, then lay there staring out at the window, waiting for the sunlight.

Khalil wasn't able to let go of the fact that he knew Mbwa was a traitor, but he couldn't say anything, not without exposing himself too. Surely his grandfather had to know a way to help him. He just had to wait for daybreak.

Khalil waited and waited, nearly shaking until he could no longer stand it. The moment he saw the darkness of the night lighten—even if he was just imagining it—he was out of bed. He hadn't even bothered to remove his clothes from the day before. He tiptoed around everyone else until he got to the door. Slowly he pushed it open, checking to see if anyone was watching. However, there wasn't a single soul except for Hamisi and Mbwa. They stood by the water well, and Mbwa was pointing into it.

Khalil wasn't sure what was going on, so he snuck closer to hear them.

"What are you showing me?" Hamisi asked, frowning as he looked into the dark water. "Nothing looks odd here."

"Are you sure?" Mbwa chuckled, gripping the hilt of his sword. "Because it's been making me sick for a long time now—"

"What in the hell are you talking about? Sick how—"

Khalil's eyes widened as Mbwa pulled out his sword and held it to Hamisi's neck. He quickly looked around, but no one was awake yet—even the lookouts were gone. Khalil turned to rush back to his room when he heard Mbwa speak again.

"Do you want to hear a sad story, Hamisi?" Mbwa sneered. "It starts with a beautiful young girl at a well. She sang there every day to earn money for her family, and word spread of how great her voice was until even the nobles wanted to hear it. It was there she caught the eye of the son of Master Hodari, the western general of the Mukundi Army, and he would not leave her be. Do you remember, Hamisi? Do you remember my *sister?*"

Khalil's eyes widened as he remembered his grandfather's story. And just like that, he didn't have any more questions. His grandfather had already told him the answer before he left—no, he'd guessed the answer.

You don't become friends with the people who kill your family.

"You were the traitor all along, Mbwa?" Hamisi gasped in utter shock. "All because of that?"

Mbwa gripped Hamisi's neck. "*That?* You—"

"You are going to bring death upon everyone here today. Who is wrong, me or you? Don't—"

"I don't care who's wrong. I just want my vengeance!" Mbwa snarled, moving to strike. Hamisi kicked away from Mbwa and pulled out his own sword. Khalil thought Hamisi had the upper hand, but in the blink of an eye, with both swords in hand, Mbwa sliced into Hamisi's throat, and the blood splattered right upon the ground like a whip. At that same moment a girl's scream coursed through the air, ripped from her throat at the sight of blood.

Mbwa turned toward the girl, but Khalil ran toward the pub.

They were here.

The Red Sun Army was already here. That could be the only reason Mbwa did this now. The sun sees all, and the sun was rising . . .

It was too late to warn anyone, ring the alarms, pick up weapons, or escape. Everyone was going to die. It was going to happen just like before, just like . . . that night. Unless Khalil could stop it.

And he only knew one way to do that.

Khalil lifted the huge map on the floor and opened the latch and he heard the screaming behind him get louder. He couldn't look back, so he jumped down, and when he did, the first thing he saw was that there were guards present and light in the tunnel. They hadn't been there before, but it didn't matter. The guards were all still sleeping. Khalil glanced above him again, then ran, not saying a word to them.

"Whoa, kid!" He ran straight into the large body of Eko. "What are you doing down here?"

"Hamisi told me to!" Khalil lied, and broke free, going down, then left, then left again, then right past three other tunnel entrances, running as fast as his legs could take him, all the while dreading his destination. But he . . . he had to do it. He had to be the one to do it. He didn't have much time.

Khalil pushed with all his might and came out onto the grass to see the orange-and-yellow sky as the sun began to rise . . . and then saw the blade pointed at his neck.

"Bastard?" one of the guards called out, recognizing him.

"What is going on? Why is there smoke coming from the village?" another guard asked.

Khalil took air into his lungs as quickly as possible before speaking. "The Reds are here! Where is the . . . where is Lord Mukundi?"

"In the tent! Get him. We need to go now!" said the first guard, already scanning the trees. "Make the call. We might be able to wait for Chima to get back."

There were usually three guards, which meant one had gone with Chima, wherever that was. As Khalil entered the tent, he once again heard his grandfather's voice.

It will never be easy for you, Khalil, because you will always be stuck choosing between two evils.

Khalil didn't get it then but thought he understood it now. When Khalil saw the boy sleeping inside, his eyes started to burn, and his throat closed up, but still, he walked over and knelt beside the impostor.

Khalil didn't want to do this.

"Mmm?" the boy muttered as he peeked through his eyelids.

"Wake up," Khalil said to him.

"Khalil? You are early—"

"Why did you do this?" Khalil cut in, watching as the boy sat up and rubbed his eyes.

"Do what?"

"Pretend to be Lord Mukundi's son," Khalil asked, pulling out the dagger from his waist and holding it tightly, never taking his eyes off the boy before him. But the impostor just stared back, not speaking. "The Red Sun Army is here . . . for Lord Mukundi's son, M'kuru. Which *isn't* you."

Immediately, the impostor grabbed Khalil's wrist, and Khalil thought the boy was going to beg him to let him go or try to take the knife. Instead, the impostor stared at him desperately.

"You have to run!" the impostor yelled.

Khalil's eyebrows came together in confusion. "What?"

"They can't catch you . . . M'kuru!" the impostor begged, yanking him off the ground with him.

"You know . . . you . . . know who I am?" Khalil stammered.

The impostor nodded and then smiled. "Don't worry. I didn't tell anyone. I couldn't believe it either. When I saw you at the tribute, I knew I'd seen you before. Years ago, Baba and I were commode diggers. We weren't allowed in the house or around your family. One time, though, you came out to practice swords with your brothers, and I saw you. You are dirtier and taller now, but your face is still the same."

Again, Khalil's head hurt. He didn't know what to say, but the impostor pulled him to the back of the tent.

"I'm sorry for pretending to be you. Hamisi found me, and I told him I wasn't, but he said we could save Madada. I really wanted to.

But I'll stay, since they all think I'm you anyway. You can make a run for it—"

"I can't," Khalil whispered, his head down.

"Why?"

"I have to save the village. As much of it as I can," Khalil said.

"How are you going to do that?"

Khalil gripped the dagger in his hand, holding his breath and trying not to be sick. Exhaling, he looked back at the impostor.

"What's your real name?"

"T'kello. T'kello Thasu."

"I promise to remember you, T'kello. I promise, and thank you," Khalil said, and with one swift motion, he pulled out the dagger and stabbed the boy in the neck. The boy's blood splattered across Khalil's face, and he watched as T'kello grabbed his neck as his body collapsed to the ground. Khalil grabbed T'kello and held him as he shook. "They won't stop until . . . they have M'kuru. I'm sorry."

Despite the pain and the blood spilling over his hands, T'kello smiled and struggled to get the words out. "Am . . . I . . . a . . . hero?"

"Yes. The very biggest," Khalil whispered as the boy's eyes closed.

"What is taking so long? We need to go now!" Khalil heard the guard yell as he entered the tent, and when he did, when he saw . . . his eyes widened, and Khalil thought the guard would move to strike him, so he grabbed the dagger from the floor. But the man didn't move to fight. He merely dropped to his knees as if someone had taken the life right out of him.

"Don't just stay there—run!" Khalil ordered, but the man didn't listen, and before Khalil could yell again, he heard a voice from beyond the tent.

"My lord, are you there?"

Khalil knew that voice.

"*Run!*" another voice screamed.

He knew that high-pitched voice also.

"My lord, if you come out quietly, I won't have to hurt your friend like I hurt your guard here," Mbwa called out, and Khalil heard the muffled screams of Ashon.

The guard inside shook as he pulled out his sword. Khalil shook his head and nodded for him to go through the back.

"I'll count to three, then," Mbwa spoke again. "One . . ."

Khalil waited for the guard to move to the back of the tent before moving to the front.

"Two . . . two and a half . . ."

"You don't have to count," Khalil said as he stepped out of the tent, looking directly at Mbwa, who stood in front of two dead guards and was holding a sword at Ashon's neck. It was red and puffy now, and he was crying.

"He's a traitor, Khalil!" Ashon tried to say through his tears. "He tricked me!"

"Such is life," Mbwa said, looking Khalil over. "If you want to keep experiencing that, I suggest you tell your little lord to come out, Khalil. I do not want to hurt you, but I will."

"The little lord is no more," Khalil whispered, staring back at him. "I killed him."

"What?" Ashon gasped.

"Do not play with me——" Mbwa began.

Khalil lifted the dagger, showing Mbwa the emblem on it. The older man's eyes widened as he dropped Ashon on the ground, right on his ass.

"How . . . Who are you?" Mbwa asked.

One day, Khalil was going to answer that question truthfully.

It was just not today.

"I am Khalil Rausi, bastard son of the Great General of the Red Sun Army."

23

KHALIL

Madada

KHALIL WAS BROUGHT INTO A MASSIVE, ORNATE tent, the ground covered in red patterned rugs and jewels that sparkled above and reflected light below. On the wooden table, before a chair made with a lion's hide, were several scrolls, books, and a golden goblet for wine. However, none of the richness could distract from the sword that was there also.

NOW OUR ENEMIES REST.

Khalil read the inscription engraved down the black blade, carved like a Liabrein tooth at the tip. The blade he knew to be Black Fang, the hilt still held by a dark, decayed, slender hand—his sister's hand.

Khalil stared. He couldn't do anything else but stare.

"It's beautiful, isn't it?"

When Khalil spun back around, the memories rushed to the front of his mind of when he'd last seen this man, sitting upon a white horse, dressed in silver, red, and gold armor with wings on his shoulders. The man wasn't in his armor now, but even without it, Khalil would never forget him or the scar on the side of his neck.

The heavens will not forgive, and Madada will not forget! The Mukundi will have its vengeance! This is our oath to you! His baba had cursed the Red Army and made a blood oath, yet the man who had killed him was still here, smiling as Khalil looked around the tent. Beside him stood a woman with skin darker than the night sky without stars.

"It's called Black Fang," Prince Effiom said as he walked toward the center of the tent. "I picked it up the last time I was in this land."

Khalil did not speak. He feared that if he opened his mouth, he'd expose everything just to curse the man for himself.

"Apparently," the prince went on, staring down at the sword as though it spoke to him, "it belonged to the Mukundi house. Would you like to hold it?"

Khalil felt his heart pounding, and he fought the urge to hide his hands behind his back. He didn't know how to get out of this, but he also knew he couldn't touch it.

Finally, Khalil tried to speak, "I am not worthy to—"

"Worthy?" The prince laughed as he looked at Khalil, gripping the sword himself with the help of Neema's decayed hand and holding it out. "They tell me you've apparently slain the last Mukundi. Who is worthier than you?"

"I—" Before Khalil could finish, the woman grabbed Khalil's wrist, forcing him to touch the blade, and just like earlier, Khalil felt as though his palm were on fire. "Ahh!"

"How?" The woman gasped and let go of his wrist, jumping back as if she were the one who had been burned.

"*YOU!*" said the prince furiously as he marched over to her, grabbing her by the throat and holding the blade to her left eye. "Did you not tell me the boy was here?"

"I saw—"

"I saw a boy as well! Everyone in that damn village did! They brought his body to my feet, and when I checked, it wasn't the right boy. And then you told me you saw something strange about *this* boy. You said it was him, yet it is not him! *So where is he?*"

Prince Effiom squeezed tighter and tighter, lifting her off her feet and then slamming her back onto the ground. "Crawl out there and find him before I get upset, Sauda."

The woman tried to pick herself up, but he kicked her back down. "I said crawl!"

Khalil watched the woman use her elbows to crawl over the red carpets to the door of the tent. Prince Effiom breathed in once through his nose before calmly walking over and placing Black Fang in the center of the table.

"Well, this is embarrassing." The prince chuckled, turning back to Khalil. "You'll have to excuse me. My seer . . . well, she sometimes has poor sight. In fact, she believed that *you* might have been the last Mukundi."

Ignoring the pain, ignoring his sister's hand, and ignoring the truth, Khalil stared back at the prince coldly. "Didn't I kill the last Mukundi?"

"Ummm." The prince snickered bitterly and nodded. "That is what it looked like. However, just like this sword, the Mukundi had a seal that was poisoned as well."

Khalil watched as the prince reached into the breast of his red robes and pulled out a thick, leather-bound patch.

"I had it shattered and carry a piece with me, close to my heart, as a reminder," Prince Effiom mused, tossing it up and catching it. "I placed it on the boy claiming to be the last Mukundi, and it burned his skin, just like yours."

"So?"

"That's evidence you and he are not of the Mukundi bloodline."

He was, though.

His father had let him hold Black Fang in the past, and it had never burned him before. He did not know why it had now, nor did he have time to think on it. Khalil was just grateful it had burned him this time.

"That settles that. Now I must face the bloodline you do seem to claim . . . as the bastard son of Great General Rausi? And that seems just as unbelievable to me. After all, if that were the truth, why are you here, looking as you do?"

"That's something you have to ask my father."

"Or your mother. Bring her in!" Prince Effiom ordered sternly, placing the leather patch back into his robe.

Khalil turned and saw his mother, held by two soldiers, being forced inside. She broke away from them and threw herself onto Khalil the moment she saw him.

"Khalil! Oh, thank the heavens, you are all right!" she cried, cupping his face and hugging him.

Except he was not all right. He'd murdered a young boy.

But he hugged her back anyway.

"If this were a play being proclaimed on the steps of the theater at Azioba, even the audience would jeer in disbelief!" Prince Effiom chuckled, watching them.

"Your Highness, I am—"

"Where is Khalaf?" Prince Effiom looked to the soldiers at the door, interrupting Khalil's mother.

"Commander Rausi is still hunting down the rebels, Your Highness," one of them answered.

"Well, someone needs to fetch him then! This is apparently more important. I cannot trust the word of a lowborn spy or a bastard and his whore mother—I mean . . ." Prince Effiom paused, looking back down at Khalil's mother. "Let me refrain from such *titles* until your identities are proven true. The last thing I wish to do is insult one of the Great General's concubines. I hold him and all his family in very high regard, no matter their rank." He turned his attention back to Khalil. "Boy, do you know the punishment for impersonating nobles?"

"A hundred whips to the back and a mark to the face for pretending to be a noble. Death by beheading to anyone who pretends to be a high noble," Khalil answered.

"Exactly." Prince Effiom nodded as he leaned in. "So, tell me *honestly*, and on account of the great deed you have done for us today, I will spare you. In fact, I will reward you and let you join the Red Sun Army. Who are you?"

But before Khalil could open his mouth, the sound of horses approached.

"Finally," Prince Effiom said, and stood up taller. It took only a moment before a man dressed in scaled black armor accented with silver horns—four on each arm, six on each shoulder, and two upon his helmet—entered the tent, and Khalil remembered him.

"Welcome back, Khalaf. Apparently, we've come across your brother!" Prince Effiom exclaimed.

Khalaf. Finally, he knew this man's name, the one who had cut off his sister's hand and stabbed his father. The first person Khalil would kill after he killed Prince Effiom. Khalil glared up at him, but the soldier did not even bother looking at Khalil.

"All my brothers are back in the capital," said Khalaf, his face devoid of emotion. "I do not know this boy."

"I did not think so. I have to question, though: even if I do not believe him, why would he make up such a lie? And how did he come upon this?" Prince Effiom said as he lifted the dagger from his waist. "Before sunrise, your spy killed Hamisi and took a Wytjrein to find the last Mukundi. But upon getting there, he found this boy covered in blood, having already slain M'kuru Mukundi with this dagger. That does seem like the loyal actions of a Rausi."

Khalaf walked up to the prince and held his hand out for the dagger. "May I, Your Highness?"

Prince Effiom gave it to him, watching him patiently. Khalaf looked over the still-blood-stained dagger before finally glancing up at both Khalil and his mother.

"Where did you get this?" Khalaf asked them.

"Your father," Khalil's mother finally spoke up, but still kept her head bowed. "You might not remember me. It has been many years. But I once worked as a maid in your house, and your father took a liking to me and made me his concubine—"

"My father has many concubines, of which a few of them were once maids, but he would not care enough to give you this dagger!" Khalaf snapped angrily. "Where did you get this? Did you steal it from my family? If you do not tell me the truth, I will kill the boy here."

"I-I took it before I was sent away!" Khalil's mother stammered, shaking more than Khalil had ever seen. He, too, shook, as that was not what she had told him. "But I swear I am your father's concubine! I am marked!"

She nearly knocked Khalil over as she turned her back to them, undoing her dirty brown top and bringing her hair over her shoulder. Khalil stepped to the side and saw a small tattoo of a sun with five spots within it on the back of her neck.

"So, it is true!" Prince Effiom said as he looked closer. "This style mark is of your house. The spots within the star clearly state your father accepted this boy as his fifth son."

Khalaf did not seem convinced, however.

"Many years ago, I bore the Great General a son, but both the child and I grew sick shortly after I got this mark," his mother replied, adjusting her top and turning back to them, her head bowed. "Your *mother* had us sent back here to Kazera, where my father remained, to heal."

Khalil noticed the way in which she sneered the word "mother," and he was sure everyone else did too.

"You both seem well, so why have you not returned?" Prince Effiom asked, a sound of rising amusement in his voice.

"We have been well for years now. I have sent letters, *many letters,* and never heard anything in return, Your Highness," she replied.

There was silence after she spoke and sudden laughter. Khalil looked at Prince Effiom, who laughed like a madman beside his commander, nearly doubled over.

"Your Highness?" Khalaf called to him.

But the prince merely shook his head, still laughing. "All this trouble. I came all this way, and all I will return with is your little brother?"

Khalaf opened his mouth to speak, but just as suddenly as the laughter started, it ended, the prince's face grim and angry as he grabbed the commander's red breastplate. *"That cannot be the story!"*

Khalil's mother winced at the prince's bellowing voice.

Prince Effiom shoved Khalaf back, then turned on his heels and moved directly to Khalil, where he dropped his hands onto his shoulders. At his touch, Khalil flinched.

"No, the story instead will be of you, Khalil Rausi. The hero of the mighty battle of Kazera!" Prince Effiom exclaimed as he shook Khalil slightly. "The slayer of the last Mukundi! You shall return to the capital with us, and all will hear of your greatness today. All will know that even if they are abandoned or forgotten, wild and unnatural, a Rausi will be a Rausi—thus bound by their blood oath."

Khalil felt the grip upon his shoulders tighten as the prince leaned into his face. "The last Mukundi is dead, and you killed him. You will tell this to the king, your father, and whoever asks. You will hold it as the truth till your dying day!"

Khalaf stood forward. "Your Highness, the Rausi are loyal to the king—"

"The concubine says she has written to your house yet was left abandoned . . . with a son, your father's *accepted* son. That story will be disgraceful at court, and I know your father does not stand for a disgrace of any kind to your name. So who do you think shall bear the brunt of his rage? I believe it might be your mother. Loyalty does not always mean the whole truth."

Khalaf's mouth clenched tightly, but Prince Effiom ignored his subordinate's distaste and looked at Khalil as he patted his shoulder. "Now, Khalil, as a hero, I must give you a reward, the first of many, I am sure. Name your wish."

Khalil looked up at the prince. "I can ask for anything?"

"Anything that is within my power, of course. What do you wish for? Gold? Glory? Your name cheered in the streets or maybe a bath?" Prince Effiom snickered.

"Don't kill them."

"Who? The villagers?" the prince asked coldly, his eyes glaring. "They are traitors, Khalil. They murdered our tribute collector, not to mention several other crimes. I know you have not been very well educated, but the Zenzele do not show mercy to those who betray us. And as a Rausi, your duty is to be our fury upon this earth. Do you understand?"

Khalil did not reply.

"Your prince asked you a question. Answer him," Khalaf snapped from behind Khalil.

"I don't know anything about your fury," Khalil grumbled, stepping out of the prince's arms. "I only know about mine and my mother's. Day after day, they mocked us, beat us, and made us suffer. And now you just want to kill them? Let them rest? No. They need to live like we did. Live and see us live better. So are you going to give me my reward or not?"

Prince Effiom's eyebrow rose as he began to see Khalil's plan. Joyful, he turned to Khalaf. "I think I will grow to like this one even more than you."

Now it was Khalaf's turn to remain silent.

"Have his mother taken care of," Prince Effiom ordered Khalaf, and focused once more on Khalil. "Come, let us see your victory."

THIS WAS THE THIRD TIME Khalil truly felt like dying.

The first night was when his family was slaughtered.

The second was this morning when he murdered T'kello.

And the third time was now, walking out into the village square, where the cobblestones were stained in blood and bodies—men, women, and children, the old and the young unsparingly. Those who didn't have the grace to die were gathered together, surrounded by soldiers dressed in black, scaled armor. No one dared speak, and every time they heard a gurgling scream from off in the distance, where the Red Sun Army tortured an enemy—their neighbor or friend or cousin—they flinched. But the worst, for Khalil, for all of them, was the sight of T'kello's body, alongside Hamisi's, Eko's, and Oringo's, impaled on spikes right outside the pub house. The second worst was the look of horror, betrayal, and confusion as the villagers looked upon him standing beside a Zenzele.

His shame felt as though it were drowning him, but he could not let it show. Khalil stared out at them, trying to seem as though he didn't care and didn't feel as defeated as they did. But he cared so much that he wished to cry for the first time in a long time.

I'm sorry.

I'm so sorry.

"You all deserve death," Prince Effiom declared as the chieftain was brought out with a rope around his neck and forced to his knees before the prince. "Especially you, chieftain. Look where you have led them to. Look at your village. None of this had to happen."

The chieftain didn't answer; he did not even lift his head.

"Luckily, this brave and *noble* young boy, Khalil Rausi"—Prince Effiom placed his hand upon Khalil's shoulder—"has asked me to spare your lives. As his prince and master, it is the very least I could do. Nevertheless, you must be punished."

Khalil inhaled, clenching his jaw tightly.

"So . . . I will take a limb from every adult male, the tongue from every adult woman, and one finger from the left hand of all the children before they are sold to slave traders . . ."

No! No! Khalil begged in his mind as the once-silent villagers broke out into screams. He didn't want this. He wanted them to live, to spare them even though he figured they'd be sold into slavery. At least slavery would be better than death. Because he could and would free them one day, but he couldn't undo death. But as he watched in horror, he knew there was nothing he could ever do to make up for this.

He looked on as the soldiers began . . . to . . .

"No! Please no!"

"Help!"

"Baba!"

"Mama!"

All the screaming cut into Khalil sharper than any blade.

"Khalil!"

His head snapped to the voice, and he saw Ashon's grandmother screaming for him as they tried to pull Ashon away from her. Immediately, Khalil moved to go to them but he felt a hold on his collar. When he looked up, he saw none other than Commander Rausi staring down at him and shaking his head.

"Friend of yours?" Prince Effiom asked him.

Khalil didn't answer.

"You can spare the Wytjrein. He'll come to the capital with us as a tribute to the king," Prince Effiom hollered and then looked back to Khalil, yawning. "All this screaming is giving me a headache. Khalil, why don't you tell me all about—"

"I need to find my grandfather," Khalil interrupted desperately, trying to tune out the world and the pain around him.

"Grandfather?" Prince Effiom repeated.

"There is a medicine man up on one of the hills." Mbwa stepped forward. Gone were his dirty clothes and straw hat, the twists in his hair had been cut off, and he was now dressed in the armor of the Red Sun Army. "After bringing the boy to you, I rushed to stop the soldiers, but I wasn't fast enough, and they had burned down the farmhouse."

Please be a nightmare.

Please be a nightmare.

Khalil said this prayer over and over in his mind. He just wanted this day to end.

"Is the old man dead?" Prince Effiom asked.

"He will not make it much longer and didn't wish to move—"

Khalil took off running as fast as he could, pushing the soldiers out of his way, which was much easier as they moved immediately for him.

"Khalil!" Khalaf called out, but Khalil didn't stop running. He wished to outrun the screams around him, but they were coming from him too.

24

COMMANDER RAUSI

Madada

AT FIRST, KHALAF WAS CONFUSED AS TO WHY the prince chose to adhere to the boy's—his *brother's*—wish to spare the villagers and why he had then demanded body parts. Now as he saw all the little bloody fingers spread out on sheepskin before the prince's woman, he understood. The prince was still secretly hunting for the Mukundi boy.

"It's none of them," the woman said as she tested the last finger on the broken seal shard.

"How is that possible?" Prince Effiom said through clenched teeth as he sat upon his lion's chair. "Isn't this all of them?"

"With the exception of the Wytjrein—" Khalaf noted.

"The one we are looking for does not have white skin!"

"I still sense him in this village—"

"Then where the hell is he?" the prince demanded once more. "Where? In the tunnels? Again?"

Khalaf did not believe that. "We have been smoking them all day, so unless he knows how to breathe without air—"

"Maybe he can! Apparently, he can disappear into thin air," Prince Effiom said, rising angrily to his feet. "Go ask if there are any other children unaccounted for—no! Wait . . . that will raise suspicion, for he is dead as far as anyone else knows."

But M'kuru wasn't dead, and Khalaf knew more than anyone else how this would haunt the prince and the whole royal family. For the boy to have escaped once already made them all look like fools and gave hope to rebels, but if the world knew they had failed a second time, they would surely believe it was the prophecy at work.

Prince Effiom inhaled deeply and looked at them once more. "The only people that know of this are me, Sauda, you, your brother, and his mother."

"What of the spy who brought you the boy's body?" Khalaf asked. He had only witnessed Mbwa carrying the boy's dead body alongside Khalil, who Khalaf did not know of at the time, to the camp at the top of the hill. By the time Khalaf had returned to the camp, Sauda had secretly informed him of what had occurred.

"He knows nothing," the woman answered him. "I checked the boy secretly."

"I really cannot believe this," Prince Effiom grumbled, rubbing the side of his head. "It almost makes me believe that stupid prophecy!"

"Your Highness, in a way, this is a good thing."

"How in all the hells is this a good thing, Khalaf?"

"Because who will believe anyone else claiming to be him?"

Khalaf replied, stepping forward. "Word of what happened here in Kazera will spread, and all will fear to join its fate. Anyone who dares to claim they are him will find themselves laughed at and without an army or people. Perhaps even stoned or given over to the Red Sun Army as an example. One person cannot bring down a dynasty by themselves. The more people forget, the more he hides, the less power he has."

Prince Effiom stared at Khalaf for a long time. Then he closed his eyes and breathed slowly. Returning to his seat, the prince relaxed comfortably.

"I wanted to bring him back alive and execute him at my father's feet and before the crown prince's very eyes. But it seems charred remains will just have to do," Prince Effiom said. "Very well. That is all, Khalaf. Go. I'm sure you have a very important letter to send to your family. We don't want them too surprised with the new addition you are bringing, especially your mother."

It was Khalaf's turn to exercise patience. He bowed his head and stepped back before turning and leaving. The air outside the tent was warm and sour, and the smell of blood and burning flesh hung in the air.

"Commander." The guards outside bowed to him, as did everyone else, and Khalaf walked farther down the muddy path to his own tent. And waiting outside of it was none other than the spy himself. Mbwa bowed his head, and Khalaf merely waved a hand for him to follow.

Like the prince's tent, the commander's was far more spacious than any other soldier's, but instead of books, jewels, and furs, Khalaf had swords, a shield, a post for his armor and spear, and a bed, which rested under a sun banner of the house of Zenzele with a drawing of his spear at the center. Unlike other noble families, the

Rausi had no official family emblem. Instead, they used the sun but always with a weapon of their choice within it.

He glanced at the dagger in his hands. *Damn Mother's jealousy!* His father would not take this lightly.

"Is Father's woman settled?" Khalaf asked as he shifted his gaze to Mbwa.

"Yes, sir. A few women from the village will serve her—"

"You idiot, she and her son just betrayed them. They might seek vengeance!"

"Lady Femi instructed me herself on the women to pick," Mbwa replied quickly.

"Did she?" Khalaf stretched out his hands to relax. "*Lady* Femi. What do you know of this woman and her son?"

"From what I have gathered, long ago, Lady Femi was meant to be the current chieftain's wife. But she did not wish to remain in such a lowly village. She had visions of something greater for herself, so she left, and no one knew what had happened to her. That is until she returned one day, ill, ruined, and with a child. She was mocked and shamed for this, so she took to drinking. From there, she mostly remained with her father and son, hated by most for her . . . arrogance."

"Arrogance for not marrying their chief?"

"That and they never understood why she could look down on them. I did not see how she did this in the past, but when the village was preparing for war, she refused to labor. So they beat her, and she still did not repent."

Khalaf chuckled, now nodding as he began to take off his breast-plate. "She never repented and looked down on them because she never stopped seeing herself as my father's concubine."

And now she probably felt that even more so. Khalaf didn't need to be a seer to know there would not be peace in his father's house once this woman returned.

"As for the boy—"

"He is a Rausi to you," Khalaf interjected coldly, glaring at Mbwa. "I may call him boy; my father, the prince, and the king may call him boy; but to you and everyone else, he is Master Khalil. Am I clear?"

"Yes, sir."

Khalaf did not know the boy, but he was blood. He would not let him be disrespected, as that would be a disrespect to his father and house. The sheer fact Khalil had been raised in the wild was enough disgrace as it was.

"Good," he said to Mbwa. "What about him?"

"Master Khalil is smart, foolishly fearless, a bit disrespectful, and solemn. And he has no problem speaking to people as though they are his equal, whether they are bigger or stronger than him."

"Like mother like son, then?"

"Yes . . ."

"You don't seem to care about those things, though."

"No, those don't concern me. What I do not understand is why he killed the Mukundi boy," Mbwa said, his eyebrows furrowed in confusion. "Just days earlier, he was adamant about fighting against the Zenzele. He stared down Hamisi, demanding to fight. There was clear hatred in his eyes."

"Are you sure it was aimed at the Zenzele?" Khalaf asked, thinking as he washed his hands in the water basin left out for him.

"What do you mean, sir?"

"Khalil has known he is a Rausi all this time, but he could not say it in these lands. He suffered and watched his mother suffer in poverty and abuse. All the while, his father is the greatest and richest general in the kingdom. Is that not cause enough for hatred and bitterness?" Khalaf was sure, from the ease with which Khalil took a life, the quickness with which he had betrayed this village, that he had endured an abundance of pain here.

"He does not hate Zenzele but . . . his own family?"

"These are family matters I shall not discuss with you. Where is he? Has he returned from his grandfather?" Khalaf had sent a few soldiers after him but had not seen them return to the camp yet.

"He is still there."

"When he returns, bring him to my tent immediately," Khalaf said, cleaning his arms.

"Yes, sir." Mbwa bowed, then stepped back to leave, but Khalaf spoke once more.

"Mbwa."

"Sir?"

"Congratulations on your revenge, but do what I say first next time. Khalil beat you to the Mukundi because of your distraction. Had it been someone else and he escaped . . . well, be grateful he did not escape." Hamisi was going to die either way, but some people could not see beyond their desire for vengeance, especially when it was right at their fingertips.

"Hopefully, there is no next time, sir."

"You never know. Revenge is a wheel that never stops turning. Those children out there may grow up and come for you one day."

"And you too, sir."

That did not scare him. Instead, Khalaf smiled, nodding. He did not mind at all, for there was no better place to be than at war.

25

KHALIL

Madada

"WHAT'S THE ENDING TO THE STORY?" HIS grandfather asked calmly, lying on the charred ground outside what was once their farm. There were no animals, no sounds, and almost no life. Everything was just black and burnt, including the skin on the right side of his grandfather's body.

The old man must have taken something for the pain, Khalil thought, and if his grandfather had done that, then Khalil knew there was nothing else he could do.

"What's the ending to the story?" his grandfather calmly asked once again.

"Grandfather, now's not the—"

"The story."

Sighing, Khalil knew—like every other time—there was no choice but to do what his grandfather wanted. "The young boy found the young nobleman, but they were no longer young. And the nobleman did not recognize the man. The man pretended to be his friend and got all his secrets, sharing them with the nobleman's worst enemy. He waited and waited until one day, just as the sun was rising, he slit the nobleman's throat. He destroyed everything the nobleman had built, finally getting his revenge."

"Do you prefer that ending now? Justice has been served."

"No, that was not justice. So many other people. Innocent . . . people . . ." Khalil had been holding it back all day. His eyes watered, and he hunched over his grandfather, trying to bite back a sob, but it came anyway. Khalil cried from the bottom of his heart, and he had not even cried like this when he lost his family.

"Revenge . . . is like poison. It can cancel out other poisons but will still bring you pain. Didn't your hand show you?"

Khalil froze, his eyes wide as he remembered the vial that had broken in the basket and burned his hand—the same hand that the prince had forced him to use to hold Black Fang. Once again, the old man had protected him. Drying his tears, Khalil glanced around the farm, looking to see if there was anything he could still use.

"I need to pick Senegalia for your wounds and—"

"Khalil."

"You can't die!" Khalil cried, the tears once again burning his eyes. "You can't . . . I still need you. Why did you stay?"

The old man answered by lifting his good arm and showing a necklace made of brown, black, and red beads . . . and Moujo's horn. It was polished smooth and held together with a wool bond thread.

"I . . . did not count on . . . dying. Your time here . . . has come . . . to an end. So, I had . . . to make this. This . . . will protect you." He had worked on it even as the fire burned, the smoke filled the air, and the roof of their home partially collapsed on top of him.

"*Nna Baba!*" It was the first time he'd ever called him that. Khalil clasped his grandfather's arm as the old man began to cough up blood, writhing in pain on the scorched earth. Khalil glanced up at the guards who'd followed him and were watching, uncaring. *"Get water!"*

"Khalil!" The old man coughed, holding on to Khalil with all his strength. "Take . . . care . . . of Femi. Plea—"

All the air left his grandfather's lungs, and his grasp eased immediately. Khalil stared at the old man's half-burnt face. Another face he'd never see again. Another person the Zenzele had taken from him.

They could not get away with it.

Khalil could not let them get away with it.

"If revenge is poison, I am going to drink a river of it, old man," Khalil whispered to his grandfather as he gently laid him on his back.

Slowly, Khalil rose to his feet and stared down at his grandfather's body under him, gripping the horn with all his rage, trying not to scream. One day, when he was big enough, strong enough, he would let out a scream that would burn down this unfair and unjust world.

"Master Khalil?"

It took him a moment to realize he was being called "master." Glancing up, Khalil met the eyes of Mbwa, who was standing only a few feet from him. "Do you wish to have a pyre?"

Khalil just stared at him, so Mbwa nodded for the guards to cover Khalil's grandfather. Khalil stepped in front of where his grandfather's body lay, placing himself between him and them.

"Master Khalil—"

"This is Madada," Khalil said coldly. "We do not burn our dead in Madada. You all have burned him enough."

Mbwa stared back into Khalil's eyes for a moment before telling the guards, "Dig a grave."

It was only then that Khalil turned back to look at his grandfather.

"If we had known you all were here, we would have gotten you all out before this began," Mbwa said from beside Khalil.

They weren't supposed to know. Fate did not wish for them to know. When Khalil first met his grandfather, he thought it crazy to believe in something so obscure as fate or that something he could not see, feel, or ever speak to was willing everything into being. Now, only a few short years later, he had come to learn that what was destined to be would be. No one could stop it.

So when the guards were done digging and had placed his grandfather deep down inside the grave, Khalil did not bother to say a prayer to the gods or to offer words to the ancestors. He simply put the horn necklace around his neck, turned around, and walked out through the half-burnt broken fence. Everywhere Khalil looked, he saw fire, ash, or blood upon the ruins that were once his home, although briefly.

"Move your asses!" hollered a guard at a row of villagers . . . or prisoners.

Slaves.

The first person Khalil noticed was the chieftain, then Ollaze, and then Ashon's grandfather, all wearing chains around their ankles and on their wrist—one arm, one wrist. They were naked from the waist down and did not even have straw shoes. But Khalil doubted they could even feel their feet with the burnt stump in place of their left arm. Even with that pain, guards forced Ashon's grandfather to lift the rolled-up sheared wool that women had been collecting just yesterday—was it yesterday?

What day is it? Khalil wondered, as it felt as though years had gone by.

"I said move it!" the guard hollered at Ashon's grandfather, who had stopped. And because he'd stopped, all the men were forced to stop as well. The old man trembled, his skinny frame soaked in sweat and his eyes rolling back into his head before he collapsed to the ground.

"Master Khalil, we must keep moving. Your brother awaits you," Mbwa said from beside him, but Khalil couldn't move.

"Cut him loose. He isn't going to make it," one guard called over to another coming with chains.

"Put him on my back," said Ollaze, huffing, his chest rising high and falling heavily, his forehead also covered in sweat. "I'll carry him."

"He's too old and too weak. Cut the old man out, and I'll end this," the guard replied, pulling out his sword.

"I said I'll carry him!" Ollaze hollered, only to be slapped across the face.

"No one cares what you say, *slave!*" the guard spat, lifting his sword.

"Prince Effiom ordered for them to be spared," Khalil spoke up, his voice so soft . . . so lifeless, that they did not hear. Only when Mbwa grabbed the guard's wrist did any of them stop.

"Master Khalil is speaking to you!" Mbwa stated.

"I do not know who the fuck that is. Release me before—"

"Khalil *Rausi*. That is who the fuck he is," Mbwa sneered into the man's face.

The man's eyes widened as he turned to Khalil and bowed his head. "Forgive me, young master. I've just arrived in the village to collect these goods. I did not see you."

"Prince Effiom ordered them to be spared," Khalil said again, staring up at him. "If he wishes to carry the old man, let him."

"It will slow them down, sir. They are already weak from their punishment. I don't think it would be—"

"I do not care what you think." Khalil looked at Ollaze, but neither he nor the rest of the men in line looked at him, so Khalil kept walking.

It was the only thing he could do. He had to keep walking the path fate had given him. Khalil wanted to look away from the horrors around him, but he didn't. He had no right to hide away from any of it. The closer he got to their camp, he made sure to see it all. The women huddled together in a cage, sobbing, blood staining their mouths and necks . . . the guards huddled around them to choose which one to rape. In another cage were Chuks and all the other young boys of the village, hugging themselves with their heads down. Khalil did not look away from any of it, or at least he tried not to, and he could not help but wonder where Ashon was.

"As you can see, the golden tent is for Prince Effiom." Mbwa pointed ahead, through the row of red-colored tents with the emblem of the spear in the sun painted upon the roof, to the golden tent in the center. The emblem there was just the sun. Mbwa then shifted his finger to the left. "The second-largest tent to the left belongs to your brother."

It was the same blood-colored tent as everyone else's but almost as large as the prince's quarters.

"Where is my mother?" Khalil asked.

"Whenever a noblewoman or concubine is in the camp, their red tent is marked with a dotted sun." Mbwa pointed to two deep-red-colored tents with a painted white sun on the roof with a single blotch in the center a little farther away from the others. Outside the door of each tent were two soldiers. "The one on the right is for Prince Effiom's concubine. The one on the left is for your mother—"

"I will see her now."

"Your brother ordered—"

But Khalil did not wait and walked toward Femi's tent.

As he stood outside, he heard giggling. Giggling? He had heard a lot of sounds today, but giggling was not one he expected.

"I haven't had such nice clothes in so long," Khalil heard his mother's voice say.

Khalil had done his best to stay calm, but hearing this, he grew angry. The scent of lilies was the first thing he noticed as he marched inside, and then it was the both of them. His mother was dressed in a bright yellow-and-blue printed robe, seated on a sheep's-wool seat in front of a small silver mirror, getting her hair braided by Ina, whose feet were shackled and who still wore her mud-soaked and half-torn dress.

"There you are, Khalil!" his mother exclaimed, turning to look at him, and he stared at her and the large smile on her clean face. "What took you so long? I wished you to pick out one of the boys to serve you until we reached Ahalon. But I wasn't sure who else you liked but the white one. I asked for him but was refused, since he is to be a tribute to the king. I managed to get Ina before they took her tongue. Look, she's done so well with my hair."

His mother looked back to the mirror, rubbing the skin under her eyes and turning her head to the side to see her new hairstyle. "Do you like it, Khalil?"

Khalil stared at her, his hands balling into fists and his chest rising and falling heavily. "Grandfather is dead."

When she turned to him, her eyes blank, he thought, for a moment at least, she'd maybe cry, but with a simple blink of an eye, she said instead, "Your brother bought me so many clothes and jewelry. Gifts from Prince Effiom—"

"Grandfather is dead," Khalil repeated a bit louder, because she might not have heard him.

"There are some new clothes for you as well. But they are with your brother. You will share a tent with him. You must get cleaned up! Look how dirty you—"

"*Grandfather is dead!*" Khalil yelled at the top of his lungs, and stepped over to her. "Your baba is dead! Half of him was burnt black, and he shook in pain! But even still, the last thing he spoke of was you, Mother."

Once more, she stared blankly and slowly blinked before turning back to her mirror. "Ina, can you wrap the edges? I do not want it to mess up in the morning."

Ina did not speak but walked over to the chest of goods behind Khalil without looking at him. It was as if she were sleepwalking. There, but not there.

"Mother—"

"Go to your brother, Khalil. You shouldn't make him wait. You need to be good, all right. Listen to him. Go."

Khalil stayed.

"Khalil, I said go!" his mother yelled at him.

Only then did he turn around and exit the tent, where he found Mbwa waiting. Khalil ignored him and walked to the second-largest tent. He couldn't help but look to see if Ashon was somewhere closer than where they kept the other prisoners, but all he saw were soldiers. Dozens upon dozens of men like ants, some in full armor, some in barely anything but their pants, others eating, and some holding women as they drank.

Khalil was invisible to most of them.

"Commander, I've brought Master Khalil," Mbwa called out when they arrived at Khalaf's tent.

"Enter."

Mbwa held open the flap of the tent for Khalil to go forward. When he stepped in, Khalil smelled spices and saw the man everyone called his brother. Mbwa walked up to him, whispering something as the man finished washing his shoulders with water from a basin.

"Very well," was all Khalaf said, then muttered something else to Mbwa before the man took his leave.

Khalil noticed Khalaf's skin was medium brown, his hair cut short, and because he wore no shirt, Khalil could see several healed wounds, some small and faint, others long and raised, on his back. Not only there, but there were also some on his arms and a few on his legs.

"Not all these came from battle," Khalaf said as he shook the water from his hands and turned to Khalil. "Father starts our training by six years, so once we are your age, we already have more than a few scars."

Khalil said nothing, just stared back, so Khalaf nodded to the food beside him. Only then did Khalil notice the spread of food on silver plates on a circular wooden table.

"I doubt you have eaten today. Come sit with me," Khalaf said, already walking over and taking a seat, pointing where Khalil should go. Khalil sat before the table. "I was unsure about what you like, so I had them bring goat, chicken, and beef. Eat as much as you like."

Khalil took only the bowl of milk and bread, noticing how warm everything still was, but he said nothing as he dipped his bread into the milk and ate.

Khalaf sighed and nodded before also picking up a bowl of milk for himself.

"If you hate us, that is fine," Khalaf said before drinking. Khalil just took another bite of bread and did not look at him. "Your hate is justified, Khalil. You and your mother have been wronged. Nevertheless, it should not be so obvious. I do not know the way in which you have lived, but I do know the way you shall live in the future. And that is with comfort, finery, and influence. So, no one will pity you. Not even Father will pity you. He's a very taciturn and harsh man. I say this to warn you, should you have had any wonderings of him. He expects only one thing from his sons, and that is for you to bring honor to our name and to the house of Rausi."

"Haven't I done that already?" Khalil finally spoke, taking a large bite of bread.

Khalaf smirked. "In killing that boy, you have. It shall be a great spectacle in the palace. However, as Father always says, 'Yesterday's triumphs mean nothing today.' And bringing honor is not always through spilling blood. There is much you must learn. The first is, when your elder brother offers you meat, you *do not* take bread."

At the tone in his voice, Khalil finally looked up at him but still ate his bread and drank his milk, making no move toward the meat. Once more, Khalaf nodded to himself.

"Very well. Be stubborn, but you'll soon learn I'm the nicest of your brothers," Khalaf replied. He rose to his feet and went to the front of the tent. He raised the flap before speaking again. "Have a bath brought in," he told someone outside.

"I'm fine," Khalil muttered, taking more bread.

"You smell of blood, piss, and shit. I can barely stomach to eat next to you. You will not sleep in here like this."

"I can sleep outside then," Khalil grumbled.

"Bring the bath," Khalaf ordered, ignoring him.

It wasn't as if Khalil did not want a bath, because he did. He also wanted to stuff his mouth full of goat, chicken, and beef, but he didn't feel right doing so. Not today, at least, not when everyone he once knew was outside crying or dying.

"Despite what we did to his village and family, the Wytjrein had no problem stuffing his face or taking a bath," Khalaf said as he tore off a chicken leg and sat back down. "He cried a lot, though, leaking from his eyes and nose as he rammed rice and chicken down his throat. I wonder what it would look like if we hung him upside down and beat him until he retched it all up."

Khalil's eyes widened as he stared at Khalaf.

Khalaf held the chicken leg before him. "It's not possible for you to have hated every last person in this village. I am sure you had one friend . . . at least. The boy seemed to consider you that friend. So let me make it clear: if you do not listen, I will take it out on him."

"He's a tribute to the king."

He shrugged. "Not all tributes make it back to the capital."

"Why do you care if I eat?"

"Because it looks like you haven't had a proper meal all your life."

"So?"

"So? What do you think will happen when you are presented to the king looking as you do? All of the court seeing a half-starved, smelly, neglected child? They will pity you, and the Rausi are never to be pitied. Eat. Now."

Khalil chuckled. "This isn't about the Rausi. This is about your mother, isn't it? If they pity me and my mother, that means they will blame yours. That's how stories work."

Khalaf's eyes narrowed. "Stories?"

"There are always heroes and villains in stories. Prince Effiom says when I go to Ahalon, I'm the hero. That means she's the villain."

"The villain is M'kuru Mukundi."

"That's just a boy who was killed by another boy. People will just laugh. Villains need to have real power, and the legitimate wife of the Great General must have a lot of it. And she used it against a weak, lowly concubine and a baby—me." Khalil lifted the chicken for Khalaf to see and tossed it back on the table. "So, if you hurt my friend, I'll eat even less and blame your mother more in front of everyone at *court*," Khalil taunted.

"How old are you, Khalil?"

"Twelve."

"I am twelve years older than you, and I did not speak as you do at your age." Khalaf frowned, glancing him over.

"Do you know how long it takes to catch, kill, and prepare a goat, a chicken, and a cow?" Khalil asked, looking over all the food on the table.

"No."

"I do. Why would we speak the same when we did not grow up the same?"

"Very true," Khalaf replied, picking up a chicken wing and taking a large bite. "Though do not think yourself grown yet."

"Sir, the bath," someone called from outside.

"Bring it in," Khalaf said as he continued to eat. It took two soldiers to bring in the circular wooden bath. They set it to the side, went back out, and Khalil then watched as several older women, all chained together by their feet, bloodstained at the mouth and covered in dirt, brought in buckets of hot water. He knew them all, but his eyes went to Ashon's grandmother.

They poured the water in one bucket at a time, and just as the tub filled, Khalaf licked his fingers clean and stood up. He moved to where Ashon's grandmother was, grabbed a fist full of her hair, and submerged her face in the steaming bath.

"What are you doing?!" Khalil screamed, rising to his feet as she thrashed under the water, trying to get out.

Khalaf lifted her face back up for him to see how scared she was, and she coughed and tried to speak.

"As I said, Khalil, there is much you must learn . . . especially about me. You do not threaten me. *Ever.*" Once more, Khalaf shoved her head back under the water. "If you do not wish to eat or listen to me, fine. You have already shown you care. I'll have men do this to her all night, then every day until we reach the capital. I'll have them break her legs, gouge out her eyes, and cut her fingers and toes."

When Khalaf yanked her from the water, Ashon's grandmother gripped the bath's edge, sobbing. When Khalaf's hand moved to push her down again, Khalil lifted the whole chicken to his mouth and took a bite.

He hated how good it tasted.

"Good," Khalaf said, pushing Ashon's grandmother to the floor, nearly taking the rest of the women down with her. Then he looked to the guards and said, "Dump this water. It's dirty. Have them fetch more."

Khalaf glanced back at Khalil, then walked over and took his seat again. Khalil just took another bite of warm roasted chicken.

"As a Rausi, you are above all these people here," Khalaf said. "But as my bastard brother, you are beneath me. Never forget your place. Never forget the strength of a *story* is in the power of the person telling it, and neither you nor your mother has any power."

Khalaf lifted his spoon of rice and ate it slowly even as he hummed to himself. "Don't just stand there. Sit down. It's a month-long journey to the capital, and I hear conversation makes time run faster. So, tell me, little brother, the *story* of your life so far."

Khalil could not remember anything other than misery. The story of M'kuru Mukundi was one of bitter misfortune, but then again, so was the story of Khalil Rausi. So Khalil told Khalaf the story his grandfather had Khalil tell anyone in the village who asked. And for the first time, he actually truly thought about him—Khalil, the real one. The boy's life he had stolen just like T'kello had stolen his. He was an impostor too. None of them were different. They were all boys trying to survive in the games of men. T'kello and Khalil died as boys, but he had to survive to become a man.

And only then would he not just play the game . . . but win it.

26

PRINCE EFFIOM

Madada

"THE DIFFERENCE A SIMPLE BATH AND SOME new clothing make," Prince Effiom said as he looked at the boy standing like a lost sheep in the middle of their camp, dressed in blue and gold wool, fresh boots that were too big, and a face so clean it shined in the sun. "Were you able to get much out of him?"

"Not nearly enough of anything important," Khalaf replied, his helmet tucked under his left arm and his grip on his sword at the right. "He only met 'M'kuru' two days earlier and was only told how to reach him and to escape should anything go awry."

"Much went awry," Prince Effiom said, his arms folded as he watched the boy watch the camp. "If there was a plan to escape, surely they planned to escape somewhere."

"He was not told—"

"He was not told, or he does not tell you?" Prince Effiom snapped, turning to glare at the commander and stepping closer. Khalaf bowed his head. "The rest of the world may never know, but we shall never forget the utter fuck-all failure this was. I did not collect the prize I came for. The two thousand dead we counted of the Mukundi Army was not nearly the one rumored to exist."

Prince Effiom's grandfather once told him the great Mukundi Army at its height had the ability to call up thousands upon thousands of men. M'Deba Mukundi had set up a private army around his private land, but they had massacred them all the last time they had been here.

"Your Highness, it has been decades since an accurate account of the Mukundi Army or any of the high noble armies has been given. There is no proof they still can call upon such numbers. There has been famine, plague—"

"Then why was Hamisi so confident in this treason?" Prince Effiom questioned, annoyed, gritting his teeth. "I cannot get my answer because your spy killed him!"

Prince Effiom wouldn't have cared had they gotten the right boy, but now, with that threat still out there, Prince Effiom could not help but wonder endlessly about what it all meant. What plans lay in the dark that he could not see? Someone had to be helping Madada.

"Your Highness, calm yourself—"

"Where is Sauda?!" Prince Effiom called out so loudly that all the camp turned to look at him.

"I am here, Your Highness," Sauda replied from behind him, and when Prince Effiom turned, she held up a small cup for him. "It is to calm your mind, sir."

Prince Effiom smacked it from her hand. "*You* are meant to do that, not tea. Follow me. Both of you."

He did not wait, just marched back to his tent.

Prince Effiom had sought to keep calm, but he could not stop worrying through the night and even into the morning. He could not make sense of it. Who had sent these two thousand men? Were they the initial forces of the Mukundi Army? Or were they all Hamisi could muster? As the son of a Madada general, surely Hamisi had connections to all the nobles of this land. Had he written to them, telling them of the impostor boy? Had they answered him? Or did they not believe him? Or *did* they believe him but didn't want to get involved? There were rumors that another noble house sought to take control of all of Madada to replace the Mukundi as heirs of this land. So maybe they did not come to Hamisi's aid in order to seize control once M'kuru was dead . . .

But he was not dead. So someone had got him out. There is no way that child could have survived all of this without help.

The more the prince thought, the stronger his headache grew, and the fury in his heart burned. He grabbed anything he could get his hands on and threw it against the opposite wall of the tent.

"Your Highness, if you act in this manner, no one shall believe the story we wish to tell," Sauda said gently, and when the prince turned to her, she once again had a cup of tea for him.

"Lady Sauda speaks the truth," Khalaf said. "For this to be a victory, you must treat it as one, especially at the palace."

Nose flared, Prince Effiom snatched the cup and drank it down before tossing it back to Sauda.

"I have been acting around those fools all my life," he said. "I do not worry about them. I worry about my kingdom!" Prince Effiom marched to his desk, ripped the map from it, and held it out for them to see. "Do you not see the boundaries? Madada, Winneba, Kossinat, and all the other lands. I have not crossed any out. Madada must fall, so the rest shall fall! Then I shall be . . ."

The prince stopped himself from speaking the words.

"Patience—" Sauda counseled.

"Do not lecture me on patience. I have had my fill of late." The prince stepped closer to her. "Be of use and tell me what you see."

Her eyes widened, and immediately she looked at Khalaf, as the prince had never asked for her vision in the company of others before. "My prince—"

"If you think he does not already know by now, then you are a fool, Sauda, and I do not care for fools."

"I only fear—"

"Commander Rausi, do you plan on betraying me?"

"Only should you betray the king," Khalaf replied unflinchingly.

Prince Effiom nodded and looked back at Sauda. "I trust him and do not plan on betraying my father, so stop wasting time and tell me what you see."

"My vision remains unchanged—you shall one day rule these lands, my prince."

Her words relaxed him, but they did not ease all his fears. Inhaling through his nose, he stood there for a moment, nodding.

"And the crown prince? What shall he say upon my return?" Prince Effiom asked her.

She closed her eyes for a moment before speaking. "Nothing."

"What does that mean, nothing? You do not see—"

"The crown prince is ill."

At that, Prince Effiom's head snapped up, and he stared at her, eyes wide.

"Ill? Of what? How ill? Shall he die?" The prince could barely contain himself.

"I am unsure, but it is severe—"

"Finally, some good news!" Prince Effiom laughed, grinning widely from ear to ear as he placed his hand on Khalaf's shoulder plate. "Gather the men. Make haste. I wish to make it back and see him as he dies!"

If only his father could also succumb. Still, he would take this—half his problems solved.

He would worry about the other half later.

27

KHALIL

Madada

"WHAT IS HAPPENING?" KHALIL ASKED HIS NEW shadow, Mbwa, as all of the soldiers were suddenly up on their feet and running from one side of the camp to the other, tearing down the tents as quickly as possible.

"We are returning to the capital immediately," said Khalaf, not Mbwa, as he stepped up behind Khalil.

"The soldiers said they were to hunt down any more rebels—"

"The soldiers do not give orders. That is why they are soldiers. If you wish to be privy to information, you stay by the commanders," Khalaf said to him. Then to Mbwa: "Find him a horse."

"I do not believe he knows how to ride, sir—"

"I do not care what you believe. He will ride as all Rausi do. If nothing else, he'll have a month to figure it out. He is far too old not to," Khalaf ordered, and Mbwa bowed his head and took his leave. It was only then that Khalaf focused his attention back on Khalil.

Khalil knew how to ride. Or, at least he'd learned already, as all children of noble blood did. However, he was supposed to have been born in a poor village, so where was he to have found a horse to learn how to ride?

Was it a trap? Another test?

Indecision plagued him as Mbwa brought a full-grown warm-brown horse with black legs and a black mane and tail before him. On its back was a leather saddle with the emblem of . . . wings. Khalil stared at the horse and then back at Khalaf.

Khalil walked around to the side of the horse, still trying to think.

"We do not have all day!" Khalaf stated.

It's a test, Khalil thought. Stepping back, he glanced back up at Khalaf. "I do not know how to get on. Show me, and I'll do it."

"You'll know how to after watching once?" Khalaf asked, eyebrow raised.

Khalil nodded. "Yes."

"Show him Mbwa, quickly."

Mbwa grabbed the saddle of the horse swiftly and easily kicked his foot over to the other side before settling onto the horse's back.

"Now you," Khalaf ordered when Mbwa came back down.

Khalil swallowed, grabbed the side of the saddle, and just as easily kicked his foot over the horse and sat in the center, but he made sure to yank on the reins harder than he needed to and dig his heels into the side of the horse, causing it to buck wildly and take off.

"*Whoa!*" Khalil screamed—not exactly feigning fear, as it had been a long time since he'd been astride a horse—as the animal sprinted forward. Once more, Khalil pulled the reins and kicked his foot incorrectly, making the horse buck more and more. Only

when he saw another solider rushing toward him did Khalil shift
and calm the horse the right way, walking it around in a circle over
and over. Then it finally stopped bucking.

"Not bad, but not at all good enough," Khalaf said, coming up
beside him, already mounted on his own dark horse. "Luckily, you
did not fall, for that would have been a disgrace that Father would
not ignore. Whether you were born in a cave or the capital, you
must know how to ride. It is in our blood."

"I'll get better, then," Khalil replied, pretending to barely control the horse underneath him. "As you said—I have a month. What
is this horse's name?"

"It's yours, now, so name it as you wish," Khalaf said as he rode
forward ahead of Khalil. "I do not have time to babysit you. Mbwa,
you are to watch over him. Explain to him what he needs to know."

Khalil watched Khalaf go, petting the neck of his horse as Mbwa
came up to him. Khalil frowned, then looked down at the man
who, only a few days ago, he thought to be some sort of brave hero.

"Are you just an errand boy?" Khalil asked him.

"I am a spy of the Rausi family," Mbwa answered as he led
Khalil's horse. "But until I am given a mission, yes, I am more of
an errand boy."

"That's pitiful," Khalil muttered, looking away from him.

"Why? Serving the Great General is an honor—"

"What good is a spy if everyone knows your face?" Khalil cut in,
not wanting to hear any praise about his so-called family. "How will
you be able to trick some other poor village next time?"

"Do you feel pity for Kazera?"

Khalil frowned and did not answer. Instead, he looked to the
red tent. "How will my mother travel?"

"All the women of nobles shall ride in a carriage. Lady Sauda prefers horseback, so an extra carriage is not present. Thus, a storage wagon will be covered and used for your mother."

"A storage wagon? What will happen to all the other stuff . . ." Khalil's voice trailed off as he looked over to the line of men, slaves now, having to carry bundles of materials on their backs. He looked away. "I understand. How many men are here?"

"Khalaf Rausi is a Silver Ray, and he is in command of three thousand men, and the prince also has one thousand personal guards."

"A Silver Ray?"

"The Zenzele military has nearly half a million soldiers. The most elite soldiers are part of the Red Sun Army. Commanders within the Red Sun are called Rays. A Silver Ray is in command of anywhere from one thousand to five thousand men."

Khalil remembered the commander who had attacked his father and helped kill his sister. His armor had been red and silver. He thought the silver was spikes but it was rays of the sun.

"And those with over five thousand men?"

"Golden Rays. Five to ten thousand men are under their command."

"And a general is everything over the ten thousand?"

"Yes."

"How many men are in the Red Sun Army?"

"One hundred thousand, I believe."

"All those men are under my father."

"Yes, the Great General moves only at the king's personal command," Mbwa replied. "You will learn more about the system at the capital."

"How did Khalaf get to be in command of three thousand already? He does not seem so old." Khalil learned from his baba that getting the title of commander took years of dedication and battle. But the Mukundi family's military ranks were not the same as the Zenzele's.

"Commander Khalaf managed to rise to command three thousand men after partaking in the destruction of the Mukundi family three years ago by the king. Though your father and eldest brother did not approve of it."

Khalil gripped his reins tightly but only managed to get out one word. "Why?"

"Why didn't your father approve? I would not dare think for your family, but I believe the Great General did not think one should rise without a true battle won. What happened to the Mukundi was more like a—"

"Slaughter," Khalil finished, but moved on from the thought.

"There haven't been any great wars here. But there have still been some battles, and rebellions. The king loves to give out rewards, so Khalaf could be promoted once more because of the Battle of Kazera. That will put him on the same level as one of your other bothers, the eldest."

Khalil frowned. He did not know much about the world beyond Madada . . . actually, the world beyond the village. Kazera got many visitors from other towns, but his grandfather always told him to avoid any news. His grandfather was dead now, and Khalil needed to know as much as he could if he was going to survive.

"Tell me everything you know. Starting with why we are returning to Ahalon instead of chasing the rebels."

"I'm sure your brother—"

"My brother has dismissed both me *and* you from his mind. So, I'm the Rausi here, and you will answer my questions."

And for the third time in his short life, Khalil found he was a new person. No longer M'kuru Mukundi of Madada, no longer the Bastard of Kazera, he was now Khalil Rausi . . . son of the greatest general on the continent, and he was going to Ahalon.

He felt like a snake shedding his skin, but instead of looking better he looked worse. Morphing into something uglier. But he would do whatever he could to survive. He would tell himself this over and over again . . .

Because nothing meant more than his revenge, even if it turned him into a beast.

28

ZIKORA

Ahalon

"ZIKORA. ZIKORA . . . ZIKORA!"

"*Mhm?*" Zikora grumbled, rolling over on her bed, grabbing the pillow, and placing it over her head. "I'm still sleeping!"

"Zikora, it's important!"

"So is sleeping!" Zikora groaned, pulling back on her blankets.

"Prince Aberash is dying!"

Immediately, Zikora sat up in bed, staring directly at the light-brown eyes of Tuliza. "I'm awake. What did you say?"

"The crown prince is—"

Zikora did not even wait for her to finish before jumping out of bed and toward the door, just as it was opened.

"Lady Zikora!" Nanny Urenna yelped, nearly tipping the basin of water over as Zikora ran past her skirts. "Lady Zikora, where are you going? You are still in your whites!"

Zikora did not care. She held up the hem of her white dress and ran barefoot down the polished amber stone tiles, in and out of one massive hall and the next. On every wall, in every direction, were paintings of the old Zenzele kings and their triumphs. It was how she never got lost.

"We should not be going," Tuliza said, running after her.

"Why did you tell me if you didn't want to go?" Zikora replied, crossing over the bridge of the inner water garden to the other side of the palace.

"So you would know, not so you could go! We will get in trouble . . . *again*."

Zikora was used to being in trouble. It did not matter if it was in Winneba or Ahalon, but being in trouble in Ahalon was never as bad because the crown prince always helped her.

And now the crown prince was sick.

"We at least shouldn't be running," Tuliza reminded her.

Normally it was against the palace rules for anyone, except for the palace guards, to run. And it was completely shameful for a woman to be seen in her whites, so the queen's rule-keeper would surely discipline Zikora for breaking two rules at once if caught. But Zikora did not think anyone would even notice, as the closer she came to the crown prince's quarters, the more and more she saw other people, mostly maids, rushing through the halls themselves. The paintings on the wall near Prince Aberash's rooms were of the king's four sons bowing to him upon the sun throne.

Just as Zikora moved toward the doors, two spears crossed in front of her face, blocking her path. She glanced up at the two guards dressed in dark-purple robes embroidered with green, yellow, and brown patterns, breastplates of iron on their chests, and swords at their sides. They towered over her, both with height and their large muscular bodies, their faces stern and unflinching. They looked exactly as guards should look, but she'd never seen them around the prince before. And she never forgot a face once she'd seen it.

Something was not right.

"You are not Prince Aberash's guards," Zikora said to them, frowning, and Tuliza tugged on Zikora's sleeve to pull her back.

But Zikora refused to be moved and stood firm before them.

The guards said nothing but still did not uncross their spears for her.

Angry, Zikora inhaled deeply through her nose and said, "My name is Lady Zikora Nnamani of Winneba, and I wish to see Prince Aberash . . . now."

Once more, they did not listen to her, so Zikora nodded, took a step back, lifted the skirt of her dress once more, and bent forward.

"What are you doing?" Tuliza said with a hiss at her.

"If I get hurt trying to get through . . . you all will be in trouble," Zikora stated, and just as she was about to run at the door, she heard a gentle voice speak behind her.

"Do you believe running headfirst into a problem will solve it?"

Zikora paused. She knew that low voice and couldn't run from her. Zikora dropped her skirt and turned back around slowly, placing her right palm over her left in front of her as she bent down slowly.

"Blessings and good morning, my queen," Zikora said with the light tone she'd been practicing for the last three years under the queen's command.

"Blessings and good morning to you as well, Lady Zikora. You may rise."

Tuliza took two steps back as Zikora stood straighter and glanced at the woman with warm-brown skin and bright brown eyes. The queen was dressed in the brightest yellow robe with green grass embroidered along the hem of her skirt. She had brown, black, and dark red embroidery of people and homes in the center of her skirt and her blouse. Around her waist were blue and white for the sky and clouds. At the very top of her blouse, its rays so large it covered her sleeves, was a bright-red embroidered sun. Like all royal and noble women, her hair was a mixture of beads and curls decorated in strings and pins of gold, and gold hung from her ears and even her nose. Everyone said Queen Esraa was the most beautiful woman in the whole kingdom, but Zikora often wondered if it was because anytime people outside the palace saw the queen, she was seated next to the king, and because he was fifty years older than her—and ugly—he made the queen, who was only nineteen, look prettier.

"Why have you left the women's court?" Queen Esraa asked, taking a step forward, and when she did, the twelve women behind her—six on the left and six on the right, all dressed in simple dark-green robes and matching scarf to hide their hair—moved with her. Only women of noble birth or status were allowed to wear their hair free, and only women with high noble birth could wear gold in their hair in the palace.

"They say Prince Aberash is ill?" Zikora was not sure if it were true, and she did not believe it.

"Who are *they*?" the queen asked her. "Who dares gossip about the health of a prince?"

"I am not sure who they are. I simply overheard it—"

"While still in your whites?" the queen pressed, her blue eyes shifting to Tuliza.

Zikora stepped back into the woman's line of sight. "I have good hearing and heard the maids speaking outside my room. Is it true? Why will they not let me see him?"

"Zikora, my dear, it is for your own safety. The doctors are unsure what has caused the prince's illness—"

"Is that also why all of my husband's guards have been changed?" came the calm yet harsh voice of Crown Princess Hasina. Her skin was dark as night, and she wore a large cape of white, red, and pink, which covered all of her body, with the exception of her neck. There she wore golden brass rings like all the women of Kéye wore. Upon her head was a golden and red headpiece that matched her hoop earrings.

Zikora and Tuliza both bowed to her. Princess Hasina made sure to place her hand on Zikora's cheek, stroking it tenderly before looking at the queen. It was at that moment Zikora quickly stepped out from between the older women. Once more, Tuliza tugged on Zikora's sleeve, and Zikora shook her off again. There was no way she would not watch this duel.

"Queen Esraa," Princess Hasina said as she placed her right palm over her left and lowered herself before her, but only slightly.

"No blessings?" Queen Esraa asked.

"What blessings can be had while my husband lies in bed ill?"

"Maybe that is why he is ill? He forwent blessing his elders?"

Princess Hasina snickered and glanced around the hall. "I see no elders here, Your Majesty, so I must be safe. Though I would feel safer if my husband's chosen guards had not been replaced."

Princess Hasina and the queen were the same age. In fact, Princess Hasina was three days older than the queen.

"Unfortunately, they have taken ill as well. But do not worry. Every guard within the palace cares for the crown prince *deeply*." Queen Esraa smiled and then turned to the guards standing watch outside the prince's door. "It seems Princess Hasina does not trust you all are capable. Please do your best despite her behavior. After all, the Kéye are *distrusting* people by nature."

"Those we distrust have rightly earned our distrust, Your Majesty," Princess Hasina replied, glaring at the queen, her jaw set tightly.

"It is because of that mentality you fret over a simple change of guards. You are supposed to be one of the future queens of this land, yet you still speak and dress as if Kéye were all that mattered. If anyone should doubt anyone, it should be us of you. Yet here we all are, rushing to see your husband in your time of distress. Your presence has dampened my spirits, so I shall come to see him another time . . . if he is still with us." Queen Esraa turned to leave.

"Don't worry, for Aberash is not going anywhere. After all, he would not leave *us*," Princess Hasina said, opening her cape to show her large stomach.

Zikora's eyes nearly fell out of her head, and Queen Esraa nearly tripped as she spun back around to see.

This is not going to be good, Zikora thought but smiled wildly and said, "You are having a baby! I just thought you were getting fat!"

Zikora took a quick step back from Princess Hasina, knowing Queen Esraa would push anyone out of the way in her rage.

"How dare you keep such a thing secret!" Queen Esraa spat.

"It is customary in Kéye not to announce until—"

"*This is not Kéye!*" Queen Esraa's voice grew even louder. Zikora did not know the queen's voice could get so loud in public. But she watched them both silently.

"Calm, my queen!" all the queen's maids begged, bowing low behind where she now stood, only feet from Princess Hasina.

"Are you not happy with the news, *my queen*?" Princess Hasina asked, staring directly at the queen and rubbing her belly. "I hear the king has been longing to hear the sound of a wailing child within these walls again. In fact, Farai . . ."

"I am here, princess." One of the princess's maids, dressed

exactly as the queen's maids except for her neck rings, stepped forward from behind Hasina.

"Have word sent to the king's court that he is to expect a grand-child *very* soon."

"Yes, princess—"

"Stop right there," Queen Esraa spoke, her voice light. "There is no need. We shall go together, and you can explain the reason you sought to hide such *joyful* news."

"Very well." Princess Hasina stepped to the side, allowing the queen to proceed.

"Lady Zikora, return to your rooms. And the next time I see you, you ought to be properly dressed," Queen Esraa ordered, and walked forward.

"Journey mercies, my queen, princess," Zikora said, sinking low before them as they took their leave. She waited for them to turn the corner before she glared back at the guards. "I'll be back."

"You really shouldn't show that you care about Prince Aberash so much," Tuliza said to Zikora as they walked back to the women's court of the inner palace.

"Why not?"

"It's clear the queen does not like him."

"The queen doesn't really like anyone . . . not even the king."

"Shh!" Tuliza's eyes were wide. "You cannot say that. And she dislikes the crown prince and princess the most."

"So? What does that have to do with me?" She knew exactly what.

"Zikora." Tuliza grabbed Zikora's hand and pulled her back, a frown heavy on her face, and Zikora tried not to laugh. Tuliza always looked like a wounded puppy when she was worried, her whole face sinking. "This could be dangerous. No, I'm sure this is dangerous. Everyone knows that you are always on Prince Aberash's side. That means you are against the queen. That's okay when Prince Aberash is there to help you, but if he dies, what's going to happen?"

"If Prince Aberash dies and Princess Hasina doesn't have a male heir, she'll have to go back to her father in Kéye—"

"I mean, what's going to happen to *you*? Have you thought about that?"

She always thought about that.

"If Prince Aberash dies, I stay here. If he lives . . . I still stay here." Zikora replied, shrugging her shoulders.

Tuliza exhaled deeply, letting go of her. "Yes . . . but the people will be meaner."

"The king likes me as well, so they won't be too mean."

"Who he likes changes every week. You have to be more cautious of everyone and make sure to stay on their good sides."

"Tuliza, the king doesn't like me like the others. He likes me as a daughter."

"The king doesn't want daughters, though—no one here does," Tuliza shot back, and it was true. It was one of the first things they had learned in the capital . . . girls were only important so they could create boys. If they could not do that, they were useless. And useless things were always ignored or destroyed. "You have to make everyone like you."

"You might as well tell me to grow wings and fly." Because it was impossible to be loved by all.

"Zikora—"

"Tuliza, if someone is nice to me, I will be nice to them and want to spend time with them. If someone is mean to me, I will avoid them. That's common sense."

"You are a high noble, so nothing about you is supposed to be common!"

But not everyone else was a high noble. If she acted like she was someone so important, if she picked sides for reasons that weren't so easy to understand, she would be playing their game, and they would know it.

That was far more dangerous.

Zikora sighed because she could not explain that to Tuliza; she did not want anyone to ever know what she was thinking. It was safer for everyone to think she was nothing but a silly girl who wanted to play.

"I'm hungry, Tuliza, can we talk about food now—"

"Zikora."

Zikora had only gotten a few feet when she saw her nanny waiting on the other side of the water garden with a pile of clothing in her hands.

"Great. We are in trouble," Tuliza whispered from behind Zikora. Even though Nanny Urenna hadn't raised her voice or even looked the slightest bit upset, both young girls knew they'd be in trouble the moment they crossed the bridge.

"We might as well get it over with," Zikora said to Tuliza, and they both grabbed their ears and pulled as they walked.

Nanny Urenna glared down at them. "I make you pull your ears so you can hear me when I am speaking. If you decide to ignore me and pull your ears later, it defeats the point."

"So . . . no punishment?" Zikora grinned, letting go of her ears only for Nanny Urenna to reach over and grab them. "*Ow!*"

"Your mother has given me written permission to punish you when I see fit. Stop giving me reasons to see fit, Lady Zikora."

"Okay! Okay!" Zikora shrank back when Nanny Urenna let go and hid behind Tuliza, rubbing her ears.

"And you, Tuliza—"

"I tried to stop her!"

"Hands down," Nanny Urenna snapped, and when Tuliza obeyed, Nanny Urenna grabbed Tuliza's ear, twisting as well. "You should have known better than to tell her at all."

"So, you knew too?" Zikora asked.

Tuliza, too, rubbed her ear in pain but would never complain about it.

"Of course. The whole palace is speaking of it, but it is none of our business. Now, come, you must change and eat," Nanny Urenna said, stretching out her hand for them.

Just as she was about to take Urenna's hand, Zikora heard someone behind her call out her name.

"Lady Zikora!"

They all turned to see a woman dressed in a simple rose-and-silver dress with light-brown freckled skin, dark-brown eyes, and shoulder-length braided hair, strands of which were tied in silver, matching her nose ring. She stood with only two maids behind her and was a stranger to Zikora. She had to be a noble, judging by her clothing and hair, which was why Zikora's nanny and Tuliza lowered themselves before her.

"Who are you?" Zikora asked.

"You stand before Lady Cyrah of the noble house of Grigah," said one of the maids, who had warm-brown skin, three tribal scars upon her left cheek, and sharp green eyes.

Zikora looked to Tuliza, as she'd never seen this woman's face before. "Who?"

Tuliza puffed up like a pufferfish as she slowly turned back to her mistress. "Lady Zikora, this is one of Prince Effiom's concubines."

"Another one?" Zikora gasped, then looked back at her. "Hello."

"Do you not know the manners of the palace, Lady Zikora? As

she is one of Prince Effiom's concubines, you are to offer blessings and greetings," the maid behind Lady Cyrah said.

"I know the manners of the palace, as I have been living here longer than you," Zikora shot back, and she felt Nanny Urenna nudge her. But neither she nor Tuliza could speak without being spoken to, and so Zikora felt free to ignore them. "I did not offer greetings because I did not know her or her status. Now that I do, I still will not, because she is a concubine, not Prince Effiom's true wife. As I am the daughter of a high noble, she offers greetings to *me*. And you are not supposed to be speaking to me. She is, *Lady Cyrah*," she finished, a bit of a question, a bit of command in how she said the name.

Lady Cyrah bit her lip and then brought her palms out before herself. "Blessings and good morning to you, Lady Zikora. Forgive my maid. She seems to have more to learn."

"Blessings and good morning to you as well, Lady Cyrah." Zikora nodded to her, then turned around. "Goodbye."

"Wait . . . please, Lady Zikora," Lady Cyrah said, stopping Zikora again. "I had just come out for a walk and saw you. I wished to come speak with you."

"Why?"

Lady Cyrah laughed slightly. "Well, as you know, I am still a bit new to the palace, and I wanted . . . I wanted to see if you would be my friend."

Zikora stared at her for a long time. Zikora could feel that this woman was not a good person. But then again, almost everyone in the palace was not a good person. "No, thank you. Bye now. I have to go eat and get changed before the queen sees me again."

"Wait!" Lady Cyrah called.

But Zikora grabbed Nanny Urenna's hand and allowed her

nanny to take her back down the hallway. No one said a word until they were safely in Zikora's rooms.

"You should not just reject her like that, my lady," Nanny Urenna said as she began to help Zikora undress.

"Something bad will happen if we stay near her." Zikora lifted her arms.

"Let me guess. Your *feelings* again?" Tuliza sighed, taking Zikora's discarded whites to fold. "You can't just say that and walk away!"

Well, she could not just say that Lady Cyrah was clearly trying to plot something and use her to do it either. Why else would she want to be friends with her? She was not a member of the royal family. Concubines in the palace were always trying to find ways to become more important. Which is why they always ended up dying. Zikora wanted no part in any of their affairs.

"How many concubines can princes have?" Zikora asked, to change the subject. "Lady Cyrah is going to be Prince Effiom's seventh. Prince Aberash only has one, and the king only has four."

"There are no limits for them," Nanny Urenna said as she bent her knees to tie the side of Zikora's dress. "They can have as many as they wish."

Zikora sighed dramatically, making her nanny giggle. "Why am I supposed to remember them all? They keep adding new ones and getting rid of the old ones."

"It is not that hard," Tuliza said as she brought over Zikora's shoes and jewels.

"I did not say it was hard. I said I do not want to remember people that do not matter," Zikora grumbled, brushing her curls off her face.

"When I first got here, the king's wife was Queen Nasera, and that wasn't even his first queen. But still I had to know everything about her and how to make her happy. Then she was killed two months after we got here. Now people are saying since Esraa has not gotten pregnant, they will get rid of her too. Then the king will get a new queen. I think I'll just call her queen number five."

"Zikora!" Her nanny gave her a stern look as she put Zikora's earrings in. "No matter how many wives the king has, you have to respect them all."

"Can't I respect them and not talk to them? It's a waste of time."

"What else are you doing with your time?" Tuliza asked her. "All you do is sleep, eat, and play."

She liked sleeping because she saw home in her dreams.

"They won't let me do anything else. I prefer to play than weave or listen to lectures," Zikora grumbled. She didn't even want to play. What she really wanted was to lift a sword or pull back on a bow, but that was considered unladylike here, so the queen had ordered her not to.

This queen, that is.

Tuliza frowned, as Zikora knew she found it frustrating too. Tuliza wanted to be a warrior, but how could she if she did not train?

She was still trying to think of a way to get the king or even the crown prince to allow them to train. But all the stupid rules for women in the palace made doing anything impossible.

"Lady Zikora. Tuliza," Nanny Urenna said gently, smiling as she petted Zikora's face. "I know it is hard. This place is different from home. But we all must do our part to get through it. Your part, my lady, is to be aware of *everyone* in the palace and the other nobles. You don't have to befriend them, but you shouldn't reject them either. You never know when they may come in use."

Zikora's mind was already full of so many things that adding more people's names made her head hurt. She reached up and rubbed it as she thought, because the problem was, once she did meet someone new, everything about their family came rushing to her mind. It was like with each new face came a history book.

"Lady Cyrah of the Grigah family. Grigah is a noble family from the Zenzele lands that goes back to the conquest. One of their ancestors helped Aksum Zenzele during the Battle of Nights. Their family emblem is four stars together as one, and they . . . ugh." Zikora winced as she rattled off all the information that suddenly appeared in her mind.

"Stop!" Tuliza grabbed her face. "Zikora, stop thinking! You're going to hurt yourself."

This wasn't the insult one might think. This is what had happened to her repeatedly over the last three years. It wasn't just with new people either. Zikora realized she knew things about lands, animals, and plants that she had only just heard of. But if she thought too hard or too long, she gave herself such a headache that her nose or ears would start to bleed. No one knew why this happened, but it was a secret among the three of them. Zikora even did her best not to show them the true extent of how often it happened.

"Sit down, Zikora," Nanny Urenna said. "It's okay. Just think of something nice, like home."

But Zikora could not. Once her mind started, it was hard to stop. But she did not want them to worry over her either.

"I am okay," Zikora lied.

"Are you sure?" Tuliza leaned in closer.

"Yes. We should go. We still need to see what is happening with Prince Aberash."

Knock. Knock.

Zikora watched as her nanny went to the door and opened it. A servant handed her a pillow.

"Who is this from?" Urenna asked.

"Lady Cyrah. It is for Lady Zikora. Lady Cyrah wishes Lady Zikora to have them, to mark Lady Cyrah's arrival in the inner palace," the servant said.

Zikora's nanny turned back and Zikora saw two golden bracelets on the pillow.

"She really wants to be your friend," Tuliza said, lifting a bracelet to see the engraving on it once the servant left.

"Princess Bahiya is not going to like this," Zikora replied as she lifted the other golden bracelet.

"I am sure Princess Bahiya won't care too much. And even if she does, she will not say anything," Nanny Urenna said.

Prince Effiom's true wife, Princess Bahiya, was the quietest of all the women in the inner palace. She was often weaving or reading by herself. Most of the fighting was always between Queen Esraa and Crown Princess Hasina. When it was not them, it was the other concubines. Princess Bahiya did not even fight with Prince Effiom's other women. She barely spoke to them, so everyone thought she was good.

Zikora, somehow, knew that wasn't true.

"Princess Bahiya is dangerous," Zikora whispered. It was that feeling again that told her.

"They are all bad in some way, Zikora," Tuliza replied, putting the bracelet down.

Tuliza had told her this almost every day, and she was right. But Tuliza thought befriending everyone was the safest why to survive. And that is where Zikora believed she was wrong.

After all, didn't Queen Nasera try to befriend everyone? The queen—the most powerful woman in the kingdom, with two young sons—was executed for treason. Her maids, whom she lavishly gave gifts to, betrayed her, accused her even of plotting against the king somehow. The princesses, whose mistakes she always covered for, said not one word in her defense when the time came.

Queen Nasera had tried to be smart and followed all the rules, only for her head to be taken off in the center of the palace, and her sons confined to their rooms, never to step out again. Since then, Zikora had never seen or heard from Prince Ayize or Prince Ehioze. But she felt as though Queen Nasera was innocent. Zikora had no proof and did not even know the queen that well, but her papa had told her to listen to her feelings, so she did.

And Zikora's feelings told her to pretend that she was nothing but a silly child, a child who did not notice or care when maids, concubines, or queens died. Not to be too clever or too eager to show any skills in anything. Her feelings told her that the king liked that she was mischievous but naïve, because that meant she was not plotting against him like everyone else.

She noticed that all the men in the palace liked when girls were stupid and cheerful. So all the women pretended to be stupid and cheerful. Well, some were really stupid. But others, like Princess Bahiya, were very smart, they just hid it.

So Zikora would hide her mind too and use innocence as her shield for as long as she could.

"Let's eat and then go get flowers for Prince Aberash! It will make him feel better," Zikora exclaimed, suddenly energetic again.

29

PRINCESS BAHIYA

Ahalon

"SO, SHE HAS FINALLY COME TO THE INNER palace," Princess Bahiya said as she weaved the thread through the loom before her. "That must mean her family has had word about Effiom. He will be here in a week's time, and they want her waiting for him when he returns."

"The Grigah family has trade routes throughout the kingdom, so their people must have reported back to them as ours did. And if they know and we know, then the king and crown prince most certainly do as well. But no one has spoken on it," said Bahiya's maid, Afuna, as she sorted the threads out before her. "This is a huge triumph for Prince Effiom. He's killed—"

"No one is speaking on it until the king speaks on it," said Princess Bahiya as she fed the thread through once more. "And when the king speaks on it, everything will change for Effiom. He'll be celebrated throughout the capital, so the Grigah want her right beside him, a fresh new toy to happily indulge in."

"What shall you do?"

"Did you prepare Lady Cyrah's rooms as I ordered?"

"Yes, the second closest to the prince. The other concubines were *not* pleased."

Princess Bahiya giggled as she dusted off the eye of the embroidered hawk she was making. "Did you explain to them that as she is the daughter of a noble, the room is her right?"

"Yes, and they were even more distressed."

Princess Bahiya smiled more and glanced at her maid. "How distressed? We would not wish anything to happen to her before Effiom arrives, now would we?"

"No, Your Highness. I also told them you expected no trouble from any of them."

"Perfect. Did Lady Cyrah say anything to you in return?"

"No, Your Highness. She barely looked at me. However, one of her handmaids asked when Lady Cyrah could come to pay her respects to you. I told her you do not wish for any. She objected, of course, but I told her you could not be disturbed by a *mere* concubine."

"That must have hurt her."

"Lady Zikora hurt her even worse."

"Zikora?" Princess Bahiya replied, pulling on a thread. "What did she do?"

"They sought her out and expected her to give them greetings, but Lady Zikora put them both in their place, saying Lady Cyrah was not his 'true wife,' so Lady Zikora was the one who ought to be greeted."

Princess Bahiya smiled and raised an eyebrow as she stared at Afuna. "One thing about that girl is she is both silly and honest. It's why the king and crown prince like her so much. That childish innocence."

"She is eleven, Your Highness, and in four years, she will be able to marry."

"Four years is still a long time, at least for anyone not named Queen Nasera," Princess Bahiya mocked, snipping the thread, her unsubtle reference to the fact that Queen Nasera was only queen for four years before her death.

"Even so, Lady Cyrah asked to be the girl's friend, and the girl said no. Lady Cyrah later gifted Zikora bracelets anyway."

"Lady Cyrah thinks she is smart, but she is a fool, so much so a little girl saw through her." Princess Bahiya shook her head.

"What I don't understand is why even approach Zikora?" Afuna asked. "What good does that do Lady Cyrah?"

"She wished to be Zikora's friend because she needs protection."

"How can that little girl protect her? Would she not need Prince Effiom's protection more?"

"She is not that stupid, Afuna. All the women in this palace know men are as fickle as the life of butterflies. Lady Cyrah was able to seduce the prince when he went to visit her father, but she was the seventh to do that. Prince Effiom will eventually find someone new if he has not already in this campaign, so she cannot rely on him alone. Nor does she wish to stay just a concubine because, even to the prince, that is a low status for her as a noble. She wishes to become his legitimate wife—they all do, in fact. But the difference between them and her is her family."

"How so?"

"Because Prince Effiom will need her father later."

Afuna thought on this but was still confused. "So why does she need Zikora?"

"Prince Effiom can't make a name for himself here at the palace with the crown prince always near. So he uses war and battle to make a name for himself. He won't be around to protect Lady

Cyrah. Queen Esraa and Princess Hasina are both in the middle of their own war over bearing a son. Now that Princess Hasina has conceived, she will be far too concerned with protecting her child and husband and won't have time to entertain Lady Cyrah. Queen Esraa fears losing her head if she cannot conceive. Then there is me, but I am her enemy, as I have the position she wishes. The only other person with any standing in the palace, albeit small, is Zikora. And as I said, Zikora has the favor of the king, the crown prince, and is a high noble of Winneba, so should anyone *truly* upset her, they could lose their heads."

"Ah, that makes sense. . . . but then why does this make Lady Cyrah stupid, Your Highness?"

"Because it is so obvious, Afuna. She all but walked in here and told me all I needed to know of her, and I have yet to see her face. How foolish. The others at least pretend they are in love and only want Prince Effiom's attention. I am sure it was her father who advised her before she came here. Only a man who has never been in the inner palace would think I am too thoughtless to notice this." Once more, Princess Bahiya snipped a thread. "I am sure he plotted to have one of the princes—he may not have cared which—meet his daughter in his home. If not, why withhold marrying her off a year ago when she became of age?"

"So, what shall you do?"

"When you put a sheep in a lion's den, what else can it do but eat?" Princess Bahiya shrugged.

"Leave it to the other concubines again?"

"No . . . let's leave it to Zikora."

"She's a lioness?"

"She certainly has teeth."

Afuna nodded. "How will you get her to do it?"

"The way to mess with Zikora, as she is nothing here, is through her loved ones, and there are only two here whom she truly cares for: that nanny and handmaid of hers."

"But will Prince Effiom really punish her for the sake of a little girl . . ."

"Zikora's family is still too important to risk over a concubine, noble or not." No, the trouble for Princess Bahiya was not Effiom. It was how to make it look like she had no hand in it while also making sure the girl was so angry, she would demand Lady Cyrah be punished.

"You do not wish to leave Lady Cyrah for now? Did you not say the prince still needed her father?" Afuna asked the princess, and the glare Princess Bahiya gave her in return was enough to make her lower her head.

Leave Cyrah? If she were any other concubine, Princess Bahiya would have. After all, she could not spend all of her energy trying to subdue her husband's urges. But like her, Lady Cyrah came from a noble family within the capital. The royal family was already seeking to add as many daughters as possible from the high noble houses to their bloodline as it was. And high noble she was not. Luckily for her, Queen Esraa and Princess Hasina were the only two of age the last time new women were needed and were therefore chosen for the king and the crown prince.

The only other girls close in age were Lady Onani of Yœngo, but she was thirteen, and Zikora at eleven. Princess Bahiya was already twenty-three. She did not feel old and neither did she think she looked it. Truthfully, she believed herself to be growing more and more beautiful, even with the birth of her sons. Still, what she thought of herself did not matter. Having sons was not enough anymore. Especially not with that witch, Sauda, always at her husband's side. It was hard enough for her to swallow her pride and allow that lowly, dirty dog to go on campaign with her prince. The only reason was she knew Effiom cared only about whatever dark abilities the woman had and did not really care about Sauda herself. Bahiya's position was not threatened by Sauda, and so she let her be. But with Cyrah?

"Effiom is free to have anyone but a rival to me," the princess whispered to Afuna as she reached into her hair and pulled out a hairpin in the shape of a golden water lily. "Send this to Lady Zikora so she remembers I, too, am here, should she need anything."

"Yes, Your Highness—"

Before Afuna could finish, the doors opened. Normally, the princess would not have accepted such rudeness, but upon seeing who it was, Princess Bahiya rose to her feet, placing her palms over each other. "Blessings and good morning, my queen."

"Spare me that," Queen Esraa snapped as she moved to take her place at the head of the table. "I need your help." Nevertheless, Princess Bahiya stepped aside before bowing to the queen and taking a seat.

"With what, my queen?" the princess asked, also looking at Afuna to bring them drinks.

"I heard you whispering. Were you not talking about Princess Hasina?" The queen spat the words as if they were venom.

"I was not—"

"What could be of greater importance than her at this moment? Surely you have heard by now she is pregnant. *Very* pregnant."

"I did hear. I sent my congratulations already—"

"Are you trying to make me upset?"

"No, you look angry enough."

"She is *pregnant*."

Bahiya tried not to smile at how uncontrollably angry she was. "So you have said."

"Bahiya, do not pretend as if you do not know she puts us at risk."

"Does she?" Princess Bahiya replied as Afuna set a cup before the queen and then before her. "How?"

"You really wish to play the fool? Very well, let me remind you that your husband does not wish Prince Aberash well. As the crown prince is now sick, your husband will be overjoyed. It's one more step closer to being king—"

"Long live King Essien, your husband—as the prince would say, for he would be heartbroken should anything happen to his father," Princess Bahiya whispered as she drank. All the while, Queen Esraa glared, annoyed.

"I, too, wish my husband to live longer. However, all men must die. And when that happens, Prince Aberash will be next in line, should he live. But if he should not, and Hasina gives birth to a boy, then that child shall be king. That would bother Effiom, would it not?"

Princess Bahiya's eyebrow rose. "Only if the baby could hold a sword or command an army."

When Queen Esraa did not speak, Princess Bahiya went on: "That baby is irrelevant to us, girl or boy, and Prince Aberash . . . well, if he dies, he dies. If he lives, my husband goes on as he always has. So nothing has changed for me. And it does not change much for you either. It is your fear speaking."

"I have been married to the king for two years, Bahiya, only months before that whore arrived, and she got pregnant before me. The king and everyone else will start to wonder, and I will not be safe once that happens. Don't you see?"

Queen Esraa's hands clenched into fists so hard her nails dug into her skin. Without another word, the queen lifted the cup and drank until it was finished. Taking a deep breath, she released her grip. "He has four sons, two he has all but forgotten exist; the other two are fighting for the throne after him, and still my life is in danger for an heir he does not need. Why?"

"Men are evil. Are you are just now noticing?"

"You and I are cousins, Bahiya."

"Maternal cousins," Bahiya reminded her. "Our houses and positions are *very* different."

"But half of our blood is the same. We were born on the same side, so tell me what I need to do," Queen Esraa whispered and leaned in. "Surely you know it better than anyone that I must live to become queen dowager and live the rest of my peacefully."

Everyone knew that. Even if the queen did not have a son, she would be considered an elder of the next king and, therefore, highly regarded and nearly impossible to be killed. The kingdom was full of horrors, but nothing was more important than respecting one's elders and ancestors. Rules Princess Bahiya knew were surely created by young men to protect themselves as old men and stay revered as dead men. "I understand you, my queen, and who does not know the king prefers to eat and sleep now in his old age than indulge in women? The king can barely make it up the stairs of his throne. Your head is in no danger. Hasina's condition does not change the fact that you are queen. You simply hate her."

"Is that so wrong? It was I who was supposed to go to Prince Aberash. Instead, I was given to . . ." Queen Esraa did not finish the words.

"You were chosen because Nérbua is bigger than Kéye—"

"In land mass, not population. Half of Nérbua is roaming lands for the elephants. The king does not need fucking elephants."

"I'll admit to not wanting a geography lesson at the moment."

"I'm saying her family did something—they must have. And now *my* life is in danger because of it? All the while, she lives happily with her sweet prince?"

"Again . . . he is sick."

"I do not care. She does not deserve it. So, cousin, how will you help me? Do not pretend like you can't."

Princess Bahiya bowed her head before the queen as she slowly saw the path to discipline her own enemy. "You overestimate me, my queen, but as your servant, I will do anything I can to help you."

Queen Esraa's eyes narrowed on her. "And what will that cost me?"

"Nothing, for as you said, we are cousins. And even if we weren't, you are queen. You serve the king, and my husband and I serve you. That is the order and is the way things ought to be. I fear I must not have shown you more respect. That can be the only explanation as to why even some maids have become so discourteous now." Princess Bahiya met Queen Esraa's gaze carefully.

"Who dares be insolent to you?"

"Not me . . . poor little Zikora." Princess Bahiya offered her a new cup of tea. "Apparently, my husband's new concubine had her maid insult the girl, demanding Zikora bow to Lady Cyrah. When Zikora refused, this maid went on to insult her in front of the other servants. Saying she was ill brought up and untamed."

"A maid speaking on a high noble's daughter? The girl is under my care, and this maid insults her raising, as if that doesn't also insult me?" The queen's eyes flared in anger. "Have you punished her?"

Princess Bahiya sighed as she held her tea. "I cannot. At least not now. The concubine has only just entered the place today, so how would it look if my first act was to reprimand her handmaid?

Everyone would say I am picking on her. Besides, you know Zikora. She does not care much for—"

"It does not matter what the girl cares for!" Queen Esraa snapped, making tight fists. "As you just said, there is an order, and this concubine clearly does not know her place in it. If she did, her handmaid would not dare speak as such. It seems, cousin, you need my help as well."

"No, my queen. This is beneath you. Let us focus on your issues. That is why you are here—"

The queen reached out, grabbing Princess Bahiya's hands. "If the men are evil, we should at least be kind to each other. I shall deal with this concubine."

"My queen—"

"Don't worry. I will not drag you into it. I'll make sure it is known I learned of her behavior from someone else. One of the other maids—"

"Zikora's nanny," Princess Bahiya replied gently. "She's very well respected by the other servants and never gossips. If they knew she told you, no one would be able to deny it."

Princess Bahiya watched as the queen nodded and slowly lifted the cup to her lips. Yes, it was important Queen Esraa survived, because she really would make the perfect queen dowager one day.

She was so easily . . . moved.

30

ZIKORA

Ahalon

"SZATU!"

Zikora called the man's name so loudly that he jumped and dropped a bucket of water on his head, nearly spilling it on the grass in the gardens.

"Must you yell my name every morning, Lady Zikora?" The man tiredly sighed as he lifted the bucket from his head and placed it down by the lavender bushes.

"Yes, or you won't talk to me," Zikora replied as she stepped up beside him and reached inside his bucket to take the ladle to help. But Szatu snatched it away angrily.

"How many times do I have to tell you that you are a lady, Lady Zikora? Talking to gardeners is beneath you, let alone trying to do their work. You should know the rules by now," he nagged, which he was quite good at.

"Everything is beneath me here. It's boring!" Zikora snatched the wooden ladle from his dirty hands, only for him to grab it back once more.

"Is that why you've come to terrorize me? Because you're bored?" Szatu said, filling the cup with water and stepping to the edge of the flower bed to pour the water inside.

"Yes, and because you always look lonely."

"Well, I am very much not lonely. In fact, I have all the friends I need here," Szatu said as he reached for more water.

Zikora glanced around the garden, where there was no one else there but them. "So you have no friends but me?"

"You are not a friend. My friend is the garden," Szatu stated as he leaned in to inspect a strange growth at the base of the flowers.

In the inner court, there were three jobs no one wished for— rodent catcher, commode cleaner, and garden keeper. They were the hardest, dirtiest, and smelliest jobs. So those positions were given to the least-liked servants at court. When Zikora first came, no servant was treated better than Szatu Osavadah, the royal messenger of her most gracious and humble majesty, Queen Nasera. But when she lost her head, all her trusted servants were either thrown out of the palace or given the most humiliating work.

"Well, you are my friend, Szatu," Zikora said as she reached into the bucket with her bare hands, making a cup and tossing the water onto the flowers.

"You will waste my water, Lady Zikora!" Szatu screeched in panic as he tried to shoo her away from his bucket. "Where is that temperamental handmaid of yours? She should not be letting you wander around the palace by yourself . . . and right now, of all times. Your nanny should have her ears. That girl is—"

"Why is right now bad to be wandering in the palace?" Zikora interrupted, causing Szatu to clamp his mouth shut and face the flowers again. So she stepped closer to him. "Szatu, is it about Prince Aberash? Do you know what happened to him?"

"I know nothing about anything other than the gardens," Szatu replied as he drew more water.

"You know everything about everything *except* the gardens. That's why algae are growing on these flowers," Zikora shot back.

He turned and gave her a confused look. "What? What do you mean algae?"

"Lavenders are drought plants. If you give them too much water, they drown and start to die."

Szatu looked at his ladle, then the flowers, and then back at her. "How do you know that?"

Zikora shrugged. "How do you *not* know after all this time?"

Szatu frowned at her for a moment before lifting his bucket and placing it back on his head, turning to leave. "Good day, Lady Zikora."

"Wait! You didn't tell me anything about Prince Aberash."

"Why would I know anything about Prince Aberash?"

Zikora ran until she was standing right in front of Szatu. She was now taller than him, so when she crossed her arms, she looked down at him. "I know you, so please tell me."

"Again, why would I know anything?"

Because he was a bad gardener, and normally, people who were bad at their jobs would be punished and given a new, worse job. Szatu should have been a rodent catcher by now, but he wasn't, so that meant someone was watching out for him. And while Zikora wasn't sure who yet, she was sure he was holding something back.

"Lady Zikora, the only thing I know is that you have no friends, can trust no one, and are better off bringing no attention to yourself. Focus on becoming a good and obedient young woman. Prince Aberash can take care of himself. Now, once again, good day—"

"*Zikora!*" Tuliza ran past Szatu so fast that the man lost balance and tipped the bucket of water on top of himself. Again.

"You—"

"Tuliza, watch out. You—"

"The queen is punishing that maid! You have to come!" Tuliza yelled in her face, grabbing Zikora's shoulders.

Zikora tilted her head to the side, not understanding why Tuliza was yelling. The queen punished a lot of people. "Why do I have to go for this?"

"The queen is punishing her because of you."

"Me? But I didn't do anything."

"Hibo is being punished because of what she said to you."

"Who is Hibo?"

Tuliza let out a deep sigh, hanging her head. "Lady Cyrah's maid, the one with her this morning who asked you to bow."

"Oh. Okay—wait! She's being punished for that?"

"Yes! The queen ordered the maid to be whipped thirty times, and the queen wants you there."

"Thirty times?" Zikora gasped. "That could kill her!"

"I know! That's why we have to go!" Tuliza grabbed Zikora's wrist and pulled her back the way she came.

"Bye, Szatu!" Zikora yelled as they started to run, breaking the rules again.

But like last time, no one was paying attention. All the petrified maids had moved toward the west side of the inner palace, making it easy for Tuliza and Zikora to know where to go.

It wasn't normal for the queen to oversee a punishment, nor for the punishment to be right outside a concubine's courtyard. But there she was, the maid from earlier, tied to an orange tree as two maids took turns hitting her back with switches. The queen stood on the third step before the doors beside Lady Cyrah, whose cheeks were sucked in from how tightly she clenched her teeth. And behind both of them was Nanny Urenna, her head down.

"Ah, there you are, Zikora. Come here," the queen called.

Slowly and carefully, Zikora walked like a lady into the center of the courtyard toward the sand-colored steps until she stood in front of the queen, and then Zikora curtsied.

"My queen."

"Your nanny let me know about this maid's rudeness to you this morning. Is it true?"

Her nanny? Her nanny never spoke to anyone unless she had to. Zikora looked to Nanny Urenna, but the woman did not lift her head.

"Zikora, I asked you a question. Was this maid rude to you today?" the queen asked again.

Zikora glanced over to Lady Cyrah, who was breathing slowly through her nose.

"She made a mistake, I think. She said I was to bow to Lady Cyrah. I—"

"She told you, the daughter of a high noble, a guest of the queen, *my guest* here at the palace, to bow to a concubine?" the queen asked Zikora, but she looked at Lady Cyrah. "What makes you so great, Lady Cyrah?"

Immediately, Lady Cyrah dropped to her knees. "Forgive us, my queen. My maid had forgotten where we were and still only saw me as a noble of the house of Grigah—"

"What makes the house of Grigah so great that a high noble would bow to you even if you were not a concubine? What lands do you govern? What armies do you have that you and your maid walk around so pompously?" the queen interrupted her. "If the Lord of

Winneba asks me why his daughter was insulted, am I supposed to explain you are from the house of *Grigah*?"

Lady Cyrah now fully folded herself upon the ground, her forehead upon the stone. "Forgive—"

"This is not your house, Lady Cyrah. This is the palace. My palace. We have an order here, and I do not care what you may have been before. What you are now is a lowly concubine. You and your maid will respect your betters. Resume the punishment! May this always serve as your reminder, Lady Cyrah."

Zikora wanted to speak up and tell them to stop, but that feeling in her told her not to, that speaking here would bring unwanted attention to herself. She did not want to watch the punishment, but the feeling told her she had to. That she mustn't shy away from painful things, because that made her weak. She wished she could describe this feeling, but it felt simply like a push or pull in her mind whenever she was faced with choices. When she was about to make a bad choice, it felt as if strings were pulling her back. When something was good, she felt like she was being shoved forward. She did not like it. But because of her baba she listened to it.

Zikora turned and watched as the maids began to beat Hibo so badly that oranges fell from the tree.

Every day at the palace felt long to Zikora, but some days, the ones that were full of bad things, felt longer than others, and today had to be the longest in a while.

By the time Hibo's punishment was finished, the medicine women had to peel Hibo's clothing from her bloody flesh with tools. The switches used in the palace were bonded with shards of black glass. The pain of it was clearly so unbearable that Hibo wet herself at the fifth whip and then lost consciousness by the tenth, only to reawaken screaming by the twentieth and to lose consciousness again. But not even then did they stop. The queen said thirty, so thirty times they beat her in front of all of the maids and servants of the inner palace. And after her apology wasn't accepted, Lady Cyrah could do nothing but bow her head, kneeling and waiting. Zikora looked up to the upper level of the palace, the balconies that commanded a view of the courtyard, to find Princess Bahiya looking down on them like birds did flies. She saw the small grin on the princess's lips, noticed by no one else because they were all so taken by Hibo's screams again.

It was only when Princess Bahiya glanced at Zikora that the smile disappear and the princess walked away.

"THEY PUNISHED HIBO TO HUMILIATE Lady Cyrah," Zikora whispered to Urenna as she laid her head on her nanny's lap. Zikora was supposed to go to her classes, but after watching the punishment, her head began to hurt, and the queen allowed her to return to her rooms for the day. "They kill servants here when they cannot kill each other, just to prove a point."

"The medicine women say Hibo will live, my lady," Nanny Urenna replied as she fanned air onto Zikora gently with crane feathers.

"But she will not be able to move, and the skin on her back is completely gone," Tuliza added, sitting beside Zikora, holding out a bowl of green grapes and peeled oranges for her. But the oranges just made Zikora think of Hibo's screams and the proud grin on Princess Bahiya's face.

Zikora shook her head, turning over onto her other side.

"Why do bad things keep happening to people here?" Zikora asked as she looked at her mother's bracelet on her wrist. "It wasn't like this in Winneba."

"Bad things happen to people everywhere, Lady Zikora, even in Winneba. Just because you never saw it does not mean it did not happen," Zikora's nanny replied.

"When do you think we can go home?" Zikora whispered. She was tired of people fighting, crying, and getting sick. She wanted to see her family, to eat in the great hall with everyone, and to laugh again.

"I want to go too," Tuliza said as she leaned against Nanny Urenna. "I want to eat my mom's cakes again."

At the mention of cake, Zikora sat up and looked at her. "Your mom bakes cakes? What kind?"

Nanny Urenna giggled, brushing Zikora's head. "You turn your head at fruits but sit up for cake? You can't live on sweets alone."

"Has anyone tried?" Zikora shot back.

"The king looks like he has. That's why he looks like this," Tuliza said, puffing her cheeks out to make them round.

"Tuliza! Shh!" Nanny Urenna knocked the top of her nose. "Have you learned nothing today? Do you want the queen to take your tongue?"

"I was only kidding—"

"Joke about anyone but those above you! You too, Lady Zikora." Nanny Urenna gave them both a stern glare. "We will one day get to go home, and on that day, I want both your parents to see that you returned to them unharmed. The palace is tense right now, especially with Prince Aberash's condition. I want you both on your best behavior all the time. If I see either of you running again, I'll have you both . . . do . . . chores."

"I already do chores," Tuliza replied as she ate her orange.

"I'd rather do chores than go to classes," Zikora said, making her nanny grab both of their ears.

"Ow!" they both cried.

"Promise me you will follow the rules," Nanny Urenna ordered.

"Promise! Promise!" Zikora squealed, and when her nanny let go, Zikora rubbed her earlobe. "I thought you wanted to return us home unharmed. I feel like my ears will fall off soon."

"Don't worry. They won't. Sleep heals everything for you, so come take a nap." Nanny Urenna patted her lap.

"Aren't we too old for naps?" Tuliza asked. However, Zikora lay back down happily. "Zikora, it's the middle of the afternoon!"

Zikora pretended to snore, but soon enough she actually felt herself drifting off. She liked to sleep, because in her dreams she saw Winneba: her family, the giants, and the cranes as they soared on the wind. She could smell the rain as it fell upon the forest all around them. Each time she closed her eyes, it was like she had traveled back home—except now.

Now everything was dark.

Zikora, the darkness called out to her.

She turned but saw nothing.

Zikora.

Zikora stretched out her hands but could not see who was speaking. It was like she had become blind, and no matter how much she blinked or walked, she could see nothing. Zikora screamed into the darkness, and it echoed.

"Zikora!"

When Zikora's eyes snapped open, Nanny Urenna was above her, staring down at her with eyes wide and her face panicked. "Are you all right?"

Glancing to the left and right of her nanny, Zikora saw her room.

"Tuliza, go get her a cup of water," Nanny Urenna ordered as she helped Zikora sit upright. "Zikora? Look at me. It's okay. You just had a nightmare."

"Here," Tuliza said as she handed Zikora the cup.

Carefully, Zikora drank the water, coughing slightly.

"Tuliza, I think she is getting a fever. Go fetch a basin of cold water."

Zikora.

Zikora glanced back up at Nanny Urenna to answer this time when she called, but her nanny wasn't looking at Zikora. She was still speaking to Tuliza, so the voice that called wasn't Nanny Urenna's.

Zikora.

Zikora looked over her shoulder as if there were a person there, but there was nothing but her own reflection in the mirror on her writing table. Zikora saw herself in her nanny's arms, her own round, brown face covered in a light sheen of sweat, her curls sticking to her skin. Everything looked the same in the reflection as it did in life, except her reflection was talking.

Finally, Zikora. You can hear us.

31
NANNY URENNA

Ahalon

ONE OF ZIKORA'S GREATEST TRAITS WAS HER resilience and joy. No matter what they had encountered over the last three years, Zikora never let it bring her down for longer than a day. They had witnessed the death of so many, from a queen to several maids, their bodies floating in the ponds or hanging from the ceiling, guards being beaten until all the air had left their lungs, yet this tiny little child managed to wake up each morning with a smile on her face. Nanny Urenna had not a clue how Zikora managed to do it, but she was nevertheless grateful each time she saw Zikora's wide grin and heard her voice prattling on about food or what game she'd played. Even Tuliza could not manage it, and oftentimes, Nanny Urenna had found Tuliza crying at night, calling out for her parents in her dreams. Though in the morning, Tuliza would pretend she was tough and smart, mostly because she did not wish Zikora to know.

In all honesty, both girls were the people who gave Nanny Urenna hope in this cruel, unforgiving palace. And that hope inspired courage in her. If girls of eleven could manage to stay positive in spite of so much, how could Nanny Urenna, a girl of twenty-six, buckle under the weight of fear?

Each day, Nanny Urenna told herself, *So long as they are all right, I am all right.* But the problem was that Zikora was not all right and had not been for several days now.

The once unstoppable, fearless, and loud child, always running from place to place, refused to get up from her bed. Zikora stayed curled in a ball, her hands over her ears and the blankets over her head as though trying to hide from something. But Nanny Urenna was not sure what Zikora was hiding from or how to help her. When Nanny Urenna asked her, Zikora would merely mutter. When Nanny Urenna tried to get Zikora to eat, Zikora would take only a few bites before having to lie back down again. Nanny Urenna had told the palace she was a little ill, which the medicine woman confirmed, saying it was a fever. However, days had passed, and now the queen was concerned.

"What is wrong with her? Why is she still ill? She must be well before Prince Effiom's return, for the king will expect us all to be in the throne room to see him," Queen Esraa said as she leaned over Zikora's sleeping and trembling form.

"Her fever still has not broken for some reason despite our treatment—"

"Then obviously you need a new treatment! Find a way to heal her, or I promise, you will never heal anything ever again," Queen Esraa commanded, interrupting the medicine woman.

Nanny Urenna did not lift her head, not daring to look at any of them. She stayed low and uninquisitive to anything or anyone except Zikora. Sometimes she even sought to breathe less so they would forget she existed, and it often worked, especially with Queen Esraa.

The woman came, inspected, and yelled at a few others before finally taking her leave. It was only then Nanny Urenna could breathe again. However, just as soon as Queen Esraa had left their rooms and Nanny Urenna moved closer to Zikora, she heard one of the maids at the doors.

"Crown Princess Hasina," the maid announced.

Immediately, Nanny Urenna moved back into place and bowed her head, seeing only the colorful strips at the bottom of Princess Hasina's skirt.

"Blessings and good evening, Princess Hasina," Nanny Urenna said in unison with everyone else in the room.

"All of you, go. I shall watch over Lady Zikora," Princess Hasina said to them.

Nanny Urenna did not feel comfortable leaving Zikora but did not dare disobey, so she started to take her leave when the princess called out to her.

"Urenna, you may stay."

"Yes, princess," Nanny Urenna replied, head still down.

"Lift your head."

"I dare not—"

"That is an order."

And so, without a choice, she was forced to lift her head and look into the deep brown face of the crown princess, who knelt at Lady Zikora's bedside, the rings around her neck matching the ones on her left wrist, the same hand she placed on her pregnant stomach.

"Whenever I see you, Urenna, I always hope my children will have such a smart and dedicated nanny."

"I do not deserve such praise."

"Oh, but you do. It is not easy to dedicate your life and future to another woman's child, whether they are royal, high noble, or not. Since your arrival, you have lived and breathed for the sake of your lady and her handmaid. It is deeply commendable, so I can only imagine how you must resent us for putting her life at risk."

At this, Nanny Urenna's eyes widened. "What do you mean, my princess? Putting whose life at risk?"

"Hers." Princess Hasina nodded to Zikora, who shivered once more. "To normal people, she is nothing but a kind and beautiful young girl. But to the royals and the nobles, she is a tool, a valuable asset, or a great weapon simply because of who her father is."

"My princess, forgive me for being so unenlightened and dull, but I do not understand your meanings here," Nanny Urenna said, and bowed her head back down. However, the crown princess merely lifted her head back up.

"Do you also not understand she has been poisoned?"

"What!" Nanny Urenna exclaimed and quickly moved to Zikora, forgetting her decorum, to place her hands on the small girl's head. "No, the medicine woman said—"

"That she had a fever that won't break . . . similar to Prince Aberash," Princess Hasina whispered softly, reaching over to touch the curls of Zikora's hair. "They wish to get rid of both him and her."

"She is but a child!"

"Did you not hear me? To you, she is a child. To others, she is a Nnamani and the daughter of the second most powerful man in the kingdom. Hurting her will hurt him."

"Hurting her will cause a war," Nanny Urenna said sternly, holding Zikora tightly to herself, the child's body giving her bravery to speak back with such convection. "No one would risk that. She is better here as a hostage, to be used against the Lord of Winneba, than dead."

"So, you *are* much smarter than you seem." Princess Hasina smiled. "Good, then listen carefully. Prince Effiom isn't trying to kill her. He's using her to get the Lord of Winneba to come here so he can kill *him*."

"Kill . . . kill the Lord of Winneba? No—"

"Do you believe Lord Winneba will stay there if he hears his precious daughter is deathly ill—which he will, once word spreads— and she is not at the banquet at Prince's Effiom's return?"

"He will not come. Lady Nnamani will—"

"Then his wife and his daughter will be held hostage here. He will not send another son either, not after already losing one. No, he will come himself, hoping his title will protect him. And then Prince Effiom will kill him. My husband discovered this plot, and now he lies dying as well. This is not a game or tale. We are balancing on a delicate rope for our lives here."

Nanny Urenna did not know what to say, so she stared at Princess Hasina in horror, rocking Zikora gently in her arms.

"I know you are scared, but I won't let anyone kill my husband or Lady Zikora. You know he is very fond of her, right?"

"I know," Nanny Urenna whispered. "She likes him too."

Princess Hasina reached over and placed her hand on Nanny Urenna's. "Then you will help me, correct?"

"Help you, my princess? How can I, of all people, help you?"

"By exposing what Prince Effiom has done . . ." Princess Hasina squeezed her hand. "We have to stop him, and right now, you are the only person I trust to help me with this."

Nanny Urenna looked down at Zikora once more. "Is there anything we can do to help her? She's been in pain."

"The antidote is with Princess Bahiya. If you listen to me, we can get it and save them both. Will you help me?"

"Yes."

For although Urenna wasn't brave, for this little girl, she could be. She would protect Lady Zikora with her life if she had to.

32
PRINCESS HASINA

Ahalon

WHEN PRINCESS HASINA WAS CHOSEN TO BE Prince Aberash's new wife after his first had died in childbirth, her father, who rarely spoke to her or any woman, even his own wife, said to her that nothing else mattered but staying alive and bearing a son. He did not expect her to write letters back home, give honors to her tribe, or show favor to their kin. Her father said ethics, integrity, and compassion were things for scholars and historians to discuss, not women.

Princess Hasina had managed to stay alive all these years but struggled to bear a son, so with her vast knowledge of medicines and poisons—a skill she'd learned from her mother, a former medicine woman—she made sure no one else within the palace could do so either. That was her way of surviving. Now that she was finally going to bear a child, she would not stop. She would make sure she lived to see her husband and son on the throne. She would not let

Princess Bahiya get rid of her as easily as she had gotten rid of Prince Aberash's first wife, and Prince Aberash would not be brought down so easily.

"No one is listening or nearby. You should not lie down so much, for it shall ruin your back," Princess Hasina whispered to the man, seemingly asleep on their bed in the dim light of her private rooms.

It took a moment before the corner of his lips turned up in a slight smile, and he finally turned his head to look at her with his light-colored amber eyes.

"Instead of telling me to get up, you should be lying down."

"It is better for the child if I stay moving often," Princess Hasina replied.

"They say the women of Kéye can give birth while running. Is that true?" Prince Aberash snickered as he sat up.

"Of course it is not. However, we are not as weak as your women here who die," the princess replied harshly.

Prince Aberash raised an eyebrow, and he extended his hand toward his wife to bring her into his lap on the bed. "Are you insulting the women of the capital in general or my first wife in particular?"

Princess Hasina did not answer, reaching up to touch his cheek, but he pulled his head back, making her giggle. "Does my prince fear I will poison him?"

"Haven't you already?"

"Was it not by your command?" Princess Hasina whispered back, placing her hand on his face. "I would have preferred a method that would not put you in such pain."

"Nothing in this world is gained without pain," Prince Aberash replied, putting his hand on his wife's stomach. "Women should understand this most of all. Just like bearing a child, bearing a king-dom brings first agony, then joy."

"I look forward to the days of joy. These days are not so pleas-ant," Princess Hasina replied before resting her head on her hus-band's chest.

Prince Aberash was silent for a moment before asking, "How is Zikora?"

"Strangely enough, she is not in as much agony as I thought she would be. She is a strong girl—one would think she is Kéye."

"You have an affinity for her."

"Don't you?"

Once more, Prince Aberash was silent. Because he did. However, he had a greater affinity for power and the throne. And for staying alive. So if he had to cause a little girl pain to get what he wanted, he would do it without guilt.

"Prince Effiom must be blessed with luck. Each time I figure out how to throw him out of the capital, he crawls his way back in with some greater victory. I never thought he'd actually find the boy. I wanted him to roam the earth for years more, but he has, and with his influence and the boy gone, the king will be elated to move on and reestablish the might of the throne."

"That does not mean he will do so with Prince Effiom. The king is the sun. He wishes to have no other light cast shadows on him. Prince Effiom does not know his place. I doubt the king will praise him much."

"It is not the king alone who makes the kingdom but the people. And Prince Effiom is becoming a hero in their eyes. I cannot have that either. Zikora is important because she is so innocent. You've done well spreading the word of how kind and generous she is to the masses. Though they have not seen her, they care for her too."

Which meant that if any harm were to fall upon little Zikora by the hand of Prince Effiom, many within the capital would see him as cruel, and the Lord of Winneba would be enraged. The king would have no choice but to punish him severely to prevent a war. Then Prince Effiom would not be a hero but a traitor.

"Don't worry. The maid believed every word I said and will get it done. Everything else is already in place."

"How lucky I am to have such a wife," Prince Aberash whispered, kissing her forehead.

How lucky, indeed.

33

ZIKORA

Ahalon

THE DARKNESS HAD TURNED TO SWIRLS OF colors, and the colors all had different voices. There were so many it made Zikora feel as if the world were spinning, and when she tried to make it stop, she heard one voice louder than all the rest.

Zikora?

"Baba!" Zikora called out to his voice, and when she did, the darkness was gone, and all around her was green. She heard the song of the crane as it flew over the water, which reflected the sun.

You wish to name your future daughter Zikora after grandmother?

She turned once more to find her father's voice, but when she looked, the man she saw did not look like the father she remembered—he looked younger. Much younger. Even his braided hair was shorter and kept in a bun with the sides shaved like soldiers did, and beside him was a man she did not know. They were both sitting around a campfire, eating fish, both shirtless and their trousers wet as they had clearly caught their meal from the river.

Yes, so all men will run in fear at the sight of her too, the other man said, and Zikora watched as her father laughed loudly.

You are not even yet married, let alone talk of being anyone's baba. *Besides, sons would be more important.*

You're our next lord, brother, so your wife can bear the family sons.

"Brother?" Zikora whispered, and clasped her hand over her mouth, not wanting her baba to see her spying. All of a sudden, she heard a chuckle from beside her.

This is the past, Zikora. They can't hear you.

She turned to see the man who was beside her baba, but older and dressed in a kaftan of white—the dress of death. His braids were free, not tied back, but long down past his waist, with beads of gold.

"Am I dead?" Zikora asked him.

Did I not just say this is the past, Zikora? Why would you be dead?

"Why would you be talking to me dressed like that?" Zikora pointed to his clothes.

Because I am dead.

"Now I'm confused!"

He chuckled and bent down before her. *I bet you are, my little niece. I bet you are.*

"Niece . . . so you are my uncle? But you are dead. And this is your memory, but I am not dead," Zikora repeated, and he nodded.

Yes, exactly.

"So why am I here?"

There are so many answers to that question that I am not sure how to reply.

"I thought the dead knew all?"

The dead only know the past, and the past is vast. Much too vast for the mind of such a little child. This is why one must be grown before receiving the Blessing of Winneba, her uncle said, reaching up and dusting off her cheek.

She was confused. "That's the ceremony for all the lords of Winneba, isn't it?"

It is the ceremony for the Kings *of* Winneba . . . *and now the* Queen *of* Winneba.

"Queen? Baba is Lord of Winneba. There is no queen there."

Yes, there is, her uncle said, and once more the world around her shifted . . . the green of the trees was gone, along with the cranes, the river, the sun, and the fish. All that remained were the two brothers. There, the baba she remembered stood . . .

And drove a dagger into his brother's stomach.

"*Baba!*" Zikora screamed at him, but she could only watch as he sobbed, holding the brother he killed until everything froze once more.

This is my last memory, her uncle said as he walked over to a dome of ash. *Your father killed me so I could pass the blessing on to you.*

"Me?" Zikora whispered and looked at the ash. "I'm in there?"

It's only been a few years. Have you forgotten?

She thought back to her father throwing her into the prison and making her drink something. But she could not remember well, and even what she could did not make sense to her.

"Why did you have to pass on the blessing? You weren't Lord of Winneba."

I was Zeikel Nnamani, true Lord and King *of* Winneba. *Your father was—is still—an impostor.*

"You're lying!"

The dead do not lie, and neither do your eyes, Zeikel said to her. *There is much you need to know, Zikora, but now is not the time for me or the rest of the ancestors to teach you. You have to get up, recover, and protect your people.*

"Recover from what?"

The poison in you, Zeikel said, stretching his hand out to her.

Zikora stared at her uncle's hand and then her baba, still frozen in agony. She did not understand, but she had that feeling, that push inside her. He was trying to help her, so she took his hand, and he brought her close before throwing her into the mound of ash.

"Ah! Ah!" Zikora coughed and tried to get it out of her face and throat.

"Zikora!" Tuliza called out, hugging her as Zikora continued to brush the ash off her face. However, nothing fell off since there was no ash, though she could still taste the grit in her mouth. "Thank all that is holy! We have been so worried!"

"Huh?" Zikora finally met Tuliza's gaze and saw that her eyes had tears in them. "Tuliza, were you crying? Why?"

"I wasn't crying," Tuliza said, despite the sniffs she was taking to cover up her tears, "but you were dying!"

"Dying? Of what?"

"A fever, my lady."

She turned to see a medicine woman offering her a bowl of something. Tuliza took it and the spoon to feed Zikora, holding them carefully.

"You have been asleep for several days, Zikora. No one knew what was wrong." Tuliza lifted the hot milk in the spoon for Zikora to drink.

Zikora opened her mouth, but she heard a voice in her head say, *Poison. You were poisoned, Zikora.*

"Was I poisoned?" Zikora asked, taking a sip from the spoon. As soon as she swallowed, her whole body twisted. That was not milk, and it did not taste good.

"Poison? No, my lady. Why would you think that?" the medicine woman asked.

No, Zikora, they cannot know you that you have found them out.

"The way Tuliza looks and is acting, I thought that had to be the reason." Zikora laughed to cover her accusation, pretending instead to tease Tuliza, but Tuliza did not say anything, just tried to offer her another bit of that wretched milk.

"Yes, your handmaid cares for you deeply," the medicine woman said. I will tell the queen you have recovered, and at the best time, for you shall be able to go to the banquet tonight and see Prince Effiom's return." The medicine woman rose and bowed to Zikora before taking her leave.

"What's wrong?" Zikora whispered to Tuliza as Zikora refused the milk again.

"How did you know you were poisoned?" Tuliza whispered back to her.

"Didn't the medicine woman say it was just a fever?"

Tuliza put the bowl down. "She's lying. Nanny Urenna wanted me to know just in case something happened to her. She said you were poisoned on orders of Prince Effiom, and I must watch over you closely."

"If something happened to her? Why would something happen to her?" Then she thought some more, and something even more pressing came to her. "And why would Prince Effiom try to poison me?"

"I don't know, but she's been close to Princess Hasina lately. I think the princess told her about it, and now they are trying to help you."

It's a trap, Zikora. Protect your people, the voice whispered.

Zikora quickly got up, knocking over the bowl as she ran from the room.

"Zikora!"

In Zikora's mind, she saw a memory of her own as she ran. But not just a memory—a feeling that gave her so much more insight than what she should have remembered. Like how she knew who Lady Cyrah was, having only her met her once. This memory was of Princess Hasina on the day Zikora had run to see Prince Aberash after hearing he was sick. Princess Hasina had pressed her hand on her cheek, and she smelled like *Melispuroa*, a small poisonous orange flower found in the fields of Kéye. Those who grew up there were unaffected by it, as they had been exposed to it all their lives, so it could be made into an oil, put on their hands, and spread to another without them ever knowing. But now she knew. Just as she knew Prince Effiom did not poison Zikora. Princess Hasina did.

So whatever the princess needed her nanny for could not be good. Zikora saw them both walking, Princess Hasina in front, her belly exposed to the world, and Zikora's nanny a few paces behind, holding a basin of water.

"Nanny Urenna!"

"Zikora?" her nanny exclaimed, dropping the basin and running to her. Nanny Urenna pulled Zikora into her arms tightly. "Oh, thank all the world and ancestors, too, that you are awake!"

"I am," Zikora said as she hugged her back, but she looked directly at Princess Hasina, who stared at her with wide eyes.

"Let me see you." Her nanny knelt and looked her over. "Why are you up? You should be resting still. Have you eaten? Look at your face. It has gotten so slim."

"Don't worry. I'll eat so much today, and it will be round again by tomorrow!"

Nanny Urenna giggled, nodding as she touched Zikora's hair. "We should quickly go wash this and style it for—"

Nanny Urenna froze in horror, and Zikora was sure she was in trouble, but Princess Hasina came to Zikora with a smile.

"Lady Zikora, how happy I am that you are well."

When Princess Hasina reached out to touch Zikora's face once more, Zikora stepped back and away, which made the princess raise an eyebrow.

Do not let her know you know, Zikora, the voice reminded her.

"Blessing and good morning to you, Princess Hasina!" Zikora said with a large smile. "Your stomach is bigger! Oh, is Prince Aberash awake yet? Can I see him?"

"My lady, please be calm. You only just recovered," Nanny Urenna said gently. "My princess, please may I go tend to her?"

"Of course, that is why you are here. We shall speak later," Princess Hasina replied, turning to walk back toward her side of the inner courtyard.

Zikora waited and watched as she left.

"Zikora, come. Let's—"

"Quickly, you must tell me what she wanted you to do," Zikora said, looking at her nanny with seriousness, something Nanny Urenna was not accustomed to seeing with Zikora. "Urenna, you have to tell me so we can stop it."

Once more, her nanny bent down to her level. "Zikora, what do you mean—"

"It was her. Not Prince Effiom. What did she make you do? Tell me *now*. It's an order."

Nanny Urenna's eyes widened, and she shook her head, confused. "She told me to beg the queen the next time she came to check on you for Princess Bahiya's sacred incense. That it would help you recover before the banquet."

"Come on. We must have it returned to Princess Bahiya quickly," Zikora said as she pulled Nanny Urenna's hand, forcing her to follow Zikora.

"Zikora, no running!" Nanny Urenna tried to tell her, but Zikora ignored her. It was far more important they reached Princess Bahiya's rooms.

Zikora could hear the voices talking again in her head. It hurt, but Zikora didn't let it stop her, and she wasn't scared of them because she now knew they were trying to help her. It was the Blessing of Winneba, and it had been trying to protect her this whole time. All the feelings, all the times she just knew things without ever learning or even seeing them before. It was the ancestors—her ancestors and her uncle. She'd always missed home, but now she could see a part of Winneba was with her. Now that she knew it, she wanted to do what her uncle said and protect her people. Nanny Urenna and Tuliza were her people.

"There you are!" the queen hollered when Zikora and Nanny Urenna reentered their rooms, forcing them to come to a quick stop. "I had just gotten word that you have recovered. I came all the way here only to find you running around in your whites once more, Lady Zikora! Do you not know how much trouble you've caused everyone? Is when you are sick the only way for you to be still?"

The queen gave Zikora no chance to answer as she continued on and on with her lecture. However, Zikora's eyes went to the iron incense burner in the shape of a firebird with one red and one blue jewel for eyes. A light-colored smoke came slowly out of its mouth.

"Are you listening to me, Lady Zikora?"

"Yes, my queen. I am sorry," Zikora said, moving to kneel when the queen pointed her finger at her.

"No! You are not to kneel and waste any more of your strength. You are to rest and prepare for this evening." The queen's eyes were hard. "You are not to trouble us any further, do you understand?"

"Yes, my queen—"

"Make sure to remind all the palace that none are to cheer for the prince until the king does so," the queen said, already speaking to her handmaid as she moved to exit the room.

"My queen!" Zikora quickly called out.

"What?"

Zikora pointed to the incense burner. "This should be returned to Princess Bahiya's room."

The queen looked at the burner, completely unconcerned by its existence. "No, it seems to have worked on you. I shall allow you to use it one more night so you may remain strong."

"Thank you, my queen, but I heard Prince Effiom obtained it especially for his wife, and she loves it dearly. Should he see it was taken from her, he may think Princess Bahiya has been unfairly forced to give up her things and grow angry."

The queen stared at the burner once more, a frown on her lips. "I do not understand all the fuss over this thing, but very well. Return it to Princess Bahiya."

Zikora tried not to release the deep breath she was holding as she watched the queen's maid pick up the burner. Then, all of a sudden, the sound of drums came thundering through the wall. Hundreds of drummers were stationed around the city to warn of an attack or a celebration, depending on how the drums were played. It was clear this was a celebration.

"They are already here! And I am not prepared! We must hurry! Move now!" the queen ordered, and she and her maids rushed from the room.

Zikora let out a deep breath and sank to the floor once the queen and the burner were gone.

"Zikora!" Nanny Urenna and Tuliza rushed to her.

"I'm fine!" Zikora replied, opening her eyes and looking up at the gold on the ceiling. "Everything is fine now."

"Zikora, I do not understand. What is going on with you? What did you say Princess Hasina did?" Nanny Urenna asked her.

Zikora looked up at their faces, trying to think of how to explain that the voices in her head, the ones that always made her feel sick, were a blessing, and they warned her of Princess Hasina's trap. She could still hear them speaking in her mind now.

Princess Hasina wished to leave poison in the burner.

The firebird burner is specially crafted so that it is difficult for anyone but its owner to know how to open it.

If Princess Hasina knew how to open it, she would have waited until this evening and placed poison in while you recovered.

She truly did not wish to harm you, only frame Bahiya and Effiom.

She'd have exposed the poison when the king inquired as to why you were not at the banquet.

She'd have said it was the same poison used for Prince Aberash.

It was a very simple plot, for why would she harm her own husband or you?

The voices went on and on, explaining, and Zikora smacked her forehead, hoping to get them to be quiet so she could think too.

"Zikora, you are worrying us," Tuliza said, forcing Zikora to sit up.

"I can't explain, but will you just trust me?" Zikora said, and it was then her stomach growled. "And please feed me!"

"Sometimes you are so odd, but I am glad you are all right." Nanny Urenna hugged Zikora, and Tuliza moved to get away, but Nanny Urenna pulled her in as well, holding them both tightly. "Don't worry. Now that the last Mukundi is gone, we will finally be able to go home."

But the voices in Zikora said in unison, *They won't free you that easily.* She did not wish to hear or believe that.

This is not over, Zikora. You must be careful.

They will not give up if this plan fails.

Tell your nanny to run. She must leave. They may still try to use her—

"*Be quiet!*" Zikora slammed her hands on her ears, and the voices were gone, just like that. Finally.

"Zikora?" Tuliza called again, concern still on her face.

"I am just hungry!" Zikora lied and smiled at them. "Everything is okay now. I promise."

34

KHALIL

Ahalon

THE WALLS AROUND THE CAPITAL WERE TALLER than thirty men standing on one another's shoulders, and when they passed through the gates, rose petals fell from the sky like rain, falling from a height that seemed impossible to Khalil. All around him, jubilation came from men, women, and children. It even felt like the animals were cheering Prince Effiom. He had slaughtered a village and made men slaves and women whores. Prince Effiom had killed Khalil's family and butchered his sister. He didn't do any of it for them, but solely for his own gain. And yet the people cheered as though the prince were some great hero. Khalil could barely stomach it. He gripped the reins of the horse he rode and glared at the back of the capital champion's head as he waved to them.

"Is there a reason why your face is so bitter?" Commander Khalaf asked Khalil from his left. As a Rausi, Khalil was allowed to sit third flank behind the prince and beside his brother, though he clearly stood out for being a boy and the only one not in armor.

"It's loud," Khalil replied. This had the added bonus of actually being true. Besides, he was still taking in the sight of the city where hundreds of brick homes seemingly stuck together went all the way up the hillside, and at the very top of the hill, behind more walls, was the palace with red roof tiles and a white pyramid in the center with a tip made of gold that reflected the sun's light. The streets were narrow and made even more so by the crowds of people on each side.

"We love you, Prince Effiom! Blessings to you, Commander Rausi!" a few women cried out in the highest of voices, making the weirdest of faces as they waved to the men around him.

"Is my daughter not beautiful, Commander Rausi? You may have her!" a man yelled, shoving his daughter to the front of the line.

"She is beautiful, Khalaf. Are you in need of a concubine?" Prince Effiom looked back, laughing.

Was she beautiful or pitiful? Her father was trying to offer her as if she were an animal, no better than a goat on the side of a street, Khalil thought.

"I am not in need, though it seems my brother is not used to such attention."

"Is that so?" Prince Effiom shifted his face to Khalil and laughed. "Yes, he does seem shocked. What say you, Khalil? Would you like a young lady? You are a hero! Just point to the one you want, and she is yours to play with."

"I'd rather play with swords," Khalil replied.

"In this city, I promise you can find a lady who plays with those too," the prince said, and Khalil could only scrunch his face in confusion. This only made Prince Effiom laugh harder before he refocused on the crowd.

Khalil ignored him and glanced back at the long march of soldiers behind them instead. The wagon pulling his mother was in the center of the procession, so he could not see beyond it, and he could not see the men at the very end of the line, the men of Kazera. He hadn't seen Ashon in days, but he was sure that since they wished to gift him to the king, Ashon would not be hurt. Khalil still did not like the fact that each time the troops marched, they were so far away. He should at least have to face the horror he inflicted on them.

Khalil would have stared longer had he not met the eyes of Mbwa, who was a few men down. Mbwa gestured for Khalil to turn around, so he did. There was no use checking right now. However, this welcome was taking far too long, and they were riding far too slowly. Khalil did not care for any of these people. If they cheered for monsters, they were monsters too.

It took them nearly thirty minutes before they reached the second gates of the palace. And once there, ten guards dressed in dark-red armor were waiting before the sun emblem.

"Who stands before the gates of the sun king, the great Zenzele?" the first man called out, and Khalil had no idea why they needed to ask such a question.

"It is I, Prince Effiom, son of the sun king and servant of the great Zenzele!" Prince Effiom called back to them with pride.

The men cheered behind him.

"Make way for our prince!" the same soldier yelled before they moved apart, and the gates opened, the emblem of the sun splitting down the middle as they did.

Once more, Khalil glanced back, and when he did, he noticed the wagon with his mother was not coming forward.

"My mother—"

"Non-royal concubines are not allowed within the palace. Now, sit straight, as all eyes are upon us. Do not forget what you were taught," Khalaf replied. On their journey back to the capital, his brother instructed Mbwa to teach him "royal manners." They were not that different from what he remembered as a boy. But there were still a lot of things he was not clear on, especially the rules involving women.

When Khalil faced forward once more, he saw the men all in different-colored robes, some dark red, some deep blue, and others purple. Mbwa had said the hierarchy in the capital was always determined by jewels and clothing, and now seeing it in person Khalil was reminded of his grandfather. When he had told him he would be foolish for going to Ahalon after the slaughtering of his family, he did not understand it then. Now he did. Everyone here dressed luxuriously in bright bold colors. Their skin was sparkling clean. He noticed even those in the capital who did not dress as colorfully still seemed cleaner than those in Kazera. Had he come then, he would have clearly stuck out.

When Prince Effiom and Khalaf got off their horses, Khalil quickly made sure to get off his as well. Then, quietly, under the watchful eye of all the old men who waited on the stairs leading up to the highest building within the courtyard, they climbed the stairs into the pyramid.

Once inside, Khalil finally knew why the king had taxed the kingdom to near death. It wasn't because he wanted them all to become slaves. It was so he could sit inside a pyramid of gold. Gold lined every inch, every corner of the walls, and the ceiling too. And it was not merely plastered but carved, engraved with all the images of kings of the Zenzele dynasty. The only place not covered in gold was the ground, which was painted with a map of the whole world. The king had put the world at his feet, right under his throne, which was a massive chair shaped like a rising sun with nine rays of light. On both sides of the throne were basins of open fire.

It was all ridiculously ugly to Khalil, but none of it could compare to the ugliness of the short, white-bearded man dressed in yellow robes, with red beads around his neck, his brown face covered in small back spots and a crease in his forehead, his hands long and wrinkled, each one with a different ring of gold. He wore a crown, also in gold, that was taller than his head, stacked like a pile of bread rolls on top of each other.

Khalil was surprised he could keep his head up under such weight.

"My blessing to you, Your Majesty," Prince Effiom called. "May your glory shine upon us like the sun does all the earth!" The prince bent the knee, as did Khalil's brother, their heads bowed down, so Khalil did the same, as Khalaf had made him practice twice every day on their journey here. He hated having to do this, but since he hated so much already, it seemed the least of his worries.

Or one more thing to add to the tally when I get my revenge.

"Is it my glory or yours? I cannot tell from the way in which the people call your name in the streets."

"It is always and forever yours, my king," Prince Effiom replied. He still did not get up, which meant Khalil could not rise either.

"Tell me, O hero, what has become of the last Mukundi?" the king asked.

"The boy is dead, but it is not I who can claim his life, my king, but the boy behind me, for he is the one who killed the last Mukundi. He is the hero of Kazera, yet none has uttered his name."

Khalil frowned. This was a lot of praise attributed to him, but it did not feel as if it were an honor. It felt like he was being used as a shield.

"This boy? Who is he? What is his name?"

"Introduce yourself, boy," Prince Effiom said to him.

"Yes. Lift your face so I may see who stole my son's glory."

Khalil lifted his head and looked at the king as he announced who he was. "I am Khalil Rausi."

"Rausi? General, you have another son?"

Khalil had heard many tales of the Great General—that he was a fierce warrior, a grotesque figure, and the bringer of death and destruction to all who dared stand against the king. So frightening that none could even look into his eyes for longer than a minute. However, when Khalil looked over at the man dressed in dark-red robes with dark-yellow trimmings; short, curly hair that was both black and white; dark, sand-colored skin; and light-brown eyes, Khalil saw no monster. Rather, he looked upon an old man with a hard face, who stared down at him with cold, expressionless eyes. Khalil stared back unflinchingly.

"Well, General? Is this your son?"

"Yes, my king," the man said, his voice sounding like two pieces of brush rubbing together. "He was born a sick child, and the medicine woman said the sickness was from his mother's blood and could only be cured upon her lands, so the woman and child were sent back to Kazera. If I knew their kin were all so traitorous, however, I would have cleared the map of their village years ago. Forgive me, my king." The Great General turned, bowing his head to the man.

"There is nothing to forgive!" the king exclaimed, quickly rising from his throne. "Your sons have brought honor to you once again, my friend. Bring the wine! Where is the food? We must celebrate with a feast and dancing! Rise to your feet, Khalil Rausi. You as well, Khalaf. All must celebrate the great hero of Kazera!"

Khalil noticed that while he and his brother were permitted to rise, Prince Effiom was still kneeling, his head still down though his hands were balled into tight fists. Seeing the prince like this, disregarded purposefully in front of so many other powerful people, should have brought Khalil joy, but it did the opposite. As Khalil turned back to see all the servants bringing in tables full of food and wine, women entering to dance as the men in red robes moved to take their seats first, Khalil realized just how massive the Zenzele dynasty was. If Prince Effiom could be so easily ignored, it meant he wasn't that powerful. And that was a gut punch, because it meant Khalil's real family, a high noble house with vast armies and men, had been destroyed by a feeble underling in the dead of night.

The more Khalil watched, the tighter the pain in his chest became. In Kazera, he had been certain he was going to get his revenge on Prince Effiom and all of the Zenzele. But as more and more people kept coming into the great hall, Khalil found himself questioning for the very first time how exactly he could do it. He had no army, no power, nothing—not even his own name.

"Do not just stand there and look the fool," the Great General said to Khalil.

Khalil looked at General Rausi, but the old man was already moving toward the first table that was set to the right of the throne. Khalil moved to follow and sit beside him when he felt a tug on his collar.

"Father sits alone. We sit behind him," Khalaf said, dragging Khalil to a table that was being prepared for the two of them.

However, just before they could take their seats, a voice hollered, "Her most gracious and humble majesty, Queen Esraa!"

All the men rose, including the Great General, bowing their heads as many women entered behind the queen, who wore a robe of embroidered yellow and a crown of gold. She was walking very slowly.

"Good, my dear, you are here!" the king proclaimed. "The Great General's son has vanquished the last Mukundi and suppressed a horrid rebellion."

"The Rausi honor us again, my king." The woman's voice was soft and low. "Welcome home, Prince Effiom. Finally, we may all have peace. All of you, drink. This is a joyous day."

Khalil turned and noticed Prince Effiom was finally able to rise from where he'd been kneeling this whole time. The prince's jaw was set, his hands were still clenched, and his nose was flared, but a woman dressed in pink with long hair tied back and held together with gold pins had come to his side and placed a hand on his wrist. It was only then that the prince let out a deep breath.

Khalil looked around to see another woman who had followed behind the queen—with gold rings around her neck and arms, her head covered with beads, and a shawl of white on her shoulders—placing her hand on a bump on her stomach. Khalil thought maybe she was a concubine, but she stood at a table closer to the king on the opposite side of them, ahead of Prince Effiom. The rest of the women had their hair tied back and stood behind their ladies.

"Where is Zikora?" the king asked angrily as they all moved to sit down once the queen had taken her seat beside the king.

"Here am I!" came a loud voice from behind the throne, which caused the king to jump slightly. Peeking in from the other side was a little girl dressed in a green dress with blue trim and not one gold pin in her hair. Instead, her hair was left free in a mess of curls that poured over her face like a lion's mane.

The queen's eyes were wide. "Lady Zikora, go to your seat—"

The king held his hand up, stopping the queen and looking at the girl hanging on to one of the sun's golden rays. "Are you trying to steal my throne, Zikora?"

"No, it's too heavy! I just wanted to surprise you!"

The king laughed, placing his hand on her head when she came around to him. "Has anyone told you it is dangerous to surprise the king? You could have been taken for an assassin and lost your head!"

"Why would anyone wish to assassinate you?" Zikora asked.

Khalil could think of a thousand reasons. He frowned, watching the girl and everyone else. He wanted to leave and find . . .

"My king!" Prince Effiom called, finding his voice again. "If you will allow it, I obtained a great many gifts for you on my return."

"I am not in need of gifts." The king's voice was stern, and he still would not look at his son. Instead, the king offered the girl a plate of grapes, and instead of taking one she grinned and took the whole thing.

"My dear king, it should still be a wonder to see them," the queen said, her soft face now glaring at the girl on his other side.

"Very well. Bring forth these so-called gifts."

"Zikora, return to your seat," the queen ordered.

The girl nodded, holding her plate of grapes as she moved from the throne, but all of a sudden she stopped, and all the people in the throne room began to whisper as a chained Ashon was brought in.

Khalil moved to get up, but Khalaf yanked him back down. "Do not move," he whispered. "Do not speak."

Ashon's white feet were covered in dirt, and his blond hair was rough and pulled in different directions. His clothes were tattered, and although he was already white, Khalil could tell the boy's face was paler, and he had been crying.

"My king, I present you the Wytjrein of Kazera!" Prince Effiom announced.

"Oh heavens," the queen gasped in horror, "it's a beast!"

"How did Kazera capture a Wytjrein?" another man called out.

"Does it speak?" another asked.

"Has it been checked for sickness? The books of old say they bring disease!" another cried out.

With each of their questions and insults, Ashon seemed to tremble more and more. Again, Khalil wanted to get up but wasn't sure what to do or say. And with his brother right beside him, he knew this was something he was just going to have to watch. The very thought made him feel like a coward, like he had when he watched his father die. And his sister. And Zereen . . .

Once more he wondered how he would ever get revenge against everyone here.

Everyone *except* that girl in green. *Zikora.* Who now stood right in front of Ashon with the plate she'd taken from the king.

"Would you like a grape?" she asked.

"Zikora, get back here before he makes you sick!" the queen shouted.

"Why would he make me sick?" Zikora said, then turned back to the king. "I do not think he's a Wytjrein."

"What would you know of these things, child?" the woman next to an annoyed Prince Effiom spoke up. "Come sit—"

"Your Majesty!" Zikora called up to the king. "Do you know that in Winneba, we have *The Book of Men?*"

"*The Book of Men?*" the king repeated. "What is that?"

"My baba used to read to me from the book," she said, not quite answering the king's question, Khalil noticed. "He said the first lords of Winneba had sent their sons to search all the lands and report of every man they came across. Many died, but many returned, and with them, drawings of men, including the dwarfs, giants, Wytjrein, Bihōng . . . and the Inaobi. I think that is what he is."

"The Inaobi? Are they not all dead?" asked the man seated beside the Great General.

Khalil noticed this man, too, wore deep-red robes with yellow trim, but his trim was only at the bottom of his robe and not at the collar like the Great General. His gray beard was braided and stopped at the center of his chest, and his head was bald but covered in tattoo markings.

"What have you heard of these people, Tsawnté?" the king questioned.

Tsawnté Tijani? Even Khalil had heard of this man in Kazera. He was the keeper of knowledge and wise man of all the Zenzele.

"The ancient books here called them skin shedders. Many years ago, before Aksum's Conquest, there were men upon this land who traded the black of their skin for magic. It was said they prayed to the heavens, and with it, they built a vast army that nearly conquered the world before they were defeated and never seen again. King Aksum forbade any mention of them in later texts, for he believed it to be heresy. Magic does not exist," Tsawnté explained, looking back over to where the girl and Ashon were. "Lady Zikora, how do you know he is Inaobi? They are a people no longer."

"That's not what it says in *The Book of Men*." Zikora giggled and tossed another grape in her mouth, and how a little girl like her could get everyone to listen, Khalil did not understand. She spoke as she skipped around Ashon. "*The Book of Men* says the Inaobi survived just as the dwarfs, giants, Wytjrein, and Bihōng do, and that they have no magic. But people still believed their skin and bone had to have power because it was different, so they began to kidnap their people to create spells. The Inaobi fought back, but lost and went into hiding so they would not lose any more people. They are not Wytjrein. They are just us with white skin."

"Do you have any way to prove that?" Prince Effiom snapped at her. "Or are we all supposed to believe the words of a child? What do you even remember of Winneba? You were nearly a babe when you left."

"I was eight. That is *not* the age of a baby." Zikora pouted at him . . . like a baby. Making Khalil slightly annoyed with her. She was a Nnamani, wasn't she? Did she not know what they did to her brother? Why was she so . . . playful with them? Khalil wondered, even as she continued. "And I remember all my baba's stories. Do you have proof he *is* a Wytjrein?"

Zikora had stopped her skipping to huff at Prince Effiom. Khalil worried that the prince would lose his temper and beat her like he did everyone else who challenged or annoyed him. But all of a sudden the king laughed, which in turn made everyone else laugh as well. Well, everyone but the Great General, who merely drank calmly, not even paying attention to any of them.

"Well, Effiom, what proof do you have?" the King asked him, and Effiom's fist clenched and his nose flared.

"The boy is white—"

"Clearly that is not enough. Maybe if you'd paid more attention to your studies than to war and women, you'd be able to answer Zikora." The king huffed as well and turned back to his wise man. "Well, Tsawnté, which *child* is right?"

"It makes more sense that the boy is Inaobi than Wytjrein," Tsawnté said, as all the attention was now on him.

"Why do you say that?" the prince asked through gritted teeth.

"The Wytjrein live across the Great Thundering Sea. How would any of them arrive on our lands and cross thousands of miles to a small village like Kazera without anyone hearing of it? The boy does not even look a full twelve summers old. Young master Khalil"—

Tsawnté glanced at Khalil, and it was the first time someone else had addressed Khalil here—"was this boy born in your village or brought?"

"I am told he was born there."

"And his mother?"

"Died bearing him," Khalil replied, then quickly thought to add, "She was only gone a year from our village before she returned pregnant."

"A year is nowhere near enough time to cross the Great Thundering Sea and return to Madada," Tsawnté said, looking out at them all. "So, it is safe to say that young Lady Zikora's thoughts on his origins are much more likely to be accurate. But if you like, my king, I can keep the boy under my charge and investigate the matter."

The king was silent as he looked over the boy. "Very well, Tsawnté," he said with a nod. "It is not as if I have a use for a boy, whether he be Wytjrein or Inaobi. Take him away."

"Here!" Lady Zikora said, handing Ashon the grapes. "Eat all of them. They are very good."

Ashon looked down at them and then at her, a small smile on his lips. However, it faded when he met Khalil's gaze. Khalil was sure the anger in Ashon's eyes would never truly go away.

He was so trapped in the enmity of his friend's eyes, it took a moment before Khalil could hear Ashon whisper, "Traitor."

And there was nothing Khalil could do but accept it. Khalil just hoped Ashon would keep getting lucky and somehow, some way, make it to see the day when he wasn't Khalil anymore.

However long that took.

35
ZIKORA

Ahalon

HE IS NOT YOUR PEOPLE, ZIKORA!

You cannot save everyone.

Prince Effiom will take it as an insult.

You have ruined his gift. He shall be furious with you.

What were you thinking? You need to listen to us.

The voices had returned, and they were angry. Very angry with her. She did her best to listen to them. But there were so many, and sometimes it felt like they were not all saying the same things. However, they were all clear that she was not supposed to help the white-skinned boy. When she returned to her seat and saw the rage in both Prince Effiom's and Princess Bahiya's eyes, she wondered if maybe she should have kept her mouth shut. At first, she really was going to listen and be quiet, but she saw how scared the boy was, and he looked so sad too. He looked the same way she had felt the first day she'd come to the capital. She just wanted to make him feel better, and in doing so, found herself defending him a little too vigorously.

Taking a seat beside Princess Bahiya, Zikora drank her water slowly, wishing to hurry up and leave.

"You cannot let them forget this glory is yours," Princess Bahiya muttered very softly to her husband in Xzishari, a language that should have been dead.

Zikora looked up at her, confused. She knew how she understood the language—well, sort of—but she did not know why or how they had learned it. Xzishari was spoken by the first peoples on the continent, before the conquest. When King Aksum declared all the houses were to speak one language, all books and writings that held any other languages were ordered to be destroyed.

"Do you not think I know that?" Prince Effiom said from behind his bowl of wine. "It is clear the king does not wish to see me honored. In fact, he rather wishes for the opposite."

"Then force him."

"How exactly do I manage that . . . *wife*?"

Princess Bahiya was silent and glanced around the hall, then her eyes finally paused.

Zikora followed her gaze to where General Rausi was sitting, not sure what she was looking at. The old man looked uninterested, as always.

"If he does not honor you, make him honor all those around you," Princess Bahiya whispered to the prince, and nodded to General Rausi. Zikora was not sure what the princess meant by that, but Prince Effiom seemed to and rose once more.

"My king," he said.

"What now, Effiom? Do you wish to present a paper dragon as a gift next?" The king openly mocked him.

"No, Your Majesty. I merely ask for your mercy and grace to be bestowed on your men who fought tirelessly in your honor,"

Prince Effiom said in return. "I ask you to reward them, especially the Rausi."

"We have no need for rewards, my prince," General Rausi replied sternly. "Our family lives to serve."

Yet the king laughed. "Must you always reject my goodwill, Khadim?"

"I reject nothing I am worthy of, but I am not worthy of a reward." General Rausi stared as he lifted his drink.

"You might not be, but your son is. Khalil!"

It took a moment, but Zikora saw a boy with short, shiny hair that was smoothed so much it had waves. He was dressed in a black-and-red robe and stood rather tall but was very skinny. His face was . . . funny—confused but angry at the same time.

Strange. Zikora had never seen this Rausi son before. And he did not seem to look like the rest of them to her. But then again, all the Rausi sons tended to look more like their mothers.

"Yes, my king?" Khalil finally said.

"You are the hero of Kazera and the slayer of the Mukundi. Your father may not think that is worthy of a reward, but I do, and since I am king, what I think matters much more. Name your reward. Anything but my kingdom is yours. Let all know that the king honors his champions!"

The boy merely stared at the king, saying nothing. In fact, he looked like he had suddenly frozen. It made a few of the other men laugh.

"Well? What shall it be, boy? Gold? Title? Land? A woman?" the king pressed, and even more men laughed, though Zikora did not understand why. Why were they so obsessed with women?

"You shall give me whatever I desire?" the boy finally asked.

"Mind your manners!" General Rausi snapped at him.

"No, do not silence him," the king said, his eyes sparkling now. "That is what I said, boy—anything but my kingdom—so what is it? Speak freely."

"I-I have no need for gold, title, land, or women right now," Khalil replied.

"Then what is it you want? There is nothing left beyond those things," the king told Khalil.

"I want a wish."

"A wish?"

"Yes," Khalil replied, his head lifting. "I am too young to know what I need right now. I do not wish to waste the king's grace, so I want you to reward me with one wish that can be granted at any time. Then, when I am older and know what I need, I will come and redeem my wish for it."

The boy is wise, the voices said to her. But Zikora was jealous. If she were given the chance, she knew exactly what she'd wish for right now. She let out a gentle sigh, which was loud since everyone was quiet, but all eyes remained upon Khalil. Everyone was waiting for what the king would say. He did not say anything at first. He merely removed the first ring on his finger and stretched it out. A servant, bowing low, took it from the king and moved to the boy, handing it off to him.

"You must return my ring the day you know what you wish for. Your wish will be granted by any and all in the house of Zenzele. I make this promise and vow as king."

There were many whispers as the boy bowed to the king and then returned to his seat.

"The boy is clever," Princess Bahiya whispered to her prince. "Make sure to remind him who it was that brought him this far. The more Rausi under you, the better."

Zikora waited, watching and eating as the king rewarded others in Prince Effiom's army. As the gold and wine began to be shared, the happier and louder everyone became. Normally, this was the time Nanny Urenna would come to retrieve her. But she never came. Zikora waited and waited, and when the female dancers arrived, and her nanny still did not come for her, she felt a sudden fear in her heart.

Zikora glanced over to where Princess Hasina was sitting. The princess hadn't said a word or even looked concerned with the fact that Prince Aberash was not here. He hadn't even been brought up. Why?

As if Princess Hasina knew she was being watched, she turned to meet Zikora's eyes and smiled warmly.

Go, Zikora. Something is not right, the voices said, and Zikora nodded, rising to her feet.

"Your Majesty, may I—"

"*Ahhh!*" The interrupting scream forced the guards to rush before the throne and Prince Effiom to jump in front of his wife as . . .

A man covered in blood, holding a sword and limping, came into the hall.

"Aberash!" Princess Hasina screamed, pushing through the guards and rushing to her husband as he collapsed to his knees, only steps into the room.

"What is the meaning of this?" the king called out, now on his feet also.

"Father . . . Prince Effiom's men . . . they've attacked the women in the inner court," Prince Aberash gasped while coughing.

"Impossible!" Prince Effiom yelled, then turned to his father. "It's a lie, Father!"

Go, Zikora! Go!

Using these distractions, Zikora ran. She held up the skirts of her dress and ran as fast as she could. Only, she did not have to get very far.

The halls and gardens were soaked with the blood of the women . . . maids, medicine women, weavers, cooks . . . and her nanny. Nanny Urenna's body was in the center of the hall, a pool of blood underneath her spreading in every direction. Zikora refused to step closer, praying it was a nightmare, that somehow her eyes were lying to her.

But they were not.

She would have stayed there had it not been for the arms of a guard wrapping around her and lifting her.

"Let go!" Zikora screamed, and punched him.

"My lady, you must wait with the king. We do not know if it is yet safe——"

"*Let go!* Urenna!" Zikora bit down on the guard's fingers as hard as she could, forcing him to let her go. From there, she ran toward her nanny's body, slipping on the blood. "Wake up! Urenna, please, please wake up!"

"My lady, you must go back to the——"

"I am not going without her!" Zikora yelled back.

The guards tried again to grab her, but she held on to her nanny's body tightly.

"We do not have time!" called a guard. "Take them both! The king will have you killed if she is injured."

A second guard came and picked up her nanny's body, and only then did Zikora move to follow them, holding on to Urenna's hand tightly and whispering for her to wake up. But Nanny Urenna wouldn't wake, no matter how roughly they carried her or how much Zikora shook her.

"Zikora!" the queen called when Zikora was finally returned to the banquet hall.

"Please help! She is not waking up! I can't get her to wake up. Help me!"

"Keep your decorum. You are before the king!" The queen squeezed Zikora's shoulders and shook her.

Reminded of who actually had power here—and seeing that the queen would not help—Zikora pushed the queen aside and ran toward the throne. Zikora quickly got on her knees and brought her head to the ground. "Your Majesty! Help me, *please!*"

"Do not worry. We shall get her the best medicine woman—"

"The woman is gone," General Rausi said.

"*No!*" Zikora screamed, her head snapping up. She looked around, but no one else was saying anything. No one else was helping Urenna. "*No! Help her! Someone help her!*"

There is no helping the dead, Zikora, you must stay calm, the voice told her, but Zikora merely shook her head over and over again, crawling back on her hands and feet to her nanny before all of the capital.

Zikora did not understand how this had happened. More, looking at the slash at Urenna's throat and the paleness of her skin, Zikora did not understand *why* this had happened. Of course it did not matter how it had happened, simply that it did. One moment, Urenna was here, and the next, she was gone. The tears poured from Zikora's eyes as she laid her head on Urenna's chest, hoping against all odds that she'd hear Urenna's heart, but it was silent. Urenna's heart was silenced.

"Your Majesty," someone said from above where Zikora lay, still trying to listen for a heartbeat, "we've caught the drunkard men of the prince's army. They did not seem to realize they were in the palace and wished to . . . have fun."

Voices clamored in protest.

"How dare they?!"

"The audacity! Is this how you train your men?"

"They should be cut to pieces for daring to enter the inner court!"

"The victims? Were they only servants?" General Rausi asked, now on his feet and quite furious.

"Five women in total, sir. Prince Aberash stopped them before they could go any further."

At the mention of Prince Aberash, Zikora finally blinked and looked over to where he now lay, surrounded by guards as his wife tended his wounds.

Prince Aberash had always been kind to Zikora.

He'd acted like her big brother here.

Zikora always visited him and he often brought treats from the city for her. He was not cruel to his women like Prince Effiom. He was the good prince. Everyone said so. And even though she did not truly trust any of them, she had thought he was not as bad as the rest. So why did she have this sick feeling in her stomach? Why were the voices telling her . . .

He did this.

"Lady Zikora. Lady Zikora?" Dabir Tsawnté knelt on the other side of Urenna, a frown on his lips. "The dead cannot remain with you. She must be moved."

Again, Zikora shook her head and held on to the woman tighter. "We are all supposed to go back to Winneba together. I promised her she'd go back. She'd get married and have children, and I'd watch over them to thank her one day. You can't take her. I have to keep my promise. I am Lady Zikora Nnamani of Winneba, and I have to keep my promises."

"I'll make sure her body is preserved so she can go home early," Dabir Tsawnté whispered back to her, placing his hand over hers.

Stay calm, Zikora.

Do not say it, Zikora.

She could feel all of the voices trying to hold her back. But she would not yield to them. She could not yield to anyone. She let go and turned back to face everyone in the throne room. "I want to go home!"

"Zikora, my dear," the queen said to her. "I know you are so very sad—"

"I want to go back to Winneba!" Zikora screamed at her. "How long is a *guest* supposed to stay, Your Majesty? Am I even a guest, or am I—"

"Take Lady Zikora to her rooms at once!" the king ordered, and there was no more opportunity to say anything else. For, just like that, she was again picked up by one of the guards.

She wanted to struggle but was so tired, and she kept seeing her nanny in her mind. How did people die so easily? How could everything change so quickly?

Soon they were back in her quarters.

"Zikora!"

Zikora turned to see Tuliza running to her, so she slid down from the guard's grasp and ran to Tuliza, and they embraced tightly. When the guards left, Tuliza whispered into her ear, "I saw it, Zikora. I saw him kill her. It was Prince Aberash."

Now Zikora knew it for sure.

There was not one good person in the house of Zenzele.

"What do we do now?" Tuliza asked her.

And she wasn't sure. This wasn't supposed to happen. She listened to her feelings . . . to the voices. She did everything right . . .

You've done nothing. She heard only one singular voice this time, and when she closed her eyes, she was no longer in her room but by the river . . . the same river she'd seen her baba sit by with her uncle, grilling fish. But her baba wasn't there. Just her uncle, once again dressed in his white kaftan, carving something before a tiny fire.

Welcome back, he said, not even bothering to look at her. *Did you have a hard day?*

Zikora's fists clenched and her teeth gritted together. "You know exactly what happened! Why are you asking that? Why are you just sitting there? Aren't you all supposed to be helping me?"

Nothing any of us could have done could have helped you, little one, he replied, still not looking at her. *Those that seek evil will always do evil. We only see what you see—*

"Then why am I listening to you? To any of you? Nanny Urenna is dead. They killed her and I wasn't even there! She died alone far from home all because . . . because—

Because you are a weak little girl, he finished, and this time when he finally looked up, Zikora hated what she saw on his face. She picked up a rock from the ground and launched it at his head. But he just smacked it away with his whittled stick. *Childish.*

Angrily she grabbed more rocks, as many as her hands could hold, and she threw them at him, one after another, over and over until her vision blurred from her tears and she sank down to her feet, hunched over and sobbing once more.

She didn't know how long she stayed liked that before she felt a rock hit her own head.

That is far too many tears for a nanny.

"Shut up!" she yelled, but when she looked up, he was crouched down right before her face.

Be childish before our enemies, not me. Not to us. Do not cry and sob before us who have buried our fathers, mothers, brothers, sisters, lovers, and children because of those people. In an instant it was as if all the world spun above her, the clear sky changing to visions of people she did not know, dying, some burned alive, others beheaded or stabbed on a battlefield filled with broken flags and blood.

We are not here to soothe your pain and hug you tight. We are here for power. Because only with power comes real strength to protect the people and things we care about. So, wipe your face and stand on your feet, Zikora, her uncle said, standing. And as he did the skies cleared again, all the visions now gone.

She did what he asked, wiping her face and rising too. But, still annoyed with him, she muttered, "Just because bad things happened to all of you doesn't mean I am not allowed to be upset."

Being upset is good. Wasting that emotion on tears is where the problem lies. He handed her the sharp stick. *Instead, you must look for vengeance.*

"I'm not sure how long you were in prison for, but people use iron now," she huffed.

It's for fishing.

"Huh? Then why would you say vengeance and give this to me?"

So we would go into the river to plot while fishing.

Zikora looked at the stick and then back at him. "Why?"

You really are your father's daughter. Both of you are very irksome, he replied, snatching the stick and heading toward the river. *Follow me.*

"Do we have to do this now?"

Yes.

Zikora sighed and marched after him. She didn't expect the water to be freezing, and nearly jumped back out, but her uncle dragged her farther towards the center.

"Will I even be able to eat these?"

Stop with the sass and catch one, he said, returning the stick to her.

She took it and stared down at the blue rainbow trout fish that swam quickly by her feet. She gripped the stick tightly and plunged it into the water . . . only to miss. She tried again and she missed once more. After the third time, she was determined and even bent down lower.

"One . . . two . . . three." She shoved the stick in.

And like before, she missed.

You lack skill and patience.

"You do it then."

He did not even have to look down once he took the stick from her. Within a second, he had caught one.

Zikora glared at him. "Am I supposed to be plotting against you or the people who killed Nanny Urenna?"

This is bigger than just your nanny, Zikora. Or have you forgotten your brother?

Zikora frowned. "I will never forget Zereen. Prince Effiom killed him."

And how will you kill the prince? he asked, pulling the fish off the stick and tossing it back into the river. She watched as, magically, the hole in it vanished as it swam again downstream.

"Kill him?" Zikora repeated. "You want me to kill him?"

Don't you want to? he asked in return. *Prince Aberash killed your nanny—don't you want to kill him too?*

Zikora froze. Because while she'd been angry and hurt, she'd never thought so far as actually killing anyone.

Blood can only be avenged with blood, Zikora.

"You all have been telling me not to bring attention to myself. To act like a child—"

And yet that act can only last for so long. What shall you do when you come of age? We thought we would have more time to prepare you for what you will need to do. But those princes are warring without care for those in their way, and it will only get worse. For them to use your nanny this way . . .

"Yes?"

Next will be your maid. And then you.

"I'll kill them!"

How?

She didn't have an answer to that.

He handed her the stick. *Once your nanny is returned to Winneba, your father will fear for your life and surely plot to come get you with or without the permission of the king.*

Zikora's eyes widened. "That will start a war."

Yes, one where thousands of men will risk their lives for you. What will you be doing then?

"What *will* I do?" She had a feeling that this wasn't the time for war. But she wasn't sure if it was her ancestors' feelings or hers. She looked up at him. "Tell me what to do."

Fish and then tell me the answer you caught.

She looked back down at her feet at the shimmers of blue gliding under the water. It had been three years since she had left home. Fortifications to Winneba should have been half-completed by now. Men would be trained . . . but that was all useless if their army came down to Ahalon. They were most powerful in their own lands. She needed to bring the war to Winneba first. But first she had to return. Except the Zenzele wouldn't let her go back now, especially after her outburst. Her only choice was to stay and fight her way out . . .

A small smile spread across her face as a plan came forward. Quickly she stuck the stick into the water, pinning a fish down.

Well? her uncle asked her.

"I need skill and patience," Zikora said, lifting the fish up. "I need to wake up and go get it."

Then awake.

ZIKORA FOUND HERSELF STARING UP at the ceiling of her room. When she looked over to her left, there was Tuliza holding a small dagger, nodding off to sleep at the side of her bed.

Zikora sat up and crawled over her prone friend, careful to not touch Tuliza or the dagger, as she was sure that was a great way to get stabbed. Quietly she moved to the dresser in the corner, where she gently pulled out the bottom drawer and dug to the very back. There she found the white owl whistle Hanif had given to her. She'd nearly forgotten about it and until now had no idea what it was supposed to do, but she was sure now was the time to use it. She moved then to the window, opening it just a crack before blowing gently on the whistle. It made no sound . . . not to her ears, at least. But she kept blowing and waiting until finally . . . a white spotted-neck owl landed in a tree in the courtyard.

There, waiting for her to give it whatever secret letter she wanted to send. All the while, she could feel the voices in her head murmuring their approval.

Because this was how the spies of Winneba sent each other information. The spies would make sure her message made it home.

36

LORD NNAMANI

Winneba

LORD NNAMANI FELT HIS DAUGHTER'S PAIN. HE could almost hear her screams and cries in the wind. It turned his stomach and boiled his blood, enraging him to the point where he wished to spill all the blood in the capital. The last straw had long been broken. This was now a declaration of war.

"My lord, what shall we do with her body?" Hanif asked him as they watched Ayubu weep over the pristine corpse of Nanny Urenna. It had surely been weeks since she was murdered, however her body seemed as if she had gone just yesterday. They had cleared the inner courtyard to give him this moment to grieve. Lord Nnamani had sent Urenna to protect his daughter, and they brought Urenna back dead upon a death altar.

"Her parents are gone, and she has no more kin. Allow Dabir Ayubu to do as he sees fit for her. She should at least be given rites by someone who loved her," Lady Nnamani whispered calmly. She looked to Lord Nnamani, her eyes filled with the same rage as his. "Will you bring back my daughter before they return her to me like this?"

"I will."

"When?"

Before he could reply, Hanif called out to him once more. "My lord."

Lord Nnamani turned to Hanif, who was now lifting the dead hand of Urenna in which she grasped a drawing of a crane. It was not abnormal for some noble houses in Winneba to follow the old ways of putting their family emblems in their palms after their passing. But it was not normally done for servants. He could see Zikora maybe doing this to honor her . . . but the slash at the throat. That was a sign.

"What?" Lady Nnamani asked, looking between them. "What is wrong?"

Lord Nnamani looked to Ayubu; "Dabir Ayubu, forgive me, but will you allow Hanif to open her mouth?"

"My lord?" he asked, confused, glancing between him and Urenna, but he nodded.

It was then Hanif cut open the stitches with his dagger and gently opened her mouth wide. He reached inside.

"What are you doing?" Lady Nnamani asked, and he did not answer. Instead he lifted out a rolled piece of paper.

"My lord," Hanif said, immediately rushing to give the paper to him. And the moment he unrolled rolled it he took in a deep breath.

Baba.

He could only read that far before gritting his teeth. His daughter had learned to call the spies and send secrets now.

Baba,

Now is not the time. Please remain calm. I am all right, I promise, so is Tuliza. Please send skill and patience. I love you all.

"Zikobi?" said his wife, who had already come to stand beside him. He knew she would know that handwriting. They had received many much longer letters from their daughter over the years. But they could never trust them. They knew everything she wrote was under the watchful eye of those in Ahalon. This felt like the first time they had truly heard from her.

"What does she mean by 'skill and patience'?" Lady Nnamani whispered, taking the letter from him with a frown. "I don't understand."

"Dabir Ayubu," Lord Nnamani said, looking to his daughter's instructor, trying to understand her wishes. "You twin sister is a member of the Seh Llinga, and her name is . . ."

"Mahira." The man nodded slowly, also trying to understand.

"Mahira means skill. Ayubu means patience."

"Yes, my lord." He nodded. "Lady Zikora calls for us?"

"I can see why she would call for Mahira. She is a fierce warrior. She will be able to protect her," Lady Nnamani whispered. "But surely she cannot understand what it means to call Dabir Ayubu. He is a man. He cannot go into the women's palace . . ."

"Not unless he loses his manhood," Hanif said to them.

"Hanif!" Lady Nnamani then looked to her husband. "Zikobi, we could not possibly—"

Dabir Ayubu knelt before them both. "Send me, my lord."

"Dabir Ayubu, you have suffered a great loss," Lady Nnamani said. "My family, my daughter, is forever in your debt, for I know Urenna protected Zikora with her life. But you are young. You may still have a family yet. You are the only son of a great family; you cannot let your line end in such a way. We shall bring Zikora home. There is no need for this. Zikobi, tell him."

"Thank you, Dabir Ayubu, truly," Zikobi said.

Lady Nnamani's shoulders dropped as she let out a breath. She said nothing as both Hanif and Ayubu took their leave.

"What happened to bringing her back, Zikobi?" she asked her husband when they were alone.

"You saw the letter."

"It was barely a letter but lines from a little girl! She does not know—"

"Do you believe you know more of her own condition than she does?!" he snapped. "If she went to this much effort, if she was willing to have the note shoved down Urenna's throat, you believe it was for lack of thought? She has managed to stay alive and unharmed for this long. It cannot be just luck. Have faith."

"I do not want faith; I want my daughter."

"And I don't?"

There was silence, then both husband and wife went their separate ways. Lord Nnamani turned the corner to find his son, his heir. Although perhaps not, for over the last three years, fewer people believed Zakee was worthy of such a title, mostly because of moments like this, where he stared out the window at the night sky like he was reading a book.

Lord Nnamani found himself doubting his son's future as well.

To many in Winneba, his father included, Zakee was the strangest of all the family because he rarely spoke in ways normal men could understand.

Like now.

"The double stars have finally met, Father," Zakee said to Lord Nnamani, not bothering to look away from the sky. "The fates of the heavens have brought them together, and with it, all the world has now changed."

"The fates of the heavens leave men to shape their own destiny," Lord Nnamani replied as he walked by.

Zakee whispered back, "That is what all men think until it's too late."

KHALIL

Ahalon

IT TOOK NINE WEEKS AFTER WHAT EVERYONE AT the capital called "the cursed banquet" before Khalil was finally invited back into the palace. The king was so enraged by what the men of Prince Effiom's army had done that he'd forced Prince Effiom to be whipped ten times in front of everyone. Even Khalil's brother Khalaf was not spared punishment, being demoted to a thousand-man command. He was not punished so far as to be stripped of his rank of Silver Ray, but any step back was considered a great shame. All other high-level officers under him were also demoted and disgraced. A few were even killed by the Great General. The king said it was an apology to the queen and her ladies for the violence brought upon them, but it was clearly all show for Lady Zikora—no, for the house of Nnamani. Who seemed to accept it, though they demanded that Lady Zikora be sent a new guardian and allowed to train under her dabir, as was custom in Winneba. The king did not seem pleased, but it was clear he had no choice but to grant their request.

Even as an outsider, Khalil realized something during his first few weeks in Ahalon. Namely, the one family that the house of Zenzele seemingly truly feared was the house of Nnamani. Which meant the one person here who could help Khalil was the one person with that name: Zikora. But getting close to any of the women in the inner palace was nearly impossible. The only way he was even allowed to today was because Khalaf sent him to take a letter to Prince Effiom, who was still under house arrest, an additional punishment on top of his beatings.

Khalil was trying to use this time to find Zikora, but he was clearly—

"Lost?"

Khalil spun around, and there was Lady Zikora, dressed in green again, and another girl behind her.

"No," Khalil said, shaking his head. "I found you."

"Me?" she asked, not afraid, but curious. "Why were you looking for me?"

Khalil reached into his pocket and handed her the bracelet she'd dropped that night of the banquet. "To give this back to you."

"My mother's bangle!" Zikora grinned as she snatched it from him and put it on her wrist. "I have searched all over for it. Where did you find it?"

"You dropped it at the banquet."

"Oh." Zikora's shoulders dropped, and her eyes filled with sorrow.

Khalil opened his mouth to speak again when Zikora's handmaid cut in, "Zikora, we must return before you're late for your lessons."

"Oh, right!" Zikora turned to run.

"Wait!" Khalil called.

"What?"

"I'm . . . Khalil!"

"I know! Bye!" Zikora said. She began to run but then stopped once more. "Thank you for returning this, Khalil. I'll pay you back later."

"I'll hold you to that," Khalil called after her, wondering why he had said that instead of, well, anything else.

As if thinking the same thing, she gave him a strange look but just nodded.

And with that, he knew he had taken the first real step toward his goal.

Toward revenge for his family.

This was his start . . .

And their end.

ACKNOWLEDGMENTS

The list of people I owe my heartfelt gratitude to is extraordinarily long, and I am not sure where to start, as it has taken me over four years to write this novel.

The very first person I told of this book was my agent, Natanya Wheeler, who over the last ten years has been my constant cheerleader, advocate, and friend. Thank you so much for all you do.

To my editor, David Pomerico, for seeing my vision and working with me to make it a reality. Thank you for hearing and respecting my voice. I'm grateful to be working with you now and in the future.

To Ajebowale Roberts, who has promoted and campaigned for my work in so many rooms I could not reach. Thank you.

To Colleen Snibson and Rogena Mitchell-Jones, my two red pens who have helped me through so many edits of my works. Thank you.

To my parents, who I never let read my books, but who always tell everyone how wonderful of a writer I am. Thank you both for your support.

To my darling husband, Stanley, who always brings me snacks when my mind is lost in adventures. Thank you, babe.

And to all the people behind this novel: Isabella Ogbolumani, cover and map artist Alan Dingman, the entire wonderful team at Voyager, as well as Elizabeth Vaziri, my editor at Voyager UK. From the bottom of my heart, thank you so much for working with me. Thank you for championing this book. *Birth of a Dynasty* could not exist without all of you.

AHKEBULIN